rw

BENEATH A PRAIRIE MOON

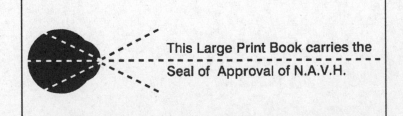

This Large Print Book carries the
Seal of Approval of N.A.V.H.

BENEATH A
PRAIRIE MOON

KIM VOGEL SAWYER

THORNDIKE PRESS
A part of Gale, a Cengage Company

GALE
A Cengage Company

Farmington Hills, Mich • San Francisco • New York • Waterville, Maine

LIBRARY OF CONGRESS CIP DATA ON FILE.
CATALOGUING IN PUBLICATION FOR THIS BOOK
IS AVAILABLE FROM THE LIBRARY OF CONGRESS.

ISBN-13: 978-1-4328-4837-8 (hardcover)

Published in 2018 by arrangement with WaterBrook, an imprint of Crown Publishing Group, a division of Penguin Random Publishing Group, LLC

Printed in Mexico
1 2 3 4 5 6 7 22 21 20 19 18

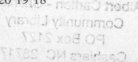

For Kristian and Allen,
who watched friendship
blossom into happily ever after.

For all the law is fulfilled in one word, even in this; Thou shalt love thy neighbour as thyself.

— Galatians 5:14

ONE

Late August 1888
Spiveyville, Kansas
Mack Cleveland

"When're you gonna have your letter ready, Mack? The fellas is gettin' fidgety. They all wanna get the packet sent off, you know."

Mack Cleveland paused in scooping nails into the scale's bowl and sent a scowl across the counter to Spiveyville's postman. The man's grin, mostly hidden behind his overgrown mustache and beard, seemed to taunt Mack. "Didn't I make myself clear the other night? I think it's a fool notion, and I want no part of it."

Clive Ackley's thick eyebrows shot upward, forming a pair of fuzzy black tepees above his watery brown eyes. "You still takin' that stand? Figured by now you'd come around, seein' how every other man in town voted yes."

9

Mack bit back an argument. Not every man in town attended the meeting. And the preacher hadn't voted yes. But Preacher Doan's vote didn't count because he already had a wife. Mack gave Clive an up-and-down look, taking in the scraggly beard dribbling across his chest and his rumpled checked shirt stretched over his round belly. "Are you sending a letter?"

Clive jammed his hands into his trouser pockets and rocked back on his heels. "You can bet your buttons I'm sendin' one." He laughed as if he'd made a joke. The scruffy facial hair couldn't quite mask a gap where a back tooth used to be or the tobacco bits caught between front teeth. "Can't hardly wait to meet up with the gal who'll be Mrs. Clive Ackley."

Mack hoped whoever arrived to claim the title would have eyesight as poor as Clive's or she might run screaming for the Pratt Center depot when she got a good look at her prospective groom. Mack dropped another clattering half scoop of nails into the tin bowl and examined the scale. Two ounces past a pound. He pinched off a few nails, and the needle jiggled a smidgen past the one. Close enough.

He lifted the bowl and poured the nails into a paper bag. After rolling the top down tight, he held the bag to Clive. "There you are."

The man kept his hands in his trouser pockets. "I think you're makin' a mistake not addin' your letter to the packet."

Mack plopped the bag on the counter and gave it a little shove toward the postman. "Do you want these nails or not?"

Clive grabbed the bag, curling his sausage-shaped fingers around the rolled edge. He pointed at Mack with the lumpy bag. "You're gonna be wishin' you done somethin' differ'nt when every fella in town except you is sayin' his vows in front of Preacher Doan."

Mack brushed bits of iron shavings from the counter and ground them into the planked floor with the sole of his boot. In his opinion, the ones wishing they'd chosen different would be all those men who trusted a matchmaker from Newton, Massachusetts, to find them wives instead of relying on the Good Lord's guidance. But he'd said all that at the town meeting and nobody'd listened to him, the same way Uncle Ray hadn't listened to Ma and Pa, so what was the sense of repeating it?

"Go ahead and send those letters, Clive. I hope it works out good for all of you."

Clive shook his head, glaring at Mack in

11

disgust, but he ambled out of the building without another argument.

Mack grabbed the broom from its spot in the corner and set to work, smacking the straw bristles against the floor with more force than needed to clear the wide planks of dust. Sweat dribbled down his temples and dripped off his chin, leaving little splotches on the floor that quickly dried in the hot wind coursing through the open front door and wheezing out the back. If he didn't slow down, he might give himself heatstroke, but he had to channel his concerns somewhere, and the floor seemed a safe target.

Why wouldn't the men in town listen to reason? Buying a bride was foolhardy. Maybe even dangerous. The fellows in Spiveyville might not be the smartest men in the state of Kansas, but they were, for the most part, an honest lot. How could they know for sure the women who came at their request were honest? Could any woman who would make herself available to travel to a town she'd never visited and marry a man sight unseen be one a decent man would want to wed? Not likely.

Some of these women could be trying to escape the law. Maybe they were women of ill repute. And the men of Spiveyville planned to send their letters and hard-earned money to a matchmaker states away without any guarantee they'd end up with a bride. Why would they be so reckless?

Mack leaned against the broom's handle and sighed. He knew why. Because they were lonely. The same way Uncle Ray had been lonely. Truth be told, Mack was, too. His thirty-first birthday had passed a month ago, and he'd operated Spiveyville Hardware and Implements on his own for coming up on ten years. He wanted companionship — a family — as much as any other man his age did.

But lonely was one thing. Desperate was another. Gritting his teeth, he put the broom to work again. Every other unmarried man in Spiveyville could participate in the scheme, but he wanted nothing to do with any mail-order bride.

Mid-October 1888
Newton, Massachusetts
Abigail Grant

Abigail drew in a deep breath, allowed it a slow escape through her puckered lips, and finally reached for the doorknob. She gave the oval etched-glass knob a twist and pushed, pasting on a smile as the door

13

opened on silent hinges.

Mrs. Helena Bingham's gaze lifted from an open ledger on the polished top of the French Empire desk and settled on Abigail. Disappointment instantly sagged her lined face. "Here you are again."

Abigail lifted her chin even though her pulse thrummed in an erratic beat. She dropped her valise next to the doorway and crossed the cabbage-rose carpet, the fraying hem of her deep-russet skirt grazing the thick fibers. "I assure you, there was no other choice. The situation there was —"

Mrs. Bingham held up one hand, reminiscent of a courtroom judge. "Let me guess. Deplorable." She raised her snow-white brows. "Yes?"

Abigail pursed her lips. The woman needn't use such a sarcastic tone. She tugged her little travel hat from her head and dropped it on the desk. A wavy strand of hair — defined as "mink brown" on her summary sheet — slid along her cheek, and she pushed it behind her ear with an impatient thrust. "Completely so. A creek for water, a dirt floor — dirt! — and a sod roof. Spiders descended onto the table during dinner." She shuddered. "The place wasn't fit for animals, let alone humans."

Mrs. Bingham closed her eyes for a moment. When she opened them, the disapproval glimmering in her pale-gray irises pierced Abigail to the core of her being. "Abigail, Abigail, what am I to do with you?"

Abigail rested her fingertips on the edge of the desk. "Stop sending me to these barbaric locations for which I am woefully unsuited." She shifted her attention to the stack of applications resting in a delicate wire basket on the corner of the desk. "Isn't there at least one request from a gentleman?"

Even as she uttered the question, her heart divulged the sad truth. No gentlemen of prominent backgrounds relied upon a matchmaker to secure a bride. Their families and close friends guided them toward equally prominent prospects. At one time, she was considered a fine catch. But her family's tumble from the social registers as a result of Father's illegal dealings sealed her fate. She hung her head, bracing herself for Mrs. Bingham's response.

"Perhaps you aren't suited to matrimony at all."

Abigail jerked, meeting the older woman's unsmiling gaze. "N-not suited to . . ." After three years of harboring Abigail beneath her roof, had the matchmaker not learned how

15

much Abigail's heart yearned for a husband and family of her own? Why, even the Bible — what Mrs. Bingham herself declared God's holy Word! — spoke of the wisdom of every man having his own wife, and every wife her own husband.

Abigail sank slowly onto the padded seat of the side chair near the desk and gaped at the older woman through a veil of tears. "How can you say such a hurtful thing?"

"Sometimes being truthful requires one to be hurtful." Mrs. Bingham's pale eyes held a hint of regret, but her lips formed a grim line. "How many times have you traveled to meet a prospective groom and returned dissatisfied?"

Abigail blinked rapidly. "I, um, I . . . don't recall."

"Six times." Mrs. Bingham aimed a barbed look across the desk and steepled her hands on the ledger. "The first time, you claimed the house was too small and was without a cooking stove. The second time, the prospective groom had rotten teeth and bad breath. The third time, the distance from town was too great and you felt insecure. The fourth time, you said you couldn't possibly marry a man with such a short stature. The fifth time, the town itself had no apothecary or millinery shops — how could you survive in such a barren place? Now, this time, the reason is a dirt floor, sod roof, and spiders descending during meals."

"If you had seen the decrepit dwelling, you —"

"Abigail, you aren't fooling anyone. Not even, I daresay, yourself."

Abigail lifted her chin and narrowed her gaze. "What do you mean?"

Mrs. Bingham reached into a desk drawer and withdrew a small square piece of paper. She waved it gently. "I received this telegram three days ago. The same day you boarded the train for the return to Newton."

Perspiration broke over Abigail's frame.

"Shall I read it to you?"

Abigail wanted to refuse. She wanted to escape. But her tongue stuck to the roof of her dry mouth. Her quivering limbs resisted supporting her weight.

Mrs. Bingham slipped a pair of wire spectacles into place and angled the page toward the lamplight. " 'Sending her back. Too hoity-toity. Give me refund or new girl.' "

Humiliation swept through Abigail, searing her from the inside out. Had others sent similar messages? First rejected by young men from her rightful social class for her father's sins, and then rejected by unworthy

17

suitors for having manners too refined. Where would she find her place of belonging? The ache for a home and family of her own engulfed her and brought the desire to cry. But she sniffed hard, blinked away the moisture gathering in her eyes, and held her chin at a regal angle, the way Mother had taught her.

Mrs. Bingham flipped the telegram into the basket and pinned Abigail with a stern glare. "Tell me the truth. Whose decision was it for you to return to Newton — yours or his?"

She patted her forehead with the back of her gloved hand. "Well, I . . . He . . ." She swallowed and gripped her hands in her lap. "I suppose it was mutual."

"Mmm-hmm."

Abigail leaned forward slightly, beseeching the matchmaker with her eyes. "I'm a city girl, Mrs. Bingham. Send me to Boston, or New York, or even Philadelphia. I'm certain all will be fine if you'll only match me with someone of similar background and breeding."

Mrs. Bingham released a heavy sigh. "The description on the telegram — 'hoity-toity' — is far too accurate, and it is your biggest detriment to finding a match."

Abigail hung her head, blinking back

tears. How could refined manners be considered a detriment? Her earliest, most cherished memories were of tea parties with her dear mother, who patiently taught her how to use silverware, to pat rather than swipe her lips after small bites of pastries or sips of tea, to utilize proper speech and decorum. Now, with Mother gone, all that remained were memories and the refinement she'd learned from her gentle mother. Was she to discard these last bits of her former life for the sake of matrimony? Abigail forced aside her thoughts and focused on Mrs. Bingham's stern reprimand.

"My clients are down-to-earth, hardworking, responsible men who are seeking down-to-earth, hardworking, responsible women with whom to build a lifelong relationship. Sending you to a city will not solve the problem, because you will take your snooty airs, fastidious manners, and unrealistic expectations with you." She raised both hands in a gesture of surrender. "I've tried my hardest, but half a dozen failures is six too many for this business. If I continue to accept money for a match that cannot possibly succeed, you'll damage my reputation as a matchmaker."

She glanced toward the door, where Abigail's carpetbag sat plump with all her earthly belongings. "Your bag is still packed. Do not unpack it. Instead, take it and —"

Abigail leaped from the chair. She clasped her hands beneath her chin, shamed by her behavior yet too desperate to do otherwise. "Please don't remove me from your list of brides. Give me one more chance. I promise it will be different this time if you'll allow me one more opportunity."

Mrs. Bingham rose and rounded the desk, determination etched into her features. "I intend to give you one more opportunity. It —"

Abigail caught the woman's hands and held tight. "Oh, thank you, ma'am."

Mrs. Bingham withdrew her hands. "Will you kindly remain silent long enough for me to finish speaking?"

Abigail whisked her hands behind her back and closed her lips. But her chest rose and fell in rapid heaves of breath she couldn't seem to control. Oh, why had Father chosen such an unsavory path? Maybe it would have been better if she had died of a broken heart as Mother had. At least she'd be spared the abject indignity of begging.

Mrs. Bingham sorted through a file on her desk and removed a fat envelope. She held it in front of her like a shield. "This envelope, sent by men from a small town in Kansas, contains sixteen written requests for brides."

Hope fluttered to life in Abigail's breast. Surely out of sixteen men, there would be one acceptable candidate for her hand.

"If the placement fees hadn't been included, I would have discarded the entire lot. The letters . . ." The woman's face pursed. "Suffice it to say, many of the writers of these missives are sorely lacking in the social niceties."

Abigail bit the inside of her lip. The hope began to fizzle.

"But sixteen requests . . . As a good businesswoman, I cannot reject the potential income. Thus, I have been striving to secure matches for each of these men."

Abigail drew in a steadying breath. She'd promised to make her next assignment work. She was twenty-five already — by next April, she'd be too old to be included as a potential match. Regardless of how unattractive the man or how dismal his dwelling, she would have to accept him as her husband.

"But I will not send any of my girls to men who indicate a distinct bent toward loutishness. This group of prospective grooms must undergo a transformation." The

21

matchmaker dropped the envelope on the desk and folded her arms across her chest. "That is where you come in."

Abigail tilted her head. "I don't understand."

"You're well mannered, well spoken, and you possess an air of authority."

If the woman meant to compliment her, the tone she used fell short.

"If anyone has the ability to mold these men into suitable husbands for my girls, it's you." The woman moved behind the desk and rustled through a drawer. "I've already checked train schedules. There is a departure tomorrow afternoon for Pratt Center, Kansas. In the morning I'll send a wire to the telegrapher in Spiveyville and inform him to expect your arrival on the fifteenth of the month."

Wariness climbed Abigail's spine as nimbly as the spiders had climbed their webs in the little sod house in Nebraska. If Mrs. Bingham was planning what Abigail suspected, she wanted no part of it. "Ma'am? I —"

Mrs. Bingham straightened and fixed Abigail with a firm glare. "You owe me a tidy sum for refunded fees and train fares. Are you able to repay me in dollars and cents?"

Abigail gritted her teeth. If she had funds available, she wouldn't have set herself up

22

as a mail-order bride in the first place. The argument she'd been forming died on her tongue.

"Then you can repay me by serving as a tutor. I'm sending you to Spiveyville to ready the grooms for their brides."

Two

Spiveyville
Mack

"Mack! Mack!"

The frantic call from the street pulled Mack from sorting his latest shipment of hinges. He darted across the floor, his boot soles pounding as hard as his pulse. He was almost to the screen door when Clive Ackley burst in. The door's wood frame slapped against a large nail keg with a resounding *crack!*

The half-inch slash of Clive's cheeks not covered by his beard glowed bright red, and perspiration dotted his forehead. He waved a slip of paper like a flag. "Got . . . got a tel . . . telegram. They're comin'!"

Mack grabbed the postman by his heaving shoulders. "Who's comin'? Is there another uprising?" To his knowledge, the Cheyennes hadn't rebelled against white settlers since

24

'78 in neighboring Comanche County, but folks couldn't help worrying it could happen again. He gave Clive a firm shake. "Get yourself under control, man, and tell me who's comin'."

"Our brides!"

Mack let go of Clive so abruptly both men staggered. Or maybe it was relief making his knees go trembly. He planted his fists on his hips and gawked at the postman. "You came hollering up the street, near busted my door, to tell me that?"

Clive danced in place, his eyes shining brighter than a pair of new pennies. "Why, sure. I hadda tell you, 'cause you're gonna go get 'em from the train station."

Mack laughed. He took two backward steps toward the crate of hinges. "No, I'm not."

Clive scurried up behind him and grabbed his arm. "But you gotta."

Mack wrenched free and stomped to the crate. He bent down on one knee and rummaged in the box.

Clive curled his hands over the edge of the crate and leaned in, poking his nose in Mack's way. "You gotta go get 'em."

Mack sat back on his heels and blew out a breath. "Clive, I've got work to do. Would you go on now and —"

25

"Listen to me!" Clive dropped to his knees on the other side of the crate. "You gotta fetch our wives. All the ranchers, they can't take a full day away from their cows to make the trip. I'm a gov'ment-employed worker, so I gotta stay at the post office an' see to the telegraph. Louis Griffin'll be cuttin' hair an' trimmin' beards on every fella who sent a letter 'cause we're all wantin' to look our best."

Mack squinted at Clive. "You're gonna let Louis trim your beard?"

"Yep." Clive combed his fingers through his shaggy beard. A few crumbs — probably from his breakfast biscuits — dropped onto his stained striped shirtfront. "Least a little. Maybe."

Mack smirked.

Clive snorted and made a face. "The thing is, you're the only one who ain't gonna be sprucin' up your house or buyin' new suspenders or seein' to livestock. The rest of us, we got duties here. But nothin' in a hardware store's so important that you can't shut down for a day to make the trip. 'Sides that, you're the only one who ain't gonna pick out a wife from the bunch, so it only makes sense for you to go."

Clive's comment about Mack's livelihood being unimportant stung, but he decided

26

not to argue the point. "How do you make sense out of me going after those women? Seems to me, since I'm not interested in them, I ought to stay out of the whole thing."

"And you can, after you've brung 'em to Spiveyville. But since you don't plan on marryin' up, we can trust you not to grab the comeliest one for yourself before the rest of us get a gander at 'em. See?"

"All I can see is that I'm being lassoed into losing a day's business and making a long drive for no good reason."

Clive angled his head like a fighting rooster. "You sayin' helpin' out your friends an' neighbors ain't a good enough reason?"

Shame fell over Mack like a sack of grain. Hadn't Preacher Doan talked on putting the needs of others above self only last Sunday? Hadn't these same townsfolk gathered around and supported him during his neediest time? His ma, bless her soul, modeled Christian love and kindness every day of her life. What would she tell him to do? He sighed. He knew what she'd tell him.

He hung his head. "When're they due in?"

Clive whooped and threw both arms in the air. "Train's set to arrive at Pratt Center's CK&N Railway station at two next Monday afternoon." He gave Mack a solid

27

clap on the shoulder. "All the fellas is gonna be right excited to see our brides, an' we're all gonna be beholden to you for bringin' 'em to us. Gotta go spread the good news now. Thanks again, Mack!"

Clive bolted out the door, and Mack shook his head, worry building an ache in his gut. *"Beholden,"* Clive had said. Well, Clive — and all the others — might choose a different response if these ladies turned out to not be *ladies* at all. He hoped his friends and neighbors wouldn't hold him responsible when the entire scheme collapsed.

October 15, 1888
Pratt Center, Kansas
Helena Bingham

Helena stepped from the passenger car's platform onto the dirt street. A gust of wind tugged at her wide-brimmed feathered hat and peppered her broadcloth travel suit with dust and fine sand. The folds of her overskirt captured tiny grains, the pale bits of grit obnoxious against the peacock-blue fabric. With a little grunt of irritation, she smacked the skirt clean, leaving a few more smudges on her gloves, which had been pristine white when she began this journey three days ago but now were the most unappealing shade of mouse gray. Swallowing another *uh!* of irritation, she lifted her gaze to the town.

The newness of the city showed in the crisp white, unpainted clapboards covering nearly every business on the wide, unpaved street. The railway station stood out with its coat of red paint and bold-yellow window casings, as proud as a cardinal in a flock of sparrows, but its cheerful appearance only served to highlight the dismal appearance of every other place of business. Unexpectedly, a thread of empathy wove through her. Perhaps she'd been too quick to judge Abigail for criticizing the previous placements. Everything within her strained to climb back on board the train and return to Newton and her well-ordered, beautifully decorated world as quickly as possible. But she couldn't leave. Not yet.

Abigail's aghast face resided in her memory, along with the young woman's shocked query — *"You intend to send me, alone and unprotected, to a gang of loutish men?"* As much as Helena hated to admit it, she'd been shortsighted in her plan to have Abigail tutor the Kansas ranchers. She held no doubt Abigail could teach the men decorum. Helena hailed from the upper society herself and understood manners and morals as well as anyone, yet she'd never met a woman who held to the standards as stringently as Abigail Marguerite Grant. But sending her alone, without chaperonage, would invite trouble. She must ensure the young woman's safety. So here she was, standing on the dirt street of an uncivilized Kansas town, with her trusty derringer weighting her velvet reticule.

Abigail descended the metal step and stood close to Helena, her slumped shoulders and dark-rimmed eyes making her seem much older than her twenty-five years. Helena recalled her own dear sister, Marietta Constance, carrying the same sorrowful countenance in her midtwenties. Now at a mature forty-one, a full eighteen years younger than Helena, Marietta's permanently rounded shoulders and the lines of unhappiness etched in her brow gave her the appearance of the older sister. Automatically, Helena chided, "Stand up straight. Tired or not, a lady never slouches."

Abigail snapped upright as if someone had tied a string beneath her chin and gave a yank. She scanned the area, her full lips set in a moue of distaste. "It doesn't seem as if anyone is waiting for us."

Railroad workers and other disembarking

passengers bustled to and fro. All seemed to throw curious glances their way — understandable, considering how their city finery contrasted the simple calico dresses and bonnets worn by other women — but no one approached them. Helena gestured to a long bench tucked against the station's wall in a patch of shade. "The answering telegram from Spiveyville assured me we would be collected from the station. Perhaps our driver has been delayed. Let's sit over there and wait for his arrival."

On their way to the bench, Helena captured the attention of a young man wearing gray trousers, a blue shirt, and the telltale brimmed railroad cap. "Would you please bring our luggage from the baggage car? Two trunks and a valise, each tagged with the name Bingham."

"Yes, ma'am!" He trotted off.

Helena guided Abigail to the bench and they sat side by side, ankles crossed, hands in their laps. Abigail's reticule dangled by its string against her thigh, but Helena kept hers nestled beneath her gloved hands in case she had need of the derringer. Some of the men striding up and down the street held a rough appearance.

A telegraph sign poked from the corner of the railway station. Perhaps she should have

31

the telegrapher send a message to Marietta and assure her they'd arrived safely in Kansas. Her dear sister would likely pace the floors until she received the news. Marietta tended to worry too much, and her active imagination always conjured the most ridiculous scenarios. Although it pained Helena to trust Bingham's Bevy of Brides to Marietta's keeping for the next two weeks, perhaps the responsibility would fill her sister's hours enough to rid her mind of invented trials. One could hope, anyway.

The railroad worker to whom Helena had assigned the task of retrieving their luggage approached, pulling a small wheeled platform. He doffed his hat, swiped a few beads of sweat from his forehead, and grinned. "Here you go, lady. Two trunks an' a carpetbag. Seems like an awful lot for just two people."

She'd taken more luggage for a four-day riverboat cruise than what now waited on the flatbed cart. She turned a tart look on the fellow. "I asked you to bring my belongings, not to offer commentary on my travel practices."

The man's grin faded. He blinked, removed his cap, and scratched his head. "What's that you said?"

Helena pinched a nickel from her reticule

and held it out. "Never mind. Thank you for your trouble."

The man pocketed the coin and then plopped his cap over his unruly hair. "Are you ladies needin' a rig? There's a livery stable about two blocks north. I can ask my boss if he'd let me run over and —"

"We have a driver coming, young man." The wind gusted and Helena grabbed the rolled brim of her hat. She'd applied three jeweled hatpins, and all three were trying to tear her hair from her head. Perhaps she should have opted for a smaller hat, similar to the little straw bowler set at a perky angle in front of the thick braid secured into a coil at Abigail's crown.

Helena frowned. "Is it always this windy in Kansas?"

"No, ma'am. Sometimes it's downright blustery an' carries a whole wall of dirt. We're all enjoyin' this nice mild weather." He tipped his cap, turned on his heel, and hurried off.

Abigail clamped her fingers over Helena's wrist. "Did he say a wall of dirt?"

Helena patted the younger woman's hand, although unease pressed at her the way the wind pressed flat the ostrich feathers woven to her hat. "I'm sure he's exaggerating. I've heard of dust storms, of course, but they

33

are more prevalent on the open prairie and during the dry months. This is October, when fall rain and early snowfalls moisten the ground. Don't borrow trouble, Abigail."

Abigail nodded, but her dubious expression brought a reminder of Marietta's constant state of uncertainty, and sympathy struck anew. Helena offered another comforting pat on the young woman's hand, and to her relief a small smile quivered on Abigail's lips.

Helena leaned against the lap siding and steeled herself against a yawn. Tiredness sent her thoughts drifting backward. She'd begun her matchmaking business partly because she'd enjoyed such wonderful years with her dear husband, Howard, and believed every woman should experience marital bliss at least once in life, but mostly because she'd witnessed the increasing sorrow in her dear sister's eyes when suitor after suitor passed her by. From a business standing, Helena should have sent Abigail packing months ago, but from a personal standing, she couldn't bear to do it. Marietta was well beyond hope, but Abigail was still young enough to march up the aisle in wedding finery. Helena vowed to do whatever she could to keep Abigail from falling into the same unhappy, dissatisfied pit in which Marietta now resided.

The engine's whistle blared, offering a welcome intrusion. Steam puffed from the smokestack, and the iron wheels groaned against the silver lines of track. The locomotive's power vibrated the platform and the wooden bench, and tingles traveled up the back of Helena's legs. The train rolled forward, the whistle continuing to pierce the air until the engine and all eight cars departed the town.

A few minutes after the last whistle faded into the distance, a horse-drawn wagon drew close to the platform, and a thick-chested man with a dapper horseshoe-shaped mustache brought the team to a halt. He set the brake with a thrust of his boot, then leaped nimbly over the wagon's edge. Dust rose when his feet met the ground, but the wind quickly whisked it away. He swatted his brown trousers and suit lapels with his palms, adjusted the ribbon at the throat of his plaid shirt, and finally lifted his gaze. It settled on Helena and Abigail. He stared at them through narrowed lids for several seconds and then gave a little nod, as if agreeing with himself about something.

He clumped up on the platform and strode directly to them, dragging his cowboy hat from his head and revealing a headful of slicked-down dark hair as he came. His blue-eyed gaze drifted briefly to Abigail and then settled on Helena. "Good afternoon, ladies. Are you some of the brides from Massachusetts?"

Helena rose and extended her hand. "I am Mrs. Helena Bingham, owner of Bingham's Bevy of Brides. This is Miss Abigail Grant." Abigail stood and dipped in a slight curtsy while gripping her reticule in front of her. "And you are . . ."

"Mack Cleveland, ma'am."

Helena pressed her memory, but the name didn't sound familiar. "Are you a prospective groom, Mr. Cleveland?"

His clean-shaven cheeks blazed red. "Um, no, ma'am. But the men of Spiveyville are real excited about you all coming." He glanced left and right. "Are the brides inside the station? It's a four-hour drive back to Spiveyville, and I'd like to get loaded and on our way as quick as possible."

Abigail flicked a puzzled look at Helena.

Helena looped her arm around Abigail's waist. "It's only the two of us."

He chewed the corner of his mustache. "You only brought one bride for sixteen men?"

Helena laughed softly. "Miss Grant isn't a

bride. She is my assistant."

He bounced his hat against his thigh, his face set in a scowl that couldn't quite mask his rugged handsomeness. Strength, as well as impatience, emanated from the man. "Then are the brides coming on the next train? I didn't expect to stay in Pratt Center for the whole day."

Helena cleared her throat. "As I said, it's only the two of us."

If his frown deepened any further, his eyebrows would form a V. "Ma'am, there are sixteen eager grooms in Spiveyville expecting me to bring back a wagonload of brides." He twisted the brim of his hat, pausing to bite at his mustache again. "I don't know what kind of scam you've got going, but I won't play a part in it."

Indignation flooded Helena. She matched his scowl with one of her own. "Mr. Cleveland, I operate an honest business. If I intended to swindle people, why would I make the long and tiring journey from my comfortable home in Massachusetts to the barren plains of Kansas?"

He peered at her for long, silent seconds with his brows tugged low and his lower lip poked out. Finally he sighed. "All right, then. But where are the brides?"

"They will come when I've assured myself

that decent, law-abiding husbands are awaiting them." Helena held her hand toward the little wagon. "Will you kindly load our luggage and help us into your conveyance? If it's a four-hour drive" — she cringed, imagining the discomfort of riding in that rattling wooden box for so many hours — "we should be on our way as expediently as possible."

Without a word, he grabbed the handle on the rolling cart and pulled it across the platform. Helena and Abigail followed.

While he loaded the trunks into the back of the wagon, Abigail leaned close to Helena's ear. "I hope the hotel offers hot baths. We'll be completely coated with dust by the time we reach Spiveyville."

Abigail had whispered, but apparently Mr. Cleveland heard, because he turned a sheepish grimace in their direction. "I hate to disappoint you, but Spiveyville doesn't have a hotel."

Wariness tiptoed through Helena's frame. "No hotel? Then perhaps a boardinghouse?"

He shook his head. "But there's a saloon-turned-restaurant. The upstairs has some rooms where the, er, working girls stayed before Governor St. John brought an end to alcohol sales."

Abigail gasped and Helena clasped her

own throat, which had gone suddenly dry.

"Over the years, a few visitors to town have made use of those rooms." The man tossed Abigail's carpetbag over the tall side of the wagon. "Athol Patterson owns the place. You can talk to him about renting a room or two when we get to town. That is" — he propped his elbow on the wagon's frame and peered at them from beneath the brim of his hat — "if you still want to ride on to Spiveyville with me."

Helena licked her lips. If she hadn't only recently lectured Abigail about being too finicky, she would order the man to put her trunks back on the platform and she would board the first train heading east. But how could she turn up her nose now without looking hypocritical? Besides, settling more than a dozen brides was too lucrative a deal to reject. The fees were appealing and, even more than that, sixteen happy grooms in one fell swoop would certainly boost her business.

She forced a smile. "Please assist us into the wagon, Mr. Cleveland, and let's be on our way. I am most eager to make the acquaintance of the men in Spiveyville."

THREE

Mack

Worry held Mack's tongue for the first hour of their journey from Pratt Center. It wouldn't surprise him a bit if the band of men gathering on the streets of Spiveyville to welcome their brides turned into a lynch mob the minute they saw the empty wagon bed. But they wouldn't string up these two women. They'd go after *his* neck.

Mack ran his finger under the collar of his shirt. October — shouldn't it be cooling down by now? The thermostat on the side of Louis Griffin's barbershop had showed seventy-two degrees when he set out for Pratt Center. It felt twice that hot now riding under a cloudless sky, all snugged up against the puffy skirts worn by the owner of Bingham's Bevy of Brides, the sun high and bright and the wind blasting him.

He risked a glance at the business owner.

Not young anymore, but not old, either. Sixty, maybe? Ma would have his hide if he asked. The woman sat ramrod straight, toes of her button-up shoes peeking out from the hem of her bold-blue dress, gloved hands clutching a lumpy coal-black pouch in her lap, and steely gaze aimed beyond the horses' rumps. She dressed like a fancy woman, the kind Uncle Ray called "wilting violets" after the Wilhelmina mess — *"All show an' no go,"* he'd mutter with disdain — but the only thing wilting on Mrs. Bingham was her hat. Or, more accurately, the feathers on her hat.

The puffy white plumes had slowly lost their fluff during the ride and turned into flattened strips that drooped down her neck. Did they tickle? If so, she wasn't letting on. He suspected Mrs. Bingham was no wilting violet, but it remained to be seen if she was a swindler.

The other woman, the younger one with puckering rosebud lips and lashes so full and thick they threw a shadow on her cheeks, clung to the edge of the jouncing seat and braced her feet against the wagon's toe board. Her pale skin bore a pink hue — sunburn. A woman who came to the plains of Kansas ought to have sense enough to wear a bonnet instead of a little straw hat

41

that covered only the front half of the top of her head. Even so, he felt sorry for her. She'd be hurting bad tonight.

He cleared his throat. "Miss Grant, if you've got a handkerchief in that bag of yours, you might want to hold it over your face."

She shot a short glare past Mrs. Bingham. "For what purpose?"

"To keep the sun off." The glowing yellow ball was on its downward trail as afternoon waned, but it was still plenty bright.

"If I release my hold on the seat to keep a handkerchief over my face, I will surely bounce over the side. This is the roughest road I have ever traveled." The wagon wheel hit a rut, and her teeth clacked. She set her jaw.

Mack chuckled, more amused than offended. "Well, I'm not sure we should call it a road. It's more of a trail, carved by cattle being driven to market. Now that the Chicago, Kansas & Nebraska Railway has a line going through Pratt Center, I figure in a year or two enough wagons will have come this way to make it an official road. I don't guess that helps much right now though, huh?"

A soft snort gave him a reply. She didn't reach for the bag hanging on her wrist.

42

"We've already determined Spiveyville has no hotel. Does it also lack a livery?"

Mack frowned. "No. Hugh Briggs — you likely got a letter from him — owns the Spiveyville livery. He's a fine farrier and wainwright. Also does a little veterinary work for the local ranchers."

"Most liverymen have carriages to rent."

Mack shifted the reins to one hand and scratched his cheek. He couldn't make sense of this conversation. "That's true enough."

"If you'd rented a carriage, Mrs. Bingham and I could be riding comfortably out of the rays of the sun. We also wouldn't have to squeeze ourselves onto such a small seat."

Hugh didn't own an enclosed carriage. The only enclosed carriage in all of Spiveyville belonged to the town's banker, Tobis Adelman, and he never let anyone else drive it. Mack shrugged. "I'll grant you it's a tight fit." His left hip ached from rubbing against the lip of the seat. "I can stop and let you climb in the back if you'd like. Either of those trunks would make a fine seat for the rest of the ride." Maybe she could hunker behind him and Mrs. Bingham, where their forms threw a shadow over the bed.

"I do not wish to sit on a trunk in the back of the wagon, Mr. Cleveland."

"But if you —"

"Abigail, Abigail . . ." Mrs. Bingham patted Miss Grant's knee and offered Mack an apologetic smile. "Please forgive my assistant. She's quite weary from our lengthy train ride, and tiredness is making her short tempered."

Mack wasn't sure, but he thought he detected a hint of warning in the older woman's tone. If so, it wasn't intended for him. "No offense taken, ma'am."

Two tumbleweeds rolled across their path, and the horses skittered sideways, rocking the wagon. Miss Grant squealed. The horses flattened their ears, and their muscles flexed. Mack double-fisted the reins and prepared in case the horses took a notion to run wild. He'd had to make several circles on the open prairie outside of town before driving into Pratt Center when the train's whistle startled them earlier that day. If he tried the same tactic now, he'd spill either himself or Miss Grant over the edge. If she went, he'd never hear the end of it. If he went, the wagon would be driverless. He couldn't decide which situation would be worse.

"Easy, easy now." He kept his voice low, calming. The horses snorted, but their ears relaxed and they settled back into a slow, steady *clip-clop*. He released a sigh, sending up a grateful prayer. Then he turned a stern look on the younger of his travel companions. "Miss, I'd appreciate it if you wouldn't do that again."

"Do what?"

"Make that noise."

"What noise?"

Did she think he would imitate her? "That one you made — the high-pitched noise."

She sniffed. "My apologies, Mr. Cleveland, but when the horses reacted to those large clumps of . . . whatever they were, it startled me."

"Those were tumbleweeds, miss, and you'll likely see more of them. They blow around out here a lot. The horses aren't fond of sudden movements, but they like sudden noises even less. Shrill noises, especially, spook 'em. If they get spooked, they might run. If they run, the wagon could tip, and then . . . Well, I figure you're bright enough to understand what could happen."

"Yes," Mrs. Bingham said, humor lacing her tone, "we wouldn't want to spill my trunks all over the prairie. My belongings could blow all the way to Nebraska."

Mack coughed a short laugh. "Well, ma'am, considering the wind is coming from the north, they'd more likely end up in Oklahoma Territory. But I wouldn't want to dump your trunks. Or anything else."

"Nor would I." Once again, the older woman placed her hand on the younger one's knee. "She will control her outbursts. Am I right, Abigail?"

"Yes, ma'am." But she sounded more aggravated than agreeable.

Mack chewed his mustache for a moment. "Ma'am, can I ask you a question?"

"Of course you may."

"Back at the train station, you said Miss Grant is your assistant. What exactly does she do?"

A sly smile curved the woman's lips. "I believe I will answer your question when we've reached Spiveyville. In the meantime, Mr. Cleveland, would you be kind enough to tell us about the town? The letters I received from prospective grooms spoke clearly of the senders', er, needs in a life partner, but none offered much information about Spiveyville as a community."

"What would you like to know?"

"Everything."

He scratched his chin, searching his mind for something interesting about Spiveyville. He shrugged. "How about I start with its history?"

"That would be fine."

Even though Mack had no connection to

any of the founding members of Spiveyville, he took pride in the little town he now considered home. He enjoyed sharing the details of Spiveyville's humble beginning as an army fort and trading post at the edge of Indian territory. "When houses started springing up around the fort — built by settlers who felt safe close to the small army base — they decided to name the area Spiveyville in honor of General Spivey, who was in charge of the fort. I never met him, but everyone says he was a fair, honest, kindhearted man who humbly served the Lord."

Both women gazed at him attentively. Their interest encouraged him to keep talking. He leaned forward, resting his elbows on his knees, and gave the reins a little flick to keep the horses moving.

"The fort was closed in 1867 by President Johnson, but the settlers stayed, and a town sprang up where the fort used to be. We have our own church and school, and a post office with a telegraph." He envisioned the main street and traveled it in his mind. "There's a bank and land surveyor's office, a restaurant, a bakery, a tailor, a barbershop, a livery stable — I guess I already mentioned Briggs's livery, didn't I? We've got a good-sized general merchandise store with grocer-

47

ies, dry goods, and household items. Grover Thompson — he wouldn't have asked for a bride because he already has one — owns the mercantile and makes sure to stock anything we need. We're lucky to have Doc Kettering. He treats people and pulls teeth as well as sees to livestock. He has a little apothecary in his office, too. Then I own the Spiveyville hardware store. That's all the businesses."

Miss Grant's fine eyebrows pinched together. The top of her nose was as bright as a ripe cherry. "No dress shop or millinery?"

Mack shook his head. "The ladies in Spiveyville sew their own clothes or order ready-made from the catalog." Her dismayed expression stole a bit of his pleasure in the telling. "I guess Spiveyville's not much of a town when compared to big cities in the east, but it's clean and made up of mostly fair, honest, good-hearted men who serve the Lord. A fitting tribute to its namesake."

"What about women?" Mrs. Bingham fanned herself with her palm. "Are there fair, honest, good-hearted women in Spiveyville? I ask because I have never in my years of serving as a matchmaker received so many requests from a single location."

Mack sat up again and accidentally

bumped Mrs. Bingham with his elbow. He excused himself and shifted as far to the left as possible. He'd be happy to get off this bench. It wasn't made for three across. "There are some women, and I'd say they fit the description I gave for the men. But every woman who's old enough to be married already has a husband. There's a handful of girls — our school has almost forty kids enrolled — but the oldest of the lot's only thirteen."

"And do you already have a wife, Mr. Cleveland?" No amusement or rancor showed in the matchmaker's expression. If he'd seen either, he wouldn't have answered.

"No, ma'am."

"Yet you didn't request a bride."

"No, ma'am."

"Because you don't trust matchmakers?"

Mack trusted the Good Lord, the only one who should be matchmaking, in his opinion, but he wouldn't insult the woman's business. Not until he knew for sure it wasn't legitimate. He cleared his throat. "The men who sent you letters have waited a long while to take a wife, and they're eager to become husbands and fathers."

Worry struck anew. What would Clive Ackley and Hugh Briggs and Athol Patterson and all the others say when he arrived

49

without their expected brides? He'd told Mrs. Bingham the men were honest, good-hearted fellows, but they might not act like it when they realized the matchmaker came by herself. Well, except for Miss Grant, who looked the right age to be getting married but wasn't available. And maybe that was for the best. Her snappy tone and thinly veiled complaints didn't endear her to him. What man wanted to marry up with a shrew, even if she was pretty to look upon? And Miss Grant was pretty. Well, except for the sunburn.

Mack bounced a nod in her direction. "When we get to Spiveyville, Miss Grant, I'll take you to see Doc Kettering."

Her eyes, with irises as brown as a doe's, opened wide. "For what purpose?"

"I figure your nose and cheeks are going to hurt something fierce tonight since you didn't shade your face like I suggested. The sun's baked it red as a clay brick." Her eyes were red rimmed, too. The sun had baked more than her face.

She clapped her gloved hands to her cheeks and stared at him, her mouth forming an O.

"Doc keeps a whole garden of aloe plants on his windowsill. If you snap off one of its leaves and rub the gooey stuff from inside

50

onto a burn, it takes the sting out." He flicked another look at her. "He might need to use more than one leaf on you."

She jerked her gaze away from him, and then she jolted and gasped. "Look at all the cows!"

Mack glanced across the rolling prairie. Sure enough, on both sides of the road, small herds grazed on the thick brown prairie grass. If they'd encountered herds, they were closing in on the town. Which meant, very soon, he'd be face to face with a whole herd of disappointed grooms.

He pulled in air until his lungs were so full his expanded chest strained his shirt buttons, held the breath for several seconds, then blew it out. He'd never backed away from a confrontation or hid behind a woman's skirts before, but depending on how the eager men of Spiveyville reacted to his empty wagon bed, today might be the first.

FOUR

Spiveyville, Kansas
Abigail

Abigail cupped her hand above her sore, wind-dried eyes and surveyed the town appearing by increments as the wagon topped a slight rise in the road. Small — not unlike some other towns to which she'd traveled and from which she'd fled — but neat, with buildings of red brick or stone blocks lining both sides of the wide dirt street that divided the town in half. No trash blew about in the wind. Spiveyville was certainly better kept than the grounds around the sod house in Nebraska, which had been littered with food scraps, animal droppings, and various broken implements.

She squinted, trying to make out the strange construction in the middle of the street. "Is there a statue in the center of Spiveyville, Mr. Cleveland?"

The man gave her a puzzled look. "Statue? No. Although the fellows have said if we ever build a town square, they'd like to have someone make a statue of General Spivey."

"Then what is . . ." She blinked rapidly, forcing her eyes to focus, and at once she realized a band of men stood shoulder to shoulder, all with heads shiny from oil. Macassar oil, if her nose was correct in identifying the scent of coconut on the wind.

Mr. Cleveland crunched his face into a scowl. "Looks like the grooms are waiting."

Mrs. Bingham adjusted her hat and brushed dust from her dress front. "How nice of them to meet us and make us welcome."

Mr. Cleveland angled a look Abigail would define as wry at the matchmaker, but he didn't say anything. What was he thinking behind those piercing blue eyes of his? She glanced at his firmly set lips. It might be better if she didn't know.

She turned her gaze to the waiting throng, and her heart began a rapid patter. Mr. Cleveland had indicated they were eager, and she saw evidence of it in their raised chins, wide grins, and twitching frames. These would be her students. Would their eagerness extend to learning the manners Mrs. Bingham expected her to teach? A

53

schoolteacher kept his or her pupils on task with threats from a hickory switch. How would she keep these grown men focused?

The panic she'd first experienced when Mrs. Bingham presented her plan returned in a rush, and her pulse bounced as wildly as a tumbleweed crossing the prairie. She grasped the side of the wagon and wished she still believed in God so she could pray for strength.

Mr. Cleveland stopped the wagon at the edge of the business district, twenty paces from the men. For a moment the group remained in a line, as if suddenly overcome with bashfulness. Then a rotund man with a full, bushy beard jabbed his fist in the air and whooped — a sound nearly as high pitched as Abigail's squeal had been. The entire smiling group surged forward.

Had Mr. Cleveland not set the brake, Abigail was certain the horses would run away. The poor animals shifted within their traces, tossing their heads and snorting in protest as the mob of men surrounded the wagon. They grabbed the sides and peeked into the bed, and then as one they raised their scowls.

"Hey!" A tall, rawboned man with a sunscorched face and the sleeves of his plaid shirt rolled back to expose thickly muscled forearms balled his hands into fists and marched to Mr. Cleveland's side of the bench. "What'd you do with our wives, Mack? Leave 'em behind?"

The men muttered, nudging each other and sending accusing glares at Mr. Cleveland. Abigail's heart pounded with such intensity she feared she would faint. She gripped the seat's edge even harder although her fingers ached badly.

A second man, as tall and suntanned as the first but wiry and wearing a dusty, threadbare suit, settled his gaze on Abigail. His frown changed to elation, and he darted at her, arms extended. "Least there's this one." Before she had a chance to react, he grabbed her around the waist, lifted her from the bench, and held her up as if claiming a prize. "I'll take you, even if you are a scrawny thing an' I requested a woman with some meat on her bones."

Abigail pounded her fists on his solid shoulders. "Release me at once, you brute!"

The fellow laughed and set her feet on the ground. "Not much meat on her, but she's sure got gumption!" He grinned down at her, his eyes nearly squinting shut. "My name's W. C., darlin'. What's yours?"

Before Abigail could answer, the men swarmed the clod. Faces pressed near, warm breath grazed her burning cheeks, and their clamoring voices pierced her eardrums.

"You got no claim to her, W. C. Let 'er go!"

"Hoo-boy, them are some fancy duds she's wearin'. This un's a real looker. I asked for a purty one. I aim to keep 'er."

"We gonna hafta draw straws to see who gets her?"

"I asked for a little gal, so she suits me fine. C'mere an' lemme get a better look at-cha."

"What color are your eyes, honey? I'm partial to green."

One of the men tapped her shoulder with his finger. "You ever saddled a horse, little gal?"

Abigail jerked away from the offensive lout, which caused her to slam against W. C.'s chest. He slung his arm around her waist and grinned like a fool. She'd never felt so exposed and vulnerable and frightened. And angry. Why didn't Mrs. Bingham or Mr. Cleveland do something? She flung a pleading look at Mrs. Bingham. The woman stood glaring down at the milling mob, her fists on her hips. Her mouth was moving, which meant she must be speaking, but her words were lost in the ruckus caused by the men.

Mr. Cleveland peered past Mrs. Bingham, and his gaze collided with hers. Grim determination steeled his features. He leaped over the side of the wagon and plowed through the group, pushing men left and right. They grunted and yelped, but they didn't try to block him. He reached the center and yanked W. C.'s hand from her waist. Then he planted both palms on the man's chest and sent him backward several feet.

W. C. caught his balance and glowered at her rescuer. "What're you doin', Mack? You didn't even send for a bride, so you got no call to —"

Mack jabbed his finger at him. "You've got no call to accost the lady the way you did. Look at her. She's scared half to death."

Abigail scuttled away from the group and hugged herself, her chest heaving as if she'd run the distance between Pratt Center and Spiveyville. She eyed the circle of men, ready to shriek louder than anyone had ever shrieked before if one of them so much as stretched a finger toward her.

W. C. squinted at Abigail, and remorse twisted his mouth. "Reckon I did come at-cha a little strong. Sure didn't mean to scare you. But you gotta understand, you're a welcome sight in these parts, miss."

The bushy-bearded man whose waving fist and whoop had begun the entire melee glared at Mr. Cleveland. "Nobody would've gone after her that way if there'd been more'n one woman with you. Where's the rest of 'em? The telegram said all our brides'd be comin' today."

"I beg to differ with you, sir." Mrs. Bingham moved to the edge of the wagon and held her hands to Mr. Cleveland. He assisted her down, and she glided across the dusty ground to the grumbling man. "Your name, please."

The man folded his stubby arms over his chest. "Clive Ackley. I'm the postman an' the telegrapher for Spiveyville."

"Where is the telegram of which you spoke, Mr. Ackley?"

He poked his pudgy fingers in his shirt pocket and withdrew a scrap of paper. "Right here. Been carryin' it next to my —" He grunted. "That is, been carryin' it ever since it come."

Mrs. Bingham beckoned to Abigail with her quirked fingers, and Abigail crossed on shaking legs to the matchmaker. The woman curved her arm around Abigail's waist, her encircling gesture much more welcome than the one from W. C., and offered a slight nod

58

at the telegrapher. "Read it, please. Loudly, so everyone can hear."

From the corner of her eye, Abigail witnessed Mr. Cleveland slip between buildings. Disappointment stabbed hard. She'd thought him chivalrous when he came to her defense, but would a chivalrous man leave two women to face an angry mob unprotected?

The telegrapher unfolded the paper, gruffly cleared his throat, and held the telegram nearly under his nose. " 'Coming . . . October 15. Arrive on two o'clock train. Please send . . . driver.' " He scowled over the top of the telegram. "See? Says right there send somebody to pick up our brides." The men began to mutter again.

Mrs. Bingham held up her finger, and silence fell. A soft smile graced her face. "Ah, Mr. Ackley, you made a presumption. How is the telegram signed?"

He shifted his scowl to the paper. "Mrs. Helennuh —"

"It's pronounced Heleena," Mrs. Bingham said.

The small amount of his face not hidden by the overgrown beard flushed pink. "Heleena Bingham."

"It doesn't say, 'The brides for Spiveyville's single men'?"

59

The man's thick brows formed one fuzzy mass in the middle of his fore-head with his fierce scowl. "I done told you, it's signed Mrs. Hel— Heleena Bingham."

The matchmaker extended her hand in a graceful motion. "I am Mrs. Helena Bingham and, as the telegram stated I would, I arrived on the two o'clock train."

"But where are our brides?" The tall man with the thick forearms shouted the question, and others echoed it with varying degrees of frustration and confusion.

"Your brides, gentlemen, are in Newton, Massachusetts."

"Massachusetts!" Half a dozen men blasted the word, and the others clenched their fists and muttered.

"Yes," Mrs. Bingham said as sweetly and calmly as if addressing the gathering of a ladies' club, "where they will stay until —"

The grumbling rose again, louder than before and with greater acrimony. The men bumped each other with their elbows, their faces red and angry. Abigail grabbed Mrs. Bingham's elbow. Should they escape to a safe hiding spot? She searched the area for a likely place in which to hide.

Clive Ackley pushed the telegram into his pocket and hooked his thumbs on his suspenders. "Listen here, lady, I —"

"Clive, watch your temper. Is that a polite way to speak to a guest in Spiveyville?"

The genial yet firm voice of a stranger came from behind Abigail. She glanced over her shoulder. Mr. Cleveland approached with another man — obviously a man of the cloth, based on his black suit, white collar, and the Bible tucked in the crook of his arm. Mr. Cleveland stopped near the horses, but the preacher strode to the shuffling group of men. Abigail swallowed a knot of regret. She'd misjudged Mr. Cleveland.

The telegrapher threw his arms outward. "Preacher Doan, this lady tricked us. We all ordered brides from her, but instead of bringin' a whole passel, she just brung one. I sent in our bride-dues — enough for a bride apiece for all o' us — an' she didn't keep up her end of the deal. I got every right to be angry."

"Maybe you do, and maybe you don't." The preacher placed his hand on Mr. Ackley's round shoulder. "Either way, remember the biblical admonition to 'be ye angry, and sin not.'"

The telegrapher hung his head and toed the ground. Many of the others snuffled or shifted their sheepish gazes to the fading sky.

Preacher Doan smiled at Mrs. Bingham

61

and Abigail. "Welcome to Spiveyville, Mrs. Bingham and Miss Grant. Mack tells me you traveled all the way from Newton, Massachusetts. You must be tired and hungry after your long journey." He turned a firm look on the group of men. "It's six thirty already, fellows, and night will fall before we know it. I think it's best that you all return to your homes."

"But, Preacher!" A short man with bright-red hair and the air of a fighting cock stomped his scuffed boot. "She ain't told us yet what happened to our brides!" More mutters erupted.

Abigail pressed closer to Mrs. Bingham, fear making her mouth go dry.

The preacher shook his head. "Vern, I know you've waited a long time for a bride. All of you have. But doesn't Romans 12:12 instruct us to be patient in tribulation?"

The red-headed man scowled, but he fell silent, as did the others in the group.

"You'll get your answers. I'll see to it." Preacher Doan sent a meaningful glance over his shoulder at the women before facing the men again. "Meet me tomorrow evening — seven thirty at the church. Mrs. Bingham and her assistant will be there and will answer all your questions." He turned a slow circle to pin Abigail and Mrs. Bingham with the same firm look he'd given the rowdy men. "Is that all right with you, ladies?"

Mrs. Bingham nodded, the scraggly feathers of her hat bobbing against her neck. "It's a splendid plan, Reverend. Thank you for arranging it."

"You're welcome." He turned to the men. "We'll see you again tomorrow, fellows. Go on, now."

Still grumbling, the men ambled off. The preacher caught hold of the arm of a stout man with thin brown hair combed from ear to ear over his round dome. "Athol, these ladies need a place to sleep tonight. Can they stay in some of your upstairs rooms?"

He shrugged. "Fine with me. The rooms likely need cleanin', though. Nobody's used 'em in a good long while. But I got nothin' against them stayin' above the restaurant."

"That meets their need for lodging, but they still need supper. What's on this evening's menu?"

"Most o' the fellas ate together while we watched for Mack's wagon, an' they cleaned me out o' salt pork an' baked beans. But there's some beef stew still simmerin' in a pot. Always got biscuits an' cold milk ready, too."

Preacher Doan arched one brow. "Do you

63

ladies like beef stew and biscuits?"

Such simple fare, but Abigail's stomach rolled over with a hunger she didn't realize she possessed. "Yes, sir."

The preacher beamed. "Good. Ladies, follow Athol to his restaurant. He'll see that you're well fed. Mack and I will carry in your luggage. He says you brought enough for a stay of a day or two."

Mrs. Bingham released a light laugh. "Mr. Cleveland presumes nearly as well as your fine telegrapher." She urged Abigail in the direction of the two-story red brick building bearing the simple proclamation Restaurant in white paint above the porch roof. "To be completely frank, Preacher, we intend a stay of half a month. But we'll discuss that at tomorrow evening's meeting."

FIVE

Abigail battled a very strong urge to escape through the restaurant's double front doors. Evidence of the building's previous purpose lurked in every corner, from the battered upright piano, its top holding a spattering of grimy shot glasses, to the twelve-foot-long bar, complete with a tarnished brass footrest, which ran half the room's length. Mother would roll over in her grave if she knew that her daughter was sitting at a blackjack table in a southwest Kansas town. At least the cards and chips had been removed.

Above them, bumps and scuffling noises gave evidence of Mr. Cleveland's and the preacher's activity. According to the restaurant's owner, each of the six rooms contained a bed, bureau, and wardrobe. Then he'd warned, *"Them rooms ain't been cleaned in a month o' Sundays, so the dust's prob'ly an inch high."* The preacher had draped his black jacket over a chair and requested a broom, bucket of water, cleaning cloths, and clean sheets. He'd then herded Mr. Cleveland up the stairs to help him ready the rooms for occupancy. Mr. Cleveland hadn't looked eager, but he'd shrugged out of his jacket and gone along without a word of complaint, and unexpectedly Abigail warmed toward the man. He respected his minister. It spoke well of him.

Balancing a dented metal tray on his wide palm, Mr. Patterson shuffled across the stained wide-plank floor that carried the slight essence of malt liquor. As he neared the table, the delightful aroma of meat and vegetables rising from the bowls on the tray chased away the other scent that made Abigail wrinkle her nose. He placed a bowl and spoon in front of each of the ladies, then plunked a basket of biscuits between them. "Milk or coffee?"

Mrs. Bingham sat with her spine straight, chin level, and one hand in her lap — the same way Abigail had been taught to while dining. Abigail had never realized how ridiculous the pose appeared in rough surroundings. "Coffee, please, and a napkin, if you'd be so kind."

The man frowned. "I ain't got napkins. Most o' the fellas who come in here to eat use their sleeves to wipe their mouths."

Abigail cringed. She would certainly address the topic of table manners with the men.

"I reckon I can bring you a wipin' towel if you like. It's some bigger'n a napkin, but it'd do the job."

"A . . . wipin' towel?" Mrs. Bingham glanced at Abigail, puzzlement in her gray eyes.

"Yes'm. What I use to wipe out the dishes before I put 'em on the shelf."

"Ah. A dish towel."

"That's what I said. A wipin' towel."

Mrs. Bingham's lips twitched. "That would be satisfactory, Mr. Patterson."

"Just call me Athol." He swung his unsmiling gaze on Abigail. "You wantin' coffee, too?"

She wanted tea, but he hadn't offered it. "I prefer milk if it's cold."

"It is. Got me a cellar under the kitchen. Keeps everything nice and cool." Pride briefly lit his features. "This was the only saloon in Pratt County with a rock-lined beer cellar."

Mrs. Bingham gasped, but she covered it with a small cough behind her hand.

Abigail swallowed her own gasp. No gentleman would discuss beer with ladies!

Worry chased away the bolt of shock. Did he keep the milk in kegs previously used for beer? If so, she shouldn't drink it. But how could she ask? She dare not utter the word *beer.* Before she determined a polite way to inquire about the milk's storage, he scurried off in the direction of the swinging door that presumably led to the kitchen.

She leaned toward Mrs. Bingham and lowered her voice to a whisper — a breach of etiquette, but she couldn't allow Mr. Patterson to hear her use such language. "Do you suppose the milk is stored in beer kegs?"

Humor graced the woman's eyes. "I suppose the milk is stored in cans. But if I have to carry you up the stairs later, we'll know otherwise."

Abigail drew back. "Mrs. Bingham!" She fanned herself with both hands.

"Forgive me, my dear, but our environment . . ." She glanced around, her brow furrowing. "It does invite one to indulge in a bit of . . . earthiness."

Abigail made a silent vow to hold tight to the manners she'd been taught by her dear, saintly mother regardless of her environment. She began exercising her commitment by dipping her spoon at the edge of the bowl and lifting a small amount of thick broth and a slice of carrot. Steam no longer rose, assuring her she could place the bite in her mouth without fear of scalding her tongue. Her face, as Mr. Cleveland had predicted, burned as if someone held a candle to her flesh. She didn't wish to experience the same discomfort on the inside of her mouth.

As she chewed the first flavorful bite, Mr. Patterson returned with two dingy-looking cloths, a plain white mug of steaming coffee, and a tin cup of frothy milk. He put the items on the table without a word and disappeared again. He didn't emerge from the kitchen until both women had finished their soup, eaten a biscuit apiece, and emptied their cups. To Abigail's great relief, the milk tasted like milk. She enjoyed every cold sip, and she informed him so when he picked up her cup.

His face streaked pink. "I didn't make the milk. The cow did all the work."

Abigail had no idea how to respond to such a statement, so she merely nodded and brushed a few biscuit crumbs toward the center of the table.

Mrs. Bingham dabbed her mouth with the cloth, dropped it over her bowl, and rose. "Thank you for a delicious supper, Mr. Patterson. Abigail, shall we go see how the

men are progressing in readying our accommodations?"

Abigail had no desire to enter a room
previously occupied by what Mother would
have called a "soiled dove," but given their
lack of options, she had little choice but to
agree. "Yes, I —"

The thud of feet on the stairs cut off the
remainder of Abigail's reply. The preacher
and Mr. Cleveland thumped into the room,
both wearing cobwebs in their hair. A little
cloud of dust seemed to hover around them,
and Abigail felt a sneeze coming on. She
quickly pressed the end of her nose to
prevent the sneeze from escaping.

Preacher Doan chuckled. "Athol wasn't
exaggerating when he said those rooms
hadn't been cleaned for a while. But he was
wrong about them not being used. Some
nonpaying critters had made themselves at
home. We knocked down a good two dozen
spiderwebs and cleaned out some mouse
nests."

Abigail's stomach began to churn. Spiders? And mice? If the webs and nests had
been removed, did that mean the vermin
were gone, too? How would she be able to
rest, fearing that such loathsome creatures
lurked in the corners?

The preacher's smile never dimmed. "But

the rooms are as clean as we could get them on such short notice. You ladies will probably want to give them another going-over tomorrow. Most likely when you open the shades to the morning's sunshine, you'll discover we left behind as much as we cleared."

Mrs. Bingham released a delicate sigh. "Preacher, you and Mr. Cleveland have been much too kind. We are so appreciative of your efforts on our behalf, aren't we, Abigail?"

Abigail forced her lips into a wobbly smile. "Yes. Thank you for . . . trying."

The two men exchanged a glance that seemed to hold hidden meaning. Then the preacher beamed his bright smile at Abigail and Mrs. Bingham. "We started to clean the rooms right at the top of the stairs, but my wife is partial to east-facing windows, so we cleaned the two looking out over the alley. You'll find a door at the end of the hall. It'll take you to an outside staircase into the backyard, where there's a, well . . ." He scratched his temple. "What you ladies would probably call the 'necessary.' "

The information was pertinent. In all honesty, Abigail had wondered about the personal accommodation but hadn't known how to ask. But to have it so casually stated caused her face to burn anew.

Without warning, the preacher's expression turned serious. "Keep the outside door locked when you aren't using it, and it would be in your best interest to never venture out alone. Stay together."

Mrs. Bingham curled her fingers around Abigail's elbow. "Are you intimating we could be in some sort of danger?"

He frowned. "Intimating?"

"Implying," Mrs. Bingham said. "Giving us a hint."

"I'm not hinting about anything. I'm saying it right out. Single ladies are a rarity in these parts, and it's better to be safe than sorry." The preacher folded his arms over his chest. "You might have a good reason for showing up here without the brides the men were expecting, but I have to warn you it could lead to unpleasantness. The fellows in Spiveyville respect women, but they're lonely and impatient and apt to be impulsive, as Miss Grant already experienced with W. C. Miller."

Mrs. Bingham huffed. "Yes. That young man certainly needs a lesson in propriety. He's fortunate that he responded to Mr. Cleveland's intervention. Otherwise I would have made use of the weapon my dear departed husband insisted I carry as a safe-guard."

Abigail gawked at her employer, too stunned to speak.

Both men's eyebrows rose high. Mr. Cleveland's gaze dropped to her reticule. "Are you packing a pistol?"

She nodded, her expression demure. "A nickel-plated Remington over-under model, and I assure you, gentlemen, I know how to use it."

Abigail gripped her throat. Her pulse pounded beneath her fingertips. "Mrs. Bingham, it terrifies me to think you carry a loaded pistol."

The matchmaker aimed an amused look at Abigail. "An unloaded pistol is useless." She lifted her chin and faced the men. "There are unsavory men in cities, too. As I promised Howard I would, I have kept my derringer close at hand since the day I buried him, and I will inform the men at tomorrow's meeting of my intention to prove my sure aim if one of them chooses to accost either Abigail or me."

An errant thought tripped through Abigail's brain. If she had a nickel-plated Remington in hand, she wouldn't need a hickory stick. A giggle built in the back of

73

her throat, and she swallowed hard lest it escape.

Mr. Cleveland grimaced. "I'm sorry W. C. scared you, ma'am, but you've got to remember the men've already waited almost two months to hear from you. Now it appears it's gonna be a while before their brides come." He looked to the preacher.

The preacher gave a grim nod. "Our sheriff got called to the county seat this morning to testify about some cow stealing over in Granger. He'll probably be back tomorrow, Wednesday at the latest. Until then, carry your derringer if it makes you feel more secure, but it'd be wise for you two to keep an escort with you." He clapped his hand on Mr. Cleveland's shoulder. "Mack's hardware store is right next door. He's a trustworthy escort. You can depend on Athol Patterson, too. Or, if you'd rather, you can ask Mack or Athol to fetch me."

"As I said, you're very thoughtful, Reverend. Thank you." Mrs. Bingham tightened her grip on Abigail's arm. "And now, if you'll excuse us —"

Mr. Cleveland stepped into their pathway. "Ma'am, before you head upstairs, I need to take Miss Grant over to Doc Kettering's office for some aloe."

Abigail drew back slightly. "I'm fine."

Mr. Cleveland scowled. "Miss Grant, you're a city gal, but haven't you ever had a sunburn?"

Mother had always insisted upon keeping the cover up on their carriage or making use of a parasol so her skin remained creamy white, and Abigail had always followed Mother's example. "No. Never."

"Then I have to tell you, it's gonna hurt worse later than it likely hurts now."

Worse? She gingerly touched her cheek, and fresh tingles stabbed like stings from a dozen hornets. She winced.

"Aloe will help." Sympathy tinged the man's tone, although not a hint of it showed in his stormy blue eyes. "Don't be stubborn. Let me take you over to the doc."

Stubbornness held no part of her reluctance. She could never traverse a dark street with a man other than her father or husband, yet to say so would seem petty and critical. Especially after the preacher had just declared Mr. Cleveland a trustworthy escort. Which was the greater breach of etiquette — to speak the bald truth or to allow him to escort her under the moonlight to the doctor's office? Why didn't Mrs. Bingham explain?

She glanced at the matchmaker and discovered the woman's eyelids were drooping.

75

Her grip on Abigail's arm, too, had become stronger, as if she relied upon Abigail to hold her upright. The older woman needed to rest after their long, wearying days of travel.

"Mr. Cleveland, I appreciate your kindness in seeking to alleviate my discomfort." Oh, how it hurt to speak, every movement pulling at the tender skin on her cheeks. Why hadn't she covered herself with a handkerchief when she'd had the opportunity? "But it's been a very trying day, and both Mrs. Bingham and I need our rest. Would you kindly allow us to retire to our rooms now?"

His entire frame stiffened and he set his lips so tightly they slipped into hiding beneath his mustache. But he stepped aside.

"Thank you again for readying our rooms, Preacher Doan and Mr. Cleveland. Mrs. Bingham and I will see you tomorrow evening at the church for our meeting with the" — she gulped — "prospective grooms."

Mack

Mack waited until the women disappeared around the bend at the top of the stairs before blasting a snort. "That is one mule-headed woman."

Preacher Doan shrugged. "It's her choice to go see Doc Kettering or not. You can lead a horse, or in this case a thoroughbred filly, to water —"

"— but you can't make her drink. I know, I know."

The men snagged their jackets from the backs of chairs and sauntered onto the porch. While they'd been upstairs swatting dust from the furniture and remaking beds, dark had fallen and the temperature had dropped at least ten degrees. Mack jammed his arms into his jacket and looked up and down the quiet, gray-shrouded street. He couldn't recall seeing the town so dark before, and it took a minute for him to figure out the reason. Sheriff Thorn was out of town, so no one had lit the oil lamps hanging from poles on the corners. Maybe he'd light them before he turned in. Those two women would need to be able to find their way to the outhouse.

A soft nicker met his ears, and he remembered he'd left his wagon and horses in the middle of the street. Putting up his team and wagon, lighting the lamps . . . He had work to do before turning in, so maybe it was best the little filly had refused his offer to take her to Doc Kettering.

He moved to the edge of the raised board-

77

walk. "Well, Preacher, I guess I oughta —"

"You had a long drive with the ladies." The preacher's serious voice chased away Mack's intentions. "What do you think . . . about them?"

Mack pushed his hands into his pants pockets and chewed his mustache. "They're both real proper. The older one, Mrs. Bingham, is a lot friendlier than Miss Grant." Mrs. Bingham had said the travel made Miss Grant cranky. Would she be less grumbly after a night of rest? He hoped so. A gal as pretty as her needed to behave pretty, too.

"I meant what you think about the reason they're here." Mack couldn't make out the preacher's face in the deep shadows, but he heard the worry in his tone. "Do you think there really is a bevy of brides waiting to come to Kansas?"

Mack couldn't say for sure. He didn't want to think the women were swindlers. Especially women as well dressed and well mannered as these two. But looks could be deceiving. He shook his head. "I don't know. I guess we'll know more after the meeting tomorrow evening."

"I think I'll bring Medora to the meeting, too. She'll probably say she needs to grade papers." The preacher's wife served as the town's schoolteacher even though she'd never had a lick of training, and everyone sang her praise. "But she's always been a good judge of character, so I want her there."

"Sounds like a good idea." Mrs. Doan wouldn't get stuck on the attractive outside of the women the way men tended to do.

Preacher Doan gave Mack a clap on the shoulder. Dust filled Mack's nostrils. Both men coughed, and the preacher backed away, waving his hands in front of his face. "I better give my clothes a good brushing before I go in the house or Medora will think I've been rolling in the street." He headed up the boardwalk, glancing over his shoulder. "Thanks for helping get those rooms clean."

"Thanks for helping get the men under control."

The preacher's laughter rolled.

Mack turned toward his store. If he intended to light the lamps, he needed some matches. His horses snorted, and he called, "I'll get to you. Be patient." The lamps came first. The horses third. Because there was something else he needed to do in between.

SIX

Helena

Despite the musty smell of the pillowcase, despite the lumpy mattress, despite the strange surroundings, Helena had fallen asleep the moment she reclined. But a sound — the scuff as quiet as a whisper in church — brought her fully awake. She instinctively slid her hand under the pillow and found her derringer. She tossed aside the cover and swung her feet to the floor. Her robe lay across the foot of the bed, and she slipped it on while tiptoeing across the creaky floorboards to the door. Holding her breath, she cracked it open, gun held at the ready.

A shadowy figure bent over in front of Abigail's door. Was he peeking through the young woman's keyhole? Helena pulled back on the hammer, and at its light *click,* the man straightened, his back to her.

"I only have one shot, but I promise I will make it count." Helena kept her voice low, unwilling to wake Abigail and frighten her, but she injected a firmness in her tone to let the man know she meant business.

He put both hands in the air and turned slowly until he faced her. Pale light from the lantern mounted shoulder high on the wall near the staircase at the end of the hall touched his face.

She gave a start. "Mr. Cleveland?" The preacher had said they could trust this man. Her confidence in the preacher plummeted. She kept the gun aimed at his broad chest. "What do you think you're doing?"

"Nothing bad. Honest." He swallowed, his Adam's apple bobbing in his throat. "Miss Grant wouldn't go see Doc Kettering, so I brought . . ." He bounced his elbow in an awkward gesture.

Helena glanced down. A clay pot holding an odd, spiky plant sat on the floor beside his feet. Understanding eased through her and she removed her finger from the trigger. "Aloe?"

"Yes, ma'am." He shifted in place, his hands in the air. "By morning her stubbornness will likely be worn out and she's gonna want something for her sunburn. So there it is."

"That's very thoughtful of you, Mr. Cleveland." Especially considering how prickly Abigail had behaved toward the man. Somehow she needed to find a way to dismantle the wall of snootiness the young woman used to defend herself against hurt. "But couldn't you have waited until morning? You're very fortunate I chose to ask questions before I made use of my weapon after the preacher warned us to stay alert."

He grimaced. "I reckon I didn't expect to get caught out here." Hands still high, his gaze never lifting from the derringer, he took a slow step forward with his heels dragging on the floor. "You . . . have that loaded and ready?"

"Indeed I do."

"You're an unusual woman, Mrs. Bingham."

"Indeed I am."

"The only other woman I ever met who carried a pistol was Wilhelmina Wilkes. She robbed a whole church full of people and came within inches of stealing my uncle's life savings after she answered his advertisement for a bride."

Although his voice — a mere rasping whisper — held little emotion, she glimpsed pain in his eyes. Sympathy sent her apprehension away. No longer threatened, she uncocked the hammer, dropped the pistol in her pocket, and folded her arms across her chest. "I assure you, I am not Wilhelmina Wilkes, and I have no intention of swindling your friends. Given your experience, you have no reason to trust my words as true, but if you come to tomorrow evening's meeting, perhaps your worries will be eased."

"I'd be welcome even though I didn't ask to be matched with a bride?" He sounded dubious, but he let his arms drift to his sides and settled his weight on one hip in a relaxed pose.

"Everyone is welcome." An idea struck as if from heaven above, and she smiled. "As a matter of fact, if you'd be kind enough to spread the word tomorrow about the meeting, perhaps other townspeople — even those who are already married — would enjoy taking part in what Abigail and I have planned for the bachelors of Spiveyville."

His gaze narrowed. "Exactly what is it you've got planned, Mrs. Bingham?"

"Oh, no." She shook her head, chuckling. "You must wait like everyone else until tomorrow evening. But for now . . ." She covered a yawn. "Thank you for bringing the aloe plant, Mr. Cleveland. I'm sure Abigail will be most appreciative when she

83

discovers it."

He glanced at the closed door, frowning. "I hope so. Don't much like to think of anybody hurting."

Clearly, Mr. Mack Cleveland was a considerate man, the kind of man she wanted for her brides. Did his resistance to marriage stem from his uncle's unfortunate experience, or did something else hinder him from seeking her services? Her curiosity would have to be sated another time because sleep now beckoned.

She stepped backward over the threshold and closed the door. The darkness of the room enveloped her, and she groped for the key. With a twist of her fingers, she secured the lock. Then she pressed her ear to the door. As she expected, retreating footsteps spoke of Mr. Cleveland's departure.

She made her way to the bed, returned the pistol to its place beneath her pillow, and lay down. She didn't rouse again until slivers of sunlight sneaked between the cracks in the shades and invited her eyelids to open. Groaning, she pushed to her feet and stretched. The need for the outhouse made itself known, and she quickly donned her robe. The little necessary sat near the bottom of the outdoor staircase, shielded by overgrown bushes, so she could make the trek in her robe and slippers.

The morning air held a chill, but pleasant aromas — coffee and fresh-baked biscuits, no doubt coming from Mr. Patterson's kitchen — reached her nostrils. She inhaled the inviting scent while descending the warped stairs, careful not to drag her hem over the deposits of dried bird droppings and tobacco stains, then held her breath during her quick venture into the outhouse. Its inside smelled nothing like coffee and fresh-baked biscuits.

She hastened back up the stairs and entered the hallway as Abigail's door opened. The young woman was completely dressed in a hopelessly wrinkled green-and-tan plaid frock. She'd twisted her braided hair into a fat bun. Obviously she'd been awake for an hour or more already.

"Good morning, Mrs. Bingham. Since our proprietor didn't see fit to fill the wash-bowls, I'm going downstairs to request fresh water." Abigail turned toward the stairway, and the toe of her button-up shoe hit the clay pot. She came to a stop and frowned at the object. "What's this?"

"It's an aloe plant." Helena picked it up and placed it on the washstand inside Abigail's door. "Mr. Cleveland delivered it last night."

"Mr. Cleveland . . . was here . . . outside my door . . . while I slept?" She touched her ruffled bodice with trembling fingers.

If Abigail had witnessed the man's concern, she wouldn't behave so timorously. "Yes, and you should be grateful."

Abigail gaped at the plant as if she expected it to do something immoral.

Helena resisted rolling her eyes. "Request the water for our washbowls, Abigail. I'll help you apply aloe to your face after I'm dressed." She closed herself in her room and chose her finest, most businesslike suit. The two-piece gown in deepest navy was far too elaborate for the little Kansas town, but she felt confident in the outfit. She would need confidence this evening when she addressed the group of eager bachelors. As she finished buttoning the bodice, someone tapped on her door. She hurried across the floor and twisted the brass knob.

Abigail stepped into the room, bringing with her the heady scent of coffee and carrying a tin pitcher. Moist rivulets slid down the pitcher's side and left a series of drips on the floor as she crossed to the washstand. She poured half the pitcher's contents into the cracked bowl on the stand and pursed her lips. "I informed Mr. Patterson we would require fresh water twice a day for the duration of our stay. He informed me where I could find the water barrel." She huffed. "This is hardly a high-class establishment."

Helena swallowed a laugh and picked up her hairbrush. "Was he in the middle of preparing breakfast for diners?"

Abigail nodded. "There are close to a dozen men downstairs. Two of them" — she shuddered — "winked at me, and they all stared as if they'd never seen a female before."

They were likely staring at the girl's sunburned face. The streaks, red and angry looking, were even brighter this morning than they'd been last night and resembled Indian war paint. Certainly the sunburn pained her. Would aloe decrease the boldness of the blotches?

Helena quickly brushed her hair, once blond but now snow white, into a thick tail. Lingering tiredness made her arms ache. She sighed and turned to Abigail. "Please help me fashion my hair, dear, and then I will apply the aloe to your sunburn."

Abigail proved amazingly adept at twisting Helena's hair into a french roll. When she'd secured the fat puff with several pins, she sat on the edge of the bed, face upturned, and trustingly allowed Helena to

87

dot liquid from the broken aloe leaves onto her face. The treatment did nothing to mask the high color. On the contrary, the residue brightened the red, making it even more obvious, but when Helena had finished coating every bit of sun-reddened flesh with the clear, gooey liquid, Abigail released a sigh.

"Oh, my. It does help take the sting away."

Helena dropped the broken leaves into a can she suspected previously served as a spittoon and dipped her sticky fingers in her washbowl. "Then you owe Mr. Cleveland a thank-you."

"Yes, I surely do." The girl brushed her palms over her skirt's wrinkles, her expression pensive. "I shall pen an appropriate note after we've finished our breakfast."

Helena needed to jot a quick note to Marietta, as well, so her sister would know they'd arrived safely. "Let's spend the morning seeing to personal tasks and recovering from our travel." Goodness, traveling had never taxed her as severely as this excursion. But she hadn't ventured beyond the boundaries of Newton since Howard's death ten years ago. Apparently nearing her sixtieth birthday was taking its toll. "Then this afternoon we can plan the lessons schedule for the bachelors. I want to have everything organized and ready to present to the gentlemen at this evening's meeting."

"Yes, ma'am."

Helena placed her derringer in her reticule and looped the strap over her wrist. Linking arms with Abigail, she guided her to the stairs. They reached the bottom of the enclosed staircase and entered the dining room. As Abigail had indicated, several men were seated at tables, enjoying what appeared to be biscuits swimming in sausage gravy. Helena recognized the telegrapher, Mr. Cleveland, and a few other faces from those who had surrounded the wagon last night. She cast a demure smile across the lot and led Abigail to a table in the corner, aware of the men's rapt attention.

As she and Abigail seated themselves, a wiry man with thick salt-and-pepper hair and a neatly trimmed beard and mustache to match rose and moved with a bowlegged stride in their direction. The tin star pinned to his leather vest caught the light as he came. He stopped next to their table and slid his thumbs into his trouser pockets, sending an unsmiling look over both of them. "Good mornin', ladies. I'm Bill Thorn, sheriff of Spiveyville. I understand you two arrived yesterday evenin'."

Helena rose and extended her hand.

"News travels quickly in Spiveyville, just as you must have to be back in town so soon. We were told you weren't expected until later today at the earliest."

His eyes, as pale blue as cornflowers, narrowed into slits. "I s'pose you was countin' on me stayin' away."

"To the contrary. I was merely repeating the information we were given." He still hadn't taken her hand, so she linked her fingers and rested her hands on her waist. "It's very kind of you to introduce yourself, Sheriff Thorn. I am Mrs. Helena Bingham, owner of Bingham's Bevy of Brides, and this is my assistant, Miss Abigail Grant." Abigail gave a slight nod, her brown eyes wary. "I am pleased you returned in time to attend the town meeting at the church this evening. I confess, it's a bit disconcerting to be without a gentleman escort in an unfamiliar town. Perhaps you would be willing to accompany Miss Grant and me to the meeting? We'd feel much safer."

He snorted. "Safer for you or for the fellas?" He glanced at the reticule with its gun-shaped lump lying on the edge of the table. "You keep that thing loaded, do you?"

She slid her fingers over the derringer's outline, keeping her smile intact. "Yes, sir, I do. But I only fire it if an ornery skunk refuses to listen to reason."

His mustache twitched and something akin to amusement sparked in his eyes. "Shootin' at a skunk's sure to raise a stink."

"Sometimes a skunk raises its own stink."

He chortled — one snort of humor that he stifled with a fist against his lips. He cleared his throat and rocked on the worn heels of his boots. "I'll walk you an' the young lady to that meetin', ma'am, an' I'll stay to hear everything you have to say. An' I'll be watchin' the two o' you. I ain't one to stand by an' allow any kind o' shenanigans in my town. A purty dress an' fancy airs don't mean nothin' to me. You break the law, you'll wind up sittin' in a cell same as any ratty ol' bum. Just wanted you to know."

Helena met the man's gaze. "The only thing Miss Grant and I intend to break, Sheriff, is the wall between the unmarried men of Spiveyville and the brides waiting to exchange vows with them." She pinched her chin and deliberately pasted on a speculative grin. "By the way, are you married, Sheriff Thorn?"

He gave a little jolt, his jaw shifting back and forth. "Uh . . . no, I ain't."

"Then might you be interested in securing a wife?"

SEVEN

Abigail

If Abigail didn't know that the matchmaker was trying to expand her client list, she'd presume Mrs. Bingham was flirting with Spiveyville's sheriff. Apparently the sheriff didn't know better, because he blushed and harrumphed under his breath. He took a shuffling sideways step away from their table, seeming as unsettled as Mr. Cleveland's horses had been when the tumbleweeds rolled across their path.

"Fellas tol' me the meetin' is set for seven thirty, so I'll fetch you ladies at a quarter after. That'll give us more'n enough time to make the trek — it's just a three-block walk from here." He glanced at Mrs. Bingham's reticule. "An' I'll ask that you not tote your weapon tonight. Might not be a 'ficial church service we're attendin', but we are gatherin' in the house of the Lord. Nobody brings guns into the church."

Mrs. Bingham drew back, clicking her tongue on her teeth. "Why, with you serving as our escort, Sheriff, I shall have no desire to . . . tote . . . my weapon." She smiled and tipped her head at a coy angle. "Thank you for your kindness to Miss Grant and me. We will be ready when you arrive at a quarter after seven."

The man's ears turned bright red. He nodded, turned, and scuttled to join Mr. Cleveland, the telegrapher, and a third man, who wore a three-piece suit and wired spectacles. The moment the sheriff plopped into his chair, the trio of men leaned in and seemingly began pelting him with whispered questions.

Mrs. Bingham seated herself. Her cunning gaze remained fixed on the sheriff and his cohorts. "Wouldn't I like to be a fly on the wall, listening to their conversation. I can well imagine it." She turned a grin in Abigail's direction. "Men like to complain that women are the gossips, but I daresay those of the male persuasion are equally guilty of indulging in tittle-tattle. Perhaps even more so."

Having been the subject of slanderous talk after her father's tumble from grace, Abigail had no desire to indulge in gossip. Mother had always cautioned her to even avoid inquisitiveness, which could be deemed as being snoopy — a vile trait. Yet curiosity nibbled. "Mrs. Bingham, did you deliberately bait the sheriff with" — should she ask? — "coquettishness?"

The woman released a soft trickle of laughter, smoothing a wispy strand of hair away from her forehead. "Why, yes, Abigail, I did. You see, it's a very useful tool for measuring a man's true character."

Abigail frowned and then winced when her tender skin panged. She forced her face to relax. "I don't understand."

Mrs. Bingham laced her fingers together and placed her hands on the edge of the table. "Sheriff Bill Thorn approached with an air of crusty authority. My mild flirtation — harmless, I assure you — uncovered a glint of amusement. Where amusement resides, tenderness is frequently a close neighbor. We need an ally in this town, and the sheriff would be the most effective one in terms of our safety. After seeing his reaction to my subtle coquetry, I feel certain Sheriff Thorn will prove a protective, helpful asset to us over the next two weeks."

Abigail had no greater understanding after the matchmaker's explanation than she'd had before, but what did she know about reading a man's character? The man she'd trusted and revered above all others had betrayed her, and on her deathbed, Mother had extracted a promise from Abigail to utilize great caution in opening her heart lest it be trampled again. Abigail vowed anew to be watchful.

"Miss Grant?"

Abigail jolted, shocked to discover Mr. Cleveland very near the table, his hat in his hands. The well-dressed man from his table stood next to him, seeming to examine her face. How had they crept up on her unaware? And while she was secretly vowing attentiveness? She clutched her throat. "Y-yes?"

"This is Hiram Kettering — the doc I told you about yesterday. He gave me the aloe plant I left for you." Mr. Cleveland's gaze roved over her nose and cheeks. "Looks like you made use of it."

Under the scrutiny of the two men, Abigail battled the urge to squirm. If she had a napkin or handkerchief available, she would toss it over her face the way he'd advised her to do on their ride from Pratt Center. Her dry tongue stuck to the roof of her mouth, denying her the ability to respond.

Mrs. Bingham smiled at the men. "I applied the aloe liberally to the sunburned

95

patches, and Abigail declared it eased her discomfort."

A slight smile creased the hardware store owner's face. "Glad to hear it. Doc wanted to get a look at you, Miss Grant, an' make sure the burn wasn't blistering."

The doctor leaned in, his thick brows pinching together. Abigail instinctively leaned back the same distance, and the doctor gripped her chin between his thumb and finger. "Keep your face to the light."

Abigail curled her fingers around the seat of her chair and gritted her teeth, painfully aware that every patron in the restaurant observed the examination. Such indignity! Shouldn't a doctor possess at least an ounce of decorum? Doc Kettering tipped her face this way and that, his unsmiling gaze so close she could see her reflection in his round glass lenses.

Finally he released her and straightened, giving a firm nod. "You got a bad burn. Apply the aloe every hour and keep a cold, wet cloth draped over your face as much as you can today and tomorrow. It'll take the heat out and put moisture in your skin. Even so, you'll likely peel." He folded his arms over his chest and shook his head, crunching his lips into a scowl. "Before you go out in the sun again, make sure you put a poke bonnet on your head, young lady."

Abigail's ire rose. Was she a child to be scolded for misbehavior? His high-handed approach required much gentling. He also needed a lesson in fashion. Poke bonnets had gone out of style in the city at least two decades ago. "I do not own a poke bonnet."

"Grover Thompson has a good selection at the mercantile. Buy one and wear it." He clomped back to his table.

Abigail turned her disbelieving gape on Mrs. Bingham. "Have you ever . . ."

Mrs. Bingham patted Abigail's wrist. "Didn't you have something you wanted to say to Mr. Cleveland?"

She'd forgotten the hardware store owner was present. Heat flooded her face, making her sunburn prickle like fire. She shifted slightly and raised her chin to meet the man's solemn gaze. "Thank you for delivering the aloe plant, Mr. Cleveland. Although I found it quite disconcerting to think of you lurking outside my door late at night when I was unaware, I do appreciate the gesture."

His mustache twitched. His eyes glittered. He sniffed, rubbed his nose, and sniffed again. "You're welcome. Glad it helped." He hustled away, his shoulders shaking in silent laughter.

97

Abigail frowned after him. "What a peculiar man."

Mrs. Bingham huffed and rolled her eyes. "What a peculiar thank-you."

Abigail held her hands outward. "Did I say something untrue?"

Mr. Patterson approached their table, coffeepot in one hand and two tin cups dangling by their handles from his other hand. "Sorry it took me so long to —" He stared at Abigail. "They wasn't kiddin' when they said you looked like somebody sandpapered your face. You'd best see Grover Thompson. He sells sunbonnets."

First the doctor and now their server. Did none of the people in this town understand advice should not be offered unless invited? Pointing out one's imperfections was particularly abhorrent. These men were too far gone for teaching. Only a fool would expend her time attempting to change them.

Abigail pushed back her chair, its legs squealing against the floorboard, and rose with as much poise as she could muster. "Mrs. Bingham, I have lost my appetite. I am returning to my room."

Bill Thorn

Bill took a noisy sip of the hot coffee.

98

Behind him, someone muttered on a moony sigh, "There she goes, fleet as a deer." He glanced over his shoulder in time to see the younger of the two city women slip around the corner to the staircase. Pret' near every man in the room gawked after her, slack jawed and starry eyed. Bill harrumphed. Those women were gonna be more trouble than the county's ne'er-do-well, Elmer Nance, when he was rip-roaring drunk.

He raised one eyebrow and turned to Mack, who wasn't staring after the little gal. "You sure you got no idea what them ladies plan to say durin' tonight's meetin'? My pa used to say forewarned is forearmed. I'd like to know ahead o' time if a full-fledged war is gonna break out right there in the First Methodist Church." 'Specially since everybody — including him — would check their weapons at the door.

Mack shrugged and dragged his fork tines through the smear of greasy gravy left on his plate. "I asked, but Mrs. Bingham said I'd have to wait like everybody else. She's a secretive woman."

And a sassy one, if Bill didn't miss his guess. He chewed the inside of his cheeks to keep from smiling, thinking about what she'd said about skunks. She might be a city gal, but she'd lived long enough to know country critters fairly well. "Don't make a lick o' sense to me why she'd show up here without the brides the men ordered unless she plain ain't got enough of 'em to go around. I'm downright fearful she's plannin' to auction off the only one she brung to the highest bidder."

"I don't know about that." Mack dropped his fork and sent a quick look at the woman, who held her glazed clay mug like it was made of fine china. "She told me to spread the word for anybody in town to come to the meeting — even married folks. I can't think she'd offer up a woman for grabs to men sitting next to their wives."

"Maybe not . . ." Bill stroked his beard, fighting a yawn. He'd hightailed it back to Spiveyville, leaving Granger hours before the sun had made its appearance that morning, and tiredness tugged at him. But he didn't dare catch a nap. Not with half the men around Spiveyville acting like lovesick coyotes baying at the moon. "But she's got somethin' up her frilly sleeve, an' I ain't gonna be able to rest easy 'til I know what it is."

"We'll find out at seven thirty, same as everybody else in town."

"Uh-huh . . ." Bill jerked. "You sayin' you're comin' to the meetin', too? Didn't figure you would, seein' as how you spoke against the fellas sendin' off for those brides."

"I reckon I'm curious, same as you." Mack fiddled with his empty coffee cup, his face screwed up all thoughtful like.

Bill sat quiet and observed the man. Although he had a good ten years on Mack, Bill considered him a friend. A dependable friend. Not prone to fits of anger over foolish things, like Otto Hildreth, the town's tailor, who once jabbed a customer with a needle for idly rearranging the spools on his spool rack. Nor so caught up in himself he lost sight of the needs of folks around him, like the banker and land surveyor, Tobis Adelman, who would probably sell the property from right under his own mama if it would turn him a dime in profit. Mack was a good man. And he'd make a good family man.

Bill poked Mack on the arm. "Hey, how come you didn't send a letter along with the others to get yourself a wife? Seems to me a young fella like you, got your own business an' all, would make a right good catch for some gal."

A slow grin climbed Mack's cheeks. "What about you, Sheriff? You've been alone longer'n me. You could've sent a letter, too.

101

Don't you want a wife?"

Bill snorted. "You sound like that fancy city lady." He forced his voice up high and squeaky. "Might you be innersted in securin' a wife?" He shook his head hard and blew out a breath. "Women ain't nothin' more'n a peck o' trouble, always wantin' to spend your money an' keep you from doin' the things you think are fun. Besides" — he propped his chin in his hand, wearier than he wanted to admit — "this badge is enough to scare most women off. Who'd wanna marry up with a fella who goes chasin' rustlers an' runs the risk o' bein' poked full o' holes from a bandit's pistol? Wouldn't be fair." He'd given up on thoughts of matrimony when he accepted the job as sheriff almost fifteen years ago, and he had no regrets. Not really.

He sat up and pointed at the younger man. "But you, Mack, you got no reason to stay alone. You goin' to that meetin' to maybe learn more about gettin' yourself a wife?"

"I'm going to the meeting to make sure Mrs. Bingham isn't a swindler. Lookin' out for my friends, that's all."

Bill examined Mack. He spoke sure, and his face didn't show signs of hiding anything. Yep, Mack Cleveland was a good man. Bill shifted his attention to the city woman, and she turned her head and caught him looking. She smiled and held up her cup the way people did when they made a toast. And just like that, the start of a poem he'd read in a book back when he was still a youngster tiptoed through his mind.

"Will you walk into my parlour?" said the Spider to the Fly.

Eyes on the woman, Bill nodded. "Yessir, Mack, I'll be glad to have you along tonight, fightin' on my side, in case things turn ugly."

EIGHT

Abigail

She had given Mr. Cleveland verbal appreciation for the gift of the aloe plant, but propriety demanded a written note as well. So Abigail retrieved her writing pad, pen, and inkpot from her satchel and sat on the edge of the bed. A desk would certainly make the task easier, but perhaps the previous occupants had no need for one. Her face flamed at her errant thoughts, and she shoved aside all reflections about the room's past use.

With the inkpot on the little bedside stand and her tablet balanced on her knee, she dipped the pen and wrote as neatly as possible given the circumstances.

October 16, 1888

Dear Mr. Cleveland,

Thank you for your kindness in providing me with an aloe plant to treat my sunburn. It was quite thoughtful of you. I appreciate your generosity.

The note seemed very short. She chewed the end of the pen, considering means of lengthening it. She could add something about his advice to cover her face, which, in retrospect, held merit. But doing so would acknowledge she regretted not heeding his words. Would he, at some point in time, hold the admission against her, the way her former fiancé had turned her heartfelt profession of devotion into a club with which to batter her emotionally?

A tremor rattled her frame. Why had Linus Hartford crept through her thoughts today? She hadn't allowed him a moment's worth of reflection for more than five years. In all likelihood, the leering grins of some of the men at the breakfast tables were too similar to her last memory of her former beau, who, despite his fine upbringing, had proved not to be a gentleman at all.

She closed her eyes and pressed her fingers to her chapped lips, willing the memories to retreat to the far recesses of her mind. When she'd sufficiently corralled all remembrances of Linus, she dipped the pen and added the closing and signature.

Sincerely,
Miss Abigail Marguerite Grant

The letters bore a slight waver, partly because of the pad's precarious location and partly because her traitorous hands continued to tremble, but she hoped Mr. Cleveland wouldn't notice. She blew on the ink until its sheen dulled, then folded the paper into precise thirds and slipped it into an envelope. As she capped the inkpot, someone tapped on the door.

Her heart fired into her throat. Hands grasping the tattered quilt, she called, "Who is it?"

"Mrs. Bingham. May I come in?"

She slumped with relief, then muttered, "Silly goose." She was giving herself over to foolish fears due to the preacher's comments about desperate men. Mrs. Bingham had her pistol. She wouldn't let anyone enter Abigail's room without giving them a reason to rue the attempt. And very soon she would leave this little town behind. But, of course, she needed to share her decision with Mrs. Bingham first.

She hurried across the floor, turned the key, and opened the door.

Mrs. Bingham swept into the room, carrying a bucket of sudsy water with a cloth draped over its rim in one hand and a broom in the other. "I thought perhaps you'd want to give your room another scrubbing. Preacher Doan and Mr. Cleveland were quite kind in their attempts yesterday evening —"

Abigail swallowed a groan. If she'd added a thank-you for dusting and sweeping to his note, the length would be more appropriate. Her appreciation would surely go far in convincing him to take her to the train depot in Pratt Center for a return trip to Massachusetts.

"— but I know it's not as clean as you kept your chamber at my home."

Strange how quickly she and Mother had learned the menial tasks of cleaning when they'd been forced to release their household staff. She took no great pleasure in cleaning, but she couldn't bear to live in squalor. *"Cleanliness,"* Mother had often lectured the maids, *"is next to godliness."* Abigail no longer believed God was near, no matter how clean she kept her lodgings, but cleanliness was the only piece that remained of the life she'd left behind. Well, cleanliness and manners. She would never release either, even if she had to don a maid's uniform herself and spend her days cleaning homes for those who'd previously viewed her as an equal.

Abigail took the items and placed them in the corner. "Thank you, ma'am. I will make use of these. If you'd like, I will come across the hall and clean your room when I'm finished in here." It was the least she could do since she intended to transfer the duty of trying to teach decorum to the rowdy men of Spiveyville to the older woman.

Mrs. Bingham waved her hand. "No need, my dear. I'll see to it myself. But thank you. I intend to write Marietta a brief missive and carry it to the post office before noon." She glanced at the envelope lying on Abigail's bed. "Would you like to accompany me? You can deliver your note to Mr. Cleveland at the same time."

Considering the preacher had advised them not to venture out alone, of course she would make the errand with her boss. "Yes, ma'am. Please let me know when you're ready."

"I will. Now, let me put a bit more aloe on your face before I write my letter."

Abigail's skin was tight and itchy from the previous application, but she sat and allowed Mrs. Bingham to dot her sunburned patches with the broken end of a fresh leaf. The older woman tossed the leaf into the trash bin and then paused in the doorway. "Before we go to the post office, let's visit the general merchandise store and purchase a poke bonnet, as the doctor advised. You truly do not want even one more sunbeam to reach your face." She grimaced and left the room.

Abigail touched her sticky cheek. The doctor had also recommended keeping a cool, wet cloth on her face, but she'd dismissed the idea. How could she function with a cloth draped over her face? She hated to waste money on something she would never wear in the city, but it would be easier to wear a poke bonnet on the drive to Pratt Center than hold a handkerchief the entire distance. Especially the way the wind blew here in Kansas.

As if hearing her internal thoughts, a gust rattled the windows. Dust found its way through tiny openings between the frame and the window casing. Abigail huffed. She might not be staying in this room for more than another night, but she would rest easier if she could lay her head on a dust-free pillowcase. She grabbed up the cleaning supplies Mrs. Bingham had brought and set to work.

An hour later, someone again knocked on the door. Mrs. Bingham must be ready to deliver her letter to the post office. Abigail snatched up her note for Mr. Cleveland and her small purse with its paltry number of coins and opened the door. "I'm ready to —"

Instead of Mrs. Bingham, a lanky man in a threadbare suit stood in the hallway. He held the saddest-looking bouquet she'd ever seen. His grin spread from ear to ear on his fresh-shaved face, and — of all things — the aroma of fresh bread seemed to cling to him.

"How-do, missy. My name's Sam Bandy, an' I own the bakery over across the way."

The unusual cologne suddenly made sense.

He thrust the dried whatever-they-were forward. "Brung you some flowers."

Abigail gripped her hands beneath her chin and leaned sideways, peering past his shoulder to Mrs. Bingham's door. "Mrs. Binghaaaaaam?" Her voice rose an octave higher than usual, fear nearly strangling her. "Would you come here, pleeeeease?" She didn't bellow, because a lady never bellowed, but she did increase the volume of

110

her voice more than she'd ever done before.

At once Mrs. Bingham's door burst open and the woman swept between Abigail and the unwelcome suitor with a flurry of skirts, as prickly as a guard dog. She carried her reticule like a shield. "Sir, your presence here is most unseemly. Please leave."

The man shifted from foot to foot, his gaze seeking Abigail. "Only wanted to get a good look-see at the little gal who come in last night since I didn't hardly get a peek with all the other fellas crowded around. Wanted her to see me, too, so she'd reckanize me at the meetin' tonight, just in case she decides to choose a beau after all."

Feet pounded on the stairs, and Mr. Patterson puffed up the hallway, arms pumping. He grabbed the baker by the collar of his suit coat and yanked him away from the doorway. "Bandy, whaddaya think you're doin'?"

Mr. Bandy held the pitiful bouquet high. Several dried leaves drifted to the floor, but his foolish grin remained intact. "Courtin'."

Mr. Patterson aimed an apologetic grimace in the women's direction. "Sorry, ladies. I didn't see him sneakin' in or I sure would've stopped him before he got up here. Glad I heard your caterwaulin' or I still wouldn't know."

111

Heat filled Abigail's face, making her sunburn sting. She'd never been accused of caterwauling. Only one day in this Kansas town and her fine manners were slipping. She needed to leave as quickly as possible.

The restaurant owner tugged Mr. Bandy toward the stairs. "C'mon, you. You ain't supposed to be anywhere near these ladies."

The baker broke loose, glowering. "What's wrong with me introducin' myself? Just 'cause they're stayin' in your rooms don't mean you own 'em."

"Never said I owned 'em. But Preacher Doan an' Sheriff Thorn told me to look out for 'em, an' that's what I'm doin'." Mr. Patterson pointed to the stairs. "Now you scuttle your skinny rump on out o' here an' stay out."

Mr. Bandy shattered the bouquet against the wall and brought up his fists. "You gonna back that up with action, Patterson?"

Mr. Patterson whipped off his apron and imitated the baker's fighting stance. "If I gotta." The pair began to circle, each hunkered low, their hands balled into fists and their faces set in horrible scowls.

Abigail's pulse thundered so wildly she feared she would faint. Such ruffians! Resorting to fisticuffs in front of ladies? Why, Mother would be appalled. Her breath released in little gasps of fear and revulsion, and she pawed at Mrs. Bingham's arm. "Ma'am, do something."

Mrs. Bingham gave Abigail a little push toward the back door. "Go down the outside stairs and retrieve Mr. Cleveland at once."

Abigail stared at her. "By myself?"

Mr. Bandy reared back and threw the first punch. Mr. Patterson ducked and brought up his fist. It caught the baker under the chin.

Abigail shrieked and covered her eyes with both hands.

Mrs. Bingham grabbed her by the wrists and threw her toward the door. "For heaven's sake, Abigail, go!"

Her heart pounding and legs wobbling, Abigail stumbled to the door with the horrible sounds of grunts and oaths and fists connecting with flesh chasing her.

Mack

Mack hung the last of the dozen new claw hammers on the pegboard and stepped back, hands on hips, to admire his arrangement. Every ball pointing east, red-painted handles perfectly aligned north to south. A colorful display. Neat. Eye catching. Not that the men who came in gave much thought to the appearance of his stock on the shelves. *"If you're going to do a job, Son, do it right."* Ma's advice rolled through the back of his mind. The men might not realize organization made a difference, but Mack did. And that's what mattered.

He scooped up the crate, now holding only the straw used to cradle the merchandise and keep the painted handles from bouncing against each other, and headed for the storeroom at the back. The front door burst open and a shrill female voice called his name.

He dropped the crate. Straw exploded over his fresh-swept floor. He took one step and slid, caught his balance, and wheeled around the corner in time to catch Miss Grant, who fell panting into his arms. She hardly weighed as much as the box had with the hammers in it. Protectiveness welled through him even though he didn't know what had her all distraught.

Her slender hands clutched at his shirt-front and her hot breath wheezed against his neck. "They — they're fighting! Please, come quickly!"

"Who's fighting?"

"M-Mr. Patterson. And Mr. . . . . Mr. . . . . Oh!" She pounded one fist on his chest, then gave a mighty tug on his shirt. "The baker! Come! Hurry!"

Mack half guided, half carried her out of the store, around the corner, and into the restaurant. Dead silence met his ears. He slid to a halt at the base of the stairs. "I thought you said somebody was fighting."

She clapped both hands to her red cheeks. "Oh, dear . . . You don't suppose they — they've killed each other?"

Mack doubted it. Sam and Athol were good friends. And they were too mild mannered to pound each other to death. "Come on." He caught her by the elbow and propelled her up the stairs, ignoring her little huffs and squeaks. They rounded the corner at the top of the stairs, and once again he stopped so fast his soles skidded.

Miss Grant gasped and covered her eyes.

He gaped, unable to believe what he saw. "What in the name of all that's sensible is goin' on here?"

NINE

Mack

Mack strode directly to the matchmaker, who stood in the middle of the hallway with her derringer aimed at Athol and Sam. The men, hands raised high, cowered against the wall. From the looks of their disheveled clothes and swollen faces, they'd fared pretty evenly in their fight.

He gently cupped Mrs. Bingham's wrist and pushed it down until the weapon's nose pointed at the floor. "What happened up here?"

"These two refused to listen to reason, so I informed them they would lose their livers if they continued to behave like a couple of uncivilized savages." The woman gave a smug nod. "Fortunately for them, they decided they preferred to keep their livers. But I wasn't going to let them depart until someone with authority escorted them out."

116

She turned her pert gaze on him. "Mr. Patterson was only coming to our rescue, but I suggest you lecture this bread maker severely about the impropriety of visiting a lady's chamber uninvited."

Mack's jaw dropped. He gawked at the town's baker. "Sam? Did you . . ."

Sam's face flamed red. Arms straight as pokers and hands high, he shook his head. "I didn't mean no harm, Mack. Just came callin', that's all."

Athol grunted and jabbed Sam with his elbow. "Nobody's s'posed to come callin'. That's what I tried to tell you, but —"

"Now, you lookee here, Athol, I —"

Mack leaped forward. "Both of you, hush your talk."

They both clamped their mouths closed, folded their arms over their chests, and glowered at Mack as if he was the one at fault. He slapped his palm to his forehead. Hadn't Sheriff Thorn said these women would be a peck of trouble? And how'd he manage to get in the middle of it? Ah. Because Miss Grant dragged him in. She might not be a swindler, but she sure was a troublemaker.

He threw his arms outward. "What's got into you fellas? Sam, Athol buys his bread from you for the restaurant. Athol, Sam eats

117

half his meals in your dining room. You help each other. You've been friends for as long as I can remember. Why do you wanna fight each other?"

Their glowers faded into sheepish grins. Athol looked at Sam, who looked at Athol. They both shrugged.

Sam scratched his cheek. "Reckon he made me mad, sayin' I had a skinny rump an' orderin' me to get out o' here an' not come back. Made me mad an' . . . an' it shamed me. In front o' the ladies."

Athol hung his head. "Guess I came on harder'n I should've when I seen you up here, all dandied up for courtin'." He blushed as red as the paint on the new hammer handles. "Seemed like you was cheatin', gettin' a jump on the rest o' us who are wantin' wives, too. An' I reckon I kinda wanted to show off for 'em. Let 'em see they was safe . . . with me."

"Well, it's all over now." Sam fiddled with his ripped lapel. "Don't guess I'll be doin' any more courtin'. 'Cause o' our tussle, I ain't even got a nice coat to wear to Sunday service."

Athol fingered his puffy chin. "Come on down to the kitchen. We'll make use o' some o' my tincture of arnica. Then I'll go with you over to Otto's, see if he can't stitch up

118

them tears. I'll even pay the tab."

Sam brightened. "You will?"

"Sure. Got some extra jinglin' change comin' since these two women are rentin' my rooms. Might as well use it to square things with you. Have we got a deal?"

Sam stuck out his hand and the two shook hands, somber. Then they broke into matching grins, lopsided from their swollen lips. They ambled off, arms slung across each other's shoulders. The moment they rounded the bend, Mack folded his arms over his chest. He peered at Mrs. Bingham out of the corner of his eye.

"Ma'am, I'm not one to tell somebody else how to run their business, but I need to know something."

She tilted her head and rested one fist on her hip. "What is that?"

"Do you really intend to bring a passel of brides to Spiveyville?"

"Yes. I most certainly do."

"When?"

She opened the reticule dangling from her wrist and placed her derringer inside. "I cannot give a definitive date. Much depends on the progress of the gentlemen in this town."

Miss Grant, who hadn't budged from her spot at the head of the hallway, gave a loud, scornful sniff. Both Mrs. Bingham and Mack looked at her. Her sunburned face glowed even redder. "Forgive my rude expulsion, but I do not understand how you can begin to use the term *gentlemen* when referring to the men of this town."

He bristled. Had she just insulted him?

"Why, they're nothing but odious oafs! You claimed they were good hearted, Mr. Cleveland, but I would call them uncouth and completely uncivilized."

Mack could argue, but what good would it do? The snooty little gal had made up her mind already. Probably even before she arrived in town. He turned a frown on Mrs. Bingham. "What did you mean by their progress?"

She smiled and chuckled, shaking her head. "Oh, now, Mr. Cleveland, you mustn't run ahead of me. All will be made clear at this evening's meeting. Which reminds me . . ." She took a step toward Miss Grant and extended her hand. "The threat has passed, Abigail. Come along now so we can organize the information for our gathering with the fine people of Spiveyville."

Miss Grant didn't budge. "I've changed my mind. These men are beyond help. I cannot subject myself to more leering grins and offers of courtship." She shuddered and shifted to face Mack. "Mr. Cleveland, may I prevail upon you to drive me to Pratt Center? I need to return to Newton as quickly as possible."

Her regal head held high, Mrs. Bingham strode across the planked floor. "To what are you returning?"

"Your house."

"For what purpose?"

The younger woman wrung her hands. She chewed her dry lip for a moment, her wide brown eyes fearful. "I'll assist in interviewing potential brides."

"Marietta is quite capable of handling that task unaided until my return, at which time I will resume the responsibility."

"Then I'll . . . I'll . . ." Tears winked in her eyes. She blinked fast and hard. "Let me go back, please? I'm sure there is something I can do that will be helpful for your business."

Mrs. Bingham shook her head. "You're needed here, Abigail, as we've already discussed."

"But I cannot —"

"You can, and you will." Mrs. Bingham gripped Miss Grant's elbow and steered her toward the room at the end of the hall. As they moved past Mack, the older woman sent him a tense smile. "Thank you again for your assistance, Mr. Cleveland. Please alert the sheriff about this morning's unpleasant encounter. Perhaps he would be wise to post a man at the restaurant doors to prevent future uninvited intrusions."

She ushered Miss Grant through the doorway and snapped the door closed behind them, but not before Mack got a glimpse of the young woman's pitiful, helpless expression. An uncomfortable weight settled on his chest — half worry, half . . . unexplainably . . . sympathy. What did Mrs. Bingham expect from Miss Grant? And why did he care?

Helena

Behind the privacy of the closed door, Helena planted her hands on her hips and gave Abigail her sternest frown. "Young woman, I am sorry you received such a fright this morning, but you and I have an agreement. I expect you to honor your word and see the commitment through to completion."

Tears spilled down Abigail's cheeks, and she grimaced. She dabbed at the moisture with her wrists. "When I agreed, I didn't realize —"

"That the men were grievously loutish?"

Helena took a handkerchief from her top drawer and pressed it into Abigail's hand. "Here, use this. And stop crying. The salt in your tears will only aggravate your sunburn." She waited until the girl gingerly dried her cheeks, then continued in a firm tone. "You're not unintelligent, Abigail. Have I ever resorted to such means with any prospective grooms in all the years of my matchmaking business? That in itself should have told you how desperately these men need gentling."

Abigail's lower lip quivered. She wadded the handkerchief in her hands. "They're grown men, Mrs. Bingham, not children to be molded and influenced. And they're so . . . so . . ." She pulled in a shuddering breath. "You've been so kind to me. I appreciate it, and I want to repay you. But . . ."

Helena waited, but Abigail fell silent, her head low. Helena emitted a soft sigh. The only reason Abigail wanted to help in this venture was because there were no other options available to her. Helena found no joy in Abigail's sorry position. The Lord in heaven knew she'd been dealt an unfair blow by her father's abhorrent decision to cheat his business partners and abscond with thousands of dollars. What young man of influence would court the daughter of a

123

known criminal? But why couldn't she lay aside her ridiculously high expectations and accept the hand of a poor but honest, hardworking man?

Why, Helena's dear Howard had been born to poor but virtuous parents who had the foresight to send him to school each day and then on to higher education, where he studied law and became a well-respected and contributing member of society. He hadn't possessed more than two nickels to rub together when they met, but she'd known instantly she would be safe with him. Security didn't come only through a large bank account. Apparently Abigail hadn't discovered that truth yet. And Helena wasn't the girl's mother. It was not her job to teach Abigail such life lessons. She would need to uncover them on her own.

Abigail sniffed and wiped her eyes again. "Trying to teach these men to be mannerly, moral gentlemen is as useless as trying to teach a bird to swim or a fish to fly."

Helena smiled. "Are you familiar with the mallard duck, Abigail?"

The girl's face creased in silent query, but she nodded.

"And the Canada goose?"

Again, a puzzled nod.

"Were you aware that both of these species of birds are quite adept at swimming?"

Abigail shifted her gaze aside and crunched her lips together.

"There is also an amazing sea creature called the Atlantic flyingfish that bursts from the ocean and glides for a distance of more than six hundred feet. It's truly an incredible thing to watch." She cupped Abigail's chin and turned her face until their gazes met. "I am not asking the impossible of you. If a feathered mallard can swim and finned Atlantic fish can fly, then you, dear, can teach uncouth men to behave like civilized creatures."

More tears wobbled on her eyelashes. "I can?"

Helena laughed and moved away from the girl. "Simply being in your presence will be a lesson in itself. The shortage of women on the plains has allowed these men to fall into boorish habits. But the presence of a lady will stir them to more appropriate behavior."

"How can you be sure?"

Abigail might not appreciate being used as bait, but this morning's melee had convinced Helena a competition would intrinsically arise between the men, each eager to claim the attractive young woman as their prize. "Because I've learned a great deal in my lifetime about the confusing yet completely irresistible creature known as a man."

She lifted the letter she'd crafted to Marietta and tucked it in her reticule. "Let's see to our errands, hmm? The post office and the general store. A poke bonnet can't cost much. Then you and I will go over my lesson notes. Once you see what I intend, you'll discover you are more than adequately equipped to conquer this assignment."

TEN

Abigail

As he'd promised, Sheriff Thorn arrived at the restaurant at a quarter past seven. He didn't offer his elbow to either Mrs. Bingham or Abigail, but he did open the doors for them. A token gesture of chivalry since the pair of doors swung on hinges and didn't even require the twist of a knob.

Dusk had fallen, but Abigail wore her new poke bonnet anyway. None of the bonnets on the shelf in the mercantile were remotely close to attractive, but she'd located a cluster of wax cherries in the bottom of a crate marked "Discards," and the mercantile owner, Mr. Thompson, made a great show of letting her have them without asking for even a penny in return. Did he really believe his behavior was gallant? Why should anyone pay for something taken from what equated to a trash bin?

But, determined to set a good example, she had thanked him profusely and then used a needle and some green thread from Mrs. Bingham's little travel sewing kit to attach the cherries to the left side of the sad brown tube-shaped bonnet. The brim shielded her face from sunlight, moonlight, starlight, and lamplight. She observed her surroundings through an odd-shaped opening, jittery since her peripheral vision was completely obliterated. For the first time in her life, she empathized with horses forced to wear blinders.

She trailed Mrs. Bingham and the sheriff past Spiveyville's businesses, careful not to step on the sweeping skirt of Mrs. Bingham's gown but staying as close as possible. The buildings didn't connect, leaving dark, narrow passageways in between where someone could easily hide. If an overeager man tried to sneak up alongside her, she wanted to be in close proximity to the sheriff. Especially since Mrs. Bingham had left her derringer in her room.

They stepped from the wooden boardwalk fronting Spiveyville's business district to a dirt street. The sheriff pointed ahead. "Church is up there yonder — sits at the corner of Second an' Adams." His saunter became a strut. "Back when we was namin'

128

streets, I come up with the idea of First, Second, an' so forth to the east o' Main an' then using alphabet letters — you know, A Street, B Street — to the west to help folks find their way around."

"And Adams, I presume, is from President Adams?" A smile colored Mrs. Bingham's tone.

"Yes, ma'am. Now, that wasn't my idea. It come from our first mayor, Ernie Emery, who's gone on to his reward. A bunch o' us wanted to take names from those who first lived in the town — Emery an' Thorn an' Adelman an' so forth — but that Ernie, he wasn't one for airs. He said to put presidents' names on the streets instead, an' everybody thought real high of Ernie, so we did as he said." He released a snort that held amusement. " 'Course, back then, we figgered Spiveyville'd get a whole lot bigger. Never thought we'd end with President Madison, Third Street, an' C Street, but that's the way of it."

Abigail wanted to examine the town, but to see beyond the bonnet's brim, she had to turn her neck at a sharp angle. Doing so meant losing sight of the sheriff and Mrs. Bingham. So she kept her gaze aimed at their backs and peeked between them at the few houses spaced sporadically along the

129

street. Despite the brim's limitation, she had no difficulty spotting the location of the church. Horses and wagons filled the yard and spilled into the street. Her pulse began to gallop. Mr. Cleveland must have followed Mrs. Bingham's instruction to invite everyone in town. And everyone must have accepted.

The sheriff led them in a mazelike path between wagons to the front porch of the chapel. Lamps glowed behind the simple two-panes-across, three-panes-down windows. Soft voices — mutters interspersed with guffaws — drifted from behind the limestone block walls. A gable not much deeper than the brim of her bonnet stood sentry above a pair of wood-paneled double doors, which were propped open with large gray rocks.

"Go on in, ladies." Sheriff Thorn gestured to the three wooden risers climbing directly to the doors. "Looks to me like ever'body's already here waitin' on ya."

Mrs. Bingham pinched her skirt between her fingers and climbed upward. Abigail did the same, but her trembling fingers couldn't quite hold their grip. Her skirt dipped, catching the toe of her shoe, and she stumbled. She caught her balance as she crossed the threshold, but her foot landed with a solid thump against the floor. As if she'd intended it to be a signal for silence, everyone stopped talking. She couldn't see, thanks to her shielding brim, but she sensed dozens of gazes pinned on her, and her face immediately heated.

Mrs. Bingham eased her fashionable wide-brimmed hat from her head. "Remove your bonnet, Abigail," she whispered. "There are hooks here on the back wall to receive millinery."

Abigail preferred to remain hidden, but she followed her employer's direction, tugging at the wide muslin ribbons with hands that shook so badly she marveled they functioned at all. She looped the bonnet ribbons on a wooden peg, then turned to face the crowd. Nausea attacked. She pressed her intertwined fingers to her stomach. Every bench was filled, mostly by men, from young to old. Expressions varied from curious to friendly. Only a few struck her as lecherous, but there were so many more people than she'd expected — fifty at least. Her practices in elocution were a decade past and had been performed in front of her peers. How would she stand in front of such a large, unfamiliar group of people and speak the way Mrs. Bingham expected?

Mrs. Bingham planted her palm in the center of Abigail's back and propelled her up the center aisle. The backless benches squeaked with the shifting weight of those seated, their faces following the women's progress the way sunflowers followed the course of the sun. When they reached the front, Mrs. Bingham stepped past Abigail onto the dais and stopped beside the preacher's podium. She skimmed a bright, relaxed smile of welcome across the entire congregation. Abigail focused on the matchmaker, willing her galloping pulse to calm and her stomach to cease its flips of apprehension before it spilled the fried chicken and corn bread she'd eaten for supper less than an hour ago.

"Good evening, ladies and gentlemen. It is wonderful to see so many of you here." She settled her smile on one area. "Mr. Cleveland, apparently you have a great talent for spreading information. Perhaps you should change your occupation from hardware store owner to newsman."

Light laughter rolled through the room. A man from the back — the same man who had plucked Abigail from the wagon seat — called out, "Stop talkin' about Mack an' tell us when we're gonna get our brides."

Sheriff Thorn strode halfway up the aisle

132

and planted himself there. "W. C. Miller, you hold your tongue until the lady tells you it's time to talk, or you can just hightail it right back to your cows." He roved his glare around the room. "This here is the Lord's house. If you wouldn't go hollerin' out at Preacher Doan, you shouldn't oughta be hollerin' out at Miz Bingham. So y'all hush."

A few people muttered, but no one argued. The sheriff bobbed his salt-and-pepper head at Mrs. Bingham. "Go ahead now, ma'am. Say what needs sayin'."

"Thank you, Sheriff." Mrs. Bingham locked her hands behind her back and paced slowly up and down the dais. Their gazes followed her, heads moving as if their noses were iron and Mrs. Bingham a magnet. "As Sheriff Thorn indicated, I am Mrs. Helena Bingham. I operate Bingham's Bevy of Brides, a matchmaking service from Newton, Massachusetts. I am here in Spiveyville with my assistant, Miss Abigail Grant, in response to several requests for brides from men residing in your community and on surrounding ranches."

As a group, their attention fixed on Abigail for a few seconds, then whipped back to Mrs. Bingham. Their seemingly choreographed movements struck Abigail as comical, and she fought nervous giggles. She bit down on her lower lip to hold the inappropriate chortles inside.

"Will the men who sent letters of request please rise?"

Men popped up like gophers from their holes, the floor squeaking in protest. Abigail silently counted. All sixteen were there. Another flutter of nervousness churned through her stomach.

Mrs. Bingham nodded, her demure smile in place. "Thank you. You may be seated." More squeaks resounded as the men settled back on the benches. "I don't wish to be rude to our other guests, but for the moment I would like to address those who rose. I am aware that most often, a matchmaker receives correspondence and a fee from a prospective groom, selects a bride who fits the groom's requirements, and sends her off to meet and eventually marry the one who made the request. As you can imagine, I become quite familiar with my prospective brides. I grow attached to them, even feel motherly toward them, and I want my girls to be well cared for. Thus, I traveled to Spiveyville in order to meet you grooms, to assure myself that you are decent, law-abiding men who will be good providers and faithful husbands to the girls who entrusted me with their futures."

A scuffle rose from one corner of the room. Abigail couldn't resist peeking, fearful Mr. Patterson and the baker had broken into another round of fisticuffs. But it was only W. C. Miller on his feet, bouncing in place and poking his hand upward like a schoolboy.

Mrs. Bingham frowned. "Yes . . . Mr. Miller, is that correct?"

"Yes'm." He jammed his hand into the pocket of his trousers. "I ain't trying to be quarrelsome" — he whisked a look at the sheriff — "but I'm wonderin' how long you're thinkin' o' lookin' us over before you bring us our brides. We're movin' into winter, a slower time for most o' us ranchers, and it'd be fine to get settled in with our women before spring comes. Durin' the spring, we'll hafta spend more hours out workin' than at home spoonin' the way new-married couples do."

Several other men nodded, and a few of those sitting next to wives hunched their shoulders and snickered. Abigail ducked her head at the image the man's comment conjured. Clearly, Mrs. Bingham overestimated her ability to bring decency into these men's lives. She longed for the courage to race up the aisle and out the door.

Preacher Doan rose from his spot on the front bench. "W. C., if I have to come back there and sit next to you, I will."

The cowboy's grin didn't fade, but he slid into his seat. Preacher Doan glowered in his direction for a few silent seconds before turning and sitting again.

"I shall now speak to every person who chose to attend the meeting this evening." Mrs. Bingham continued her slow back-and-forth trek, her heels clicking softly on the raised wooden platform. "God Almighty Himself created the institution of marriage, claiming that man and wife should become as one. Contrary to Mr. Miller's inference, being a husband means more than having the freedom to enjoy the physical side of the relationship. Certainly a husband should be his wife's lover —"

The benches squeaked. Whispers, some shocked and others holding notes of elation, filtered to the rafters. Abigail closed her eyes and wished the floor would rise up and swallow her.

"— but being a lover goes beyond the physical. A woman's heart is a precious thing. Women wish to be cherished, to be wooed."

"Even by their husbands?" A short, red-haired man in rancher's attire squawked the query.

A female voice from the center of the crowd answered. "She sure does!"

More mutters and self-conscious laughter rang.

Mrs. Bingham raised her voice. "I wish to make certain my girls are met by men who can pass the test on how to treat a lady. Miss Grant?" Abigail reluctantly met the match-maker's gaze. "Will you please —"

Clive Ackley bounded upright. Hands balled into fists, he leaned toward the dais. "The ad you put in the *Dodge City Courier* didn't say nothin' about us havin' to pass no test."

Abigail paused with one foot on the dais, the other on the floor, her flesh tingling. The air held the same tension as the minutes before a thunderstorm descended.

Across the room, men — the same ones who'd stood at Mrs. Bingham's invitation a few minutes ago — bolted to their feet.

"Clive's right. You ain't bein' fair."

"I ain't no snot-nosed schoolboy who needs learnin'."

"What kinda test can figure out what kind o' husband I'll be?"

"I want my woman now!"

In two broad strides, the sheriff reached

the front of the church and held both arms in the air. "Settle yourselves down!" The furor continued.

Preacher Doan rose and faced the crowd. "You heard the sheriff! You aren't in a saloon or a barn. Have some respect. For the love of all that's holy, sit down and be quiet!"

The men continued to mutter, but one by one they plopped back onto the benches. The preacher positioned himself at one end of the dais, the sheriff at the other. From the corner of her eye, Abigail observed Mr. Cleveland shifting to the foot of the center aisle, inside the doors. He planted his boots wide and crossed his arms, his serious gaze darting left and right. The room fairly crackled with compressed fury, but finally all was quiet, and the preacher nodded at Mrs. Bingham.

She held her hand to Abigail again, and on shaking legs Abigail stepped up next to her. She faced the crowd, her stomach jumping the way popcorn kernels explode inside a kettle on a hot stove. Mrs. Bingham guided Abigail to the preacher's podium and then stepped aside.

Abigail curled her fingers around the edges of the simple wooden podium and held tight. "I . . . I am Miss Abigail Grant, and I've come to Spiveyville at Mrs. Bingham's request" — should she be truthful and admit she'd been coerced? — "to conduct classes in social dancing, dining, courtship, conversation, and commonsense etiquette."

Too late she realized she'd left the note concerning the classes in her pocket, but she didn't think she'd omitted anything. She cleared her throat, eager to finish and return to her dismal room above the restaurant. "Although only the men who requested a bride from Bingham's Bevy of Brides will be required to attend the classes, anyone in the community is welcome. This includes couples who are already married but who might like to broaden their horizons and strengthen their bonds of matrimony."

All across the room, jaws dropped. Eyes grew wide. Most of the women looked eager, but she was certain if she wasn't a lady and Sheriff Thorn wasn't standing guard, the men would stampede her and chase her out of town. She licked her dry lips and forced herself to finish the speech she and Mrs. Bingham had planned.

"The classes will take place Monday through Friday evenings, for a duration of no more than two hours per night, and —"

"Wait, wait . . ." Mr. Ackley bounded up

again, waving both pudgy hands. "Where're we gonna be doin' these classes?"

Abigail looked at Mrs. Bingham, and Mrs. Bingham looked at Preacher Doan. The matchmaker held out her hands in query. "Do you have a suggestion, Reverend?"

The preacher lifted his shoulders in a slow shrug. "I s'pose you could use the church for the classes on conversation, courting, or — what'd you call it? — et . . . et . . . ."

"Etiquette," Abigail and Mrs. Bingham said at the same time.

"That's it. Etiquette. But there's not room in here for dancing or dining."

Mr. Patterson spoke up. "Makes sense to do the dinin' in my restaurant, long as you don't get in the way of me seein' to my customers."

A man in the front row, the best dressed of any of the men in the room, slapped his knee. "A barn's always a good place for dancin'. Maybe Hugh Briggs'll letcha use the loft in the livery stable."

A shy-looking man with a prominent nose unfolded himself from a bench on the opposite side of the room. "That'd be me." He gulped. "I'm Hugh Briggs, I mean. An' sure. If you wanna dance in my loft, I don't mind." He sat so quickly the bench popped.

A small flutter of excitement worked its

way through Abigail's center. They were co-operating, more than she'd expected. Perhaps this idea would work after all.

Another man, this one holding a cowboy hat against his chest, stood and aimed his unsmiling gaze at Abigail. "Little gal, I'm willing to excuse you 'cause you ain't from these parts, but the town fellers ought to know that me an' the other ranchers can't be traipsin' into town ever' night for classes on dancin' or dinin' or that etta-whatever. Leavin' your spread unattended is an invitation for rustlers to come sweepin' in."

"You tell her, Firmin," W. C. said, and several others nodded.

The pretty, dark-haired woman who'd sat quietly at the end of the first bench next to Preacher Doan stood and shook her finger at the complaining men. "Firmin Chapman and W. C. Miller, I'm ashamed of both of you, pickin' on Miss Grant this way. I know your mamas taught you better, and so did I."

Firmin sat and W. C. slunk low in his seat.

The woman joined Abigail on the dais. "Miss Grant, I'm Medora Doan, Spiveyville's schoolteacher. It won't be an easy thing, teaching this motley crew, but I'm more than happy to help if you need it."

Abigail wouldn't reject an ally. Especially

one who could make W. C. be quiet. "Thank you, ma'am."

Mrs. Doan tapped her lips, her brows furrowing. "It is a problem, however, to expect the men from the ranches to come to town every day. Are you willing to teach each of the classes more than once?"

Abigail and Mrs. Bingham had discussed the possibility of repeating a class if the men didn't thoroughly grasp the concepts of manners and morals in one setting. "I'm not averse to the idea."

A bright smile broke across the woman's face. "Then I suggest focusing on one subject a week. The ranchers could choose a day to come in when their closest neighbor stays home so the spreads aren't left completely unattended. Townsfolk who want to take the classes can join in whenever it suits them. Surely over five days, each of the men who requested a bride will be able to come at least once."

Abigail's mouth fell open. A full week per topic? But there were five topics in all. That would mean remaining here in Spiveyville for more than a month. "Oh, I —"

Mrs. Bingham clasped Mrs. Doan's hand. "What a splendid idea. We'll make a schedule chart and post it on the message board at the post office. The ranchers and towns-

Welcome to Albert Carlton -
Cashiers Community Library
Sylvia Barrows
You checked out the following
items:

1. **Beneath a prairie moon**
   Barcode: 39493108302540
   Due: 9/10/2020
2. **Seeds of hope**
   Barcode: 39493108301625
   Due: 9/10/2020

You Saved
$66.00
by borrowing from the library!

Albert Carlton - Cashiers
Community Library
8/20/2020 3:17 PM
Telephone: 828-743-0215
Tue&Wed: 10am-5:30pm
Thurs: 10am-7pm
Fri: 10am-5:30pm
Sat: 10am-4pm
Closed Sun & Mon

people can sign up. You're brilliant, Mrs. Doan."

The woman blushed prettily. "I've learned how to organize my students into groups so I can meet all their needs." She laughed and lowered her voice. "As you've probably figured out from listening to them fuss this evening, teaching these men won't be much different than teaching children. Except you won't be able to make them stand in the corner if they misbehave."

The humor in her expression faded. She flicked a look across the room, then leaned close to Abigail. "I'll make sure either Sheriff Thorn or my husband attends the classes, too, Miss Grant. We want to keep you . . . safe."

143

ELEVEN

Bill

The church sanctuary buzzed with excitement, every soul yammering either in a whisper or out loud. Bill didn't try to hush them since the three women on the platform along with Preacher Doan, Hugh Briggs, and Athol Patterson had their heads together, all yakking at each other. He scanned the group, looking for signs that somebody was ready to bust into something more than talk, and thought over what he'd heard from the fancy women.

He wasn't sure what he'd expected them to say, but their talk about classes for manners and so forth took him by surprise as much as it did those who'd sent off for a bride. Not that the fellows in town couldn't benefit from a little settling down. They were mostly cowpunchers, after all, not city gentlemen. But the comments about what a

144

woman wanted from a husband surprised him the most.

His pa'd been a strong man, a hard worker who took pride in seeing to his family's needs, and his ma had never voiced one word of complaint. At least, not where Bill heard. But Ma'd always been quiet, going about her work without many smiles or laughter. Could it be she'd felt cheated somehow? The idea niggled like a bad itch.

Mrs. Bingham stepped to the edge of the platform and raised her hands. "Excuse me. Excuse me, please."

Everybody quieted and looked to the front, including Bill.

"Since it will take a few days to ready our locations for the classes, we will begin with the first topic, commonsense etiquette, on Monday, the twenty-second, at six thirty in the evening right here in the First Methodist Church."

Groans broke from several of the men. Vern O'Dell jumped up and balled his hands on his skinny hips. His face was as red as his unruly hair. "Aw, c'mon, lady, we've already waited two months. Let's get these classes done so our women can get here." Mutters rose.

Bill stomped his foot, ending the complaints, and pointed at the red-haired man.

145

"You want a wife, Vern, you gotta follow the rules."

The fiery rancher grumbled some, but he sat.

Mrs. Bingham went on just as easy as if nobody'd said a word. "I'm not unsympathetic to your eagerness, but by waiting until next week to begin, each of you will have sufficient time to visit the post office and place your name on the day that best meets your personal schedules. It will also allow time for those of you who have children or animals you cannot leave untended to make arrangements for their supervision."

W. C. jabbed his hand in the air again. "When you gonna have that list ready?"

"Mrs. Doan, Miss Grant, and I intend to create the charts this evening. They will be posted the moment Mr. Ackley opens for business tomorrow."

"Ackley shuts down early, though. Some o' us can't get into town before five o'clock."

W. C. didn't know when to hush up, but he made a good point. Bill cleared his throat. "There's two businesses in town that stay open late to accommodate the ranchers — Patterson's restaurant an' Cleveland's hardware store. Mebbe the charts could go up in one o' them places instead."

Athol broke into a toothy grin. "Sure. Post

146

'em on the wall in the restaurant. I don't mind."

Vern shook his head, making his thick cowlick bounce. "Nuh-uh. Patterson's tryin' to score points with the ladies. He's already puttin' 'em up in his rooms. Most likely he's hostin' the dinin' class, too."

"I sure am." Athol rocked on his heels, smug as could be.

"Then the scales ain't balancin' too good." Vern swung his glare at the other hopeful grooms. "Anybody else thinkin' Patterson's got too much goin' with the ladies?"

All across the room, heads bobbed in agreement.

Bill sighed. "You fellas are like a bunch o' kids fightin' over one licorice whip." He pinned his gaze on Mack, who stood quiet and serious at the back of the church. "Mack, will it bother you any to put the charts in your store? None o' the men are likely to accuse you o' scorin' points since you ain't even asked for a bride."

Mack gave a half-hearted shrug. "I can find a spot on a wall, I reckon, if it'll help you out, Sheriff."

Mrs. Bingham beamed. "It will help us greatly, Mr. Cleveland. Thank you." She let her big toothy smile drift over every person in the room, including Bill and Mack. That

147

lady'd make a fine politician. Or snake oil salesman. "Thank you, everyone, for your attendance here this evening. Miss Grant and I look forward to becoming better acquainted with you during the classes. Good evening."

Folks started shuffling out, the wives holding on to their husbands' arms and smiling up, all hopeful like. They wanted to take the classes. Wanted to — like Mrs. Bingham said — strengthen their bonds. Maybe if somebody'd come along and offered that kind of help to his pa and ma, Ma would've been happier.

He trailed the group, making sure they all got out to their wagons without somebody starting a scuffle. Cantankerous men. Worse than schoolkids. He called after them, "You get signed up, now, you hear me? Don't be disappointin' Miz Bingham an' me."

Louis Griffin shot a grin over his shoulder. "You planning on takin' the classes, Sheriff? Betcha that lady could find you a wife, too."

Bill flapped his hands at the barber. "Get on home, now, an' don't talk nonsense." What would he do with a wife? And why all of a sudden did his stomach hurt?

Mack glanced at his pocket watch and gave a start. How'd the morning hour go so fast? He should have unlocked the front door to customers two minutes ago. He hurried across the floor, dropping the watch into his trouser pocket as he went, and turned the key a brisk half turn. A resounding *click* announced the release of the locking mechanism. He swung the door wide and gave a second jolt. Mrs. Bingham and Miss Grant waited on the other side of the doorway. At least, he assumed the second woman was Miss Grant. The poke bonnet was the same one Miss Grant wore to yesterday's meeting, and the slender form under the dress as dark red as a male cardinal's chest — as well as the stiff-shouldered way she held herself — matched Miss Grant. But he couldn't see anything of her face behind the bonnet's wide brim.

He pushed the screen door with one hand and gestured the ladies in with the other. "I'm sorry. I hope you weren't standing out here too long." A gust of cold air chased them over the threshold. Seemed as though last night's wind finally carried fall to the plains. He'd better toss a few shovelfuls of his precious coal into the potbelly stove. If

149

the wind didn't die down during the day, he'd want some heat in the building.

He closed the door and turned to find Mrs. Bingham holding up a rolled tube of paper.

"These are the schedule charts Mrs. Doan, Abigail, and I constructed after the meeting. Six of them in all. I am very grateful for your willingness to post them."

"Six?" He'd cleared an area, but he wasn't sure there'd be room for that many. He might have to move another display.

"Yes. One for each day of the week, and one with the subject and location for each week's class." The older woman's gray eyes twinkled. "Perhaps having the charts in your store will tempt you to sign up for a class, too."

Sheriff Thorn had already talked Mack into going to the classes on the nights the sheriff or Preacher Doan couldn't to serve as an unpaid, unofficial protector and — there was no other word for it — spy for the women. Just in case they proved double dealing. But the sheriff asked him to keep quiet about watching for evidence of a scam. So he chuckled nervously and shrugged. "You never know."

Mrs. Bingham smiled and glanced around. "You have a very neatly organized store, Mr.

150

Cleveland. I see a great deal of pride of ownership. Don't you agree, Abigail?"

Miss Grant loosened her bonnet strings and let the oversized bonnet slide back. He tried not to stare, but it was hard not to. The skin on her nose and cheeks was bubbled like the surface of boiling water. No wonder she'd hidden behind the brim. Her wary gaze moved across the rows of shelves and lineup of barrels. "Yes. It's quite nice."

Quite nice? She couldn't have any idea how much work it took to keep everything clean and orderly. But he shouldn't pat himself on the back. Ma always said the satisfaction of a job well done was reward enough. He suddenly realized she was holding out a square of paper. He took it. "Another chart?"

She picked at her chapped lip. "A thank-you note."

He frowned. "What for?"

She turned her face aside, almost touching her chin to her shoulder. "The aloe."

From the looks of things, it hadn't done her much good. Unsure what to say, he slipped the envelope into his shirt pocket and brushed his palms together. "Let's get those charts hung, huh?"

On his way across the floor, he snagged a

hammer — one of the new ones he'd taken down to make room for the schedule charts — and a handful of tacks. "The only place I could put 'em was on the back wall. I hope folks won't mind walking all the way through the store to sign up."

"I'm sure the location will be fine." Mrs. Bingham matched him stride for stride, but Miss Grant trailed behind, her head low. She hung back while Mrs. Bingham unrolled the pages and held the first one flat against the wall.

Mack tapped the tacks into place over all four corners. Then he stepped back and looked it over. "You made this?"

Mrs. Bingham nodded toward Miss Grant. "Abigail did, using Mrs. Doan's suggestions. She possesses a very neat hand, yes?"

"As neat as anything a printer could do." Every line was straight, the letters evenly spaced. If he got a ruler and checked, he'd probably find they were all the exact same height, too.

A slight flush darkened Miss Grant's red cheeks. "Both penmanship and elocution were stressed at the school I attended in Boston. Father always said even a girl should be able to express herself and make herself understood whether in spoken word or on paper." Her face crumpled, like someone had stabbed her.

Mack thought he understood. "No need to talk if it makes your face hurt, Miss Grant. That sunburn'll heal up soon enough."

She turned her back on him. "I'll wait for you by the door, Mrs. Bingham." She scurried off, slipping her bonnet into place as she went.

Maybe he shouldn't have said anything about her face, but he'd only meant to comfort her.

Mrs. Bingham touched his sleeve. "Shall we hang the rest of the charts? I'm sure you have other work to do."

He always had work to do. He and Mrs. Bingham finished putting up the charts. By crunching them together and making two rows of three each, he didn't need to clear any more merchandise from the pegboards. When they finished, he glanced toward the front of the store, then leaned close to Mrs. Bingham.

"I didn't mean to embarrass Miss Grant. She's probably pretty self-conscious about her face right now."

Mrs. Bingham gazed at Miss Grant and sighed. "I doubt it's her face that's paining her at the moment, but it's very kind of you to be concerned." She held out her gloved

153

hand and he took it. "Let me thank you again for your assistance with the classes, for transporting Abigail and me to Spivey-ville, and for coming to our rescue yesterday morning when we had need of a protector. If you change your mind and decide to make use of my services to match you with a wife, I shall happily waive half the fee."

Only half? Maybe she didn't appreciate him as much as she said. He swallowed a laugh. "No, thank you, ma'am. I'm content to let things happen the old-fashioned way."

"And what way is that?"

He shifted her hand to the bend of his elbow and escorted her to the door. "Well, like you said in the meeting last night, God's the one who planned for man and woman to come together. I figure that means He's the best one to bring whoever's supposed to be my wife across my path."

Her smile turned impish. "But what's to say God can't use a matchmaker to aid Him in His work? After all, did He not use a fleece to speak to Gideon and a donkey to speak to Balaam?"

Oh, this one was wily. Sheriff Thorn was smart to keep watch on her. He stepped away from her and opened the door. "I'll take down the sign-up charts at the end of the day Saturday and bring 'em over to you, ma'am. You and Miss Grant" — the younger woman still stood with her back to him — "have a good day now."

TWELVE

Abigail

Abigail braced her palms against the restaurant's swinging door, eager to get in out of the cold. To return to her room. To work on lesson plans and scrub her mind of reminders of her father.

Mrs. Bingham caught her elbow. "I'd like to visit the telegraph office and send a quick message to Marietta. Come with me."

A rush of cold air whooshed along the boardwalk and lifted the tails of Abigail's wool shawl. She shivered. "Wouldn't you rather wait until later in the day, when the sun has climbed a little higher? Surely the temperature will rise as the day progresses."

"Once I'm in, I'll wish to stay in. I'd rather see to all errands now." She gave a little tug. "Come, Abigail. It's only next door. We won't be in the cold for long."

Swallowing another protest, mostly because Mrs. Bingham was her boss and partly because the preacher had advised them not to venture out alone, she allowed herself to be drawn along.

A few other townspeople were already waiting for a turn at the counter. Abigail and Mrs. Bingham moved to the end of the short line. Mr. Ackley huffed like a train engine as he hustled from one end of the little post office to the other, retrieving mail from cubbies or pasting stamps on envelopes. As others turned to leave, they offered smiles and simple greetings to Mrs. Bingham and Abigail. Mrs. Bingham responded to each, but Abigail angled her head and feigned great interest in the "Wanted" posters on the wall. Mr. Cleveland's comment about her sunburn rang in her memory. She shouldn't subject anyone else to the unpleasant sight.

Finally Mrs. Bingham took her place at the counter. "I'd like to send a telegram, please, to Newton, Massachusetts."

Mr. Ackley's round face lit with eagerness. "To our brides?"

"Mr. Ackley . . ." Abigail didn't have to look to know the woman wore a disapproving frown. "I am aware I must tell you the contents of my message in order for it to be sent along the wires, but communication between two parties should at least be given the pretense of confidentiality."

The man scratched his furry cheek. "What's that you said?"

Mrs. Bingham sighed. "Never mind. May I have a piece of paper and pencil, please?"

Abigail paced in front of the window while Mrs. Bingham scratched words on a paper. "There you are."

"All right, lemme make sure I can read it all okay."

If he was unable to make it out, the blame would lie on his eyesight, not Mrs. Bingham's penmanship. The woman wrote almost as neatly as Abigail.

" 'Marietta,' " Mr. Ackley recited in a monotone, " 'date for brides' arrival estimated for November 26.' "

The twenty-sixth of November, if Abigail remembered correctly, was a few days before Thanksgiving Day. A time when families and friends gathered and counted their blessings. A perfect occasion for the men of Spiveyville to meet their intended brides for the first time. A deep ache built in the center of her chest, recalling the past lonely Thanksgivings without a home and family of her own. Future ones held no promise of happiness either. A tear slid down her cheek, stinging her sunburned skin. She sniffed and dried the trail with her gloved fingertip, hoping the bonnet hid the evidence of her heartache.

" 'Letter for . . . fort . . . ' "

"Forthcoming." Mrs. Bingham cleared her throat. "The word is *forthcoming.*"

" '. . . forthcoming. Love, Helena.' " A huge sigh wheezed from the man's mouth. "Twelve words'll be ten cents."

Abigail, ready to make her departure, inched toward the door while Mrs. Bingham retrieved her little coin purse from her reticule. The wood door swung inward, and a stocky man with coal-black hair and a matching mustache burst into the post office. His gaze landed on Abigail, and he drew back as if someone had jabbed him with a sword.

"Howdy, Otto," Mr. Ackley called out.

The man eased past Abigail, keeping a wide berth, and scuttled to the counter.

"Ladies, you remember Otto Hildreth, don'tcha? He keeps us fellas all patched up an' lookin' dandy. O' course" — the postman barked a short laugh — "soon as we all have wives, we'll be lettin' them do our stitchin'. Save a few pennies." He thumped his fist on the counter. "Guess what, Otto? Miz Bingham's set the arrival date for our brides. They'll be here by Thanksgivin', just in time to cook us a big celebration dinner."

Abigail gasped. The audacity of the man to not only announce the contents of Mrs. Bingham's telegram but also expect the newly arrived women to immediately step into a role of servitude.

"Missssster Ackley." Mrs. Bingham's tone echoed Abigail's shock. "It is most unseemly to share a private telegram with everyone who comes through the door."

"I didn't share with everyone. Just Otto here."

Abigail aimed a disbelieving look at the postman, viewing the scene through the tube-shaped opening of her bonnet.

Mrs. Bingham pursed her lips. "Not to mention it is an estimated date. There is no guarantee the men will have completed the classes to my satisfaction by then. I merely need my sister to be prepared, just in case."

Mr. Ackley's jaw dropped. "But they gotta —"

The tailor leaned halfway across the counter. "What was that you said about lettin' the women do your stitchin'?"

Mr. Ackley shrugged and shifted his attention to Mr. Hildreth. "Makes sense, don't it? Stitchin' is part of a wife's duties."

"So what you're sayin' is you an' the other fellas is gonna stop comin' to my shop?

160

Gonna put me out o' business? Is that what you plan?"

Mrs. Bingham hurried across the floor and took hold of Abigail's elbow. The women departed the post office and pulled the door tightly closed behind them, but the men's angry voices carried past the brick walls to the boardwalk. Mrs. Bingham flung a glance over her shoulder and shuddered. "You will have quite the challenge, taming these hotheads into gracious gentlemen. We may still be here well into the beginning of the new year."

Abigail swallowed a moan. Useless . . . Trying to tame these men was completely useless. "Wouldn't it be easier to simply return to Newton? There will be other requests for brides."

"It's too late for that. The men paid their fees, and a sufficient number of women are ready to leave the crowded cities for a new start in the West. I have every faith that with you as their instructor, they —"

A crash sounded in the post office.

Mrs. Bingham cringed. "— will change." She linked arms with Abigail and scurried up the boardwalk.

In the privacy of her room, Abigail removed the bonnet and laid it on the dresser top. She glanced at her reflection in the

161

round mirror hanging above the dresser and quickly turned aside, repulsed. Oh, such a sight. As much as she missed her genteel mother, gratitude eased through her that Mother needn't witness the ugly blisters. Gathering her courage, she faced the mirror again and gingerly picked at the loosest pieces of skin. She gritted her teeth against the prickling sting and continued pinching away every tissue-like bit.

When she'd removed all the pieces that had bubbled up, she leaned close to the mirror and examined her cheeks and nose. Now her face bore patches as pink as boiled shrimp, each dotted with light speckles. Not what she would call an improvement. Maybe she shouldn't have picked at it after all.

Moving away from the mirror, she scooped up the notes she'd begun jotting last night. Mrs. Bingham had suggested focusing on one subject at a time and giving it her full attention, but she wanted to have a firm outline in place for each of the five weeks. After all, Father always said early planning was the key to success. Mother took the advice to heart, beginning preparations for dinner parties nearly a month ahead of the dates. Everyone praised Mother for her well-organized and orchestrated gatherings. The last one before Father's arrest was particularly successful, making it a bitter-sweet memory. If Abigail expected to earn her employer's praise, and perhaps a recommendation for a position when they returned to Newton, she should plan well, too.

She sat on the edge of the bed and spread the notes out beside her. She chose the page titled "Commonsense Etiquette" and read down the list of topics, adding further explanation behind some, rewording a few definitions, and clarifying the importance of others. She drew an arrow from "Physical altercations are singularly abhorrent," which was in the middle of the list, to the top of the page so she'd remember to cover it first. Apparently the men in this town needed the reminder.

Shortly after noon, someone tapped on her door and then cracked it open. Abigail jolted to her feet, apprehension striking hard, but only Mrs. Bingham peeked in. She dropped back on the edge of the bed with a sigh.

"Are you ready to go down for lunch?"

Abigail touched her mottled cheek. "Couldn't you bring a tray up here? I . . . I'm quite busy." She gestured to the pages.

The woman stepped into the room and glanced across the scattered papers. "I'm glad you're taking this assignment so seriously, but you do have several days to prepare. You don't intend to stay sequestered up here the entire time, do you?"

She wanted to stay sequestered until her face healed, but that could take longer than a few days. "I might."

Mrs. Bingham folded her arms over her chest. "Don't be ridiculous. If you want people to feel comfortable taking these classes, they need to have the chance to get to know you. You can't hide the way you did in the post office this morning."

Heat flooded Abigail's face, making the raw patches burn. "I . . . I wasn't hiding."

"Please don't tell falsehoods." Mrs. Bingham crossed to the bed, shifted the pages aside, and sat. "I realize it's uncomfortable for you to be in a strange town, surrounded by unfamiliar people."

Warmed by her kind understanding, Abigail nodded. "Yes, ma'am. It is."

"But you only succeed in making others uncomfortable when you refuse to acknowledge their presence. You really must set aside these self-important airs, Abigail. They benefit you not a bit, and now is not the time to be off putting."

Could the woman not see the source of Abigail's angst? She crossed to the mirror and peered at herself, willing the awful pink patches to magically disappear.

Mrs. Bingham shifted, and the bed springs twanged. "You know, if you put some effort into making friends, you'll be much happier with yourself."

Abigail spun to face the matchmaker. "And with whom do you suggest I pursue a friendship? Mrs. Doan? She's a very nice lady, but she's at least fifteen years older than I, married, and the mother of three. We have nothing in common. I have nothing in common with any of the women in this town because they —"

"Are poor?"

Abigail bit her lower lip to hold back a groan. Yes, they were poor. And uneducated. And probably nearly as uncouth as their husbands. She didn't belong in this town with these people. But she didn't belong in Boston anymore either. Oh, if only Father hadn't resorted to thievery. If only Linus Hartford hadn't proved to be unfaithful. If only she'd had the chance to become a wife before Mother died and the house was sold and the foundation of her carefully ordered world crumbled. If only . . .

Mrs. Bingham stood and crossed to Abigail. She placed her hands on Abigail's shoulders and fixed her unsmiling gaze on her face. "I am well aware of your privileged upbringing. I am also well versed in the kind of instruction you received concerning mixing with other social classes. I heard it thrown at me when I fell in love with a man whose name was not on the social registers. Later, when my Howard had established himself as a trustworthy lawyer and we were an accepted part of the upper crust, I heard the disparaging mutters aimed at other people. Not all the instruction was bad. Manners, morals — they are fine attributes. But being mannerly doesn't make you better than others, Abigail, merely better behaved."

Abigail frowned, puzzled by the woman's comment. "Isn't better behaved . . . better?"

"As long as 'better' is not perceived as 'superior.' "

Abigail hung her head. "I'm not superior to anyone. Not anymore." Father's tumble had taken his entire family with him, and there was no climbing out of the pit. She met her boss's gaze. "But at least I can honor my mother and my upbringing by modeling the manners I was taught."

Mrs. Bingham sighed, squeezed Abigail's shoulders, then lowered her arms. "It's lunchtime. Let's go see what Mr. Patterson

166

has prepared for today's menu. Given the change in temperature, hot soup would be a welcome choice today."

Abigail trailed Mrs. Bingham down the stairs. If Mr. Patterson served soup, she would have an opportunity to demonstrate the correct way to utilize the spoon. Yesterday she'd seen half a dozen men, one woman, and two children pick up their bowls of milky morning porridge and slurp from the rim.

Mrs. Bingham stepped around the corner and paused, scanning the room. Abigail peeked past her. The restaurant's dozen tables were already occupied. The aroma of something savory stirred Abigail's hunger, but at the same time relief swooped in. She touched Mrs. Bingham's sleeve.

"We'll have to come back a bit later, when some of the customers have departed." If they waited an hour or so, every table would be empty and they could eat without men gaping at her or offending her by chewing with their mouths open and smacking their food.

Mrs. Bingham nodded. "I suppose you're right." She turned toward the staircase.

"Ma'am?" Mr. Cleveland sat alone at the table closest to the stairs. He gestured to them. "You ladies can sit with me, if you don't mind sharing a table."

Mrs. Bingham's face broke into a smile. "That's very considerate of you, Mr. Cleveland." She caught Abigail's elbow and drew her to the table.

He jumped up and pulled out chairs for both of them. A few of the other men in the room pointed, guffawed, and nudged each other, but Mr. Cleveland didn't seem to notice. He stood close by until Mrs. Bingham and Abigail sat, then he plopped back into his own chair and picked up his fork.

He jabbed the fork into a mound of greasy-looking sliced potatoes and grinned. "You ladies are new around here, so you couldn't know the Wednesday special is the most popular with the men in town. It runs out quick, so everybody comes early."

Mrs. Bingham raised her brows and peered at his plate. "What exactly is the Wednesday special?"

"Fried catfish, fried potatoes, stewed tomatoes, an' corn dodgers."

Abigail sneaked a look at the wrinkled skin, picked-clean bones, and smears of grease decorating Mr. Cleveland's plate. Her stomach gave a little lurch. "H-how unfortunate that it runs out quickly. I suppose we'll have to eat a sandwich instead." She hoped a sandwich — something other than fried fish — was on today's menu.

"Athol can always make you a sandwich if the fish is all gone and you don't want to order the chicken 'n' dumplings." Mr. Cleveland smiled, the corners of his mustache curling upward with the gesture. "There's always chicken 'n' dumplings the day after fried chicken, which is Tuesday's special. It lets him use up the leftover chicken. Of course, the dish is always a little heavy with dumplings since there's never much chicken left."

"That will likely change once the brides arrive in Spiveyville." Mrs. Bingham rested her linked hands on the edge of the table and glanced across the other patrons. "Many of the diners seem to be those who have requested a bride. They will likely eat fewer meals in Mr. Patterson's restaurant and more meals at home when they have a wife cooking for them."

Unease attacked Abigail. She recalled Mr. Hildreth's reaction to Mr. Ackley's comment about the wives taking care of the men's stitching. The arrival of the brides would change the balance of the entire town. Were the town's businessmen prepared for the change?

THIRTEEN

Mack

Mack swallowed the last bite of potatoes and pushed away from the table. "I'll go see what's keeping Athol. You ladies enjoy your lunch now." He headed for the kitchen, weaving between tables. Several men called out teasing comments about him cozying up to the city ladies, but he ignored the taunts and kept going. His pa had taught him a quiet answer turned away wrath, and he saw no sense in inviting more ridiculous comments by responding to them.

Athol was at his massive cookstove, stirring something in a big pot while sweat poured down his face. He shot a frown at Mack. "What're you doin' in here? You know I don't like nobody comin' in my kitchen."

Mack grinned. Athol would have to change that tune when the future Mrs.

Patterson arrived in town. "Wanted to let you know you've got some new customers out there. Mrs. Bingham and Miss Grant are ready for lunch."

Athol groaned. "I plumb forgot about them two, what with keepin' up with every-body's orders for fish. I gotta keep stirrin' this milk for tonight's pudding or it'll scorch. You s'pose they'll mind waitin' a little longer?"

Mack doubted Mrs. Bingham would com-plain about a wait, but Miss Grant didn't seem too keen on staying in the dining room any longer than necessary. Not that he could blame her. Half the fellows gawked at her like they'd never seen a woman before. With her face all blotched up like a leper from the Bible, she probably felt more self-conscious than usual. He peeked into the pot. "You want me to stir that while you go take their orders?"

"Baked puddin' is a particular thing. I gotta take this milk off the heat at just the right time or the puddin' won't set. If you're bound to help, I'd rather you took their order an' served 'em."

Mack already knew what they wanted. "Where's the chicken 'n' dumplings?"

Athol bobbed his head toward a huge kettle at the other end of the stove.

Mack grabbed two crockery bowls from a shelf and dipped plump dumplings into each. Then he fished through the creamy broth for as many chunks of chicken as he could find and added them to the bowls. He plopped the bowls on a tray and frowned. Sure didn't look like much. "Where do you keep your pickles, Athol?"

"You're a real pest, Mack, you know that? Pickle crock's in the cellar."

Mack headed for the cellar door.

"Take a saucer with you. An' put some o' my pickled onions on the plate, too. They go real good with dumplin's. They're in a smaller crock next to the cucumbers."

Mack reversed his steps, snatched up a saucer, and took the dirt stairs to the cellar. The smell under the kitchen was so heady — a combination of all the foods Athol had cooked over the past two days plus the tang of pickles — he was tempted to stick around and sniff. But the women were waiting.

He pinched out four good-sized pickles and added a full dipper of onions to the plate. The vinegary smell teased his nose as he headed back upstairs. He put the saucer on the tray along with two spoons and forks and some checked cloths that looked clean. As he lifted the tray, he realized the ladies didn't have anything to drink. He paused beside the stove. "Should I take 'em coffee?"

"Mrs. Bingham likes coffee. Miss Grant is partial to cold milk."

Mack had no idea why, but thinking of Miss Grant drinking a glass of frothy milk made him want to smile. "I'll come back for their drinks. Don't want these dumplings to get cold."

"Thanks, Mack." Athol swiped sweat beads from his forehead with his arm and kept stirring, his gaze aimed into the pot.

Most of the men had cleared out during Mack's time in the kitchen, leaving dirty dishes scattered over the tables and their chairs all askew. He eased between the tables, bumping chairs out of the way with his hip. He grinned and settled the tray between the two women. "Here you go. I forgot your drinks, but I'll get those now. Coffee for you" — he bounced a nod at Mrs. Bingham — "and milk for Miss Grant."

The younger woman blushed, her newly sprouted freckles almost disappearing beneath the red flush. "I'm fine, Mr. Cleveland. Thank you."

He hadn't meant to embarrass her. "You sure? I don't mind." He chuckled and smoothed his mustache. "It'd give me an excuse to go back into Athol's cellar. The good smell down there makes a man want to take up residence."

Miss Grant turned her face away. Her blush increased. Mack frowned. What had he said now?

Mrs. Bingham chuckled. "Not to rob you of your opportunity to partake of the cellar's, er, unique aroma, but we don't wish to trouble you any further. Thank you for delivering our lunch, Mr. Cleveland. As usual, you are most accommodating to us ladies in need."

"You're welcome." He dug out payment for his dinner and dropped it on the table. "I guess I'll get back to my store now. You ladies enjoy your dumplings."

"Thank you. I'm sure we will," Mrs. Bingham said.

Miss Grant still wouldn't look at him. Mack headed for the door, shaking his head. She was one peculiar woman.

Abigail

Abigail hadn't forgotten the previous purpose for the cellar. Just when she'd begun to think there was one man in town who possessed a modicum of decency, Mr. Cleveland admitted he liked the smell of malt liquor. Disappointment sagged her shoulders. After the way he'd pulled out their chairs, engaged them in conversation, and served their lunch, she'd held on to a thread of hope that the other men could be taught manners, too. But underneath the polite surface lurked one who found pleasure in the smell of alcohol. He'd let her down.

Mrs. Bingham bowed her head, and Abigail followed her example even though she only sat quietly instead of offering a prayer of thanks for the food. Her heart was too heavy to craft a prayer.

They had finished their meal before Mr. Patterson emerged from the kitchen and began stacking dirty plates on a large tray. "You ladies get enough to eat?"

Mrs. Bingham dropped the cloth over her empty bowl. "Yes. The dumplings were quite flavorful. You're an excellent cook, Mr. Patterson."

"Thanks, ma'am. Miss Grant, did you like the dumplin's, too?"

"Yes, sir. They were very tasty and filling." Abigail chose not to add that the simple fare was very different from the dishes her childhood cook had prepared for her family. Could Mr. Patterson roast a leg of lamb or prepare quail stuffed with chestnut dressing? Her mouth watered, thinking of her favorite childhood meals.

Mr. Patterson ambled over, his smile wide. "Well, you're in for a treat tonight. I bought some beef tongue from the Fletcher brothers, Melvin an' Millard — they run the Crooked F Ranch out west o' town."

Abigail's stomach rolled. Tongue? These people ate a cow's tongue?

"Gonna roast it with carrots, taters, an' onions. I ordered up a batch o' fresh rolls from Sam, an' for dessert there'll be plum puddin'. I just now tucked it in the oven for a slow bake. It'll set up thick as a cake. You wait an' see." He beamed at them. "Don't that sound good?"

"*Doesn't* that sound good." Abigail snapped the correction, hoping to chase away the awful images parading through her mind. They remained.

He nodded. "Glad you think so."

She swallowed against the desire to gag. How could she possibly eat tongue? "W-what else do you plan to include on tonight's menu?"

"Why, nothin'. Can't imagine why anybody'd order something else. Besides, it takes a heap o' planning to roast the tongue an' vegetables an' get that puddin' just right. I only got two hands." He held up his

176

large hands and examined them as if he expected them to perform some marvelous trick.

Mrs. Bingham rose. "I'm sure it will be a great relief to you when your wife arrives and assumes some of the cooking duties."

His eyes bulged and he drew back. "She ain't gonna step up to my stove. Huh-uh. She's gonna be servin' customers, clearin' tables, an' doin' up the dishes. I'm the cook in this restaurant. That ain't gonna change."

He would have his wife serve food? Such a disagreeable position for a lady. Abigail fanned herself. "Mr. Patterson, surely you don't mean —"

Mrs. Bingham placed her hand on Abigail's arm. "Thank you again for the fine lunch, Mr. Patterson. Miss Grant and I will likely be down midafternoon for a cup of tea, if that won't inconvenience you."

"Not at all, long as you bring your own tea to put in the hot water. I only make coffee."

"Of course. I forgot. We'll enjoy a cup of coffee." She urged Abigail toward the stairs. "Have a pleasant afternoon, Mr. Patterson."

When they reached the top of the stairs, Abigail sagged against the wall. She clutched Mrs. Bingham's wrist. "Ma'am, did you hear his intentions? He wants his wife to be a server in the restaurant. A server! No decent woman would take requests in a public eatery. He might as well hire a . . . a saloon girl." She shuddered.

Mrs. Bingham patted Abigail's hand. "Add it to your list of commonsense etiquette — a lady does not wait tables outside of her own home." She tipped her head. "Puzzling, isn't it, that a task so appropriate and necessary in a home is considered immoral in a public setting? Sometimes I wonder where these rules of decorum originated."

Abigail didn't know, but she could never take up such a position. Nor would she expect it from any of the young women Mrs. Bingham sent to the western towns. "It's common sense, ma'am."

"Yes, I suppose so . . ." Mrs. Bingham moved toward their rooms at the end of the hall. "Would you like to come in and practice your presentation for the first class? I would be happy to offer constructive criticism."

Abigail paused with her hand on the tarnished brass doorknob. "I'm not quite ready." She needed to set aside all thoughts of beef tongue and Mr. Cleveland's desire to sniff malt liquor before she could focus on the classes. "Tomorrow morning, maybe?"

"Very well."

Despite Abigail's intentions, she begged off on practicing in front of Mrs. Bingham on Thursday. She didn't practice on Friday or Saturday, either, instead spending Saturday alone in the First Methodist Church sanctuary, pacing on the dais in front of an imaginary audience in an attempt to squelch her rattled nerves. She knew the material well. She'd been taught by the most well-mannered and morally sound woman she knew — her own mother. All she needed to do was remember Mother's voice and repeat what she'd been told. But she hoped her memory would function correctly when she came face to face with the unmarried men of Spiveyville.

Sheriff Thorn had walked her to the church and promised to return at suppertime to walk her safely back to the restaurant. She stepped down from the dais at a little after five even though she knew he wouldn't come until closer to five thirty. In case he arrived early, she didn't want him to catch her mid-presentation. She sat on a bench near the doors and reviewed her notes while she waited.

At twenty past five, the *clomp* of boots on the stairs alerted her to the sheriff's arrival.

She unhooked her shawl and bonnet from pegs on the wall. The church door opened, allowing in a blast of surprisingly cold air, and Otto Hildreth clattered in with it. The tailor sent a scowl as black as his mustache across the empty sanctuary, slammed the door into its frame, and planted himself in front of it.

"Miss Grant, I'm needin' a word with you."

Mr. Hildreth wasn't a large man — not like Mr. Ackley or Mr. Patterson — but his surly stance intimidated her. Instinctively, Abigail reversed several feet. The back of her knees connected with a bench and brought her to a halt. "M-Mr. Hildreth, the sheriff will be here soon."

"Didn't come to talk to the sheriff." His tone matched his harsh appearance. "Wanna talk to you."

She'd intended to give him a warning, but obviously he hadn't caught the subtle hint. Her heart pounded so hard her entire body quaked, but she soothed herself with the reminder that the sheriff was coming. If she could keep Mr. Hildreth talking until then, perhaps he wouldn't accost her. "For what purpose?"

"About these women you an' Miz Bingham're bringin' in. They all know how to stitch? To fix tears an' such?"

Nearly every woman she knew had the ability to perform at least rudimentary garment repair. The poor learned stitching out of necessity, and the wealthy weren't incapable. Nearly every little girl from a high-society family learned the art of embroidery. She'd discovered that her embroidery skills transferred well to stitching small tears or replacing a button. She stared into his narrowed gaze, afraid to say yes but unwilling to tell a fabrication. *"One always speaks the truth"* was one of Mother's most oft-quoted principles by which to live.

She licked her lips and forced a calm, even tone. "I . . . I am certain they do."

He balled his hands into fists and growled. "Then Clive's right. They're gonna put me out o' business." His face blotched red, and he took one step toward her, his dark eyes spitting fire. "You gotta tell 'em they ain't allowed to do any sewin' for their hus—"

The church door flew open and Sheriff Thorn came in with a fresh gust of cold wind. He nearly plowed into Mr. Hildreth's back. With a frown, he grabbed the tailor by the collar of his jacket. "Otto, what're you doin' in here? You best not be pesterin' Miss Grant."

Mr. Hildreth wriggled loose. "Wasn't pesterin'."

"Then what?"

Mr. Hildreth sent a quick glare at Abigail before answering. "Don't matter." He shrugged, settling his jacket in place, and charged out the door.

Sheriff Thorn stared after him for a moment, then slammed the door and whirled on Abigail. "He looked plenty upset."

"Yes, he certainly was."

"Did you give 'im reason to be?"

She'd never been a tattler and didn't care to start now, but Mr. Hildreth's verbal attack had left her unsettled, and now it seemed the sheriff was blaming her for the tailor's behavior. She wouldn't accept responsibility for yet another man's choices. She sent him a caustic look. "Of course I didn't. You might inquire after me. After all, he barged in here uninvited and . . . and . . ."

The sheriff stiffened. "Did he hurt you?"

At the man's quick shift from condemnation to concern, the indignation seeped from Abigail. She shook her head. "He didn't lay a finger on me. I'm fine." So why did she continue to quiver?

He frowned at her for several seconds as if trying to decide whether to believe her or not. Then he gave a brusque nod. "Let's get you back to Athol's." He held out her shawl and bonnet. "Tie them things on good an' tight. A storm's been blowin' in this afternoon. Wind strong enough to carry a body into the next county an' cold enough to freeze your eyeballs."

Abigail peeked out the window, stunned to discover the sky had turned gray and menacing during her hours in the church building. The sturdy rock walls had done a fine job of muffling the wind. She wished the frigid blasts had kept Mr. Hildreth at bay. She gave the knot at her throat a firm yank, adjusted her bonnet to better protect her face, and took the sheriff's bony elbow. "Why didn't you come for me earlier if you were concerned about a storm?"

"Oh, I peeked in at you around three."

Embarrassment struck hard, and Abigail gulped. "You . . . peeked in?" Had Otto Hildreth stood outside and observed her while she was unaware, too?

"Yep. Saw you wavin' your arms an' walkin' up an' down. Figured it'd be best not to disturb you since you seemed as wrought up as Preacher Doan when he's warnin' us all about the evils o' sin." He pressed his elbow to his ribs, trapping her hand. "Now you hold tight an' I'll getcha to the restaurant safe an' sound."

The wind stole Abigail's breath the moment they left the church. Oh, so cold! And so strong. She should have left the church hours ago. She could have saved herself an unpleasant encounter. She clung to the sheriff's arm with both hands and kept her head low. Gusts forced her bonnet brim flat against her face, pulled at her shawl, and plastered her skirt to her legs, making it difficult to walk, but Sheriff Thorn kept a steady pace, and within minutes they entered the warmth of the restaurant.

Abigail collapsed into a chair, releasing a mighty breath. "Thank you for accompanying me, Sheriff. I appreciate your stalwart presence very much."

He rubbed the underside of his nose. "Well, now, I know what a wart is. Have had a few of them in my day. But stalwart, you say? I ain't too certain about that. But since it come from your mouth, I'm gonna take it as a compullment."

"You should. *Stalwart* means trustworthy and dependable. Excellent qualities. Especially for someone in a position of leadership." She removed her bonnet and smoothed stray wisps of hair into place. How the wind had reached her hair even beneath the bonnet's wide brim, she couldn't understand, but it had, just as it now wheezed between cracks in the rattling windows and whisked beneath the solid door.

The sheriff crossed to a window and peered out. He fidgeted, his movements tense and jerky. "I'm guessin' there won't be many who come to the restaurant for supper. They'll be securin' their shutters an' stayin' in to eat hardtack." He sent a grin in her direction. "I got a load of buckshot in the back o' my left thigh when I was a boy, an' it's let me predict a rip-roarin' storm ever since. We're in for a bad'un, my leg's tellin' me. So you be smart, Miss Grant, an' don't go roamin' no place else tonight. All right?"

The windows rattled again. Cold air crept under the door and across her ankles. Otto Hildreth's fury-reddened face flashed in her memory. She shivered. "Yes, sir, I'll stay in. I promise."

FOURTEEN

Mack

Mack removed the tacks holding the sign-up charts on the wall, doing his best not to tear the charts' corners. Only one corner tore away, and he used a pair of scissors to smooth the rough edge before tamping the charts into a neat stack. Then he stood with the stack in his hands and argued with himself about what to do with them.

He'd promised to deliver the pages to Mrs. Bingham and Miss Grant at closing time on Saturday. Which was now. He made it a practice to keep his word, the way he'd been taught. The way he knew his heavenly Father would approve. But just this once, he wished he could ignore his conscience and stay in.

The wind howled worse than a pack of prowling wolves. Dust formed billowing clouds outside the window, thick enough to block the evening sun. He looked at the charts and then again out the window. Did the women really need the names today? Couldn't it wait until tomorrow, when the storm had passed?

He nibbled the tip of his mustache and argued with himself for several minutes, but in the end, he knew he wouldn't rest unless he honored what he'd said. He had to take these charts to the restaurant.

With a mighty sigh, Mack laid the charts aside and buttoned his jacket all the way to the collar. The restaurant was right next door — only twenty paces from his front door to Patterson's. He wouldn't get lost even in a blinding storm because he was smart enough to follow the buildings. He just didn't like the idea of being out.

"But a promise is a promise." He rolled the charts into a tube, gripped them tightly in one hand, and marched himself out the door.

The wind hit with such force he staggered backward several steps. He'd intended to lock the store behind him, but who else would be foolish enough to be out? Bending forward, one shoulder braced against the wall, he pushed against the gusts. Twice he bounced free of the building's lap siding, and both times confusion struck him with the sensation of being suspended in a whirlwind. After the second time, he pressed himself flat to the wall. It made for slower progress, but he felt safer knowing exactly where he was.

When he reached the narrow alleyway, he nearly fell into the opening. He regained his footing, plowed forward, and connected with the corner of the restaurant. Another twelve deliberate steps, and his shoulder found the door. With a groan of relief, he stumbled into the restaurant and directly into the table where Miss Grant and Mrs. Bingham were accepting crockery bowls from Athol. All three gaped at him with identical looks of disbelief.

He held out the charts, still rolled but bent and dented from their journey. "Here. These are yours." He dropped the charts onto the table. The pages uncurled into a larger tube and rocked back and forth.

Athol shook his head. "What're you doin' out in the storm? Did you lose all your senses?"

Mack forced a laugh. "I don't know about my senses, but I lost my balance. Three different times. That wind's as strong as a twister."

Mrs. Bingham's forehead pinched into lines of worry. "You don't suppose the storm will bring real damage, do you?"

Mack shrugged. "It's hard to say. We can get some pretty rough storms out here, but most of the time they blow through pretty fast. And you ought to be safe here with Athol. His restaurant's snug in the middle of the block between a rock building and my hardware store, so it's protected." A mighty gust of wind rattled the windows. The building moaned. He cringed. "Just in case, he's got a cellar where you can hide away if things get real bad."

Miss Grant pinched her lips tight, the way a person who'd tasted a lemon might do. She must be nervous about cellars. Probably because of spiders. He said a quick prayer that the women wouldn't be forced to seek protection under the ground.

Athol put spoons on the table and tucked the empty tray under his arm. "Nobody else's gonna be comin' in tonight, Mack, so my pot o' ham an' beans is gonna go to waste. Unless you want some, too."

Mack grinned. "Have you got corn bread to go with it?"

"Don't I always make corn bread to go with my ham an' beans? It oughta be ready to come out o' the oven right about now."

"I'll take a bowl then. Thanks." He began unbuttoning his jacket and turned toward

189

an empty table.

"Mr. Cleveland," Mrs. Bingham said, "there's no sense in dirtying up a second table. Join Miss Grant and me."

He paused. The last time he'd been around the two ladies, Miss Grant hadn't acted too keen on having him near. He glanced and discovered she was still holding her lips all pursed up. "Are you sure?"

"Of course we are." Mrs. Bingham spoke so staunchly Mack couldn't help but smile.

"Well, all right, then. Does seem kind of silly to make Athol clean more than one table. We might even convince him to sit and eat with us."

"I heard that." Athol bustled toward them. His tray held two bowls, four tin cups, and a plate of mealy squares of corn bread stacked high. "An' I don't mind at all sittin' down with you, long as you ain't got no objections."

Miss Grant wrinkled her nose. "Don't have any."

Athol frowned. "What's that?"

"Don't have any objections."

"Good." Athol plopped the tray in the middle of the table, squashing one end of the rolled papers, and took the chair across from Mrs. Bingham.

Mack eased into the last chair, which

faced Miss Grant. She was all pink in the face, but he didn't think he'd caused it this time.

Athol shot him a questioning look. "You wanna say grace for us all, Mack?"

Mack folded his hands, bowed his head, and closed his eyes. "Dear Lord, thank You for giving us a place where we're safe from the storm. Thank You for this food and for the hands that prepared it. Please bless it that it might nourish our bodies. Amen."

"Amen," Athol echoed. He grabbed two squares of corn bread and crushed them on top of his beans. Crumbs exploded, reaching as far as Miss Grant's hand.

She made her pinched-lips face and brushed the crumbs toward Athol's bowl. Athol flipped them to the floor, picked up his fork, and pushed past the corn bread to the beans. Sitting across from Miss Grant, Mack couldn't help but notice the graceful way she dipped her fork and carried no more than three beans to her mouth. She made eating look like a ballet dance. Especially when compared to the mess Athol was making.

Mack helped himself to a piece of corn bread and broke it into little pieces over his beans, careful to keep his crumbs to himself. The whistling wind and groaning boards made the hair on the back of his neck stand up. The women seemed apprehensive, too. Only Athol ate with enjoyment, apparently unmindful of the storm. Or maybe he was too hungry to care about it. Either way, Mack thought somebody should put the ladies at ease. Since Athol didn't seem inclined to do it, he'd better.

"Are you ready to start teaching classes, Miss Grant?"

She visibly jumped, and a bean fell from her fork into the bowl. Her face glowed red, and she lowered her head for a moment. When she lifted her face, a steely determination glowed in her dark eyes. "Yes, I am."

"How many times've you taught these classes?" He forked up a bite of beans and chewed.

She sent a sideways glance at Mrs. Bingham.

The older woman smiled and set her fork aside. "This is the first time Abigail has taught the subject of decorum."

Mack frowned. "But you told everybody at the meeting how you like to make sure the men are prepared to be loving husbands."

"That's true." Mrs. Bingham reached for a piece of corn bread and put it on the edge of her bowl. "I am accountable for placing my girls with men who will treat them well and give them a chance for a happy life. Most often, I can ascertain a man's character through written correspondence. In this case, however" — she cleared her throat — "a face-to-face visit seemed a better choice."

"Why?" Athol barked the question, his cheek puffed from food.

Mrs. Bingham broke off a small piece of corn bread, carried the bit to her mouth, and chewed and swallowed. "Let me ask you a question, Mr. Patterson. Miss Grant and I have been staying here above your restaurant for five days now. Would you say you know us well?"

He chomped twice, swallowed, and shook his head.

"Why is that?"

He shrugged. " 'Cause we ain't really talked."

Miss Grant shook her head slightly. "Because we haven't talked."

Athol nodded. "That's what I said. We ain't spoke much. Except to find out what you wanna eat."

Miss Grant closed her eyes for a moment, and Mack stifled a chortle. Poor Athol. He had no idea she was correcting his grammar. And poor Miss Grant. She must feel

193

useless as a teacher if the pupil didn't catch on.

"Five days," Mrs. Bingham said, "and still we aren't well acquainted, because you've had other distractions with your business, and Miss Grant and I have been otherwise occupied, yes?"

"Yep." Athol jammed another huge bite into his mouth. "But that don't answer how come you're in town makin' us fellas take classes."

Mrs. Bingham lifted her fork again. "With every other match, I've dealt with an individual. I can correspond with an individual and draw conclusions. But with so many of you, it would take months to become acquainted one at a time. By coming to town and having you attend classes, we can hasten the process and bring you together with your brides in a more expedient fashion."

Athol gaped at her with his mouth slightly open.

Miss Grant sighed. "You'll be able to meet your brides faster."

He gave her the same open-mouthed stare for several seconds. Then he closed his mouth and grimaced. "Sure don't seem very fast. Been a long time already, an' now you're sayin' it'll be another whole month

194

to do the classes." Hopefulness lit his face. "You don't reckon you'll change your mind? Let our brides come early, will you? I could sure use help around here. Doin' the cookin' an' the cleanin' an' everything else is just about to wear me out."

Mack understood Athol's complaint. Sometimes he wished for someone to come alongside him and help in his store. But Athol was missing something important. "Athol, if all you want is somebody to wash dishes and clean up in here, you aren't looking for a wife. You could hire somebody."

Athol turned the dumbfounded look on Mack. "I'd hafta pay 'em though. A wife'll help out for free."

Mrs. Bingham lowered her forehead to her hand as if she'd suddenly experienced a headache.

Miss Grant sat up, pert as a spring robin, and frowned at Athol. "Mr. Patterson, a hired helper is much less costly than a wife. That is, if you truly love your wife and wish to please her. You needn't house and clothe and shower gifts upon an employee, but these are the things you'll be expected to do for a wife. Additionally, a man should seek companionship, compassion, and love above a clean house and mended socks. Life can be a dreary journey, but a warm, loving

195

companion brightens the path."

Mack stared at Miss Grant with as much stupor as Athol. How had she managed to define what he wanted someday? He couldn't trust a matchmaker to bring someone so special to him. Only God Himself could make a heart-match. The kind of match Pa and Ma modeled, sticking together through good times and bad. Even the baddest time, when Wilhelmina Wilkes swooped in like an enemy army.

He nodded so hard his neck popped. "Yes. Yes, that's exactly right." He shifted his attention to Athol. "A wife is a gift, Athol. Heaven's best gift, my pa always said. If you can't appreciate the gift, maybe you shouldn't ask for it."

Red streaks of anger climbed Athol's cheeks. He pushed away from the table. "If all you're gonna do is pick at me, I'm goin' to the kitchen. Least in there I've got some peace." He grabbed up his bowl and stomped off.

Mack turned an apologetic grin on the women. "I'm sorry. I didn't mean to ruin your supper."

"You did not ruin my supper, Mr. Cleveland." Mrs. Bingham used her staunch tone again, and she coupled her words with a genuine smile. "It's refreshing to meet a young man who understands the complexities and unique qualities that make marriage the beautiful union God intended."

Mack turned to Miss Grant. "All that you said to Athol, is that what you plan to teach the men?"

She nodded. "In part."

He looked at Mrs. Bingham. "Have these women you're bringing to Spiveyville taken the classes, too? They understand they'll need to give as much as they get?"

"I very carefully select my brides-to-be." The woman's serious expression and voice held Mack's full attention. "They undergo an intensive interview intended to reveal their beliefs about marriage, family, and household responsibility. I don't seek perfection. No one can be perfect. But I want girls who are modest and sensible and who possess self-control and a good work ethic. When a girl passes my interview, I invite her to reside in my home until a suitable match is found. Even if one misleads me with her words, I can glean a great deal about a girl's character when I sit across a dinner table from her on a daily basis."

She pushed her bowl aside and rested her hands on the edge of the table. "My goal, Mr. Cleveland, is to help two people meld into one, to build happy, lasting relation-

197

ships. If I fail in that attempt, my business crumbles. Thus, any woman who does not meet my strict standards is not sent out as a bride. Likewise, any man who refuses to grasp and act upon the concepts of loving and caring for his wife will not be matched with one of my girls. I will not be part of establishing doomed-to-fail relationships."

"Not even if they" — he hesitated, not wanting to offend her, but he had to ask — "pay the fee?"

She raised her chin. "Not even then."

While Mrs. Bingham spoke, Miss Grant had slowly shrunk back, the way a porcupine hunkered low when something threatened it. An uneasy thought tickled in the back of his mind. Could it be Miss Grant hadn't met Mrs. Bingham's standards? She was a smart girl. The way she talked, the words she used — even the way she tried to correct Athol's speech — let him know she'd had plenty of schooling. She planned to teach the men about courting and caring, which meant she knew how marriage was supposed to work. So why wasn't she trying for a match? He wished he could ask, but Ma had taught him it wasn't polite to ask pushy questions. Saying, "Why aren't you part of Mrs. Bingham's bevy of brides?" would be pushy. Especially after everything he'd just asked Mrs. Bingham. Sometimes he wished his conscience wasn't so sharp.

He sighed. "Well, ma'am, I'm gonna pray that these stubborn men in town will pay attention to Miss Grant's teaching and decide to be the kind of husbands you want for your girls. Because if your girls are all you say they are, the men would be downright lucky to marry up with them."

Mrs. Bingham smiled. "I like to think so."

Mack leaned back and hooked his elbow over the back of the chair. "What you described reminds me a lot of my ma. She's a kind woman. Sensible. She has a good disposition, too — hardly ever gets angry. She tries to be like the woman from Proverbs. You know the one I mean?"

"The one who 'looketh well to the ways of her household'?"

He nodded. "So her husband and children would 'arise up, and call her blessed.' That's her. Pa adores her. I do, too." Loneliness for his parents hit hard. He lowered his head. "I miss them."

Mrs. Bingham curled her hand over his wrist. "Clearly, they set a good example for you. I can see you'd make a fine husband. Are you sure you —"

He gently removed his arm from her touch. "I'm sure. But thanks." He rose and looked out the window. Dust was still blowing, but it didn't look as heavy as it had before. "I better get home before it's full dark." He grabbed up his jacket and strode to the doors. Then he glanced back. "Will I see you ladies in church tomorrow?"

"Most certainly." Mrs. Bingham gave a firm nod. "I never miss."

He looked at Miss Grant. "And you . . . too?"

She nodded, but not with any enthusiasm.

Something was bothering her, maybe making her sad, and he wished he knew what. But he didn't ask. He couldn't be pushy.

FIFTEEN

Helena

Helena awakened with a start. She sat up and looked around, groggy and confused but uncertain why. Finally awareness dawned. The horrendous wind that had rocked the building and caused it to groan like a wild thing during the night was still. Instead, the cheerful single note of a songbird graced her ears, and she smiled. "Ah, the calm after the storm."

She slipped out of bed and reached for her dressing gown, chuckling. After Howard's untimely death, she began the silly habit of speaking out loud to herself. The large house she and Howard failed to fill with children had been far too quiet without voices, and hearing her own voice was better than hearing no voices at all. Now the house was generally filled to the brim with prospective brides awaiting their opportunity to travel west, but the habit of speaking to herself remained. A harmless habit, most certainly, but she would be embarrassed if someone overheard her.

She donned silk slippers for her morning trek to the necessary. When she opened the door to the outside staircase, she froze in place and gasped. The entire yard was littered with tumbleweeds, clumps of dried grass, and what appeared to be broken shingles. She stepped to the edge of the little landing and peered both directions, examining the buildings for signs of damage.

The patter of footsteps came from behind her, and Abigail joined her on the landing, clutching her robe closed at the throat. Helena gestured to the mess in the yard.

"The wind carried more than dust in its stead. I can't see the roof of the restaurant, but I hope those shingles came from a different building."

Abigail's brown eyes widened. She gripped the railing and gazed downward, seeming to examine every tumbleweed and piece of displaced wood. She pointed. "What is that next to the necessary's wall?"

Helena squinted, and then she laughed. A pair of matted long johns lay in a crumpled heap snug against the outhouse's lap siding. "Someone neglected to take his clothes off the line, and the wind stole his underwear. At least, we can hope it was stolen off a line and not off a person."

The pale pink patches where Abigail's face had peeled blazed red, making them stand out like roses on a bed of snow. "Oh, my."

Helena took the younger woman by the arm. "Let's finish our morning ablutions and hurry to the dining room. I suspect we'll hear many stories about the storm's damage from those who come in for breakfast."

Her supposition proved true. Men complained about downed fences, broken windows, and missing shutters. Each seemed determined to top the previous one's report, but everyone fell silent when Preacher Doan entered the restaurant, his face stricken.

Mack Cleveland left his eggs and bacon on the table and hurried across the floor to the minister. "What's wrong, Preacher?"

Several others repeated the question, and Helena set aside her cup of coffee and gave the minister her full attention.

Preacher Doan pulled in a breath that expanded his chest, held it for a few tense seconds, and blew it out in a whoosh. "I needed to let you know church services are canceled this morning."

"What? How come? You sick, Preacher?"

The confused, concerned voices carried from every corner of the dining room. The men's genuine disappointment gave Helena an unexpected lift. If missing a worship service pained them, there was decency in them.

The preacher slid his hands into his trouser pockets and aimed a sorrowful look around the room. "The church lost part of its roof in last night's storm."

Abigail released a little gasp and planted both palms on her bodice. "Oh, no. Did a tornado come through?"

Preacher Doan offered a sad smile. "It wasn't a twister, Miss Grant. Just good ol' Kansas wind. But it was strong. Strong enough to tear off a good number of shingles and lift the sheathing underneath. It broke some windows, too." He hung his head. "The sanctuary's a mess with dust and dried grass blown in all over. I can't have anybody in there until we get things cleaned up and the roof repaired."

Helena experienced a jolt of guilt. Were the shingles behind the café from the church roof? She hadn't intended to wish damage on the house of the Lord. She hoped God wouldn't hold her errant comment against her. She stood. "How can we help?"

A clatter of offers to do whatever they

could rose. Helena's heart flooded. Yes, despite their crusty exteriors, these were good-hearted men underneath, as Mr. Cleveland had said.

Preacher Doan lifted his face. His eyes glittered with unshed tears. "I was hoping you'd ask. Sheriff Thorn's making the rounds right now, finding out how many other places suffered damage. He'll come see me when he's done, and we'll put together a list of all the folks who'll need help with repairs."

Hugh Briggs shuffled from side to side. "We don't need to wait for the sheriff, Preacher. No matter what'n all else needs doin', the church comes first. Let's get started."

"Hugh's right." Mr. Cleveland placed his hand on the preacher's shoulder. "There's no sense in waiting. Let's get the church done. Then Sheriff Thorn can post the other places that need fixing. Folks can come in and sign up — just like they did for Mrs. Bingham's classes — to give our neighbors a hand."

Helena's heart had lifted at the men's eagerness to restore the chapel to its proper order, but now worry descended. The classes on etiquette were to be held in the church's sanctuary. Would they face a delay?

If so, her time in Spiveyville might be extended yet again.

Bill

Consarn wind.

Bill wasn't much for cussing. Every now and then his pa had let fly. Generally when he was aggravated to the point of fury. But his ma had frowned at it. So Bill tried not to do it. But as he stood looking at the dozen dead chickens in Norm Elliott's yard, he cursed the uncontrolled wind and the damage it'd left behind.

Norm toed the ground, his head low. "Took the whole coop, Sheriff. I heard the splinterin', but with the dust so thick, I couldn't tell what had busted apart. So I stayed inside an' prayed the house would hold. If I'd knowed my chickens were blowin' around, I would've come out. Least tried to save 'em."

Bill pointed to the planks and boards thrown all over the yard. "An' you might've got clonked in the noggin an' would be lyin' there alongside your chickens if you had." He slapped his arm across the man's shoulders. "Hard as it is to lose the birds, it'd be a lot worse if we'd lost you."

Norm nodded, but he didn't look too

206

sure. Everybody knew how fond he was of his livestock. Treated the critters more like pets. He grew corn, the only one to farm instead of raise cattle because he didn't like the idea of sending his animals to slaughter. Some of the fellas in town made sport of Norm and his tender heart, but Bill couldn't think of a one who would see anything funny about the dead birds.

"Lemme help you bury your chickens, and then I gotta be headin' on. Checkin' everybody else's spreads."

"No, you go on. I can tend to 'em myself." He sniffed and wiped his sleeve across his watery eyes. "But I wouldn't turn down help in buildin' a new chicken coop. A sturdier one this time."

Bill pulled the little pad of paper where he'd recorded others' needs and added Norm's request — *Bild chicken cup for Norm Elliott* — to the list. He slipped the pad into his shirt pocket. "I'll make sure some fellas come out an' lend a hand. Wouldja be willin' to help out at other places, too?"

"Sure will, Sheriff." He eased in the direction of the barn. "Gonna get my shovel now an' put these birds in the ground. Thanks for checkin' on me. I appreciate it."

Bill swung himself into the saddle and clicked his tongue on his teeth. His black-

and-white paint, Patch, broke into a steady canter that carried Bill off the Elliott land, past the fallow cornfields, and up the road toward Firmin Chapman's place. Surprisingly, the only damage at Firmin's ranch was a downed sign — the one Firmin had carved to announce Double C Ranch. The wind had tore the sign from its post. Firmin didn't need any help, but he promised to come in and help repair the church's roof. Bill thanked him and headed on.

By late morning, he reached the Circle L, Clifford Lambert's ranch. Cliff wasn't there. He'd probably gone into town expecting to attend church services. Bill snooped around on his own and made a note about a downed fence and some broken shutters on the barn. He stood in the sunny yard with the breeze — calm now but cold — raising gooseflesh on his arms and examined the list. Except for Firmin, every rancher within a five-mile reach of Spiveyville would need some help putting things back to right on their property. Bill scowled at the lengthy list. It'd take a heap of days to fix everything. He'd supervise it all to make sure nobody got neglected.

He jammed the pad into his pocket and aimed his boots for Cliff's porch, where he'd tied Patch to the railing. So many broken things in need of mending. It'd take a goodly chunk of time to organize it all, which meant he'd have less time to keep an eye on the city women. He'd bumbled, letting Otto sneak in on Miss Grant. Or maybe Miss Grant had been tryin' to pull something on Otto. He wasn't quite sure which way that situation leaned because neither of them was talking. If he was tangled up in these repairs, it'd leave the women free to do some swindling or leave them open to some rowdy fella taking advantage. Neither thought set well. Sometimes wearing this badge was a bigger burden than he wanted to admit.

He passed Cliff's chicken coop, and the image of the dead chickens and Norm's sorrowful face swooped in. He paused and pulled out his pad.

Git chickens for Norm.

With a nod of determination, he returned the pad to his pocket and trotted across the hard ground to his waiting horse.

Mack

"Hey, Athol, toss up another bundle o' those shingles, wouldja?" Mack braced himself at the edge of the roof and held out his hands. With a grunt, Athol heaved the

209

bundle skyward. Mack snagged it and sat back on his haunches. "Thanks."

"No problem." Athol shielded his eyes with his hand. "Be careful up there, huh? Don't need anybody fallin' off the roof."

Mack had no intention of falling. He tucked the bundle under his arm and crab-walked to Sam and Hugh, who sat ready with a bag of nails and hammers from Mack's store. "Here you go. This ought to finish 'er up."

"Good thing you had these extra bundles, Hugh." Sam grinned at the livery owner. "They've sure come in handy."

Hugh's narrow face flushed pink. "Kinda embarrassed about how I fussed at ol' Tobis for miscalculatin' how many I'd need when I added on to the livery. Even thought maybe he'd told me to get too many on purpose so my loan'd be higher at the bank."

Sam chortled. "Oh, that Tobis, he does enjoy droppin' a penny in his coffers."

"Yep. But I ain't unhappy about it no more. Seems like God knew this wind'd be comin', an' He made sure we were ready for it."

Whistling, the pair set to work, Sam holding the shingles flat while Hugh secured them with square-head nails. Watching

210

them, satisfaction filled Mack. This — this was why he'd decided to stay in the small town instead of going back to Kansas City after Uncle Ray died. Maybe Spiveyville didn't have conveniences like cable cars or a variety of restaurants or an opera house, all the things some folks held important. But Spiveyville had something better. Camaraderie. Community. Compassion. As much as he missed his parents and wished he could see them every day, he wouldn't move back to Kansas City. And not because he was still mad at how folks in the church turned up their noses at his family. Spiveyville was home.

He inched to the edge again and sat with his legs dangling. Every person who'd been in Athol's restaurant had left their plates and breakfast behind and trailed Preacher Doan to the church. Inside, women dusted and swept. Outside, men raked debris and cleaned up broken glass and climbed all over the roof. Their industry matched that of a busy ant colony. By evening — with the exception of the broken windows because they'd have to order panes from Pratt Center — the church would be as good as new and ready for meetings again.

As soon as they were done, Preacher Doan would probably invite everybody in and lead them all in hymns of thanksgiving. He'd read Scripture about the joy of brothers coming together in a united cause. Seemed as though Paul had mentioned such things in his letters to the Colossians. Or maybe the Philippians. Preacher Doan would know, and he'd share it with them. Mack looked forward to the service. Especially since they'd had to skip the morning worship.

A horse and rider came up the street, and Mack squinted against the sun. He recognized the tall tan hat and the black-and-white horse. Sheriff Thorn on Patch, back from his visit to the local ranches. Mack waved, and the sheriff waved back, but he looked weary. An uneasy feeling tiptoed through Mack's chest. He shifted to the ladder and climbed down, then met the sheriff at the edge of the churchyard.

"Is everybody outside of town all right?" Despite damage to property, no one had been hurt inside Spiveyville. But out on the open prairie, the wind could've caused even more harm. He sent up a prayer for his neighbors' well-being, the action as natural as drawing a breath.

"Didn't lose no people, but Norm Elliott's whole flock o' chickens got killed when the coop collapsed on 'em." Sheriff Thorn

212

shook his head, sorrow in his pale-blue eyes. "Sure don't like to see helpless critters in that kind o' state. Was pretty hard on Norm, too."

Harriet Thompson, carrying a broom and dustpan, stopped next to Mack. "Did you say Norm Elliott lost all his chickens?"

"Yes'm. Not a one of 'em survived the storm."

She shook her head and clucked, much like a hen. "That's so sad. I'll ask around town, see how many folks'd be willin' to cull one or two from their coop. There aren't that many of us who keep chickens in town, so we can't probably give him as big o' flock as he had before, but at least he'll have a few hens peckin' in a pen again."

Another wave of warmth flowed through Mack. "That's kind of you, Mrs. Thompson."

She shrugged, a sheepish look on her face. "Well, now, Norm gave my Betsy a chick for her Easter basket one year. It turned out to be the best layin' hen we've ever had. He's done the same for others around town. Reckon it won't hurt a thing for us to gift him in return." She hurried off.

Mack rubbed Patch's nose. "The church'll be all repaired by evening, thanks to the town's help."

Sheriff Thorn surveyed the church and grounds. He sat tired in the saddle, but Mack glimpsed approval in his eyes. "That's good. That's real good. Gettin' God's house fixed up first is the right thing to do."

Mack nodded. "It meant a lot to Preacher Doan, how everybody stepped up. It made Mrs. Bingham happy, too, since she and Miss Grant need the building for those classes they're giving. Preacher Doan said they could use it once it was all fixed again."

The sheriff's brows pinched down. He shifted in the saddle, making the leather squeak. "About them classes . . ." He grimaced. "I'm gonna ask Miz Bingham to hold off until all the damage in town an' at the ranches is tended to. If folks work together, like you done here at the church, it shouldn't take too long to get everybody took care of. Mebbe a week. Mebbe a little longer. But the ladies — an' the grooms — are just gonna hafta wait."

Sixteen

Abigail

"An entire week's delay?" Abigail hugged herself and paced the length of her small room. How could Mrs. Bingham be so calm in the face of such calamity? "That means we must remain in Spiveyville until early December." Of course, there wasn't any reason for her to return to Newton. Perhaps she should celebrate the extension in this Kansas town. If she hadn't had a nightmare about Otto Hildreth chasing her with a pair of scissors, she might be more amenable to the idea.

"I'm not any more pleased at the prospect than you are, dear." Mrs. Bingham sat on the edge of Abigail's bed and followed her progress back and forth with her gray-eyed gaze. "But honestly, the delay gives us a very unique opportunity."

Abigail stopped and frowned. "What op-

215

portunity?"

She smiled. A slow, complacent smile that made Abigail wish she could pinch her on the end of the nose. "To see the men's character."

"What?"

Mrs. Bingham sighed. "Abigail, you were sitting at the table with me when I explained to Mr. Cleveland why I invite the women who apply to become brides to reside in my home during their time of waiting."

Abigail tightened her arms against her rib cage, wishing she could shrink into nothingness. She'd wanted to crawl under the table when her employer spoke of observing the girls and gleaning their true character. What had Mrs. Bingham determined about Abigail? She wanted to believe the woman had seen something worthwhile. After all, of all the girls in the house, Abigail was the best educated, the best groomed, the most mannerly. She knew she'd initially been given favor, because Mrs. Bingham had sent her to prospective husbands. But not anymore. Now she'd been delegated to the unpalatable task of attempting to tame untamable men. She was doomed to failure and then to expulsion. What would she do then?

She closed her eyes for a moment — allowing her cramped, unembellished surroundings to hide behind her lids — and deliberately searched her memory for images of happier times. To her chagrin, the pictures refused to rise. She popped her eyes open and glared at Mrs. Bingham. "We would have every opportunity to observe them during classes, to monitor their participation, to measure their willingness to change. A week holed up in this room while they rove from house to house and ranch to ranch will gain us nothing at all."

Mrs. Bingham stood and crossed slowly to Abigail. A hint of determination showed itself in the firm set of her lips, but something else glimmered in her eyes. Sympathy? Or was it sorrow? She cupped Abigail's cheek in her warm palm and shook her head. "I hadn't intended for us to stay holed up here. I intended for us to help."

Unease attacked. "Us?"

"Well, of course." The matchmaker lowered her hand and smiled again, this time with humor twinkling in her eyes. "Did we not help at the church?"

"Yes, with sweeping and straightening. The damages listed on the chalkboard Sheriff Thorn brought into the restaurant will require much more than cleaning skills. My education, although well rounded, hasn't prepared me to mend a fence or secure shutters to a barn or build a toolshed."

Mrs. Bingham clicked her tongue on her teeth — a somewhat sympathetic *tsk-tsk.* "My dear, you've only substantiated my belief that you are unsuited to being matched with one of the rugged men residing in the West. The wife of a rancher or farmer won't limit herself to household duties. She will be expected to assist her husband in every aspect of caring for the land and animals."

Shame brought searing heat to Abigail's face. How petty she must sound. How incompetent. The same crushing weight of unworthiness inflicted by Linus Hartford's rejection returned anew. "I . . . You . . ." She had no defense against the matchmaker's presumption. Mrs. Bingham's words were far too true.

The woman waved her hand as if dismissing Abigail's feeble stammering. "I don't intend to ask you to wield a hammer, but the workers will need sustenance. Mr. Patterson has offered to supply sandwiches to those assisting in the repairs, but his duty is here at the restaurant. I volunteered to deliver the food to the various work locations, and Mr. Cleveland has given the use of his horses and wagon to do so."

Mrs. Bingham and Sheriff Thorn had met together for only half an hour after the evening service at church. How had they managed to make so many arrangements in such a short amount of time? Abigail should have stayed in the dining room with them instead of coming up to her room to change out of her dusty dress and freshen herself. Then these plans would not have taken her by surprise and she needn't feel so foolish and inept.

Her tone turned sharp, evidence of her inner angst. "I was not aware that you knew how to drive a team and wagon."

"It's been several years, but my husband used to allow me to take the reins when we went on drives through the countryside on sunny afternoons. I'm sure I shall be able to recall enough to get us safely from one place to another, if need be."

Worry rapidly descended. "Both Preacher Doan and Sheriff Thorn warned us not to venture out alone." She never would again. Not after her foul encounter with Mr. Hildreth.

"Which is why the preacher will accompany us on each excursion. He will ride his horse and lead our wagon and then participate in the workforce." Mrs. Bingham folded her arms over her chest. "Pouting and bemoaning the extra days will not change the fact that the wind blew in Kansas last night. Sometimes plans must change. People who can adapt to changes are much more content than those who are rigid. Please give that some thought."

Abigail slumped on the end of the bed. There were too many changes for her to absorb at once. First having to extend their stay and teach one subject for an entire week rather than a single day, and now being forced to delay the start of classes. Another concern struck with force.

She shifted sideways to meet Mrs. Bingham's gaze. "What is it going to cost for us to stay here several additional weeks? Will you have any profit at all from these matches after paying for a room and lodging for such a lengthy period of time?"

The sly curve of the woman's lips made Abigail's flesh tingle. She considered putting her fingers in her ears to block whatever she would say next, but deliberately ignoring someone was the height of ill manners.

"Mr. Patterson and I discussed ways to minimize my bill, and he agreed to provide meals free of charge in exchange for help in the restaurant. Beginning tomorrow, you and I will keep the dining room clean and the dishes washed."

Helena closed herself in her little room and crossed to the window. She peered out, looking at nothing, and sighed. Abigail would end up alone and bitter, just like Marietta, if she didn't change her ways. Why was the young woman trapped in such a rigid mind-set? At times Helena wanted to take Abigail by the shoulders and shake her until her stiff spine was as floppy as an old rope.

She should ready herself for bed — it was after eight already according to her jeweled watch — but Marietta needed to be apprised of the latest happenings. So she pulled the little bedside table from the corner, laid out paper, ink, and pen, and began to write.

Sunday, October 21, 1888

Dearest Sister,
An unfortunate wind beset the little town of Spiveyville yesterday and through the night, causing much damage. To our great relief, no one was hurt in the vicious storm, but the prospective grooms must now apply themselves to repairs instead of attending the classes

for which Miss Grant has so diligently prepared. The sheriff has asked me to allow a full week of attention to putting things to right, thus the proposed arrival date sent in my telegram is no longer valid.

I am aware this will disappoint the brides, who are eager to make their new start,

She paused and frowned. For the first time she realized the delay left her business in Marietta's hands for an even longer period of time. Worry tried to nibble at her, but she pushed it aside. Marietta was capable, Helena well knew, because she'd helped raise her. Eighteen years separated them in age, and their parents had died shortly after Marietta's twelfth birthday. It was only natural she and Howard would take her in, and Helena made certain her sister received the same education Helena had been given. When matrimony passed Marietta by, she provided for herself by serving as a nanny, the most recent position caring for a set of twins. Keeping watch over adult women was less strenuous than chasing an active pair of five-year-olds. Maintaining the accounting ledgers would be Marietta's biggest challenge. She had never liked anything remotely connected to arithmetic, but even so, she had the knowledge to complete the task.

Helena dipped the pen and continued.

and for that I sincerely apologize. I leave at your discretion allowing some of them to answer other requests that appear to be compatible matches as long as a sufficient number of suitable girls are available for the journey to Spiveyville when we've deemed the men ready to receive them.

May I again express my gratitude to you, my dear sister, for stepping into my shoes during this time. Does it not seem fortuitous that your little charges were enrolled in the private kindergarten just as I had need for a replacement? God most certainly put the elements in place, and I trust He has a purpose in keeping Miss Grant and me in this small Kansas town.

Helena gave a little start and stared at her final line. The words had flowed so easily, even without true conscious thought. God knew the men would not be able to attend the classes all at once. God knew the wind would blow and the repairs would need to be made. God knew, well in advance, the number of days she and Abigail would be in Spiveyville. God knew, and He no doubt had a purpose beyond smoothing the rough edges of these cowboys' behavior.

With a smile, she completed the letter.

I shall write again later this week with an update on our progress here, and I look forward to receiving a letter from you with a good report of your "settling in" as the administrator of Bingham's Bevy of Brides.

I love you dearly, Marietta. I pray for you each morning and night, and I trust my name is mentioned in your daily prayers as well.

Your loving sister,
Helena

She carried the letter and her capped ink-pot to the dresser and laid them on top. Tomorrow she and Abigail would take over the cleaning chores in the restaurant, but she didn't anticipate it taxing them overly much. All the girls took turns at chores in Helena's house, and Abigail had proved adept — to the point of fastidiousness — despite her affluent upbringing. If she'd been unable or unwilling to perform menial tasks, Helena would not have allowed her into the program. But Abigail had demonstrated an ability to keep a neat house. Now if only she could learn to be a content companion and helpmeet.

Not for the first time, Helena pondered the girl's inability to bond with people. From what she'd said in her entrance interview, she had enjoyed a close and loving relationship with her parents as well as a large circle of friendships. Of course, her father's unfortunate choices had certainly affected her. Sympathy coiled itself through Helena's heart when she considered how much it must have hurt Abigail to realize her father was not the morally upright man she'd believed him to be. Could it be she was holding all men accountable for her father's sin? Fear of being hurt again would certainly encourage one to build a protective barrier.

Helena hurried across the floor to the dresser. She uncapped the inkpot, dipped her pen, and turned the page to add a postscript.

P.S. Please keep Miss Grant in your prayers, Marietta. She carries a deep wound that affects her day-to-day associations. She is an unhappy young woman, and I do so want her to find joy within herself. Her longing to restore her previous lifestyle cannot be honored. "Polite" society won't allow it. So somehow she must accept a different kind of life and find contentment in it. I know, with your tender heart, you will hold her up to our heavenly Father. Thank you, dear sister.

Helena smiled as she closed the inkpot yet again. With both her and Marietta praying, surely they would see results. And putting Marietta's focus on someone else would take her mind off her own loneliness, which could inspire joy to bloom for her, as well. She aimed a teary smile at the ceiling.

"God, I suspect You have a plan. I trust You to see it through."

SEVENTEEN

Mack

Mack gave the front door to Patterson's restaurant a good yank. With the arrival of colder weather, the old wood swelled. Made a fellow work to get into the place, but at least its tight fit kept the warmth inside and the cold air outside.

His body gave an involuntary shudder as he stepped over the threshold. Orange glowed between the slots in the iron door of Athol's stove. He moved directly to the stove and held his hands toward the warmth. A sigh eased from him. The heat sure felt good. He glanced around the quiet room. No customers sat at any of the tables, but dirty plates and displaced chairs let him know the restaurant had been busy already.

The door to the kitchen swung outward, and Mack aimed a smile in that direction, expecting to tell Athol he'd take an order of

227

ham and eggs. But Mrs. Bingham, followed by Miss Grant, came from Athol's hallowed space. Mack drew back and stared at the pair. They both wore stained aprons over their dresses. Mrs. Bingham's sleeves were rolled partway up her arms, and Miss Grant's apron bore damp splotches. Why were they working in the kitchen? Had something happened to Athol?

He took one step toward them. "Is everything all right?"

"Right as rain." Mrs. Bingham pointed to a table that had been recently vacated, and Miss Grant scurried over to it. She began clearing the plates, cups, and silverware, stacking it all as skillfully as he used to stack his toy blocks.

Mack followed Mrs. Bingham to a second table. "Where's Athol? Is he sick?"

"No, he isn't sick. He's at his stove, his favorite place to be."

"Then why . . ." He gestured to Miss Grant and the table in front of him.

Mrs. Bingham clanked forks and spoons onto a plate. "Abigail and I have agreed to lend a helping hand in the restaurant for the duration of our stay in exchange for our meals." She smiled. "A mere business agreement that benefits both of us."

"Ah, I see." Considering they'd be stuck

here in Spiveyville for longer than they originally planned, they'd been smart to work a barter. "So do I tell you what I want?"

Miss Grant breezed by, amazingly graceful considering her full hands. "Absolutely not. We clear the tables. We do not act as servers." She disappeared into the kitchen.

Mrs. Bingham chuckled. "Miss Grant holds to the convention that ladies do not wait tables, so we are leaving that duty to Mr. Patterson. But please have a seat. I'll let him know you're here." She headed to the kitchen with her armload.

Mack settled at a table closest to the stove. Moments later, Athol bustled out, wiping his hands on his apron.

"Hey, Mack. Most ever'body was in an' out early today — wantin' to get busy at the Rockin' E. They all decided gettin' Norm a coop built for the chickens folks're plannin' to give him would be the best place to start."

Guilt pricked. Mack wanted to help at his friends' places, but the preacher and the sheriff had convinced him having his store open would be the best help. Folks making repairs might need the stock from his shelves. "Norm will appreciate it, I'm sure."

"Oh, yeah. 'Specially gettin' some new chickens. Him an' his critters . . ." Athol shook his head. "Whoever marries up with him better have a fondness for animals. Whatcha wantin' this mornin'?"

"You have any ham and eggs ready to fry? That sounds pretty good for a cold morning."

"Comin' right up." Athol bustled off.

Miss Grant entered the dining room and began collecting dishes from the remaining dirty table. With no one to talk to and nothing else to watch, he turned sideways in his chair and observed her careful stacking. Midway through, her hands started to tremble, and she shot him a wary look. "Am I doing something wrong?"

He scratched his cheek. "Not that I can see. Appears to me you've helped in a kitchen before. Am I right?"

She lined up the forks like a row of soldiers on top of the plates. "I've never held a position of servitude in a place of business. But during the last two years of my mother's life, I did the cooking and cleaning in our home."

He sensed a story underneath her brief explanation. He leaned forward slightly. "Because she wasn't able to do it anymore?"

Her brows pinched together. "Because our kitchen staff departed and Mother was too delicate for manual labor. If we intended to eat, someone had to cook, so I taught myself."

He was pretty sure he didn't have the whole story, but she'd given him enough to draw some conclusions. And he'd asked enough questions. He was getting close to being pushy. So he smiled. "I'm sure your mother appreciated your efforts."

She picked up the stack and left without a word, but her pursed lips and furrowed brow spoke volumes. Somehow he'd hit a nerve. Once again he wished he could be pushy. She stirred his curiosity.

The dining room door banged open and a tall man in dirty, rumpled clothing stumbled inside. A string of smelly catfish hung from his hand. He scanned the room, and his dark gaze landed on Mack. "Where's the owner?"

Mack raised his eyebrows. He hadn't seen this fellow in Spiveyville for quite a while. Hadn't missed him any either. Elmer Nance wasn't the friendliest sort. "In the kitchen."

"Fetch him."

Before Mack could rise, Athol sauntered into the dining room. He came straight at Mack, carrying a plate hidden beneath a slab of ham, fried eggs, and biscuits. He plopped it on the table. "I need to make another pot of coffee, Mack. Sheriff Thorn

231

took my last one with him out to Norm's. Said he'd need it to keep everybody warm. As soon as it's ready, I'll —" He wrinkled his nose, sniffing the air. He turned, seemed to notice Nance, and immediately prickled. "What're you doin' in here?"

The rough-looking man advanced, holding out the string of fish like a prize. "Sellin' these fish. Figgered you could serve 'em up for lunch or dinner."

Athol held up both hands and leaned backward. "I got my own catfish pond at the edge o' town. I got no need for them. 'Sides that, they look like they was caught a week ago. They're smellin' up the whole place. Get 'em out o' here, Nance."

Nance waved the string around. "There's nothin' wrong with these. Only fifty cents for the whole string."

Athol balled his fists on his hips. "I wouldn't pay a nickel for them things. If you don't take 'em out o' here an' take yourself with 'em, I'll sic the sheriff on you."

The man's grin turned menacing. "You're bluffin'. I heard you say the sheriff's out o' town." He pushed the string of floppy fish at Athol. "I'll leave when you've done gave me what I'm askin'. Fifty cents."

Athol's shoulders stiffened. "Git, Nance."

The man leaned in. "Make me."

Mack pushed his chair back, ready to leap into the melee if Nance threw a punch.

"I suggest you do as Mr. Patterson requested." Mrs. Bingham pushed between Athol and Nance and aimed the barrel of her derringer at Nance's chest.

His glower dropped to the gun. "What're you doin', woman? Put that thing down."

"I will as soon as you vacate these premises."

Where the city woman got her nerve, Mack didn't know, but apparently Nance believed she intended to use the weapon. He backed up, his heels scraping against the floor.

"All right, fine. I'm leavin'." He threw the string of fish on the floor and pointed his filthy finger at Athol. "But I ain't gonna forget this, Patterson." He yanked the door open and stormed out.

Athol trotted after him. "Don't show your grimy face in my restaurant again." He slammed the door and brushed his palms together. "That's good riddance."

Miss Grant peeked out from the kitchen doorway. "Who was that very disagreeable man?"

Athol snorted. "Name's Elmer Nance. He has a ranch near Coats, but every now an' then he wanders into Spiveyville." He

233

stooped over and pinched the string holding the catfish between his fingers. "Trouble always seems to come with him." He angled a grin at Mrs. Bingham. "Sure am glad you had that derringer handy. Ain't much Nance'll back down from, but the firin' end of a pistol works real good."

"Real well," Miss Grant said.

Athol nodded. "It sure do." He held the fish at arm's length. "Gonna throw these things out to the alley cats an' check on your coffee, Mack."

"That's fine. Thanks."

With the excitement over, Mrs. Bingham slipped her derringer into her apron pocket and headed for one of the empty tables.

Mack bowed his head, said a short prayer, then reached for his fork and knife. While he ate, he watched Mrs. Bingham scrub tables with a soapy sponge. He grinned and couldn't resist teasing her a little. "I've never seen Athol attack the tables with so much enthusiasm. You might wash the finish right off."

She aimed a mock scowl at him and then laughed. "It's quite obvious they've been given not much more than a half-hearted swipe with a dry towel."

"There've been times my elbows got stuck to the tabletop."

234

She shook her finger at him. "Never place your elbows on the table."

He swallowed a bite of eggs, covering a chuckle. "That sounds like something Miss Grant would say. Sometimes I think she invented manners."

Mrs. Bingham's face clouded. She went still. "Yes. Yes, I know."

"Not that there's anything wrong with having manners." Mack cut a piece of ham free and lifted it to his mouth. He chewed and swallowed. "My ma was a stickler for doing the polite thing. She'd tell me, 'Mackintosh' —"

Mrs. Bingham's eyebrows rose. "Mackintosh?"

Fire exploded in his face. He flicked a glance right and left. "The only one who calls me that is my ma."

"But it's such a stately name, Mr. Cleveland." She crossed to his table, dripping suds on the way. "Mackintosh Cleveland. It has the sound of royalty."

Mack grimaced. "If you promise not to tell anybody, the whole thing is Mackintosh Horatio Cleveland. It's not quite as bad as W. C. Miller's real name. He's Wendlesora Clotilde."

She gaped in open-mouthed silence for several seconds, and then she burst out laughing.

He laughed, too. "Awful, isn't it? No wonder the poor man goes by W. C. As for Mackintosh Horatio, you might think it has the sound of royalty, but it's the kind of name that can get you into fistfights in a school yard. So I'd rather go by Mack."

She covered her mouth and brought her laughter under control, but the corners of her eyes stayed crinkled. "Your secret is safe with me. But what was it your mother used to tell you?"

He'd forgotten what they were talking about. He rolled his eyes upward and searched his memory. "Oh! She'd tell me, 'Mackintosh, there are always two ways to respond to people — the polite way and the rude way. No matter what others do, always choose the polite way. Then you'll carry no regrets.' " He huffed a brief, sad laugh. "She led by example, too. I never heard her say a rude word to anyone. Not even to someone who really deserved it."

Mrs. Bingham's expression turned thoughtful. "You come from good stock, Mr. Cleveland. Were you raised here in Spiveyville?"

"No, ma'am. I grew up in Kansas City, Missouri. I came out here to Spiveyville to help my uncle start his hardware store."

He'd never admit he came not as much to help as to escape a mighty anger. "Halfway through building it, he took sick and died."

She slid into a chair. "Oh, how sad."

"It was a hard time, I won't deny." Mack fiddled with his fork, memories of those difficult days marching through his mind. "Even though we were newcomers, folks rallied around me. Helped me finish the store and convinced me to add a little apartment off the back where I could live." They'd restored his faith in people, that was for sure. "By the time we had it all finished, I'd decided I wanted to make this town my home. So I didn't go back to Kansas City." He shrugged. "I miss Ma and Pa, but I don't want to live in the city again. I like this prairie. Even when the wind blows."

Unsmiling, she seemed to search his face. Then she stood. "Mr. Cleveland, thank you for sharing this with me. You've given me much to consider."

He didn't know what he'd said that was so important, but he had enough manners to know how to respond. "You're welcome, ma'am."

She returned to the table she'd vacated, and Athol came puffing across the room, carrying the coffeepot and two cups. Athol splashed coffee in both cups and sat across from Mack with a big smile.

"Miss Grant's in there doin' up the dishes, so I got time to sit. Mind if I join you?"

"Not at all." Mack took a slurp of the strong brew. "Mmm, that tastes good." The eggs had grown cold, but he chopped off another piece and popped it into his mouth. He swallowed the bite and tipped his head in Mrs. Bingham's direction. "It's nice of you to work out a deal with the ladies. I imagine it'll cost you some."

Athol poked out his lips. "Some." He leaned in and dropped his voice to a husky whisper. "To be honest, I'm not sure how I'll keep two of 'em busy. They work a lot faster'n I expected 'em to. It'd be better for me to keep the deal with only one, but it'd seem spiteful to go back on my word now. So unless somethin' comes along that takes 'em elsewhere, I'm pretty much stuck with 'em."

Mack pushed the last piece of ham around on his plate. "They'll be busy with those classes, won't they?"

"In the evenin'. But not durin' the day." Athol held his big hands wide. "Up 'til now, they've stayed in their rooms all day. But since we decided to barter, they're down here askin' me for things to do. It's only the first day, an' I'm already wonderin' what

I'm gonna do with 'em."

Mack slapped the table. "I know."

Athol jumped. "What?"

Mack grinned. "Let me talk to Mrs. Bingham first. In case it won't work. But if it does, we'll both be happy." He scooted back his chair, leaped up, and marched toward Mrs. Bingham. "Ma'am, I have an idea."

Abigail

"Now, are you sure you'll be all right?"

Abigail smoothed her hands over her green-and-tan plaid skirt front and met Mr. Cleveland's gaze. His apprehensive tone and the lines of worry marring his brow didn't inspire confidence. If he didn't believe she was capable of manning his store for a few hours, perhaps he shouldn't have asked.

She pressed her palms against her jumping stomach and forced a smile. "As you said, Mr. Patterson is right next door, and Mr. Ackley only beyond that if Mr. Patterson is unavailable. I don't expect to bother them, though." She'd never heard of anyone robbing a hardware store, and every able-bodied man was applying his hands to Sheriff Thorn's list. She needn't fear anyone accosting her today. "I'll record any purchases in the log, the way you showed me.

239

As long as customers don't expect me to carry something heavy, I shouldn't have any trouble at all."

"Well . . ." He fiddled with the door handle, his uncertain gaze drifting from corner to corner. Then he ducked his head and laughed. A short laugh, full of self-deprecation. "A person would think I was leaving you in charge of my newborn baby." He peeked at her. "Sorry."

He looked so boyish, she battled a smile. "It's all right, Mr. Cleveland. You're proud of your store, and you've operated it on your own for many years. You should feel . . . protective. And possessive. I understand." She had very little left of her former life. She clung to those few things as if they were her very breath.

Finally he smiled, the ends of his neatly trimmed mustache twitching and his blue eyes beneath his thick dark brows sparkling. "Mrs. Bingham said you're responsible and hardworking. I won't worry one bit about you."

His statement filled her with unexpected pleasure.

He opened the door. "I better get the team hitched. Athol promised to have sandwiches out to the work crew by noon, and it's almost eleven thirty already." He put one foot out on the boardwalk. "You enjoy your afternoon, Miss Grant, and if anything — anything at all — goes wrong, just hightail it to the restaurant and get Athol." He hovered there, one foot in and one foot out.

If she didn't give him a shove, he might stay forever. She hurried from behind the counter to the door. "Goodbye, Mr. Cleveland."

He sent one more slow look across the store. "Bye now, Miss Grant." He stepped out of the building.

Abigail closed the door behind him, then leaned against it, shook her head, and laughed. She'd seen this kind of reluctance before. Twice she'd gone to her father's office with him when she was on break from school and Mother had other obligations. On both occasions, he'd given her a simple task — the first time alphabetizing a stack of contacts, and the second time addressing envelopes to send to clients — to keep her occupied. Both times he'd hovered near, watchful, as if anticipating she wouldn't be able to complete the assignment without his supervision.

Memories of Father erased all hints of amusement. She hung her head, unpleasant thoughts torturing her. Had Father not trusted her? Or, even more distressing, had he been trying to hide illegal dealings from her even then? She bolted upright and strode to the counter. She didn't want to think about Father. She'd learned long ago that busyness prevented her from thinking, so she snatched up the feather duster from beneath the counter and set to work swishing the feathers over every item on every shelf in the store.

When she'd finished dusting, she located a broom in the closet at the rear of the store and applied it to the floor, meticulously attacking every corner and reaching as far as possible beneath the sturdy shelves. She recovered very little dust, a testament to Mr. Cleveland's impeccable care, but what little she found she pushed out the door, across the boardwalk, and into the street, where the wind could carry it away.

Back inside the store, she stood with her hands on her hips and tried to decide what to do next. Organize things? She set off on a slow exploration up and down the walk space between shelves, examining the little crates of hinges, bolts, doorknobs, cabinet pulls, and dozens of what she called "what-have-yous." Nothing seemed out of place. Mr. Cleveland's perfectionism almost rankled, but she wasn't sure why.

She locked her hands behind her back and

strolled to the spot behind the counter. She tamped the stack of scrap papers he used to tally up a customer's purchases. Sharpened every pencil in the cup next to the cast-iron cash register and swished the shavings into a waste can. Carried the waste can to the back and emptied it. Tamped the scrap papers again.

She peeked at the clock hanging on the wall. Not even one thirty? Mr. Cleveland planned to work until dusk. She still had hours to burn. And absolutely nothing to do. She chewed the inside of her cheek. Might Mr. Cleveland keep a book or two lying around somewhere? If so, she could sit on one of the nail kegs and read. She started toward the closet.

The door swung open and Abigail turned in its direction. "Good day. Welcome to Spiveyville Hardware and Implements."

A barrel-shaped man wearing a three-piece suit as well made as those Linus had worn strode importantly across the floor and looked her up and down.

Instantly she broke out in gooseflesh. She darted behind the counter and picked up the feather duster. A dismal weapon, but holding something gave her a modicum of confidence. "May I help you?"

"I'm Tobis Adelman." He spoke with the

243

arrogance of someone who expected to be instantly recognized.

She'd heard the name, but she'd heard so many names in the past few days, the significance was lost. "What can I do for you, Mr. Adelman?"

He grunted and stared at her through slitted eyes beneath heavy, almost-black brows. "Not a thing. Athol Patterson sent me in to check on you. He thought you might be hungry an' wondered if you wanted a sandwich."

Her stomach chose that moment to growl. Embarrassment smote her, and a nervous titter escaped. "Um, yes, I suppose it is past lunchtime. Did Mr. Patterson want me to come to the restaurant or —"

"I'll bring it to you. While you eat, there's somethin' I wanna talk at you about."

Oh, these men and their shoddy way of structuring sentences. Without thinking, she corrected, "Something I would like to discuss with you."

His brows pinched even deeper. "Are you makin' fun of me?"

She hadn't intended to make fun. But shouldn't a man who wore the most up-to-date suit and combed his hair away from his forehead in a dramatic wave use speech that matched his appearance? He was glowering at her, waiting for a reply.

"No, sir."

"That's good, 'cause I wouldn't take kindly to it."

An uneasy thought struck. He surely didn't intend to ask her about matrimony, did he? She swallowed a nervous giggle burbling in her throat. "I'm not making fun of you, sir. Honestly."

He glared at her for another few silent seconds, then spun on the heel of his highly polished boot. "I'm gonna sit down, have something to eat at the restaurant. When I'm done, I'll be in with a sandwich. Then we'll talk."

EIGHTEEN

Bill

Bill tugged his hat a little lower on his head so the breeze wouldn't carry it to kingdom come and reached into the back of the wagon for the first of the half-dozen wired cages. Each held a clucking hen. The chickens had kept up their ruckus the whole drive from Spiveyville.

He frowned at the speckled white hen jabbing its beak against the wire and clucking like somebody'd set her tail feathers on fire. "Now, settle yourself down. You'll be out an' peckin' soon enough."

The bird started running back and forth, rocking the cage. Bill took a stumbling step and almost dropped the thing. "Whoa there!"

Laughter exploded behind him, and someone reached around and took the cage from his hands. Bill glared over the top of the wire at Mack. "What're you doin' out here? I thought I told you to stay in your store so's folks could get what they needed."

He grinned. "You'll be happy I came when you see the stack of sandwiches Athol sent out with me. Cold beef tongue and ham and roast turkey."

Bill's mouth watered. He slid a second cage from the wagon bed and followed Mack toward the brand-new chicken coop standing proud in Norm's yard. "I thought the ladies an' Preacher Doan was gonna bring them sandwiches. Somethin' happen to keep 'em from comin' out?"

"Nope. Mrs. Bingham's with me, but I asked if I could take the preacher's place. I plan to stick around, help finish putting up the pen around the coop." Mack heaved a happy sigh. "I like being out here, helping my neighbors the way they helped me when I first came to Spiveyville. Remember?"

Bill remembered a sullen-faced young man with a big burden to bear. Mack had grown some since then. In lots of ways. "Sure do, an' I ain't surprised about you wantin' to help. But I gotta say I'm disappointed your store's closed. Might delay some other fixin' gettin' done."

Mack placed the cage on the ground and turned toward the wagon. "No it won't."

Bill plopped his cage on top of Mack's and trotted after him. "How come?"

" 'Cause I didn't close it." He grinned. "I asked Miss Grant to keep store for me."

Bill's stomach gave a flip. "You did?"

Mack nodded. He lifted a cage holding a red hen and handed it to Bill. "I figure someone as educated as Miss Grant ought to be able to add up purchases and keep records. Athol was running out of things for her to do at the restaurant, so I put her to work at my place."

Bill rocked back and forth with the cage balanced against his belly. Should he tell Mack what the banker told him first thing that morning? He might not've believed it if Tobis hadn't shown him the article from a back issue of the *Boston Times* from five years ago. Funny the things that Tobis held on to. Inside his house Bill had seen empty oatmeal tins stacked up like totem poles, a small mountain of shoes — most of them had seen more'n enough use — in the corner of the kitchen, and a wardrobe full from bottom to top of newspapers.

Most folks put their old newspapers in the stove or the outhouse instead of stock-piling them. If Mrs. Adelman hadn't decided she wanted the wardrobe for her spring dresses, the newspaper with the article that got Tobis all worked up might never've been seen. But Tobis had seen it, and he'd shown Bill, and Bill couldn't put it out of his mind. Now, knowing Miss Grant was all by herself in Mack's store with access to the cash register, Bill faced a dilemma. Telling Mack would probably wipe the smile off his friend's face, but he had to say something.

Mack grabbed another cage and took a step in the direction of the coop. Bill moved into his path. "Uh, Mack?"

"What?"

The peaceful contentment on his friend's face stung Bill. He cleared his throat and made himself be honest. "Tobis come to see me this mornin'. Said he had some news about one o' the city ladies that needed tellin'."

"What was it?"

Bill cringed. Right now Mrs. Bingham was handing sandwiches around and smiling, talking, carefree as a lark. She sure didn't look like a swindler. But what successful swindler would look like one? He shoved his hands in his pockets and rocked on his heels. "Now, most times I wouldn't pay no mind to Tobis. I dunno how he keeps that bank runnin' when he's got so little common sense. If it hadn't been for me findin'

Miss Grant closed up in the church with Otto Hildreth, an' Otto all worked up about somethin' she didn't wanna talk about, I'd just ignore it, but . . ."

"C'mon, Sheriff, what're you trying to say? I'd like to get these cages set down and get a sandwich before they're all gone."

Bill gathered up his gumption and let the secret spill out. "Tobis said Miss Grant's pa is sittin' in a Massachusetts penitentiary for stealin' from his business partners."

Abigail

Even if Mr. Adelman hadn't brought a sandwich with beef tongue between the thick slices of bread, she wouldn't be able to eat. Disgrace weighted her, nearly bending her in two. Her legs turned wobbly, and she sank onto the closest nail keg and stared at the yellowed newsprint bearing her father's stoic image. A two-column article filled half the front page, outlining his wrongdoings, quoting statements made by the trial judge about him, and proclaiming his sentence.

"Is that your kin, young lady?"

For one moment, Abigail considered denying it. But Mother had taught her to never tell a falsehood. She swallowed the bitter bile filling her throat and nodded.

The man folded his arms over his chest, his smile smug. "I thought so. When I seen the name Grant on the paper an' saw how he was from Massachusetts, same as you, I figured he had to be kin. I'm guessin' he's your pa. Right?"

Miserably, she nodded again. She hadn't realized her father's sins would be known even on the plains of Kansas. She folded the paper to hide Father's face and handed it to the banker. "Have you told anyone about . . . him?"

"Yes, I did." The man bounced the folded pages against his thigh. "The sheriff needed to know there's a thief here in Spiveyville."

Indignation chased away her humiliation. She sat upright and glared at him. "I am not a thief."

"You come from a thievin' family."

She couldn't argue that statement.

"To my way of thinkin', the apples don't fall far from the tree. My pa was a banker. Now I'm a banker. Sam Bandy's pa was a baker. Now he's a baker. Your pa's a thief. So now . . ."

Fury filled her. Fury at her father for putting her in this uncomfortable, undeserved position. Fury at the banker's pompous attitude. Fury at her helplessness to refute the facts. She curled her hands into fists and rose from the keg. "I cannot deny that my father made a dreadful error of judgment. He is paying for his crime." So had Mother. So was she. "But I can assure you I was taught right from wrong, and I have never — never! — engaged in unlawful activities nor dabbled in behavior one might consider even remotely indecent. I greatly resent your implications, Mr. Adelman, and I will ask you to take your vile suppositions out of this store."

He backed up two steps, his eyes wide and his mouth slightly open.

Fortified by his cowardly retreat, she took one step in his direction and pointed at his florid face. "Furthermore, I insist you keep this information to yourself, or you may find yourself facing charges of slander."

His face remained blotched with red, but he blasted a snide laugh. "You can't charge me with slander for tellin' the truth."

"The truth about my father does not extend to truthfulness about me, sir, and you would do well to remember it or I shall have need of contacting my lawyer." She had no way of following up on such a threat. She knew lawyers, of course. Linus Hartford's father was one of the finest in Massachusetts, and she'd once believed he

252

would be her father-in-law. But where would she find the fees to secure his services? She could only hope Mr. Adelman didn't know she was nearly penniless and therefore wouldn't call her bluff.

Her bluff . . . Shame swooped in again. Where had she learned to mislead someone so? Maybe she possessed some of her father's unsavoriness inside her after all. The thought did little to cheer her despite the banker's continued uneasy harrumphing and blushing.

He stomped to the door and aimed a glare over his shoulder. "The sheriff'll be watching you, young woman, an' I will be, too."

"Go ahead and watch, Mr. Adelman. But watch in silence if you don't wish to be brought up on charges of defaming my character."

He charged out of the store.

The door's slam stole her bluster. Her legs gave way, and she sank back on the nail keg. Her pulse pounded in her ears so fast and loud she battled dizziness. They would be watching her, the banker said. She buried her face in her hands. How unfair that she should pay for the sins of her father. How unfair that her mother's legacy of appropriate, upright, moral living should be tarnished through no fault of her own.

She sat up and stared across the quiet store, blinking back hot tears of both anger and anguish. Somehow she would set things right. Somehow she would force the short-sighted banker and anyone else who dared to make suppositions about her to cast aside their concerns. She would rise above Father's illicit choices and erase all vestiges of his mistakes from everyone's mind.

She clenched her fists and vowed anew, "They will find no fault in me, for I shall exhibit nothing but unblemished refinement."

Mack

Mack finished securing the latch on the gate to the brand-new chicken pen and stepped back. A cheer rose from the men who'd spent the day building the coop. Norm Elliott stood in the middle of the group, grinning from ear to ear.

"Let's take the chickens out o' their cages now an' let 'em run," Norm said. "Poor hens — they sure ain't been happy all closed up in those little boxes o' wire."

W. C. Miller gave Norm a sock on the arm. "Prob'ly feels like jail to 'em." The men roared in response, but Mack didn't laugh. There wasn't anything funny about jail.

Especially not today, with the truth about Miss Grant's father fresh in his mind.

Sheriff Thorn had returned to town and took Mrs. Bingham with him right after lunch. Before he left, he'd filled Mack's ears with all kinds of troubling ideas fed to him by Tobis Adelman. Such as maybe Miss Grant meant to take the fees from Spiveyville's hopeful grooms or sneak off with the contents of Athol's cashbox. Sometimes people did steal because they'd learned it from the one who should've been teaching them better.

Worry nagged at him. His cash register drawer was pretty full. He'd developed the habit of making one big deposit the last day of every month, so the bills and coins got stacked fairly high by this time of the month. If someone had come in and made a cash purchase and Miss Grant opened the drawer to drop in the coins, she'd notice what was in there. Would it tempt her?

He didn't want to think such things about Miss Grant. Didn't he know all too well that some accusations were made without real evidence? He'd never forget how folks his family had known his whole life accused Uncle Ray of partnering with Wilhelmina Wilkes when all he'd done was innocently place an ad.

He groaned under his breath. This was all Tobis's fault. That man's money-hungry ways trickled over into ridiculous suspicions. Why should anybody listen to him?

"Hey, Mack."

He gave a jolt. Melvin Fletcher stood close, a wiggling brown hen tucked under his arm.

"Couldja step aside? We're gonna let these cluckers loose."

Mack stepped back and the men dropped the hens one by one into Norm's pen. The chickens explored every inch of their new patch of ground and fresh-built coop, wings flapping and feathers flying. The men pointed and laughed like they'd never seen such entertainment. After their long day of work, they deserved some cutting up, but their jollity rankled when Mack considered the sheriff's worries about Miss Grant.

Melvin threw his arm across Mack's shoulders. "One down, thirteen to go."

Confused, Mack frowned.

Melvin grinned, showing a gap between his front teeth. His brother, Millard, had a gap exactly like it but one tooth over. "Thirteen more projects. Still a couple hours of daylight left. We're headin' over to the Circle L, gonna at least get a count on the busted fence posts. You comin'?"

There were half a dozen men besides him on the work crew. How many would it take to count fence posts? Shaking his head, Mack eased away from Melvin. "I think I'd better get to town, make sure everything's all right at my store."

Melvin smirked. "It's likely gone all to pieces, what with you leavin' it in the hands o' that little city gal."

Mack broke out in a cold sweat. The sheriff wouldn't have told the other men about Miss Grant's father. That would be a vindictive thing to do, and Bill Thorn had never been vindictive. But Mack wouldn't put it past Tobis to spread gossip. He'd done it before. Mack forced his dry throat to release a sharp question. "Why do you say that?"

Melvin shrugged. " 'Cause she ain't likely ever had to mind a store before. Who knows what kind o' mistakes she might've made."

Mack nearly collapsed with relief. Before he'd left, Miss Grant had stated she understood why he'd feel possessive and protective of his store. He caught himself feeling protective now, and he thought he understood why.

He nodded and forced a grin. "You're right, Melvin. I better go make sure the place is still standing."

Melvin's laughter followed Mack to his wagon. He climbed in, released the brake, and flicked the reins. He wouldn't hurry the horses. Hurrying them wasn't a safe thing to do. But he couldn't deny eagerness to get to Spiveyville as quick as possible to assure himself all was well. Not with the store. With Miss Grant.

NINETEEN

Helena

Helena hung the last of her and Abigail's laundry on the line strung from the corner of the restaurant to the corner of Mr. Patterson's smokehouse. The dresses, petticoats, slips, and camisoles filled every inch of the line and flapped gently in the breeze, sending out the scent of roses from the bar of soap she'd dissolved in the tub of hot water. She wanted to wash their sheets, too, but the line wouldn't accommodate even another sock. She would have to wait for another day.

She picked up the empty basket Mr. Patterson had loaned her for transporting the wet clothes to the backyard and climbed the stairs. Abigail would probably be embarrassed when she realized Helena had gone into her room and gathered up her soiled clothes for washing, but Helena had time to

259

spare and the wash needed to be done. Perhaps she'd allow Abigail the privilege of washing the sheets tomorrow to help her feel less beholden. The girl's intense sense of honor disallowed her owing anyone a favor.

Helena dropped the basket on the landing inside the back door and entered her sleeping room. She crossed to the dresser, picked up her comb, and smoothed some stray hairs into place. Her reflection revealed a smile she didn't even realize she was wearing. She released a soft chuckle, recognizing its source. She'd enjoyed the day — her morning in the restaurant, the drive to Norm Elliott's Rocking E Ranch, engaging in casual conversation with the men. They used uncultured speech, which occasionally made her cringe, but she'd seen their unfettered willingness to help a friend, and it had heartened her. Even dipping the clothes in the hot, scented water proved pleasant. How nice to be busy rather than stuck in this dismal room, staring at the plain walls.

Had Abigail enjoyed her day of usefulness, too? She glanced at her little pendant watch, which hung from a pin on her left shoulder. Mr. Patterson wouldn't need her for another half hour, so she had time to go next door and check on Abigail. She slung her shawl around her shoulders and headed down the stairs, out the front door, and across the short expanse of boardwalk to Mr. Cleveland's hardware store.

A bell above the door jangled merrily as she entered, and she smiled in response to it. But when her gaze fell on Abigail's tense, unsmiling face, her joyful spirit received a splash of cold water. Clearly, the girl had found reasons to complain. Mostly manufactured reasons, Helena presumed. She strode to the counter and braced one fist on her hip. "What has upset you this time?"

Abigail's chin quivered. With her face still blotched from the healing sunburn, she made a pathetic picture. But Helena determined not to give way to sympathy. Without intervention, this girl would succumb to self-pity and pettiness the way Marietta had so many years ago.

Helena arched an eyebrow. "Do you intend to answer me?"

Abigail angled her gaze aside. Her chin stopped its quiver and gained a stubborn tilt.

Helena sighed. "Let me see if I can guess." She glanced around. Nothing seemed out of place. The store was quiet. Peaceful, even. She turned to Abigail again. "All right, I confess, I'm flummoxed. You'll have to tell me what has displeased you."

Hinges squeaked, a door slammed into its case, and boots thumped from the back of the store. Abigail sucked in a breath and gripped her clasped hands to her throat. A puzzling reaction. Helena shifted her attention to the rear entry, and moments later Mr. Cleveland strode in. His rugged face wore an expression of determination, and his squared shoulders and ready fists gave the impression of one prepared for battle. His gaze skimmed from Abigail to Helena, and he gave a little jolt that halted his progress.

"Mrs. Bingham . . ." His thick eyebrows descended slightly. "I didn't expect to find you here."

"I came to check on Abigail, to assure myself her day was going well." She glanced at Abigail. Her face had gone white except for the pale-pink patches of peeled skin. The freckles that had sprung up in those patches seemed even bolder. "I presume it didn't, but she refuses to talk to me." An idle thought trickled through her mind, and a smile tugged at the corners of her lips. "Perhaps she will tell you what transpired to bring about her doldrums."

Abigail whirled, pinning a fierce glare on Helena. "I have no doldrums."

Mr. Cleveland grimaced. His hands relaxed, and he slid his fingertips into the pockets of his tan trousers. He sauntered forward, his blue-eyed gaze seemingly pinned on Abigail's face. "Did the sheriff come talk to you?"

Tears swam in Abigail's eyes. Helena's irritation melted in light of the girl's true distress. "Why would the sheriff have need to speak with Abigail? Did someone harass her?" She addressed her questions to Mr. Cleveland. Despite the sheriff's dire warnings about Abigail or her being harassed, she hadn't experienced a smidgen of unease until that moment.

He stayed focused on Abigail as if Helena hadn't spoken. "Did he?"

Abigail shook her head.

He groaned. "Then did Tobis?"

Helena's patience flew out the window. She stomped her foot. "Would you please stop tiptoeing around the subject and tell me what has transpired?" Abigail was her employee. If whatever happened would affect her business, she had a right to know.

Mr. Cleveland sighed and settled his weight on one hip. "Mrs. Bingham, do you know where Miss Grant's pa is?"

If Abigail's face lost any more color, she would collapse. Helena darted behind the

263

counter and put her arm around the younger woman's waist. "Yes. I do."

Mr. Cleveland looked grim. "Well, so does our town's banker. He told Sheriff Thorn. And I'm guessing that Tobis, being Tobis, couldn't keep from coming in here and asking Miss Grant about her father's crimes. Am I right?"

A single tear slid down Abigail's cheek, and she batted it away with a vicious swipe of her hand. "He not only asked about my father, he accused me of . . . of following in his footsteps." Her entire body trembled, and Helena tightened her grip. "I am not a thief."

Mr. Cleveland jutted his jaw and chewed his mustache, his brows pulled low.

Words formed on Helena's tongue — words of anger toward Tobis Adelman, who dared to accost a helpless woman, words of frustration toward Abigail's father, who'd caused such turmoil for his child, and words of defensiveness. If she'd thought Abigail was capable of stealing, she would never have accepted her into her program. Abigail had many faults, the worst of which were perfectionism and haughtiness, but she was honest. Helena would staunchly defend her against any allegation to the contrary.

Her verbal attack formulated, Helena

264

opened her mouth to speak.

Mr. Cleveland blew out a breath. "Tobis Adelman's pa helped found Spiveyville. The older Mr. Adelman loaned money to nearly every rancher and business owner in the area, so a successful town means money in his pocket. Tobis inherited the bank and inherited the loans, and he's protective about the town — the way you said I was about my store, Miss Grant."

Abigail lifted her pale face and aimed an aghast stare at Mr. Cleveland. "Are you saying he was correct to come in here and . . . and threaten me?"

Helena gasped. "He threatened you?"

"Yes. He said he would watch me." Abigail stretched to her full height and angled her head in a regal manner. "I told him he would be wise to keep silent about his ridiculous notions about me or I would file charges of slander against him."

Helena burst out laughing. She knew she shouldn't, but she'd met Mr. Adelman. At least six feet tall and built like a bull, he cut an intimidating figure. But Abigail — petite, civil, nonthreatening Abigail — had stood her ground. She gave the girl a squeeze. "Good for you. I'm proud of you."

Mr. Cleveland rested his elbows on the counter, his back curving into an apostrophe. Worry creased his face. "Sheriff Thorn will probably come talk to you two about what Tobis said. He'll want to assure himself there's no reason for anybody in town to worry about Miss Grant doing something . . . illegal."

"And I will most certainly assure him." Helena grabbed Abigail's limp hand and gave it several brisk pats. "You have nothing to fear, Abigail. You've done nothing about which to be ashamed."

The girl hung her head. Tears filled her eyes again, turning her lashes into moist spikes. "I appreciate your efforts to cheer me, but I cannot accept your statement as fact. It's true I've done nothing illegal or immoral, but that meant nothing in Boston. My father's guilt spilled over on Mother and me regardless of our innocence. We lost our home, we lost our friends, my fiancé rejected me . . . The officials came to auction our belongings and sell our home, and our former friends swept in like buzzards to oversee the bidding so they could be sure they would be recompensed for their losses, little caring about what we lost. Even when Mother died, no one came to offer condolences or apologies for abandoning us in our time of deepest need."

She lifted her head, and the pride that

Helena had come to associate with her returned. "I thought coming to the West would mean leaving my past and its dark stains behind, but now I know they will always be with me. I am forever tainted by my father's foul actions. I . . ." Her brave countenance, or perhaps her moment of vulnerability, crumbled. She took a stumbling step toward the door. "Now that you have returned, Mr. Cleveland, I shall leave your store in your capable hands." With her fist pressed to her lips, she fled.

When the little bell stopped its clamor, Helena turned a stern look on Mr. Cleveland. "Sir, I must ask you to keep in confidence everything Miss Grant disclosed. She is a very private person, and only deep duress would compel her to share something so intimate with someone who is basically a stranger to her."

He stared at her with wide, disbelieving eyes. "Is all that she said true? Her intended and her friends all abandoned her because her pa stole?"

Helena pursed her lips. Would Mr. Cleveland understand the inner workings of the elite? "He didn't merely steal, Mr. Cleveland. He stole from his business partners, who were also his friends. He betrayed an entire circle of people who are not in the habit of forgiving disloyalty."

He waved one hand at the door. "But that shouldn't have anything to do with her."

Helena smiled sadly at his vehemence. "Ah, have you not read the accounts of Moses's conversations with God found in the book of Exodus? God is loving and compassionate, but even He remembered the father's sins unto the third and fourth generations. Do you truly believe mortal men, who lack God's deep compassion, would do anything less?"

Mr. Cleveland folded his arms over his chest. "It's not fair."

"No. No, it certainly isn't." There were many unfair happenings in her small corner of the world. Was it fair that Marietta was passed by for matrimony, leaving her alone and bitter at an age when love rarely bloomed? Was it fair dear Howard was taken from her long before she was ready to bid him goodbye? Was it fair for a weather calamity to strike the community and postpone bringing brides to the eager grooms of Spiveyville?

She sighed. "Life is often unfair, and we cannot change it. We can only do our utmost to make the best of what we've been dealt and perhaps try to bring a little happiness into others' lives. Isn't that what the

Bible advises — to love one's neighbor as oneself?"

He scowled, but Helena believed it was a thoughtful rather than a vengeful scowl. "Mrs. Bingham, I know what it's like to be alone. It happened to me right here in Spiveyville when my uncle died. If the folks in town hadn't rallied around me, I don't know what I would've done. And the folks here didn't even hardly know me yet. It pains me that people she'd called friends turned on her. I know how it —" He pushed upright and gazed toward the door, which Abigail had left ajar in her haste to depart. "It seems to me what Miss Grant needs more than anything is a friend."

Warmth flooded Helena's chest. "Are you volunteering to be her friend?"

He looked at her, both indecision and determination playing in his expression. "If I did befriend her, it might go a long way in convincing the other businessmen in Spiveyville they don't have a reason to suspect her. I have" — a delightful self-conscious flush stained his cheeks — "a good reputation in town, so . . ."

She rounded the counter and placed her fingertips on his upper arm. "I am deeply touched by your concern and your willingness to befriend Abigail. Especially considering your standing in this community and how it could be tarnished if Mr. Adelman's suppositions about her character were proved true."

"They're not true, though, are they." A statement, not a question.

She liked this man more with every passing minute. "No, Mr. Cleveland. They are definitely not true. Abigail has resided beneath my roof for a little over three years, and not once in that time has she dipped so much as her little toe into the pool of impropriety. She is honest, sometimes to a fault, and staunchly moral. Her father's choices will never be something she emulates."

He gave a firm nod. "Then I'm gonna have a talk with Sheriff Thorn about Tobis. And I'm gonna do what I can to let Miss Grant know she can depend on me to stand up for her if need be. Like you said, we're called to love our neighbors as ourselves." He grinned. "I guess, for me, that includes you and Miss Grant since you're living right next door."

TWENTY

Abigail

Her only saving grace, as Mother would have called it, was that Tobis Adelman had a wife to cook for him, so Abigail didn't need to worry about him coming to the restaurant for his dinner after their unpleasant exchange. Thus, she relished her evening of peace. Well, if not peace, at least an evening with enough busyness to distract her from thoughts of the pompous man and his untrue assumptions.

She stacked dirty dishes and carried them to the washtub in the kitchen. Mr. Patterson, large metal fork in hand, looked up from his spot at the massive stove. "Everything goin' all right out there?"

The mingled savory and sweet aromas of fried pork chops and brown sugar-glazed carrots made her mouth water. After her foul encounter, she hadn't expected to be

271

hungry, but now she wished she'd had the chance to sit down and eat before the restaurant owner put her and Mrs. Bingham to work. "Everything is fine. The men seem to be enjoying the pork chops." She paused in the doorway, ignoring the *drip-drip* from the sudsy scrub cloth. "Do you think you'll have enough for . . . everyone?"

He grinned. "I already set aside two nice thick chops for you an' Miz Bingham. Don't worry."

How had he known what she meant? Embarrassed, she scurried out of the kitchen and nearly plowed into Mr. Cleveland. "Oh! Excuse me."

"Excuse me." He held his hat flat against his stomach with both hands. "I was gonna holler in to Athol that I'll take the special. It smells pretty good."

She skirted around him. "Yes, it does."

"But not as good as the cellar. Have you been down there yet?"

Why did he have to mention the place where the previous owners had stored their kegs of beer? Had she not suffered enough angst today? "No, I haven't, nor do I intend to. Excuse me, Mr. Cleveland." She hurried to the table she'd cleared and gave its top a thorough scrubbing.

As she turned to take the cloth back to

the kitchen, she discovered Mr. Cleveland in her path again. She started to step around him, but he held out his hand.

"I wanted to tell you . . ." He shot a glance across the dining room. He leaned down slightly. "I talked to Sheriff Thorn, and he said he'd make sure Tobis doesn't pester you again."

She wanted to be grateful, but his comment about the cellar was too fresh. But even if she didn't feel grateful, she could be polite. "Thank you."

"He also told me you had some kind of fracas with Otto Hildreth at the church. Was it about the same thing?"

Abigail gritted her teeth. How many conversations had the men in this town had about her? "No."

"Then what?"

She sighed. "I have work to do. Would you excuse me, please?"

"You're right. I shouldn't bother you when you're working." An easy smile spread across his face. "And I'm sorry if I'm a pest about trying to send you to the cellar. But it's the most amazing thing. All the good smells from Athol's kitchen must soak through the floorboards and settle down there. The cellar smells like Christmas dinner."

Abigail blinked twice, uncertain she'd heard him correctly. "It doesn't smell like . . ." She couldn't say beer.

"Not musty, like you'd expect from a cellar. No, I'd say Athol's cellar is one of the best-smelling places in the whole county."

A laugh burbled in her throat and found its way out. She clapped her hand over her mouth.

He grinned. "What's so funny?"

She couldn't possibly explain. She waved the cloth. "I need to rinse this. And I see there's another table that requires clearing, so please excuse me." She hurried off, but she couldn't squelch her smile. He hadn't wanted to send her down to sniff beer after all. The thought gave her heart more of a lift than she understood.

While rinsing the cloth, she envisioned Mr. Cleveland's serious face as he'd claimed Mr. Adelman wouldn't bother her again. If only he could promise she'd never see the obnoxious man again, but that was impossible. Their paths would certainly cross. Mrs. Ethel Adelman had signed herself and her husband up for Thursday evening classes. For the first time, she welcomed the delay in beginning the classes. Would a few days of separation allow her to recover her wits and prepare for the moment when she would be face to face with the banker again? She hoped so. It wouldn't do to dissolve into a puddle of anxious tears or give vent to the anger still coursing through her. Mother had taught her not to prove herself to be the one in the right, but in this case she was sorely tempted.

She paused with her hand in the tepid water. She needn't prove herself right. Mr. Cleveland had already taken care of it for her by involving Sheriff Thorn. Her heart fluttered. Why had he defended her? She didn't know, and propriety forbade her from asking, but she couldn't help but wonder. Perhaps he could go along to wherever she went next and be her defender there, too.

At that thought, she dropped the cloth in the basin and scurried out the door to gather the dirty dishes. Until Mrs. Bingham finished carrying in their laundry, she was solely responsible for the cleanup. She wouldn't earn her pork chop dinner by dawdling.

The supper hour flew by. Even with Mrs. Bingham's help for the last half, after being on her feet in the restaurant in the morning and behind the counter at Mr. Cleveland's store all afternoon, Abigail was ready to sit by the time the last few diners straggled out the door.

"Let's get these tables cleared and the dishes washed," Mrs. Bingham said, "and then —"

"Them dishes can wait." Mr. Patterson scuffed toward them carrying two plates containing pork chops still sizzling from their time in the pan and a mound of beautifully browned carrot coins. "Set yourselves down an' eat while this is hot. Nothin' worse'n cold pork chops, to my way o' thinkin'."

Abigail licked her lips. "Oh, even cold, these would be wonderful, Mr. Patterson." She'd eat the pork chops cold before she'd eat the roasted beef tongue hot.

He grinned, set the plates on a table, and returned to the kitchen.

Mrs. Bingham sat and Abigail joined her. Mrs. Bingham bowed her head and offered a brief prayer. At her "amen," she picked up her fork and knife and cut into the pork chop.

Abigail speared a carrot coin and carried it to her mouth. The sweetness melted on her tongue and she released a murmur of pleasure.

Mrs. Bingham smiled. "He's a very good cook, isn't he? I wonder if he will ever choose to relinquish those duties to someone else. Even to his wife."

"He says no." Abigail took two more bites, forgoing placing her fork on the table in between.

"Well, then, I shall have Marietta review the applicants for the Spiveyville grooms." Mrs. Bingham cut into her pork chop. "Every now and then, one of the prospective brides indicates a lack of enthusiasm toward cooking. I don't quite recall, but it seems as though Delphine Peabody wasn't keen on kitchen duties because she'd spent half her childhood serving as a cook's helper. Perhaps she would be a good match for Athol."

Abigail nearly swallowed her tongue. Had Mrs. Bingham just referred to the restaurant owner by his first name?

"But we will have to wait and see. Just as we won't know if Jemima Willoughby will take a shine to Norm. Remember Norm, from the Rocking E? His and Jemima's mutual love for animals leads me to suspect they would be compatible, but —"

Abigail dropped her fork. "Mrs. Bingham, forgive me for interrupting, but why are you referring to the gentlemen by their first names?" She'd been betrothed to Linus Hartford and she hadn't called him by his given name except in those rare moments they were alone and no one would overhear.

"Isn't it a bit too, er, familiar?"

Mrs. Bingham shrugged. "*Familiar* is merely another word for *friendly*, don't you think? I need to be friendly with these men in order to get to know them better." She stabbed a carrot coin with her fork and held it up the way a schoolteacher held a pointer. "You might discover it's easier to connect with them during the classes if you call them by their given names."

Abigail drew back. "Oh, no, ma'am. I couldn't. It would feel much too unseemly."

Mrs. Bingham chewed a piece of carrot and swallowed, her face a study of contemplation. "Hmm, given your position as instructor, you might be right. Especially considering some will be in the company of their wives. So a more formal bearing is appropriate there." Then she brightened. "But let's discuss the men who aren't taking the classes. Would it hurt, or be too unseemly, for you to relax and allow yourself to be friendly with those who don't intend to sit beneath your tutelage?"

Abigail searched her memory, but she extracted only one man. Mack Cleveland. Heat flooded her face. "I . . . I don't know if I could. I . . . I . . ."

Mrs. Bingham reached across the table and took Abigail's hand. "My dear, I think you could. Even more than that, I think you should. You might find it quite freeing to bend your stiff rules in this one instance." She withdrew her hand and picked up her fork and knife again. "I am quite certain Mr. Mack Cleveland would not be offended nor find you improper. Considering his kindness toward you, using his given name even seems an appropriate response."

Abigail lowered her gaze to her plate, but in her mind's eye she saw Mr. Cleveland's smile when he questioned what she'd found amusing. An inviting smile rather than condescending. So different than the expressions her former fiancé sometimes turned in her direction when she'd said something of which he disapproved or found uninteresting.

"Abigail?"

She pulled herself from her reverie and looked at the matchmaker. "Yes, ma'am?"

"We still have tables to clean and dishes to wash. We should finish our dinner and see to our responsibilities."

"Yes, ma'am." She cut into the pork chop. As she lifted the bite to her mouth, she allowed herself to think the simple name *Mack. Mack.* She gave a start. "Mrs. Bingham, do you think Mack is really Mr. Cleveland's given name? Generally Mack is

279

the shortened version of a formal name, such as Mackenzie or Macauley."

An odd, teasing smile appeared in the woman's eyes, but her mouth remained in a serious line. "Perhaps, Abigail, that is a question you should ask the man yourself."

Tomorrow afternoon Abigail would return to the hardware store so Mr. Cleveland could help one of the ranchers with repairs on his barn. Maybe, if she was able to gather her courage and if Mother's admonitions didn't prove too difficult to overcome, she would bend the rule about avoiding inquisitiveness and ask.

Mack

Tuesday morning Mack awakened early, before the sun had so much as peeked over the horizon. The room was dark as pitch, but he rolled out of his cot anyway and felt his way to the table where his oil lamp waited. Familiar with his surroundings and the process, he lifted the globe, struck a lucifer against the underside of the table, and touched the flame to the lamp's wick. A warm glow filled the room.

He settled the globe in place and crossed to the single window in his one-room apartment. A half moon hung high and bright in the dark cloudless sky, surrounded by stars that reminded him of the freckles scattered across Miss Grant's cheeks. Funny how the sun had left its mark behind in those pale-brown dots. The freckles, coupled with her petite frame, made her seem years younger than her true age, which Mrs. Bingham had divulged was twenty-five.

He frowned, drawing circles where his warm breath had fogged the windowpane. If the article Tobis showed Sheriff Thorn was five years old, that meant she was twenty when her father went to prison. Twenty . . . the same age he'd been when Wilhelmina Wilkes bilked his family's church out of its benevolence fund. Only a year younger than he was when he made the trek to Kansas with Uncle Ray. A tender age. What Ma would call a blooming age. Mack had bloomed here in Spiveyville, thanks to the community's open acceptance. But Miss Grant hadn't been given the chance to bloom. She'd been forced to wither instead.

Wither . . . into bitterness.

He swallowed the bitter taste that filled his mouth. He must still be half-asleep to let his thoughts get so morose. He busied himself making his bed — not as neatly as Ma would have done it, but he couldn't bring himself to leave the covers all rumpled. He dressed in his usual tan trousers and blue plaid button-up shirt. After tugging on his boots over thick gray socks knitted by Ma and mailed to him last Christmas, he made a dash to the outhouse. The temperature had dropped even more during the night, and he created little clouds with his huffing breaths on the trips to and from the little wooden structure.

Back inside his warm apartment, he stood at his tin washbasin and used his toothbrush and powder to clean his teeth. A lot of the men in town didn't bother with the toothbrushing, but he'd seen too many of them with gaps in their mouths where teeth used to be to ignore the childhood habit Ma instilled in him. The sweet taste of the powder rid him of the unpleasant flavor from his long-ago memories.

Fully dressed and with his morning chores complete, he was ready for breakfast. But according to the windup clock on his bedside table, Athol wouldn't open his door for another half hour. So he plopped down at his little table with the most precious book he owned — Ma's Bible.

He riffled the worn, gold-stamped page edges with his thumb, hooked a spot, and let the Bible fall open. An underlined passage caught his attention, and he leaned in and began reading aloud. " 'Though I speak with the tongues of men and of angels, and have not charity, I am become as sounding brass, or a tinkling cymbal . . .' " He continued reading, his low voice welcome in the otherwise quiet room. He read the entire chapter of 1 Corinthians 13, and when he reached the end, he followed the words with his fingertip. " 'And now abideth faith, hope, charity, these three; but the greatest of these is charity.' "

Mack could hear his mother's voice in his head, reading these same words to him before tucking him in at night. He remembered Pa standing behind her, listening while she read, nodding at times. When Ma finished, Pa always sat on the edge of Mack's bed and prayed with him. Pa didn't speak with the eloquence of the Bible, the way Ma could thanks to the schooling she'd received, but he always sounded confident — like he knew without a doubt God was close and listening. The same warmth that carried Mack into dreamland as a boy filled him now in the remembrance. Good memories . . .

But what kind of memories did Miss Grant carry? Before her pa's arrest and conviction, had her childhood been warm and loving? Had someone prayed with her before tucking her in at night? She'd been taught manners — that much he knew — but had she been taught to love Jesus?

Once more, the Scripture Mrs. Bingham had mentioned whispered through his heart. *"Thou shalt love thy neighbour as thyself."* Words spoken by Jesus Himself. Mack had come close to discarding the whole idea yesterday evening. Miss Grant held him at a distance the way he'd avoid someone who'd been sprayed by a skunk. But maybe God woke him up early and let the Bible open to verses about love for a reason.

He wouldn't give up. He'd be Miss Grant's friend. Because she — like every other person ever born — needed faith, hope, and charity. Maybe she needed it even more than most, caught in the shadow of her father's sins.

TWENTY-ONE

Bill

Bill stood back and admired the lay of crisp new shingles on Jerome Reed's barn. Here it was, only Wednesday afternoon, and the wind-caused damage was set to right. Not only at Jerome's place, but at every ranch and house in Spiveyville. By splitting up and scattering across the area, the townsmen had finished Bill's whole list in half the time he expected.

In the patch of sunshine beside the barn, men whooped, tossed their hats in the air, and pounded each other's backs, as lively as spring calves playing in green grass. If Bill wasn't wearing a tin star on his chest, he'd join them, but a sheriff shouldn't be undignified. He couldn't help grinning at the raucous lot, though.

Jerome trotted over and tilted back his hat to better view the roof. "Looks fine, Sheriff.

Mighty fine. Better'n it did before the wind hit, I'd reckon."

Bill wouldn't say anything, because he wasn't the rancher's pa or his boss, but Jerome tended to be a little lazy about upkeep. His barn likely wouldn't have lost so many shingles if the first ones had been applied the correct way. "Yep. An' now that I've crossed your barn off the list, we're all done with fixin' jobs."

Jerome's tanned face lit like a firecracker. "That mean we can get started on them classes the city lady is makin' us take?"

Bill scratched his cheek. "Well, I —"

Jerome whirled to face the group of men who'd started gathering up their tools. He waved both arms over his head. "Fellas! Fellas! Ever'thing's done! We can get them classes goin' now!"

Bill grabbed Jerome's arm. "Now, I didn't say —"

The men swarmed him, all clamoring. "Whoopee! Gonna get our brides! Let's git to town an' tell the ol' city gal we're ready!"

Bill pawed the air, the way Preacher Doan did when he wanted the congregation to listen, but nobody paid him a lick of attention. They took off for their horses and wagons, still prattling, still smiling, still poking their fists in the air and jumping up to

286

bounce their heels together. Worse than schoolboys on the first day of summer vacation. He wouldn't be able to do anything with them now.

With a harrumph, Bill yanked his hat low and quickstepped it to his horse. He'd better beat them all back to town and give Mrs. Bingham a word of warning. She'd likely run for the hills if the whole squabbling crowd swooped in on her at once. Good thing his Patch had good wind and strong legs.

By giving Patch the freedom to gallop, Bill made it to Spiveyville ahead of the men. He slid to the ground, looped the horse's reins over the restaurant's porch rail, and burst through the door. Six or seven fellows — those who'd worked somewhere other than Jerome's Double Diamond Ranch — were sitting at tables enjoying bowls of beans 'n' bacon and corn bread. They all looked up, and two of them rose out of their chairs when he turned the lock on Athol's door. He didn't mean to scare anybody, but he wanted to keep that eager throng out long enough for him to talk to Mrs. Bingham.

He balled his hands on his hips. "Where's the ladies?"

Louis Griffin pointed to the kitchen.

Bill stomped in that direction. A few of

the fellas called out questions, but he kept going and pretended he didn't hear. Mrs. Bingham was at Athol's washbasin, up to her elbows in cloudy-looking water that smelled so strong of lye it stung his eyes from ten paces away. He wrinkled his nose and stepped close.

"Ma'am, in another few minutes, there's gonna be a gang o' men poundin' through the door, expectin' you to be able to start teachin' them classes tomorrow instead o' waitin' 'til Monday."

She straightened and met his gaze. "To-morrow?" She didn't look too rattled or even surprised.

"Yes'm. 'Cause they've finished up all the fixin'."

"My goodness, they must be fast work-ers."

The lye smell was about to choke him. He covered his mouth and nose with his shirt collar. "Yes'm, they are. So —"

Bang-bang-bang!

Bill cringed. That'd be fists on the front door. "What do you want me to tell 'em?" More banging — louder and more insistent — came.

Louis Griffin stuck his head into the kitchen. "Sheriff, these men're wantin' in bad. Can I unlock the door?"

288

Athol turned from the stove and shot a frown at Bill. "Why'd you lock 'em out? They better not be tearin' my door down."

"I'll see to 'em." Bill inched backward in the direction of the door, still waiting for Mrs. Bingham's answer.

"If you want us to start the classes tomorrow evening, Sheriff, then that's what we'll do."

He blew out a mighty sigh and grinned. "You're an accommodatin' woman, Miz Bingham. Thank you." He trotted to the door, scowling at the impatient men with their faces pressed to the restaurant windows, and twisted the lock. He threw the door open and flung his arm in a gesture of welcome. "Git in out o' the cold, fellas, an' set yourselves up to a table. Eat hearty. An' those've you who signed up for Thursday classes . . . you'd best plan on bein' at the church tomorrow at six thirty."

A cheer rose that could've sent Athol's roof into the heavens if it weren't firmly secured. Yes, indeed, that Miz Bingham was an accommodating lady.

Abigail

Abigail climbed the cellar steps, balancing a large crockery bowl of pickled cucumbers against her ribs. She hated to leave the pleasant space. Cool but not cold, quiet, and — just as Mr. Cleveland had indicated — full of wondrous smells. As she entered the kitchen, cheers, laughter, boots thumping, and chair legs screeching assaulted her ears. She paused in the cellar doorway, nervous but uncertain why.

"Bring me them pickles." Mr. Patterson quirked his fingers at her in an impatient gesture.

She hurried across the floor and set the bowl on the worktable. She peered in the direction of the dining room. "What's going on in there? Is it someone's birthday?"

He shook his head, pinching pickles from the bowl and placing one on each of the waiting plates. "No. Miz Bingham's got the men all excited." He was trying to be grumpy. He held his lips in a firm downturn and crinkled his brow, but his eyes were shining. "She says we can start the classes tomorrow since all the work's done around town."

Abigail's pulse gave a leap. "Tomorrow?"

He nodded and finally broke into a smile. "If I didn't have a heap o' cookin' to do yet, I'd be out there doin' do-si-dos with the others. Sure am glad we can get these classes done an' bring our brides to town."

He stuck out his arm, lined plates along its reach, and headed for the dining room. More cheers erupted at his arrival.

Abigail crept to the doorway and peeked out. The men had pushed two tables to the corner and were using the empty space to clomp in circles in a clumsy dance. They waved their hats and hooted. She clutched her throat. Such childish behavior! Had they no sense of decorum at all? Where was Mrs. Bingham? She scanned the room, but the matchmaker was nowhere in sight.

She ducked back around the corner and pressed herself flat to the wall. Tomorrow . . . Tomorrow she would begin teaching these raucous, lively men. She had the lessons on commonsense etiquette prepared, but their unrestrained frivolity made her wonder if any of them would listen or respond to anything she said.

Mr. Patterson burst back into the room. "Miss Grant?"

"Yes?"

He jumped. He turned around and scowled at her. "What're you doin' there, hidin' like a sneak?"

"I . . . I was merely —"

He shook his head. "Never mind. Sheriff Thorn's walkin' Miz Bingham over to Preacher Doan's to let him know about the classes startin' up tomorrow. She said to tell you to go up to your room an' study. She'll take care o' the cleanin' chores by her own self when she gets back."

Abigail peeked into the dining room. Any man who wasn't eating was cavorting as if he'd had access to a barrel of malt beverage. How would she find the courage to walk past the boisterous bunch to the stairs? She'd rather stay in the kitchen and wash dishes until they all went home.

"You goin' or what?"

"I . . ."

"Miz Bingham said —"

"Yes, yes, Athol, I heard you." She gasped and clapped her hand over her mouth. How could she have called him by his given name? These men's improper ways were seeping into her being. She jerked her hand downward. "I'm going."

With her shoulders back and head high, she forced her feet to carry her out of the kitchen and around the corner. She eased along the wall toward the front of the restaurant, as far as possible from the dancing men. The long bar provided a welcome barrier between her and the diners. Once behind it, she considered crouching low and waiting until everyone left, but fear of discovery compelled her to dart to the opposite end.

As she stepped clear of the bar, the dancers stopped their stomping and formed a circle. They linked elbows, swayed from side to side, and broke into a rowdy song about buffalo gals dancing by the light of the moon. She had no idea what a buffalo gal was, but she feared it described the kind of women who'd once lived in the upstairs rooms. Her face flamed at the thought.

Some of the diners clapped, others sang, and still others bobbed their heads and smiled. None seemed to take notice of her, however, and she continued her trek for the stairs. She'd made it halfway across the front wall when her familiar nemesis, W. C. Miller, latched gazes with her. With a broad grin, he broke loose from the swaying circle and wove between tables, still singing, and made a beeline for her. She sped her steps, and he did, too, but by lifting the hem of her skirt and running — how she hoped Mother wasn't peering through one of heaven's portals to witness her unladylike display — she made it to the stairs before he reached her.

His laughter carried around the corner. Although W. C. called for her to come back and join the fun, she clattered up the stairs, the patter of her feet echoing against the plaster walls in beat with the thrum of her pulse in her temples. She reached the top and dashed the distance to her room. At her door, she glanced up the hallway and nearly collapsed in relief to find it empty. Laughter rang from the lower level, but apparently none of the men had followed her. She fell through the doorway and locked the door behind her.

Now that she was safe, her limbs went as limp as noodles. She staggered to the bed and sank onto its edge. Tomorrow she would have to face some of that uncivilized crowd again. To teach them manners. Manners they sorely needed. W. C. hadn't molested her, but his deliberate pursuit had frightened her, which was disrespectful at best and debauched at worst. These men must be made to understand that ladies were to be treated like ladies and not like "buffalo gals."

Her pulse finally calmed. She believed her legs would support her again, so she rose, crossed to her washbowl, and splashed tepid water on her face. Cold water would have been better, but the moisture revived her somewhat. She patted her skin dry with the length of rough toweling Mr. Patterson had provided, then laid it aside. Her gaze drifted to the dresser, to the stack of charts she and

Mrs. Doan had constructed. Which of the men who'd behaved so callously this evening would be in tomorrow's class?

She hurried to the dresser and pulled the Thursday chart from the stack. She held it up and read down the list.

Mr. and Mrs. Tobis Adelman
Otto Hildreth

She groaned. Mr. Adelman and Mr. Hildreth in the same class? How would she face both of them at the same time? Images of their faces — one superior and condemning, the other fierce and threatening — filled her memory. Her hands began to shake, rattling the page. She read the rest of the names.

Firmin Chapman
Mr. and Mrs. Saul Sandburg
Vern O'Dell
Mack Cleveland

She gave a little jolt. Mr. Cleveland intended to take the classes? But hadn't he said he wasn't interested in securing a bride? Then fondness rolled through her as sweetly as Mr. Patterson's white sauce flowed over waffles. Mr. Cleveland . . . her protector. With him in the group, she needn't fear Mr. Adelman or Mr. Hildreth or Mr. O'Dell or any of the others.

She hugged the list to her beating heart

and whispered, "Thank goodness for Mr. Cleveland." The utterance wasn't a prayer. Not quite. But almost.

TWENTY-TWO

Mack

"Hey, Mack, what're you doin' here?"

Mack closed the church door and removed his hat. He hung it on a peg, lobbing a grin at Firmin Chapman, who lounged on the back bench, which was shoved against the wall — the only place a person could lean back and relax. Did the rancher intend to sleep through Miss Grant's class the way he sometimes slept through Sunday services?

Mack pushed his open jacket flaps aside and hooked his fingers in his trouser pockets, offering Firmin a half shrug. "Same as you, I reckon."

Firmin's green eyes widened. "Takin' the class? But you don't hafta. You didn't order a bride."

"I know."

Firmin chuckled and patted the spot next

to him. "All right, then. Why don'tcha join me?"

Mack would sit in the front, where he could keep an eye on Miss Grant, the way Sheriff Thorn had asked. "Thanks, Firmin, but I'll hear better from up front."

Firmin snorted softly, but Mack chose to ignore him. He ambled up the center aisle to the front benches. Tobis and Ethel Adelman sat next to the aisle on the left, with Otto Hildreth on their far side. They didn't seem inclined to move, so he plopped onto the end of the right-hand bench next to Saul Sandburg and his wife, Amelia. The couple wore their Sunday best, the same way he had, and it pleased Mack. He greeted both of them with a smile and gave Saul a firm handshake.

Sandburg tugged at his collar and worked his lips back and forth as if he had food stuck in a tooth, the picture of a man who wanted to be somewhere else. But Mrs. Sandburg sat snug against her husband's side, her hands curled around his forearm, with a content smile lighting her face. Why had the Sandburgs come? They had to be in their midforties already, married for more than twenty years, with four children at home. What could Miss Grant teach them about marriage that they didn't already know?

He glanced across the aisle to the Adelmans. They'd gotten married three or four years ago. If he remembered right, Mrs. Adelman was the daughter of a friend of a second cousin to Tobis's mother. Tobis had bragged up and down the streets about the city girl he'd hooked, as if he'd won some sort of contest instead of being lucky enough to have folks arrange a bride for him. Mack couldn't honestly say he'd ever seen Ethel Adelman smile in Tobis's presence. Those two could probably use some tips from Miss Grant on improving their marriage. But where was Miss Grant?

Mack glanced at the pendulum clock *tick-tick*ing on the wall. Six twenty-five. Shouldn't she be here by now? Somebody'd come and readied the church for the class. The sanctuary was well lit, all twelve lanterns glowing from their spots on the painted walls, and the space was warm with the potbelly stove blazing from the back corner. Nearly everyone who'd signed up for Thursday was here, so they hadn't gotten confused about having a class tonight. All they needed was the teacher.

He cleared his throat, and people on both sides of him jumped. He smoothed his mustache, hiding his smile. "I wonder what's keeping Miss Grant."

Firmin laughed, the sound echoing from the rafters. "She's prob'ly still wore out from last night's dancin'."

Tobis Adelman turned sideways on the bench. "Where was there some dancin'?"

"At Athol's. A bunch of us had a real good time last night."

The hair on the back of Mack's neck stood up. Before he could question Firmin, the church door opened. A cold breeze whisked up the aisle and made the lanterns flicker. Miss Grant, Mrs. Bingham, and Sheriff Thorn came in. The sheriff pushed the door closed behind them, and Mrs. Bingham placed a thick brown folder on a bench. While the women removed their wraps, Sheriff Thorn bounced a serious look across everyone seated.

"S'posed to be eight folks here tonight. Who're we missin'?"

"Dunno," Firmin said.

Mrs. Bingham picked up the folder and opened it. She began calling names, the way a teacher took roll, and like obedient schoolchildren, they raised their hands when their names were called. "Vern O'Dell?"

Firmin poked a plug of chew in his lip. "Vern ain't here."

The sheriff frowned. "Firmin, take that outta your mouth. This ain't a barn, it's a church." Firmin grumbled but obeyed. Sheriff Thorn bobbed his head at Miss Grant. "You go ahead an' get started. I saw Vern lollygaggin' outside Kettering's place. I'll fetch him for you." He stomped outside, letting in another whoosh of cold air.

Mrs. Bingham seated herself at the rear of the chapel across the aisle from Firmin, and Miss Grant scurried to the front as if propelled by the breeze. She stepped up on the dais with a little hop, placed the folder on the podium, and then turned a tight smile on the group. "Good evening."

"Good evening," they all echoed, except for Tobis, who'd folded his arms over his chest and glared at the ceiling. His wife bumped him. He grunted and growled out, "Evenin'."

Miss Grant opened the folder, and from Mack's spot, he got a good view of the dark-brown leather. He'd never been a big fan of brown. The color of dirt. But Miss Grant wore a brown dress, a shade darker than her hair and a shade lighter than her eyes. Suddenly brown didn't seem so plain anymore.

"This evening's focus will be on commonsense etiquette, which is essentially manners." She stepped beside the podium, linked her hands against her skirt, and lifted her chin. She'd probably stood that way to recite poems when she was a little girl. "It has been said that manners make the man. Manners are more than a list of rules. They are behaviors that help define a person's character. Guarding one's conduct is a way of showing respect, and respectfulness is always in fashion. Let's begin by discussing the various ways a gentleman shows his intended that he respects and values her."

She moved behind the podium again and placed her finger on the top page. "A gentleman will never reach for a lady's hand but will wait for her to offer it. A gentleman always tips his hat to a lady in passing. A gentleman always opens doors for —"

The church door banged open. Sheriff Thorn came in, escorting Vern by the collar of his jacket. "Brung your last pupil, Miss Grant." He gave Vern a little push.

The wiry, red-haired rancher stumbled forward several feet, then turned and glared at the sheriff. "I could o' got here on my own."

"Just makin' sure." Sheriff Thorn touched the brim of his hat, nodded at the ladies, and strode out. The slam of the door rattled the building.

Vern stayed in the middle of the aisle, his face as red as his hair.

Miss Grant cleared her throat. "Please have a seat, Mr. O'Dell, and I shall review what you missed."

He took one sideways step and plopped down.

Everyone shifted their focus to Miss Grant again.

She repeated all she'd said before, checked her notes, and drew a breath. "A gentleman always opens doors for a lady. A gentleman assists a lady from a carriage by taking her hands, not her waist." Pink tinged her cheeks. She kept her head low. "A gentleman offers his arm when he and a lady go for a stroll. A gen—"

"What's a stroll?" Firmin lobbed the question with the same force that a cowboy flung a lasso.

Mack started to tell him to hush, but Miss Grant spoke first.

"A stroll is a leisurely walk. You might stroll up the street or through a park. The purpose of strolling is to enjoy one another's company."

Firmin laughed. "You can cross that'un off your list. We don't got a park."

Abigail frowned. "Don't have a park."

"I know. An' if I come to town, it's to shop

303

at Mack's or the mercantile or get me somethin' to eat at Athol's restaurant. I got a ranch to run. I don't have time to stroll."

Vern and Tobis murmured their agreement.

Miss Grant's cheeks splotched pink. "When your work is done for the day, and the sky is beginning to fade from blue to pink, your wife may very well wish to enjoy a stroll around your ranch grounds with you. As a gentleman, you should offer her your arm. Please remember it."

Firmin snickered, but he hushed when Mack shot him a glare.

Mrs. Bingham got up and moved closer to Firmin, who scooted an equal distance away. Mack growled under his breath. Maybe he should have sat by Firmin after all. The rancher leaned against the wall, propped his ankle on his opposite knee, and grinned at Miss Grant.

"Go ahead, ma'am. I'm listenin'."

Miss Grant, still pink cheeked, glanced at her paper again. She swallowed, lifted her gaze, and seemed to focus on the window above the church doors. "A gentleman never interrupts a lady when she is speaking."

Mack covered his mouth with his finger to hold back a chuckle. That advice was well timed.

"A gentleman does not resort to fisticuffs to settle a disagreement. He does not brag. He chews with his mouth closed. He habitually uses *please* when making a request and *thank you* when the request has been met."

The list went on for quite a while, and though some of the rules seemed a little picky, Mack agreed with a lot of what she said. Some manners — such as *"A gentleman controls his temper"* — came straight from God's Word. He hoped Firmin was awake in the back row. Miss Grant was almost preaching a sermon.

After a half hour of listening, some people started fidgeting, the same way they did midway through Preacher Doan's sermons. Miss Grant must have noticed, because she paused, bit down on her lower lip, and sent a slow look across the audience.

"This seems a good place to stop and practice a bit of what I've presented." She gestured to a little table and two chairs tucked at the corner of the dais. "Who would like to demonstrate the proper way to escort and seat a lady at the dinner table?"

Mrs. Sandburg looked hopefully at Saul, but he pinched his lips and sat as stiff and still as a stone. Mrs. Adelman looked aside instead of at her husband. Vern shifted his feet against the floor, a sound like sandpaper on a board. Otto seemed to be trying to drill a hole through Miss Grant's middle with his steely glare. Mack decided not to look at Firmin. He was probably asleep.

Miss Grant stood next to the podium with her fingers clasped. She seemed lonely. Helpless. Forlorn. The way he'd felt eleven years ago when people turned their noses up at his family.

Sympathy propelled him from the bench. "I would."

Abigail

Abigail's heart fluttered. She'd expected Mr. and Mrs. Sandburg to volunteer. Although Mr. Sandburg hadn't smiled once, he'd kept his gaze aimed on her and appeared as attentive as his wife. Mr. Cleveland's offer touched her deeply but also made her very nervous.

Her lips trembled, making it difficult to smile. "Thank you, Mr. Cleveland."

Mr. Chapman chortled. She risked a glance and discovered him smirking. Her nervousness increased. She aimed a pleading look at Mrs. Bingham. "Ma'am, would you like to . . ."

Mrs. Bingham rose, but she shook her

306

head. "No, thank you, Miss Grant. You go ahead and demonstrate with Mr. Cleveland. When you're finished, perhaps Firmin and I will attempt to emulate you." With a determined stride, she crossed to Mr. Chapman and sat next to him. "Pay attention, now, Firmin."

The rancher coughed into his hand, but he sat up and turned his scowl to the front of the church.

Mr. Cleveland stood beside his bench, fingertips in his pockets, shoulders high. A boyish, embarrassed pose. He'd volunteered, but he seemed riddled with apprehension. She should put him at ease. And she would, as soon as she convinced her stomach to stop jumping.

She forced a little laugh and stepped down from the dais. "Perhaps, before we go to the table, I might prevail upon you to demonstrate the art of strolling?" A walk around the church circumference might settle both of their nerves.

A relieved smile broke across his face. "That's fine, Miss Grant." He yanked his right hand from his pocket and extended his elbow.

Swallowing an anxiety-induced giggle, she slipped her hand into the bend of his arm. She involuntarily jolted. She'd held Linus

Hartford's arm dozens of times, but Linus's forearm had not prepared her for the feel of Mr. Cleveland's firm arm. Tendons stood out like rope, his flesh taut beneath her fingers even through layers of fabric. She battled another giggle and cleared her throat to control it. She braved a glance at his face. "Mr. Cleveland, a gentleman always leads."

TWENTY-THREE

Abigail

Mr. Cleveland nodded and guided her toward the dais. At the front of the church, he angled her to the right and they moved to the north wall. She deliberately didn't look at their audience, but she sensed them following their progress, the way everyone had watched her and Linus glide around the dance floor during her betrothal party. Her stomach whirled, much the way it had when he'd spun her in a promenade. She squashed all thoughts of Linus.

Mr. Cleveland turned right again and led her along the entire length of the wall. He kept a leisurely pace, tempering his stride to match her shorter one. As they moved beneath the lanterns, light fell on his dark hair. The oil he'd used to tame the thick strands into place shone like flashes of silver. Would moonlight bring out that same shimmer?

At the back of the church, he turned and moved toward the center aisle. She anticipated taking the aisle to the front and prepared herself for another turn, but he passed the aisle and went instead to the south wall. They strolled past Mr. Chapman and Mrs. Bingham, and to her surprise, Mr. Chapman seemed to study them with real interest. His change in attitude encouraged her, and she couldn't resist giving Mr. Cleveland a genuine smile. Her chest went fluttery again when he returned it with one of his own.

When they reached the front of the church, she experienced a touch of disappointment that the stroll had to end. But the feeling whisked away when he took her hand and assisted her onto the dais. He stepped up beside her and placed his hand gently on her lower spine.

"Are you ready for dinner, Miss Grant?" His tone held a hint of teasing, but his fervent blue eyes held something completely alien to amusement.

She gulped. A jumble of strange emotions vied for prominence. Why hadn't Mrs. Bingham offered to participate in this playacting that was beginning to seem far too real?

"Miss Grant?"

She gave a little jolt. Her students were watching. She had to continue. "Yes. Yes, I'm ready."

His broad, warm palm — firm, possessive, welcome — guided her to the table. He pulled out a chair, and she squelched another giggle as she slid into the seat. He rounded the table and sat across from her. She hadn't requested tableware because she intended to dedicate an entire class to table manners next week, so there was little they could do except gaze at each other. If they began such an activity, she might not have enough wits to continue the class.

She turned sideways in her chair and faced the audience. "Mr. Cleveland has done a fine job of demonstrating how to stroll, how to assist a lady from one level to another, and how to seat a lady at a table. Let's applaud him for his attention this evening." She patted her palms together more enthusiastically than the observers, but the firm contact chased away the strange web that had wrapped itself around her. She stood.

"Since Mr. Cleveland has brought me to the table, perhaps I will take this opportunity to share a few dining manners before we have the next couple practice." She hurried to the podium and retrieved her notes about dining protocol. "I shall begin with the art of mastication."

Every man in the room, with the exception of Mr. Cleveland, burst into laughter.

Abigail banged her fist on the podium. "Quiet. Quiet yourselves, now."

"She said to hush up."

At Mr. Cleveland's roar, the clamor ceased, leaving a deathly silence in its stead. Torn between gratitude and humiliation, Abigail offered him a tight smile and then turned a stern look on the audience.

"Perhaps you find humor in the subject of proper chewing, but I can assure you, if you will master it, the lady with whom you find yourself dining will greatly appreciate your efforts."

"I should say so." Mrs. Adelman voiced the firm statement, and her husband squirmed in his seat. She nodded at Abigail. "Go ahead, Miss Grant. Tell him how it should be done." She poked Mr. Adelman's shoulder with her finger. "And you listen, Tobis."

The man's face blazed, but he looked in Abigail's direction.

Abigail maintained an even, firm tone as she compared gobbling, chomping, and smacking to a herd of swine feeding at a trough. She then outlined gentlemanly manners, including draping one's napkin over the knees rather than tucking it into the collar of one's shirt, never using a piece of bread as a sponge to absorb grease or gravy — oh, how they needed that piece of instruction — and keeping one's elbows tucked close instead of splayed widely as if guarding one's plate. She concluded with, "A knife or fork is not a spear to be gripped in one's fist. Handle these pieces of cutlery the way you would wield a fountain pen and you are much less likely to push food over the edge of the plate onto the table or into your lap."

A few of her listeners appeared to fight off grins, but she finished the presentation without interruption.

She dared a glance at the wall clock. The hands showed forty-five minutes past seven. The class was scheduled to end at eight thirty. She should allow the others to practice before they ran out of time. Stepping to the edge of the dais, she flicked her fingers. "Will you all stand?"

The women rose with eagerness, but the men showed their reluctance by slowly unfolding from their seats.

"Please pair off. Of course, Mr. and Mrs. Adelman and Mr. and Mrs. Sandburg will want to stay together." The expression on

Mrs. Adelman's face refuted Abigail's statement, but there was little Abigail could do for the unhappy woman. "Mrs. Bingham, you partner with —" She paused. Both Mr. O'Dell and Mr. Chapman had exhibited mild scorn toward her, but Mr. Hildreth's icy glare made her stomach tremble. She didn't want to take his arm.

"— Mr. Hildreth, please. Mr. O'Dell and Mr. Chapman, if you will exhibit patience, another gentlemanly virtue, I will take turns partnering with each of you."

Mr. Chapman snickered. "That sure beats what we have to do at barn dances, huh, Vern?"

Mr. O'Dell nodded, smirking. "Seems like you had to wear the apron at the last dance an' be the gal, didn't ya, Firmin?"

"Which would make it your turn tonight."

Mr. O'Dell aimed his smirk at Abigail. "Didja bring any aprons with ya, Miss Grant?"

Completely confused, she shook her head.

The man shrugged. "Then we'll take turns strollin' you around the room." His shoulders shook in silent laughter.

Mr. Cleveland took two wide strides that brought him to Abigail's side. "I'll watch to be sure you treat Miss Grant like a lady, the way a gentleman should."

Mr. O'Dell held up both hands as if under arrest. "Easy, Mack, I was just funnin'. I admit, I ain't keen on havin' to do these classes — seems kind o' silly to my way o' thinkin' — but I'm wantin' my wife, so I intend to earn my passin' grade." He stuck out his elbow. "C'mon, Miss Grant, let's you an' me stroll, an' then I'll set you loose on ol' Firmin over there."

By the last evening of the commonsense etiquette classes, Abigail knew an exhaustion beyond anything she'd discovered before. Not a physical exhaustion, but one that went deeper, into the core of her soul. Preacher Doan and Medora had come to the Friday class, and afterward Abigail had confessed to Medora a new appreciation for teachers. "I will be giving the same lesson again and again, but you teach several subjects at several different levels every day. How do you do it?"

Medora had patted her hand. "It's all a matter of getting used to it. Practice breeds confidence, they say, and I've found it's true. John and I are praying for you, Abigail. The Lord will carry you through to the end."

Abigail clung to Medora's encouragement and promise of prayer while resting over the weekend. On Saturday, more than a dozen new couples from young to old came to the restaurant and asked to be added to a class list. Abigail considered their interest a compliment. After all, people must have talked about the classes in a positive way for others to want to join. But the number of attendees for the Monday, Tuesday, and Wednesday classes grew until by the fifth presentation, a total of twenty-five people crowded together on the church benches. To her surprise, Mr. Cleveland was among the number.

The fifth presentation went much more smoothly than the first even though triple the people attended. She credited it in part to having memorized the material, allowing her to maintain eye contact with her audience the entire time. But she believed the greater reason was the number of women in the audience. The presence of females had a positive effect on the single men. The women were still outnumbered, of course, but none of the prospective grooms — not even one of the Fletcher brothers, who had been part of the rowdy circle of revelers in the restaurant — made snide comments or huffed or argued. Instead, they listened. Respectfully. Even, it seemed to Abigail, intently.

As had happened the first night, when time came to demonstrate, Mr. Cleveland volunteered. But unlike the first night, he didn't wait to see if anyone else would come forward. The moment she requested a volunteer, he bolted to his feet with his hand in the air, as eager as a child offering to taste a new batch of taffy. Several people tittered and one of the Fletcher brothers blasted a guffaw, but Mr. Cleveland strode to the front of the church with a smile and held out his hand.

He took her on the same stroll around the periphery of the sanctuary, and no nervous flutters attacked her this time. Medora Doan's comment that familiarity bred confidence proved true. Her level of comfort in his presence was surely due to their increased contact during the past six days. On two different occasions he'd joined her and Mrs. Bingham in the restaurant for the evening meal, both times exhibiting the manners she'd stressed in class. Sunday afternoon he'd spent nearly two hours at the restaurant, engaging her in a friendly game of checkers as well as conversation.

He informed her of common practices in the community — including some men donning aprons and assuming the female partner at barn dances so they could at least all participate — and entertained her with stories involving skunks building a den beneath his apartment or snakes sleeping on the top edge of screen doors and dropping on unsuspecting people who crossed the thresholds. Some of the stories had made her shudder, but they painted a vivid picture of small-town Kansas prairie life, and she'd found herself both intrigued and impressed by the men and women who'd chosen to make the plains their home.

She and Mr. Cleveland completed their stroll around the church, and she took his hand without a moment's pause at the edge of the dais. He escorted her to the table and seated her with the same ease as before, but when he stepped around the table, his fingers brushed a path across her shoulder blades, sending a shaft of reaction down her spine and to her fingertips. She found herself momentarily discombobulated. Had he touched her intentionally? Sitting in front of a group of watchful attendees, she couldn't ask. She couldn't even give him a questioning look lest she inspire their curiosity. But her pulse pounded and her mouth went cottony, making it difficult to start her spiel about table manners.

When Abigail finished sharing appropriate dining behavior, she invited everyone to break into pairs and practice what they'd learned. The nine married couples immediately latched arms and began moving to the outer edges of the sanctuary. The seven single men without a partner gathered near the dais, looking sheepishly at each other. She and Mrs. Bingham had developed the practice of taking turns partnering with the prospective grooms, but with so many of them this evening, they might not all get a chance to practice.

She offered the men an apologetic grimace. "Gentlemen, Mrs. Bingham and I will do our utmost to take a turn with each of you, but it might be necessary for two of you to partner up, with one taking the role of the lady."

Mrs. Harriet Thompson, the mercantile owner's wife, drew her husband to a halt in their progress around the benches. "Miss Grant, what if some of us" — she waved her hand and indicated the other wives — "took a turn with the fellows? We can practice with our husbands at home. Matter o' fact, they can stroll us all the way home."

Light laughter rolled and Abigail joined in, surprised at how easy she found it to do so. "That's a splendid idea, Mrs. Thompson, as long as you're all willing and your husbands don't mind sharing you."

A white-haired man with twinkling hazel eyes caught his equally white-haired wife by the shoulders and set her aside. "You can borrow my Judith. Jest don't bring her home past nine 'cause you'll hafta carry her. She's always asleep by eight forty-five."

Judith gave her husband's chest a light slap, but she laughed so merrily they all laughed with her.

"All right." Abigail arched her brows and placed her hands on her hips. "Gentlemen, please offer your elbows."

With one accord, they jabbed their elbows outward, some offering their left, others their right.

Abigail *tsk-tsk*ed. "Right elbows, please."

With some good-natured grins and teasing remarks, they all stuck out the correct elbow.

Judith and Harriet were the first to take hold, choosing Mr. Cleveland and one of the Fletcher brothers, respectively. Other wives moved away from their husbands until every unmarried man, even bashful Hugh Briggs, had a partner. Two couples remained linked, and those two led the group in a stroll around the church.

Abigail stayed on the dais and watched the parade. Mrs. Bingham, who wasn't needed with so many other women in the group, joined her. The matchmaker slipped her arm around Abigail's waist.

"Things are going well, Abigail."

Abigail's cheeks hurt from smiling, her flesh still tender from the scorching it had received, but she didn't attempt to squelch the smile. "Yes, ma'am. I'm so relieved."

"As am I, but I am not surprised." Her arm tightened slightly, an almost hug — something Abigail hadn't experienced since Mother died. "I knew you'd be able to bring decorum to the men."

Abigail basked in the woman's praise. She blinked rapidly to stave off tears of pleasure. "Thank you, ma'am."

"As a matter of fact" — the woman's tone turned musing — "you'd make a fine teacher."

Abigail tucked the comment away in the corner of her mind to contemplate later.

At eight thirty, Preacher Doan arrived, and everyone except Mr. Cleveland left with a flurry of farewells and women holding their husband's elbows. The preacher beamed a bright smile at Abigail. "That looks to be a happy bunch."

She hugged herself, reliving the successes of the evening. "Yes, sir. They all seemed to enjoy the class."

"That's good. Let me extinguish the

lanterns and see to the stove, and then I'll walk you ladies to the restaurant."

Mr. Cleveland stepped forward. "I'd be glad to escort the ladies, Preacher. I've gotta go that way anyway."

The minister seemed to notice Mr. Cleveland for the first time. "Why, Mack, I thought you were signed up for the Thursday class."

He shrugged. "I am. I'm here tonight for —"

Abigail held her breath, anticipating hearing her name.

"— Sheriff Thorn."

Preacher Doan frowned. "But the sheriff is signed up on Mondays and Wednesdays."

Mr. Cleveland nodded. "I know. He expected to come tonight, but he got called out to the Double Diamond. Something about a barbed-wire fence that got cut. He wasn't sure he'd make it back to town in time for the class, and he wanted somebody watching Miss Grant, so I said I'd do it."

Chills flowed through every inch of her body, as if her blood had turned to ice. The sheriff had assigned Mr. Cleveland the task of watching her? Was that why he'd joined her and Mrs. Bingham for dinner? Why he'd spent Sunday afternoon with her? He'd assured her no one would bother her, but she was more bothered by this news than she'd been by Otto Hildreth's dire warning or Tobis Adelman's foul statements. Because she held no fond affection for the tailor or the banker.

She took a shaky step toward the door. "Mr. Cleveland, I'd rather walk to the restaurant with Preacher Doan."

Mr. Cleveland's eyebrows rose. "Is there something you need to discuss with him?"

"No." She hugged herself again, a feeble attempt to hold herself together.

"Oh. Well, then . . ." He took his hat from a peg and settled it on his head, his movements slow and his puzzled gaze locked on her. "I'll see you tomorrow evening in the restaurant for the dining class."

He needn't look at her as if she'd done something wrong. She turned her head aside and stared at the wall. His heels scuffed against the floor, and the door clicked closed.

TWENTY-FOUR

Bill

Bill reined in at the livery stable and swung down from the saddle. He groaned, his stiff muscles resisting straightening.

Hugh trotted from the barn and took hold of Patch's reins. "Hard day, Sheriff?"

Bill massaged his lower back with both hands. "Hard ride. Make sure ol' Patch gets double oats. He earned his keep today." The paint had carried him almost seven miles along the fence line, bucking a cold wind the whole distance. If Patch was half as weary as Bill, the animal deserved a treat.

"Will do."

Bill gave the horse's white rump a pat and aimed himself for Athol's. If Patch was getting a treat, Bill should have one, too. Coffee. Lots of it. And maybe something sweet. Even though it was almost nine and the sun had gone to bed over an hour ago, Athol's place was still lit like a Christmas tree. The man must use a gallon of coal oil a day to keep all his lamps burning. Somebody — probably Mack, if Bill didn't miss his guess — had lit the streetlamps, too, so Bill had no trouble finding his way to the restaurant.

He creaked the big door open and stepped in out of the cold, giving a shudder of relief when the warmth hit him. Athol and Mrs. Bingham sat at a table near the potbelly stove. Bill ambled over and plopped down with them. His backside hit the chair, and Athol bounced up like the two of them rode a seesaw. Athol headed for the kitchen.

Bill called after him. "Where are you goin'?"

"Gettin' the coffeepot, a cup, an' the last piece o' sweet-tater pie. Looks like you can use it."

That Athol was a good man. Bill sighed, popped off his hat, and dropped it on the table. He rested his elbows on the table and locked gazes with Mrs. Bingham. "Everything go all right at the church this evenin'? Sorry I couldn't be there." Truth was, he could've been. Jerome's fence hadn't been cut at all. The fool man just hadn't dug down deep enough when he set the fence posts, and the cows knocked a few of them over. The fella had no business ranching if

325

he couldn't take care of a place any better than that.

"Everything went well. There were twenty-four in attendance. Twenty-five if you count Mr. Cleveland, but we probably shouldn't since he was there in an official capacity."

Did he detect a hint of sarcasm in her tone? "You can't hardly call him official, because he don't wear a badge. He's just dependable an' willin' to help out now an' again."

Athol ambled over and put a wedge of golden pie in front of Bill. He splashed coffee into a cup and handed that over, too. He held the pot to Mrs. Bingham, but she put her hand over her cup and shook her head. Athol set the pot next to Bill's elbow. "Gonna go chop up that day-old bread for tomorrow's bread puddin'. Sit an' visit as long as you like." He sauntered back to the kitchen.

Bill picked up his fork, eager to dig into the pie. "Did we break some rule by havin' Mack in the class twice? After all, Preacher Doan sat through two sessions, too."

Mrs. Bingham tilted her head and pinned a suspicious look on Bill. "Yes, now that you mention it, the reverend attended one session with his wife at his side and a second on his own. Was that at your bidding, too?"

Bill jammed a huge bite in his mouth. Sweet filling, flaky crust. As good as the pie his mama used to bake. He chased the bite with a swig of coffee, strong and hot, just the way he liked it. Athol sure knew how to cook. He swiped his mustache with the back of his hand. "Yep." He forked up another bite.

"Why?"

Bill paused with the chunk of pie halfway to his mouth. " 'Cause it seems smart." He pushed the pie in his mouth and chomped down.

"Why?"

With a sigh, Bill dropped his fork. "I'm not generally in the practice of explainin' myself to folks, but since you're a lady an' what my mama would call one o' my elders, I'll tell you. It's my beholden duty to keep folks safe in my town. Mack come complainin' that Tobis Adelman went into his store an' got Miss Grant all upset. I caught her an' Otto Hildreth in some kind o' disagreement in the church."

The woman's eyebrows shot up. "You did? When?"

He waved his hand. "Don't get all het up. She said she was fine, an' I been keepin' an eye on her. Otto ain't bothered her again."

"But why would he —"

He'd never get to finish his pie if she didn't stop asking questions. "He didn't say, the stubborn cuss, but I speculate he was fussin' at her about these wives you're bringin' in. Him an' Sam Bandy an' Louis Griffin are all worryin' about the women doin' the sewin' an' bakin' an' hair trimmin' once they get here. Lots o' mumbles goin' on from them three."

She pinched her lips shut and stayed silent, so he grabbed a quick bite of pie and spoke around it. "An' take Tobis Adelman. He can be a real thorn in my side. He's too spoiled for his own good an' that's a fact. He likes to talk, an' even though I've warned him to keep quiet about Miss Grant's pa, I'm waitin' for him to let the news fly an' get everybody all stirred up. If a riot breaks out, I want somebody around to keep you an' that little gal from gettin' hurt."

He sneaked another bite and chased it with a swallow of coffee. "Then there's the unmarried ranchers. Now, they ain't really dangerous. Not criminal-like dangerous. But they can get high spirited from time to time, an' havin' a pair o' pretty women in their midst when they're grumbly about their brides not bein' here is askin' for them to not use good sense." He shrugged. "I figgered it's smart to have somebody in every class to help keep 'em in line."

Mrs. Bingham was frowning, but she'd lost some of the spark in her eyes. "Are you trying to tell me that you stationed men at the church not to watch Miss Grant but to watch out for her?"

"Ain't that what I already said?" He chopped the last chunk of pie in half and jabbed one piece with his fork. It went down good, so he followed it with the other. Then he sat back and let out a little burp behind his hand. Guess he'd eaten too fast. "I can't spend ever' night keepin' watch, so I asked Preacher an' Mack to help me out. That's all."

The woman lowered her head. The lamp swinging from a chain overhead painted a ring of light on her hair. Like a halo. He swallowed a chortle. This one could be both angel and devil all rolled into one the way she went from sweet to tart to sweet again. If he was bride shopping, he'd want a sweet and sassy woman. To keep things livened up.

When she looked up, all the devil was gone and only angel remained. "Please forgive me, Sheriff. I feared — and Miss Grant did, too — that you placed Mr. Cleveland at the church tonight to make sure she didn't engage in anything illegal." She made a face. "Unfortunately, the treatment she's received in the past has raised her defenses and made her prone to thinking the worst. I fell into the trap with her, but I should have known better. I do believe you are an honorable man."

Bill's chest went tight. Folks in these parts appreciated him. He knew that because they kept electing him every year, but they weren't much for saying it out loud. Miz Bingham was a city gal. Educated, and with more years on her than he had. Oh, she wasn't old enough to be his ma, but old enough to hold his respect. Her words felt good. Real good.

He sniffed, then grabbed up his cup and took a swallow so she wouldn't think he'd gone soft. "I've pret' much give up on worryin' about the two o' you bein' swindlers. Did some checkin', an' seems your business is a fair an' honest one."

Her cheeks went pink and she smiled all wobbly. Gave him some pleasure to know he'd pleased her. He took another quick slurp and shrugged. " 'Sides, it ain't fair to blame Miss Grant or think ill o' her for what her pa done. Mack said so, too, an' he was real forceful about it. Prob'ly 'cause o' what happened with his own pa before he come

330

to Spiveyville. That's why I knew he'd be willin' to take my place."

Mrs. Bingham jolted like somebody'd poked her in the back with a stick. "What happened with his pa?"

Bill had said too much. He drained his coffee cup and reached for the pot to fill it again.

She grabbed the pot first. Bill stuck out his cup, but she held the pot hostage. "He told me about his uncle, who was nearly taken in by a dishonest woman. But he hasn't mentioned anything about his father."

Bill bounced his cup. "An' I ain't gonna mention nothing more about it neither. That's Mack's story to tell if he wants to."

She stared at him, a hint of the devil returning, but finally she sighed and poured coffee into his cup. "You're a mule-headed man, Bill Thorn."

"An' you're a mule-headed woman, Helena Bingham. An' I reckon it's served both of us pretty good over the years."

She smiled. A soft smile, the kind Ma used to wear at the end of hymn singing at Sunday morning service. "Yes, I suppose so. I would like to ask you a favor, though."

He took a sip of the coffee, squinting at her over the rim of his cup. "What's that?"

"If Mr. Cleveland is going to continue to attend more than one class a week, please have him explain his purpose in being there to Miss Grant."

"Why can't you tell her?"

"I think it will mean more coming from Mr. Cleveland."

"Why?"

Her smile turned sly. "I have my reasons, but I believe I will keep them to myself." She stood and draped her hands over her chair's back. "We'll use the dining room for lessons on the subject of proper table manners."

He remembered his burp. He took another gulp of his coffee.

"I excused Abigail from kitchen cleanup and sent her to her room after class to ready her notes for tomorrow's lesson, but I'm sure there are still some dishes to be washed, so I'd better go help Mr. Patterson. May I presume you won't attend the class tomorrow since Mr. Cleveland has signed up for Thursdays?"

"I might be in here havin' my dinner. I eat most o' my meals with Athol an' put it on the town's tab. But I won't listen in." Maybe he should, though. If all the other fellas in town started putting on airs and minding their manners while he didn't, he'd stick out like a possum in a canary cage.

"Very well, Sheriff. I'll leave the pot with you in case you want another cup of coffee." She rounded the corner, the hem of her skirt skimming the floor and making it look like she glided.

Bill held his cup between his palms and stared after her. She was a handsome woman. Smart. Sassy. Even funny. Granted, she wasn't what his pa would call a spring chicken anymore, but she still had plenty of life left. She was busy matching up other women with fellas. Why didn't she try to latch on to one her age for herself?

Abigail

Abigail lay on her back on the lumpy mattress and stared unseeing at the gray ceiling. She was so tired — emotionally spent, Mother would have said — but sleep wouldn't come. Her mind refused to stop dredging up memories of the evening following Father's arrest. She and Mother had sat alone in their parlor, too anguished to speak, and then the door chime rang. With hope rising in her chest, she dashed to the vestibule and peeked out. Her heart had rolled over in relief when she spotted Linus Hartford on the small square porch.

He'd dressed impeccably, as he always did, in a three-piece suit of charcoal gray with a crisp white shirt and a deep golden-rod cravat nearly the same color as his hair lying just so at his throat. She opened the door and spoke on a sigh. "Oh, Linus, I'm so happy to see you." How she'd needed him, and here he was. Tears of joy and relief sprang into her eyes. She tipped her cheek for his customary hello kiss, but he stepped past her, stopped in the center of the foyer's marble-tile floor, and turned to face her.

Believing his formality was to appease Mother, who could hear and see everything from her spot on the settee, Abigail held out her hands. "May I take your hat?"

He pushed his hands into the pockets of his jacket and shook his head. "I won't be staying."

She slowly lowered her hands and linked them behind her back. "Not even for a cup of tea? Or an apple tart? The cook baked apple tarts this afternoon. Your favorite treat, yes?" Surely the promise of an apple tart, and her consideration in saving one for him, would bring a change to his stiff de-meanor.

His cold expression remained unchanged. "I don't care for tea or an apple tart. I've come to end our betrothal."

The words struck like blows, stealing her ability to breathe. She stumbled sideways and connected with the wall. She pressed her frame to the gold-brocade wall covering, her entire body breaking out in a cold sweat. "W-what? But why?"

He rolled his eyes. "For heaven's sake, Abigail, what else would you expect after today's fiasco at the bank?"

She couldn't answer. The pain of Father's admitted illegal activities was still too raw.

"Would I choose to wed the offspring of a murderer? Or a drunkard? Of course not, because I couldn't give my fine name to someone of such low bloodline. The same applies to the child of a professed thief. I'd forever watch you, wondering when the temptation to steal would rise in you. I'd forever worry about my name being sullied. No." He shook his head, the action adamant. "I cannot honor our agreement. It is customary for gifts to be returned, but I shan't request the brooch. It's too late to return it to the jeweler, and I would never be able to gift another with it, so you might as well keep it."

She touched the lovely brooch pinned to her left shoulder, imagining its stone of smoky quartz, as large as an apricot pit, and its circle of delicate gold rope. Smoky quartz . . . the color of her eyes. The color of Father's eyes. She couldn't bear to keep it.

"No. No, you take it." Her hands shook too badly. She couldn't unfasten the clasp.

He gripped the doorknob and gave it a wrench. "I shall have a retraction of our agreement printed in the newspaper by the end of the week. Goodbye, Miss Grant."

He'd slammed the door on his departure, and Abigail gave a jolt on her lonely bed in the dark room even though the slam was only in her memory. Tears came. Tears of mortification and heartbreak from that night, and tears of humiliation and anger for having been forced to live it again.

"I'd forever watch you," Linus had said.

"He wanted somebody watching Miss Grant, so I said I'd do it," Mr. Cleveland had said.

Neither of them trusted her. Linus Hartford was long gone from her life. Mr. Cleveland was much too close.

She rolled to her side and closed her eyes tight, willing sleep to come, but her thoughts refused to quiet. If only Mother were alive to sit on the edge of the bed and sing. If only God hadn't abandoned her family. Then she could talk to Him about her aching heart. If only . . .

336

TWENTY-FIVE

Helena

After church on Sunday, Mack offered to walk Helena and Abigail to the restaurant. But just as she'd done on every other opportunity to be in the hardware store owner's presence, Abigail declined him before Helena had a chance to reply. The man settled his hat over his thick dark hair and strode off without a word or even a flicker of anger on his face, but the heavy set of his boots against the ground told Helena he wasn't as unaffected as he pretended to be.

Helena secured the tails of her shawl — the wind was, once again, blowing from the north — and looped arms with Abigail. "Come along, dear." They set off in the direction of the restaurant. The cold wind wheezing between buildings and throwing dried grass and dust in their path inspired Helena to hurry, but Abigail moved stiltedly, the opening of her bonnet aimed at Mr. Cleveland's retreating back. She kept them a good twenty paces behind him.

How long would Abigail hold herself aloof from the man? Helena admired him for his persistence and continued kindness in the face of Abigail's rejection, but she wouldn't blame him if he abandoned the efforts. Temptation to scold the girl and very emphatically inform her that she was mistaken pulled hard, but Helena resisted. Abigail, despite her fine manners, was one of the most head-strong people she'd ever met. At times, the trait served her well. It had given her the courage to care for her mother after her father's incarceration and to march into Helena's office while still in the throes of mourning her mother's unfortunate passing and request the opportunity to become a western bride. It held her on task in a roomful of restless listeners. But at other times, such as this one, it kept her from seeing beyond her jaded expectations to the truth.

As much as Helena wished to intervene, she would allow Abigail to discover on her own that Mack was trustworthy. Helena believed it with every ounce of her being. The man's faithful attendance to church services and polite, friendly bearing each time their paths crossed proved to Helena that he wasn't a cad, but Abigail's hurts ran deep. It would take time for her to overcome her distrust. So Helena wouldn't lecture. Even if she bit off the end of her tongue in her attempts to keep it still.

Mack passed the restaurant and stepped into the gap between Athol's building and the hardware store. The moment he disappeared from sight, Abigail's breath whooshed out and formed a little puff of condensation at the end of her bonnet. Despite her intentions to stay silent, Helena couldn't stifle a chuckle.

Abigail halted, forcing Helena to stop, too. The ridiculously large brim swung in Helena's direction, and she got a glimpse of Abigail's frowning face.

"What is funny?"

Helena swallowed against the urge to chuckle again. "Have you ever heard the saying 'He cut off his nose to spite his face'?"

She huffed, creating another little cloud. "Of course I have."

"Perhaps you should take it under consideration. How many times over the past three days has Mack tried to talk to you and you've rebuffed him?"

Abigail toyed with her bonnet ties, lifting

her chin in an insolent manner. "As if I would keep count."

Helena had kept count. "Seven." She gave Abigail's elbow a little shake. "Seven times, which seems apropos when one considers the biblical admonition Preacher Doan shared with us this morning to forgive seventy times seven."

Abigail turned her face forward, and once again the bonnet hid her from Helena's view.

Helena stepped in front of the girl and bent slightly to peer at her through the tube-shaped opening. Wind pressed at her back, encouraging her to enjoy the restaurant's welcoming warmth, but inside they would be surrounded by listening ears. This conversation was best suited to the privacy of the porch.

She gripped Abigail's upper arms. "It is quite obvious to me that you wish to be at ease with him again. Why not set aside your stubborn pride and allow him to be your friend? You'll be much happier."

Abigail wriggled free. "I came to this town to teach the men proper behavior. I did not come to form friendships. Please allow me to focus on my duty so I might complete it with excellence." She marched past Helena and entered the restaurant.

Helena raised her gaze skyward and shook her head, sighing. "She's cutting off her nose to spite her face, but it's her nose, so . . ." Her attempt at apathy fell flat. She cared about Abigail the same way she cared about all her girls and wanted the best for them. The letter she'd received from Marietta in yesterday's mail, a letter proclaiming her pleasure in readying the brides for their placements and the belief that something new and exciting waited around the corner for her, included a promise to pray for Abigail. Helena trusted her sister to honor the pledge.

Of course, Helena would continue to pray as well. But what would it take for Abigail to release her fear of betrayal and to trust again? She was running headlong on a pathway to loneliness and unhappiness, and she seemed determined to continue despite the many signs warning her of its dangers.

Standing out here in the cold wind wouldn't solve the problem. With a shiver, Helena reached for the doorknob. As her fingers closed around it, the *clop* of hoofbeats approached and someone called her name. She turned, her smile intact, but it faltered when she recognized the tall, disheveled, sullen man sitting astride the roan horse.

She moved to the edge of the porch. "Mr. Nance, why are you in Spiveyville again?"

He didn't remove his hat but gazed at her from beneath its low curved brim through slitted eyes. "I come to see you. Word is you're bringin' a batch o' brides into Spiveyville to marry up with ranchers. Is that true?"

"It is indeed."

"I need one, too."

Helena shivered again, but she wasn't altogether sure she could blame it on the cold wind. She automatically reached for her reticule, but of course her derringer was in her room. No one carried weapons to church. "Mr. Nance, would you mind if we stepped inside the restaurant? It's chilly out here." The diners could serve as witnesses if this man proved as bad tempered as he'd been on his previous visit.

His scowl deepened. "How long's this gonna take? I left my youngsters alone an' promised I'd be back before dark, so I don't got a lot o' time."

So he was a widower. Despite his ill-mannered behavior, a thread of sympathy wove its way through her. Perhaps losing his wife had embittered him to the point of surliness. Mourning had a way of changing

342

people. "It shouldn't take long. Please come in."

He growled under his breath, but he slid down from the saddle, wrapped the reins around the porch railing, and followed her inside. Every table in the restaurant was already taken, but Abigail sat alone at the one closest to the enclosed staircase. "Follow me, Mr. Nance. We'll join my assistant." He followed her so closely, his hot breath stirred the fine hairs on the back of her neck. She hurried the last few feet and sat.

He yanked a chair from the opposite side of the table, turned it backward, and straddled it. "Get on with it, then."

Abigail paused in eating and sent a wary glance at Helena.

Helena forced a smile. "Miss Grant, you remember Mr. Nance, don't you? He rode over from nearby Coats. He is a widower who would like to remarry."

"Never said I was a widower." The man spoke so sharply Helena believed his words could chop wood. "My wife took a notion to try city life an' left my two boys behind when she took off. Got some papers in the mail last week that we ain't married no more. I'm needin' a woman to see to my boys an' take care o' the household chores. She don't have to be pretty. Just strong."

He looked at Abigail. "Not spindly like this one."

Abigail visibly bristled. She placed her fork next to her plate and angled her head in the proud way Helena had come to recognize as her fighting stance. "Mr. Nance, first of all, size has nothing to do with strength. Second of all, it sounds as if you're looking for a house servant and nanny instead of a wife. Third —"

A thunderstorm was blooming on the man's face. Helena squeezed Abigail's wrist. "There is an application process before I can consider matching you with a bride."

"I figured you'd ask for money." He yanked off his glove and shoved his hand into his jacket pocket. He withdrew his fist and slammed his hand flat in the middle of the table. When he lifted his palm, two silver dollars and a spattering of smaller coins lay in a heap. "Got that much now. When I sell some calves in the spring, I'll have more. But you take that as my down payment an' fetch me a woman."

Helena gingerly pushed the coins toward him. "Sir, let's discuss the application first, shall we? If you would be so kind as to send me a letter explaining your needs in a wife and how you intend to see to her well-being, it will help me greatly in finding an appropriate match for you."

"A letter? You mean all writ down?"

Was he unable to write? There was no denying this was a foul individual, but inexplicably, sympathy pricked again. "Yes, sir. Please mail it to the post office here in Spiveyville rather than to my home in Massachusetts, since I will likely be here for another three weeks. As soon as I have it —"

He thumped the table with his fist again, and the chatter at other tables abruptly stilled. He leaned in, his expression reminding her of a snarling dog. "Ain't you listened to anything I said? I don't got time to write letters. I don't got time to wait. We been by ourselves for comin' up on three weeks now. My boys an' me 're needin' somebody now."

"Nance, what're you doin' in here?"

Helena jolted to her feet and rounded the table, placing herself between Athol and Mr. Nance. "I asked him to come in because it's too cold to visit outside. Mr. Nance is interested in acquiring a bride."

Athol folded his arms over his chest and appeared to puff up. "You got some nerve, Nance, comin' back in here after I told you to stay out."

Mr. Nance jutted his chin. "She brung me in. Besides, I ain't sellin' nothin'. Nor or-

345

derin' nothin'." He flicked a glower at the other diners, and a hungry look crossed his face.

"You sure ain't. An' you ain't gonna take up one o' my chairs, neither." Athol angled his bulky frame in front of Helena. "You want a bride, you do what the rest of us did an' send a letter askin' for one. Now get on out o' here."

Nance lurched upright and shoved the chair aside in one smooth motion. The legs screeched across the floor, and several people drew back. He leaned toward Athol, raising his clenched fists, and instinctively Helena reached for Abigail. The girl clung to her hands. Athol held his ground. He didn't even unfold his arms. After several tense seconds of both staring into each other's scowls, Mr. Nance sent a snarling glare across the entire dining room and took a backward step.

"I gotta get back to my spread." He pointed at Helena. "You got my down payment. Get me a wife." He turned and stomped out of the restaurant, leaving the door open.

One of the diners jumped up and closed the door. Then, with a nervous laugh, he turned the lock. At the click, everyone in the place began talking at once, creating a cacophony that drowned out the frantic pulse beating in Helena's ears.

Athol put his hand on her shoulder. "You all right?"

Helena forced a laugh. She released Abigail and pretended to smooth a wrinkle from her skirt. "We're fine, Athol. Perhaps a little rattled, but there was no harm done. I'm sorry I invited him inside. I thought I would be safer talking to him in here than out on the porch."

Athol shook his head, his lips set in a grim line. "There's no safe place to try an' reason with a man like Elmer Nance. He's been banned from half the towns in Pratt County. Everywhere he goes, he causes trouble."

Abigail's brown eyes widened. "But why?"

"How should I know?" Athol shrugged, and the noisy chatter of moments ago quieted. It seemed everyone in the room was listening to the restaurant owner. "Mebbe he's got grudges against certain people. Mebbe he's just plain mean. Some people are, you know. He's stayed overnight in every jail in the county at one time or another on account of bein' disorderly. I'd trust a rattlesnake before I'd trust that feller."

The silence, along with Athol's explanation, sent a shudder through Helena's frame. "Such a temper. If he behaves so badly in a public place, what must his poor family witness in the privacy of their home?"

Athol grimaced. "Nothin' good. He's a bad 'un for sure. Wouldn't be surprised if he even raises his hand to his wife."

"He no longer has a wife." Abigail's voice quavered. "He said she left him and sent divorce papers."

"Good for her." Athol retrieved the chair Mr. Nance had slid aside and brought it close. He sat and propped his elbows on his knees as if suddenly weary. "I'm gonna send one o' the fellas for Sheriff Thorn. I want you to tell him everything Nance said. An', ma'am, don't you fetch that man a wife no matter how much he begs or how much money he gives you. No woman should have to put up with the likes o' Elmer Nance, an' that's a fact."

TWENTY-SIX

Mack

Canned beans made a sorry Sunday dinner, but at least they filled his stomach. Mack clanked his plate and fork into the tin washbasin and dipped water from his water barrel over them. He'd figured out letting his dishes soak for a while made the cleanup a lot easier. He liked keeping things neat, but he also liked little tricks to make the job go faster. It left him more time for his store.

Even though he was never open on Sunday — the day of rest, Pa always said — he usually checked the inventory on his shelves on that day. It was quiet then. No customers or clanging bells. Just him and the stock and the smells of wood and leather and turpentine. Not a mixture that would sell in a bottle, but he liked it. And it was easier to focus when he didn't have to worry about someone coming in and distracting him. He

349

grabbed his ledger and a pencil from under the counter and headed for the shelves at the front of the store.

A horse and rider pounded past the windows. He got only a glimpse, they went so fast, but the rider was bent forward over the horse's neck and must have been pulling hard on the reins, because the horse's mouth was open and its eyes rolled even as it galloped.

Mack pressed his face to the glass and looked after the rider, then searched the street. When someone ran a horse that hard, they were either chasing someone or trying to avoid someone. But he didn't see anyone else, so he said a quick prayer for the man's — and the horse's — safety and turned his attention back to the shelves.

He'd barely made it halfway down the first section when someone pounded on the door off the alley. He left the ledger and pencil on the shelf and trotted to his apartment. Sheriff Thorn peered at him from the other side of the filmy material serving as a curtain over the square pane of glass in the door.

Mack grinned and swung the door wide. "Hey, Sheriff, did you come for a game of checkers?" He'd enjoyed teaching Miss Grant how to play the game last weekend, but he wouldn't need to give the sheriff any lessons. The man won more games than he lost.

The sheriff entered the apartment and dragged his hat from his head. "No time for checkers today. Sorry."

Mack doubted Miss Grant had time, either. She didn't have time for him anymore for anything. He'd made a promise to Mrs. Bingham to befriend the younger woman, but she didn't make it easy. "What do you need?"

"I come to ask you a favor."

"What's that?"

"I need to ride over to Coats tomorrow, take some money to a fella who left it behind over at Athol's." Sheriff Thorn rolled the brim of his hat while he talked, a nervous gesture. "Gettin' to Coats ain't an unreasonable distance, but there's no tellin' how this fella will take to gettin' his money back, so there's a good chance I won't be here to sit in on the dinin' room lessons tomorrow. I'd ask Preacher Doan, but Sunday's a busy day for him an' he generally takes his rest on Monday, so . . ."

Mack gave the sheriff a pat on the shoulder. "It's no problem. I'd be glad to keep watch."

Sheriff Thorn grimaced. "An' about

351

that . . . Make sure you don't say you're keepin' watch over Miss Grant. I guess she got kind o' prickly about it, thinkin' we was watchin' her."

Mack frowned. "Aren't we?"

"Well, sure." He scratched his head. "Miz Bingham said it this way — watchin' out *for* her."

"Ah . . ." Such a small difference, but Mack understood why it mattered. And now he understood why she'd gotten, as the sheriff put it, prickly. "I'll be careful what I say."

He grinned, his graying mustache lifting at the corners. "Ladies can be hard to please, but there's no sense in goin' out o' our way to offend her, seein' as how she's a guest in town."

Mack hadn't meant to offend her, and he'd be sure to tell her so when he saw her next. If he could get her to stand still and listen.

Helena

"Athol, I refuse to argue with you about this." Helena gave the apron strings a firm yank, securing the bow. She pointed to the doorway leading to the dining room. "If you're to take the class, you need to be sit-

352

ting at a table, not coming in and out of the kitchen all evening."

Athol stared at his stove the way a mama stared at a baby reaching for a stranger. "But I ain't never let anybody else cook at my stove. It feels plumb unnatural."

"It's only for one night. Tomorrow you can return to cooking and serving, but tonight you are not a cook. You are a student." She gave him a little push toward the door. "So let me take care of things in here, and you pay attention to Miss Grant."

He scuffed across the floor, his shoulders slumped and his head hanging low. "Ain't bad enough Miss Grant picked the supper menu for these classes. Now I got somebody else cookin' up the food."

Helena couldn't resist laughing at the dismal picture he painted. "You will survive, Athol. Trust me."

He flung one last forlorn look over his shoulder, then entered the dining room.

Still chuckling, Helena set two frying pans on the stove and reached for the crock of bacon drippings stored on a shelf nearby. She hummed as she spooned milky-looking fat into the pans. When Howard was still alive, she'd prepared elaborate dinners for the two of them, finding joy in his appreciation. For the past several years, she'd allowed the girls who were awaiting matches to take turns with cooking chores in her home, and they chose the same simple fare to which they'd grown accustomed in their childhood homes. She'd nearly forgotten the joy of cooking.

Not that she was preparing anything elaborate tonight. Abigail had requested ham steaks and seasoned root vegetables, with rolls from Sam Bandy's bakery. Helena had retrieved the rolls from the bakery and listened to Sam's sad soliloquy on how his business would likely come to ruination when all the brides arrived so he'd better enjoy selling buns while he could. She wasn't sure her pat on his bony shoulder and verbal assurance that many would still enjoy the convenience of bakery-bought bread had helped. But there was little else she could do, so she might as well focus on the task at hand.

She inhaled deeply. The chopped carrots, yams, and turnips were already in the oven, sending out a heavenly aroma of rosemary and thyme. A ham from Athol's own smoke-house was sliced and ready for the frying pan. She chuckled again, recalling his reluctance to leave his stove. How could he remain so proprietary when he'd done all the preparation and left her with nothing more than heating the steaks?

The grease popped, announcing its readiness, so she carefully laid a steak in each pan. Grease bubbled around the slices, leaving a lovely brown, crispy edge. She flipped them, allowing both sides to pick up a slight sear, and then transferred them to a large roasting tray at the far end of the stove, where they would stay warm until serving time. She developed a rhythm of forking the slices into the pans, watching the sizzle, flipping, and transferring. Grease spattered the front of her apron and the stove top, joining countless other stains, and the smell rising from the pans made her mouth water.

From the dining room, Abigail began her strident instructions. "We've already determined the proper way to assist a lady into her chair, so tonight we will cover appropriate table manners. First, let's discuss the 'nevers.' Never eat peas or any other food with a knife . . . ."

The list was long, giving Helena plenty of time to lay out eleven dinner plates and arrange a slice of ham, a large spoonful of vegetables, a roll, and a little dome-shaped lump of creamy butter on each. Sweat dripped from her temples and tickled her cheek, but she ignored it, determined to do as well as Athol so he wouldn't be disappointed in her.

She nearly laughed at the thought. Would she have considered worrying about such a thing before coming to this town? Somehow these men — rough and unsophisticated as they were — had won her affection. They were striving to please her and Abigail, and she wanted to please them in return.

Just as she filled the eleventh plate, Abigail poked her head into the kitchen. "We're ready."

Helena flashed a triumphant smile. "As am I." By placing four plates on a tray, she was able to serve everyone in only three trips. When she put the last plate in front of Athol, he gave an approving nod that warmed her from her toes to the top of her head. She shifted aside with the tray tucked under her arm, ready to assist Abigail if necessary.

Abigail roved around the room, creating a weaving path between the tables. "Please pick up your fork in your left hand and your knife in your right." The attendees shuffled with their silverware, a few good-natured chuckles sounding. "Puncture the ham with your fork tines approximately a half inch from the edge of the steak. Now, holding your knife at a downward angle and using your pointer finger to guide it, slice off a piece of ham."

Mack raised his hand holding the knife. Lamplight bounced off the blade, creating a flash of white.

Abigail's lips twitched into a stiff smile. "Yes, Mr. Cleveland?"

"Excuse me, but isn't there something we ought to do before we cut into the ham?"

Her face glowed pink, and she fussed with her skirt. "Oh, yes, please forgive me. Mr. Patterson didn't have enough, er, wiping cloths to go around, but it is very proper to place a napkin across your knees before picking up your utensils."

He shook his head. "That's not what I meant. If we're gonna eat, we need to say grace first."

The pink in Abigail's cheeks changed to a fiery red. Helena hurried across the floor and took her hand. "I'd be glad to say grace. Everyone, please bow your heads."

Abigail

Ashamed, and angry because she felt ashamed, Abigail stood as stiff as a statue while Mrs. Bingham thanked the Lord for the food. She'd asked one of the men in attendance at each of the previous classes on dining to offer a blessing for the food. Hav-

357

ing Mr. Cleveland seated at a table, even though he wasn't signed up for Monday, had sent her longtime habit scuttling to the back corner of her mind.

Not once in all her childhood had she and her parents sat down to a meal without giving God thanks. Father in particular formulated lovely prayers with flowery phrases, his voice eloquent in its delivery. She at once longed to return to those days and wished she could forget them. Had he meant any of those prayers?

"Amen." Mrs. Bingham gave Abigail a nod. "Go ahead."

But now her stomach fluttered with nervousness brought on in part by Mr. Cleveland's presence and partly by her little foray into the past. She cleared her throat, attempting to clear her head, and forced herself to concentrate. "Cutting meat . . ." She pulled in a breath, then released it. "Holding your knife and fork as I previously instructed, cut off a slice of meat. Please take note of the slice. Is it larger than an inch square?"

She paused to give everyone time for examination. "If so, please make another cut, removing a one-inch portion from the larger slice. Then, when you've accomplished it, carry that piece to your mouth without shifting your fork to your right hand. This is achieved by lifting the fork, rotating your wrist, and placing the meat in your mouth."

While they followed her directions, she slowly moved around the room again. "Remember our 'Never cut up the entire piece of meat at one time'? This is what I want you to practice. Cut a single bite, put it in your mouth, lower your fork to the table, chew with your mouth closed, swallow, and then cut another bite."

Clive Ackley spoke around a piece of ham. "This is takin' forever. We'll spend the whole night at the table if we hafta cut an' eat one bite at a time."

Abigail clicked her tongue on her teeth. "Mr. Ackley, you are forgetting 'Never talk with food in your mouth.' "

He raised one eyebrow, but he chewed and swallowed with his mouth closed.

"What about these vegetables, Miss Grant?" The barber, Louis Griffin, pointed to the roasted vegetables with his fork. "Do we spear 'em up one at a time, or can I scoop up more'n one?"

"Never shovel your food," Mr. Ackley said, again with a piece of ham in his mouth.

Sam Bandy snorted. "I ain't gonna poke 'em or shovel 'em. Turnips? Phooey. That's food for pigs."

Mr. Griffin raised his hand. "I don't remember. Is there a 'Never ask what's in the food'? 'Cause I'm wonderin' what're all these little sticks stuck to the sweet taters."

Abigail stifled a sigh and looked directly at Mr. Bandy. "Never extravagantly praise nor criticize any food upon your plate."

Mr. Griffin frowned. "But is askin' criticizin'?"

Mrs. Bingham hurried over to the barber and touched his shoulder. "It's rosemary, Louis, a seasoning. It's actually quite flavorful."

"Thank you, ma'am."

"You're very welcome." She sent Abigail a smile and nod.

Abigail drew another fortifying breath. "Let's move on to the bread, shall we?" More grumbles rose when she informed them to tear off a bite-sized piece, apply butter, and then eat the small portion. Even Mrs. Pendergraff, a kindly-looking older woman, asked why she couldn't butter the whole slice at once. "It saves so much time."

Abigail gave the woman a smile she hoped appeared sincere. "Dinner should be an enjoyable event, not a rushed affair."

Mrs. Pendergraff shrugged. "That sounds real nice, honey, but the truth is I've still got chores waitin' after supper. The longer I sit at the table, the later I get to bed, an' I still gotta rise with the rooster no matter what time I put my head to the pillow."

Abigail feigned a seeking glance across the tables. "Oh, it seems we've forgotten the salt and pepper shakers." She didn't even know if Mr. Patterson had duplicate sets of shakers to place on the tables, but it didn't matter. She needed an escape. "Please excuse me." She darted into the kitchen.

Out of sight of the diners, she leaned against the wall and closed her eyes. She still faced two more evenings of dining rules. The reactions to her list of "nevers" were no different tonight than they had been during the previous classes. None of the men wanted to take the time to cut individual pieces of meat. None of them wanted to tear their bread into bite-size chunks and butter the chunks individually. None of them wanted to engage their wives in talk about current events. They only wanted to eat.

"Miss Grant?"

She let out a squeak of surprise and popped her eyes open. She planted her palms against the wall and glared at Mr. Cleveland. "Never creep up on someone that way."

"Is that one of the 'never' rules?" A teasing grin lifted one corner of his mouth.

The impish grin irked her because she found it appealing. "It shouldn't need to be a stated rule. It should be common sense." She bolted past him and began searching through Mr. Patterson's cupboards.

He followed her. "I wanted to tell you not to be discouraged. The rules are good. They're things we should all know for when we sit down to eat in a fancy restaurant or at someone else's house."

She angled a frown over her shoulder. "But . . ."

He shrugged, grimacing. "But for everyday sitting up to the table, maybe they're a little too . . ."

An unpleasant accusation from the past seared her. "Hoity-toity?"

He shrugged again, his expression apologetic. "Maybe."

She turned her attention to the cupboard and pushed cans around.

"The thing is, Miss Grant, I think" — he moved closer behind her — "you're teaching city rules to country folk. The rules aren't bad or wrong. They're just not something we're used to."

She spun around and faced him. "Why are you in here? Is it to comfort or encourage me, or is it to make sure I don't take something that isn't mine?" Hurt and fury roared through her. She plunked her fists on her hips. "Are you watching me again, Mr. Cleveland?"

TWENTY-SEVEN

Mack

He'd prayed for the chance to set things
right, and now it was looking him straight
in the face, spitting fire and ready to attack.
At least she didn't carry a pistol, so he
didn't need to worry about her shooting his
foot off. Mack took a breath and spoke the
truth.

"I am watching you, but not for the reason
you think."

Her gaze narrowed. "And how do you
know what I think?"

"I guess I can't know for sure, but I can
speculate. Your pa did something wrong,
and afterward, people started treating you
different. Watched you. Distrusted you." He
made sure to speak gently so she wouldn't
think he was casting stones. Ma was always
real firm about not casting stones. "Am I
right?"

Her brown eyes filled with tears, and her chin quivered. She nodded.

"Well, that's not what's happening here. Not from me." He'd learned a long time ago to treat people the way he wanted to be treated. He'd suffered mistreatment after the oldest Batson boy claimed Pa stole a silver tea set — *"It had to've been Chester Cleveland. He probably learned to steal from his no-good brother Ray"* — when he was painting woodwork in their family home. Even after the investigation proved Everett Batson pawned the set himself to repay a cardsharp, some people still looked at Pa — and Mack, because he'd been at the house helping Pa — differently. Mack had carried a chip on his shoulder all the way to Kansas. So he understood Miss Grant's feelings. He also understood they wouldn't do her any good.

He took a single step toward her, keeping his gaze locked on hers so she'd see the sincerity in his eyes. "You grew up in fine society. You aren't used to men who get a little rascally sometimes. Not mean or bad, just rascally. So the sheriff asked Preacher Doan and me to help look out for you, to step in if need be. That's all."

She held his gaze for several seconds. Then she hung her head. "Please forgive me, Mr. Cleveland. I am so ashamed. My mother taught me to seek the best in people and make allowances for the bad, remembering we are all sinners in need of grace, but I . . ." Tears ran past her freckles.

He pulled his handkerchief from his pocket and gave it to her. To his surprise, she took it without a moment's pause. He waited until she'd dried her cheeks. "You got hurt, so you built a wall."

Her face lifted and her wide eyes spoke of wonder. "Yes. How did you know?"

"Because I built one, too." He hadn't expected to share his hurt with her. He'd kept it hidden except from those he considered good friends — Preacher Doan and Sheriff Thorn. But the story about Miss Wilkes becoming Uncle Ray's intended and then using her pistol to convince Uncle Ray, who served as the church's accountant, to empty the safe holding the benevolence funds, and the way everyone in the congregation started viewing his family as untrustworthy, came out so easy he had to believe it was God's prompting.

He slipped his fingers into his trouser pockets and gave a nod. "That's why when Uncle Ray decided to come to Kansas to start a new life without the shadow of Wilhelmina Wilkes hanging over him, my folks sent me with him. To get me away from the source of hurt and let me heal. It took some time, a lot of prayers" — his and his parents' — "and this community rallying around me when my uncle died. The people in town proved the goodness in folks' hearts, so I got better." He took the handkerchief from her hand and used it to wipe the last tear trailing down her cheek. "And you will, too, in time."

She looked so hopeful and so doubtful at the same time, he wanted to hug her until all the doubt went away. But he couldn't. She was too proper to accept a hug. And it might give him ideas he shouldn't entertain. But he had to do something.

He pinched the corner of the handkerchief and swished it at her. The fabric barely grazed the tip of her nose, but she drew back as if he'd snapped her with it. Her mouth fell open, and she stared at him for three startled seconds and then broke into laughter.

He laughed, too. He couldn't help it. "You ready to go back in there and finish up your class, Teacher?"

Every bit of humor in her expression dissolved. "I suppose I should, although it all seems useless. As you said, they likely won't ever use the manners I'm teaching." She sighed. "But I have nothing else to offer, so I shall continue." She straightened her shoulders and strode determinedly into the dining room.

Bill

Bill unlocked the door to the sheriff's office and stepped inside. The office was dark, the way it should be at eleven o'clock at night, but light from the lamppost came through the windowpanes and let him see well enough to find the match tin on the stand next to the door. He pried the lid up and poked around, but the tin was empty.

"Consarn it!" He clapped his hand over his mouth and sent a quick look right and left. Then he snorted. "Ma's not in hearin' range, an' neither is nobody else. Get that lantern lit."

Guided by the dim lamplight, he inched his way to his desk and yanked upon the middle drawer. Black as pitch inside it, but he pawed until he found another tin of matches. Gripping the tin in his fist, he started for the lamp, then groaned and flopped into his squeaky chair. Why waste the oil? He rested his head on the chair's high back, closed his eyes, and sighed.

He sure hadn't intended to spend near

the whole day in Coats. But when Nance wasn't at his ranch, he hadn't known where else to look. Puzzling . . . Nobody in town had seen Nance in at least a week. The Nance boys were at the schoolhouse, but when he asked them where their pa was, they acted scared and said they didn't know. Most troubling of all, the post office clerk vowed Nance hadn't gotten any mail. So he'd fibbed to Miz Bingham about getting divorce papers. Yet he'd ordered a bride. So did he or didn't he still have a wife? Bill didn't much like the ideas running in his head.

The coins Miz Bingham had given him weighted his pocket. He needed to put them in Nance's hand. So where'd that no-good skunk gone off to? Having somebody with his temperament roaming wild left an uneasy feeling in the pit of Bill's stomach. He yanked off his hat, slapped it onto the desk, and ran his hands through his hair. He was tired. So was Patch. But tomorrow he'd saddle up and take another trip to Nance's ranch. The sooner he returned the money and gave the man a stern warning about staying away from Spiveyville, the better for everybody.

The smell of pancakes and sausage greeted Abigail's nose when she entered the dining room Tuesday morning. Although still early — the sun's rays hadn't even climbed above the horizon — Mr. Patterson was already at work. Why hadn't she stopped to consider the hardworking attitude he possessed? Such an admirable trait. All she'd seen was his stained apron. All she'd heard was his uncultured speech. But last night, as she'd pondered the sad tale that had brought Mr. Cleveland to Spiveyville and the change he'd experienced thanks to the community's acceptance, a different picture of Spiveyville and its residents had emerged.

Mr. Patterson had a good heart. She'd seen it in his concern for her and Mrs. Bingham when the vile Nance banged on their table. She'd seen it in his service to his fellow townsfolk. She'd even seen it in his reluctance to let someone else assume the cooking duties, a responsibility he considered his own. Somehow Mr. Cleveland's simple statement — *"The people in town proved the goodness in folks' hearts"* — awakened her to look beyond their outsides to their insides. She had misjudged many of them, and she determined to make amends.

370

Starting with Mr. Patterson.

She called his name as she moved through the kitchen doorway, and he looked up from the large pan, where four pancakes sizzled in bacon grease.

"Miss Grant . . ." He ran his free hand over his nearly bald head. "Didn't expect you up so soon. I was fixin' myself a little somethin' before everybody starts stormin' the door."

She smiled, touched by his nervousness to be alone with her. "I don't want to interrupt your routine. I only wanted to tell you how much I appreciate your help with the dining classes. I know it's been an inconvenience for you, yet you haven't uttered a word of complaint. Thank you, Mr. Patterson."

"Well, I . . . um . . ." He removed the pancakes from the skillet and stacked them on a plate that already held three sausage links. He gestured to the plate with his spatula. "You hungry?"

She tipped her head. "What did we discuss in commonsense etiquette? When someone thanks you, the appropriate response is . . ."

His round face flushed. "You're welcome." He shrugged. "But I don't know that I did anything worth thankin' me for. Only did what I always do. Cooked. An' served."

She closed the distance between them and touched his rolled sleeve. "Uncomplaining service is worthy of gratitude. So please accept my thank-you."

He harrumphed. "Accepted. Now, since you're here, you want them pancakes?"

She'd never eaten breakfast so early in the day, but the smell was too tempting to ignore. "Yes, thank you. But it's far too much for only me, and I'd hate to see it wasted. Should we share?"

His eyes bulged. "Sh-share?"

"Yes. If I may have a fresh plate, I'll take one pancake and a piece of sausage. You may have the rest."

He blinked so fast it almost made her dizzy. Then he broke into a grin. "All right."

He grabbed a plate from the shelf, transferred a pancake and sausage link to it, and handed it to her. She picked up the second plate, too, and headed for the dining room with him shuffling alongside her. At the doorway he paused and reached into a basket. He held up two wiping cloths and grinned. "Gotta have napkins, right?"

She smiled. "Right." She set the plates on the table closest to the kitchen and started to sit, but he thrust out his palm. "Wait!"

Dumbfounded, she froze in place, and he

bustled around the table and held her chair for her. She laughed. The most inappropriate response she could possibly give to a gentlemanly gesture, but it bubbled up and spilled out on a note of joy. She slid into the seat and beamed at him. "Thank you."

"You're welcome." Still grinning, he hurried to the opposite chair and sat. Jugs of maple syrup already waited in the center of each table, and he offered theirs to her first. She poured a bit of the thick brown syrup on her cake, then gave him the jug. He flooded his plate in syrup, licking his lips the entire time.

Oh, such manners! She'd exhibited better behavior at the table by the time she was three, but somehow his childish enjoyment brought amusement rather than annoyance. Perhaps it was the nearly empty dining room, the early hour, or the simple surroundings, but she had no desire to correct him.

Mr. Patterson said a short prayer, and the two of them ate. To his credit, he ate one bite at a time — bigger bites than she would have recommended, but he did have a kitchen to run — and he only talked with food in his mouth twice. While they ate, he told her about growing up in a family of all sisters, all older, who had no idea how to treat him like a boy, so he learned to cook and clean and sew as well as any of them.

"Now it's all I know," he said with a shrug. "But knowin' it has let me make a good livin', so I can't complain." He scowled, painting lines of worry across his broad brow. "Some o' the fellas are certain-sure that when all the wives get here, our services won't be needed no more. I don't know nothin' else except cookin'. Kinda scares me to think of nobody comin' to my restaurant an' orderin' up a plate o' fried catfish or a bowl o' ham an' beans."

Abigail set her fork aside and gave the cook her full attention. "Mr. Patterson, the city in which I lived before coming to Spiveyville had dozens of bakeries, tailors, barbers, and restaurants. The city was filled with married couples, yet the businesses — all of them — continued to thrive."

His eyes widened. "That so?"

"Yes. Instead of worrying about decreased patronage, perhaps each of you should consider how having a prosperous business in place makes you a very desirable match for a woman. You'll also be able to grow your businesses with a wife who partners with you in your ventures."

He held the fork like a spear, his mouth slightly agape, and stared at her.

She wiped her mouth and placed her rumpled wiping cloth next to her plate. "But if I might be quite frank with you, Mr. Patterson, I believe nearly every woman will want to do more than wash dishes and mop the floor for you."

"You mean she'll wanna do some cookin', too?"

Abigail shook her head. "That's not what I meant, although it's possible. You see, you've dedicated all day every day to your restaurant. But when you're married, you'll want to have time with your wife, and she will want time with you." She laced her fingers together and placed them on the edge of the table. "Have you ever considered taking a day off? Many restaurants in cities are closed on Mondays or Sundays, sometimes both. So the owner has a break."

"Well . . ." He scratched his cheek, still ruddy from his morning's razor. "Seein' as how so many o' the fellas didn't have nobody else to cook for 'em, I stayed open to make sure they'd get fed. I gotta cook for myself anyway, so it wasn't much to cook for them, too. But you're right. If I've got a wife, I'm gonna want time with her for talkin', like you an' me are doin' now, an' . . . an' . . ." He looked aside.

Heat filled Abigail's face, but she finished

the sentence for him. "Spooning?"

He nodded.

"And you'll need time for such. It's all part of the marriage relationship." Sadness descended, stealing some of the pleasure of her early-morning chat with Mr. Patterson. As a child, she'd never been embarrassed to witness her parents' affectionate behavior. It had given her a sense of security, knowing they loved each other and weren't afraid to show it. At the end, when Father was taken away, how much of Mother's mourning was for her lost lover and how much for the shame of betrayal?

"I'll do some thinkin' on what you said. Might be once all the fellas have their wives, I won't need to keep my doors open every day." Mr. Patterson's expression turned thoughtful. "These women, they'll bring lots o' change to Spiveyville, won't they? Otto's the most scared. Clive told 'im the men'll ask their women to do their stitchin' an' such. I think he's half wishin' we hadn't sent for 'em, but it's too late now."

Someone rattled the doorknob.

Mr. Patterson jumped up. "Plumb lost track o' time sittin' here." He trotted toward the kitchen. "Unlock the door, Miss Grant, an' let 'em in. I gotta fry the cakes."

TWENTY-EIGHT

Abigail

Mrs. Bingham had asked to be excused from restaurant duty to wash sheets, and Mr. Patterson agreed even though he voiced his surprise that they needed washing again after only a week's worth of sleeping. Abigail cleared and cleaned tables and washed dishes on her own. Between chores, she watched for Mr. Cleveland. He ate nearly every meal in the restaurant, and she felt certain he would come in for pancakes and sausage. The spicy and sweet aromas mixed together was the most wondrous perfume, and it had surely drifted to the hardware store with as many times as the front door opened and closed.

At a little past seven thirty, he entered the dining room, sweeping off his hat as he cleared the threshold. Her heart gave a leap, and then shyness attacked. She'd given Mr.

Patterson her thank-you. She owed one to Mr. Cleveland, as well, and she would give it. But it would take more courage than it had taken to address Mr. Patterson. Because even though she liked Mr. Patterson, he had no effect on her pulse.

To her chagrin, Mr. Cleveland didn't sit at the lone empty table by himself but joined Louis Griffin and Clive Ackley. Abigail couldn't deliver a personal message in front of the other two men. Deflated, she entered the kitchen.

"Mr. Patterson, Mr. Cleveland has arrived."

Mr. Patterson flipped pancakes, sweat pouring down his face. "I'll get to him when I can, but I'm behind on servin'." He flashed her a hopeful look. "Sure would help if you'd carry out some o' these plates."

Abigail bit her lower lip. Serving in one's home was acceptable. On the cook's day off, she and Mother had taken turns serving dinner. But in a public restaurant? Never had she even seen a female server in the restaurants she'd visited with her parents. A man named Harvey utilized only female servers in his chain of restaurants, which had been met with varying reactions of shock to horror from Mother and her friends, but this wasn't a Harvey-owned establishment.

Mr. Patterson sighed. "Never mind." He handed her the spatula. "Watch them cakes an' don't let 'em burn. I'll be right back after I've served these an' took Mack's order."

Chastened by his tone, she kept careful watch over the pancakes and removed them before even a hint of scorching appeared on their edges.

Mr. Patterson puffed back in, wiping his hands on his apron. "As I figured, Mack wants a stack o' cakes an' sausage, like pret' much everybody else." He grabbed the spatula and moved between her and the stove. "I hope them jugs o' syrup is holdin' out. Couldja check 'em an' replace 'em if they're runnin' low?"

Eager to return to his good graces, she hurried out to obey. All five jugs were considerably lighter than they'd been at the beginning of the morning. She took the one from the empty table and carefully added its contents to another jug, but the other three jugs were in the middle of diners. She didn't want to take those.

She returned to the kitchen and crossed to the stove. "Mr. Patterson, do you have more syrup jugs in the cellar? If so, I'll trade them for the half-empty ones."

"Not in the cellar. It's too cool down there." He plopped pancakes into a stack on a plate and added several sausage links. "I keep the syrup in the smokehouse's little add-on, where it'll stay warm enough to pour. Go ahead and bring in a couple more jugs." He hurried in the direction of the dining room.

Abigail opened the door leading to the backyard and stepped outside. After being near the heat of the stove, the cold made her wish she'd grabbed her shawl. She hugged herself and half walked, half jogged across the yard. The clothesline stretched from the restaurant to the smokehouse. One sheet flapped on the line, and the basket with the other wet sheets lay on its side on the grass. Clean sheets spilled across the ground, picking up dirt. She released a little grunt. Oh, the wind! Did it have to topple the basket?

She righted the basket and scooped up the damp sheets, searching the area for Mrs. Bingham. The woman wasn't in the yard. Maybe she'd gone to her room, or maybe she was in the outhouse. Either way, the sheets were speckled with bits of dry grass and dirt. They couldn't go on the line. Abigail dropped the wadded lump of fabric in the basket and picked it up. She would take the sheets inside to the washtub.

Balancing the heavy basket against her stomach, she turned for the stairs and spotted the container that held the clothespins. It lay upside down near the back alley. Wooden clothespins were scattered all across the grass, creating a trail from where she stood to the alley. Chills attacked her that had nothing to do with the cool morning. She turned a slow circle, her pulse pounding like a woodpecker's beat on the tree.

"Mrs. Bingham?"

No answer came. Fear soured the pancake in her stomach. She dropped the basket, clattered up the stairs, and burst into the hallway. "Mrs. Bingham? Mrs. Bingham, where are you?" The matchmaker's room was empty, the bed stripped. Abigail checked her own room, but she found only a bare mattress, evidence that the woman had been in.

She raced back down the stairs, her feet pounding, and pushed on the outhouse door. It opened without resistance. Mrs. Bingham wasn't there. She explored every corner of the yard, calling and calling, but her boss didn't answer. Once again she looked at the clothespins, at the way they formed a trail, much like the bread crumbs in the story of Hansel and Gretel. On quivering legs, she followed them to the alley, where flattened grass and Mrs. Bingham's treasured jeweled watch glinting in the sun told a story Abigail didn't want to read.

Grabbing up her skirts, she raced for the restaurant, screeching Mr. Patterson's name at the top of her lungs.

Helena

Hog-tied and gagged in the back of the rattling wagon, Helena rued having left her reticule in her room. If she'd had her derringer handy, Mr. Nance wouldn't be able to sit on the wagon seat. He wouldn't be able to sit anywhere for a good long while. How could she have let him overpower her? She rolled and kicked, struggling against the ropes that bound her ankles and wrists. When she managed to get loose, lady or not, she would claw his eyes out.

"Stop floppin' around back there. Won't do you no good." The man spoke amiably, much more so than at their previous encounters. "I tie knots that no critter can break, an' cows're a lot stronger'n any ol' lady. When we get to where we're goin', I'll cut you loose. Until then, just be still an' get comfortable."

Comfortable? Lying on warped, splintery lengths of wood, being bounced like a sack of grain, with her hands tied behind her back? How could anyone get comfortable given those circumstances? She wanted to ask him where he was taking her, what he wanted with her, if he really thought he would get by with stealing her away, but the handkerchief he'd tied over her mouth cut off any sound. She tried to keep her tongue from touching it. The taste of dirt and sweat made her want to retch, and if she retched, she would choke.

She really had little choice but to follow his instruction, so she tried to do what he said — be still. And she prayed.

Mack

Such a ruckus in the kitchen. Louis and Clive craned their necks around and stared at the doorway. Everyone else stared, too, even though Miss Grant had told them all during the commonsense etiquette class how impolite it was to stare.

"Whatcha think's goin' on in there?" Clive's mouth hung open. Syrup dotted his whiskers.

"Dunno," Louis said, "but sounds like

somebody's tryin' to put a cat in a sack."

Several men laughed, but they were nervous laughs.

At the next table, Doc Kettering stood. "Do you think we should go in? If that's Miss Grant making all the noise, she might've hurt herself."

Fear exploded in Mack's gut. Of course Miss Grant was the one crying, but he hadn't considered she might be physically hurt. He thought she was mad enough or upset enough to drop her usual poise and let fly. But the doc's question brought him to his feet.

Louis grabbed his arm. "Best stay here, Mack. Athol's let them women come an' go, but he gets all wrought up when most folks step foot in his kitchen."

Yes, the kitchen was Athol's domain and he didn't appreciate people invading it. But the sobs and cries were too full of anguish to ignore. He had to know what had happened to Miss Grant. He strode for the door. Doc Kettering followed him.

"Miss Grant, you gotta calm down. You ain't makin' any sense." Athol held her by the upper arms. She squirmed and babbled brokenly between sobs. When Mack and Doc stepped near, relief flooded his face. "Oh, glad to see you fellers. Doc, she's been

384

carryin' on like a mouse with its tail caught in a trap since she come in from the yard. Somethin' about clothespins."

Doc touched the back of his hand to Miss Grant's forehead. "Are you feeling poorly, Miss Grant?"

She slapped his hand away and choked out, "She's gone! There are clothespins all over the yard, all the way to the alley, and there's — there's —" She sobbed too hard to continue.

Mack touched her shoulder. "Who's gone, Miss Grant?"

"M-Mrs. Bingham." She drew several shuddering breaths and grabbed his hand. "Come!"

Too stunned to do otherwise, Mack let her pull him to the back door. Doc and Athol came, too, and the three of them followed Miss Grant along a winding trail of clothespins to the alley.

Her hands flew around in wild gestures. "I came out and the sheets were on the ground and I couldn't find Mrs. Bingham anywhere. Then I followed the clothespins, and this is what I found." She crouched and picked up a piece of jewelry. Cradling it between her palms, she bit her bottom lip and rocked slightly.

Athol moved to the edge of the flattened

patch of dried grass. His face went white. "Somebody's been scufflin'."

Mack stepped beyond the flattened area and looked up and down the alley. Fresh wagon tracks carved two lines in the nearly knee-high dried grass. He swallowed a knot of dread. What had happened out here?

Doc Kettering turned and headed for the restaurant. "I'm goin' after Sheriff Thorn."

"He ain't in town." Athol stared at the grass as if he expected Mrs. Bingham to suddenly appear. "Knocked on my door real early for some biscuits an' set off for Coats."

Miss Grant bolted up and skittered to Mack's side. "We've got to do something. She could be anywhere. With anyone. Who would have taken her?"

Doc trudged around the flattened patch, his face set in a scowl. "Vern O'Dell and W. C. Miller weren't happy about having to wait so long for their brides. Maybe one of them took her, thinking they could convince her to bring the brides sooner."

"Then there's Otto, who's been worryin' worse'n anybody about how he's gonna lose his business, thanks to those wives comin'." Athol held his hands wide. "You think he might've took her, thinkin' it'd scare the rest of 'em from showin' up?"

Mack gritted his teeth. It would take

hours to check with Otto and every rancher around Spiveyville. Mrs. Bingham was likely scared half to death. The quicker they found her, the better. What would Sheriff Thorn do if he were here? He wouldn't stand around and do nothing, that much was sure.

He slapped his leg. "Doc, go get Preacher Doan."

The doc took off at a run.

"Athol, let everyone in the restaurant know Mrs. Bingham is missing and have them round up all the men in town. Tell 'em to meet in your dining room."

Athol started across the yard.

Mack remembered something. "Athol!"

The cook paused.

"Have 'em come armed and either on horseback or in a wagon."

Athol nodded and broke into a clumsy trot.

Mack turned to Miss Grant. "Ma'am, as for you, you're gonna —"

She aimed her tear-stained face at him. "If you are planning to say I'm going to stay here and wait, you might as well save your breath. If you're going after Mrs. Bingham, I'm going, too."

TWENTY-NINE

Abigail

Mr. Cleveland put his hands on his hips, and Abigail imitated his stance. He might be a foot taller and at least seventy pounds heavier, but she wouldn't let him cow her. Not when her only friend had been kidnapped. She swallowed a knot of anguish. What would she do if Mrs. Bingham never came back?

"Listen, Miss Grant, I know you're worried, but —"

"Of course I'm worried!" Now that she'd exhausted her tears of fright, anger filled her and left her quivering with indignation. "Who knows who has her, what he plans to do with her. One of these so-called good-hearted men of Spiveyville certainly proved his duplicity." Had she really intended to issue thank-yous to the men in this town? She shook her head and groaned, betrayal increasing her ire to a level that stole her ability to think rationally.

Clive Ackley huffed toward them. "Athol told us Miz Bingham's been took. Miss Grant, you reckon we oughta send a telegram to her sister?"

A new wave of grief swept over Abigail. Marietta had no family other than Mrs. Bingham. She would be devastated by this news, yet she had to be told. She grabbed Clive's elbow. "Yes, let's do that now." She pointed at Mr. Cleveland and gave him her fiercest glower. "Do not start a search party until I have returned!"

The man's eyes turned stony, but he didn't argue.

Abigail pulled on Mr. Ackley's arm. "Come on. Let's hurry."

At the post office door, Mr. Ackley fumbled with a ring of keys. Abigail gritted her teeth and resisted scolding, but when he finally located the correct key and couldn't seem to fit it into the lock, her patience ran out. She snatched the ring from his hand, jammed the key into the slot, and twisted it. The latch clicked. She opened the door and gave him a not-so-gentle nudge over the threshold. "Get me some paper."

He waddled behind the counter and brought out a square piece of paper and a stubby pencil. Abigail grabbed the pencil and bent over the page, her mind racing. A telegram had to be short, but how she hated divulging such distressing news without offering sentences of assurance. She scratched out a message.

Marietta, Helena has been kidnapped. Search parties forming. Will advise as able. Abigail

She cringed. So blunt. *Dear God, prepare Marietta's heart for this message and give her comfort.* She jolted. The prayer had come effortlessly, as if it had been lying in wait for the opportunity to emerge from her heart.

"Got it ready?" Mr. Ackley wrung his hands and shifted from foot to foot.

"Yes." Abigail pushed the note into his hands. "Please send it right away. I'm going back to the restaurant." Mr. Cleveland better still be there.

She ran the short distance, not caring that her raised skirt exposed her feet and ankles. Several horses were tied to the railing, and a wagon was rattling to a stop as she reached the restaurant porch. The driver of the wagon called, "Hold up there, Miss Grant, an' lemme get the door for ya."

She slid to a stop, torn between tears and laughter at the man's solicitous intention. He clomped across the boardwalk and opened the door. Abigail burst into the room and joined a small throng of milling men, all jabbering, all with pistols on their hips or rifles cradled in their arms, all with shoulders squared and faces set with determination. Preacher Doan and Mr. Cleveland stood in the center of the group.

"Excuse me, excuse me." Men shifted aside, tipping their hats as she pushed her way through to the middle. She tugged at Mr. Cleveland's sleeve. "Where will we look first?"

He gave her a look that communicated both admiration and aggravation. "As long as you understand 'we' means the men only, I'll tell you."

She stomped her foot. "As I already told you, I will not be left behind. Mrs. Bingham is in peril. I cannot be left here to pace and worry. I want to help."

Preacher Doan shook his head. "We don't know who took Mrs. Bingham, but we can surmise he's dangerous. We won't put you in harm's way."

Abigail bit back a groan. "Your concern is touching, but as you recall, the sheriff was concerned about leaving me without supervision because something might happen to me." She flung her arm to indicate the band of men. "If you take every man in town out for the search, who will remain here to keep me safe? Would it not make more sense to take me with you and, therefore, keep watch over me?" She glared at Mr. Cleveland, silently daring him to argue with her.

He grimaced, turning his sheepish gaze on the preacher. "Much as I hate to admit it, she could be right. If we left her here all alone and then came back to find her gone, too, I —" He gulped. "I promised the sheriff I'd keep her safe. So I'll stay here in town while the rest of you search."

Abigail clenched her fists and huffed. "That's not what I want! I want to help look for her!"

Mr. Cleveland bent his knees slightly and grabbed her shoulders, looking her right in the eyes. "A lady has no business on a search party. You're staying put, and that's that." He abruptly straightened. "Preacher, it looks to me like everyone's here. Let's get this search organized."

Mack

Mack felt Miss Grant's glower as the preacher divided the men into groups of

392

three and assigned them a direction to search. She could frown and pout and cry and scream all she wanted to. He wouldn't give in. It was his beholden duty, assigned by Sheriff Thorn, to keep her safe, and he'd do it. Including keeping her safe from herself and her fool notions.

They'd quickly ruled out Otto Hildreth as Mrs. Bingham's kidnapper. He didn't own a wagon, and even if he'd borrowed one to haul her away, his clean, unrumpled appearance lent strong evidence that he hadn't been rolling in the alley. Preacher Doan intended to check at the Miller and O'Dell ranches himself, figuring — rightly, to Mack's way of thinking — that the men would hand Mrs. Bingham over without a fuss if the preacher made the request. Mack half hoped either W. C. or Vern had snatched her. At least he trusted they wouldn't outright harm her. Beyond scaring her, anyway.

Preacher Doan gripped Clive's round shoulder. "Send a telegram to the Coats telegrapher for Sheriff Thorn. He needs to know what's going on here. Then you stay in your office and watch for an answer."

Clive scuttled out.

The preacher turned to Athol. "Let's have you stay here in town, too. The search groups will return here to report any findings, and they'll need hot coffee and snacks."

Athol bobbed his head. "They'll get what they need, Preacher. You can count on it." He bustled to his kitchen.

"As for the rest of you . . ." Preacher Doan gestured, drawing the men near. "We're going after a man who's brazen enough to grab a woman during daylight hours, which means he's capable of anything. Stay with your partners. I don't want anyone facing him alone."

Mack ground his teeth. Mrs. Bingham was facing the kidnapper alone. He reached for Preacher Doan's arm. "Before the men set out, I think we ought to pray. For everybody's safety." He glanced over his shoulder at Miss Grant. She stood ramrod straight, chin high, but she was hugging herself. "And for Miss Grant, too."

Preacher Doan bowed his head, and every man in the room whipped off his hat and pressed it to his chest. Mack bowed, too.

"Our dear heavenly Father, we praise Thee for Thy boundless love and care for Thy children." A peaceful hush seemed to descend on the room. "We entrust Mrs. Bingham into Thy keeping and ask that Thou guard her from harm. Be with each of these men as they seek our lost friend. Protect them. Guide them. Surround those seeking and those awaiting word with a peace only Thou can give. We love Thee, our Lord, and we ask that Thou bring us all safely together again. Amen."

A rumble of "amens" sounded, including a higher-pitched, raspy one from Miss Grant.

Preacher Doan patted the weapon on his belt. "Remember to fire three shots in the air if you find Mrs. Bingham, two shots if you find yourself in trouble. If you hear the signal, ride in the direction of the sound." He caught Sam Bandy by the elbow. "Let's go."

The thunder of boots on the floor was nearly deafening, and when the last man slammed the door behind him, silence fell like a wool cloak. Mack turned to Miss Grant. Her jaw quivered, and her entire body seemed as tense as a new spring. He'd need to keep her busy.

He held his hand to her. "How about you and me rewash the sheets and get 'em hung? When Mrs. Bingham gets back, she'll likely be tired. Wouldn't it be best to have her bed all made up and ready for her?"

Her brown eyes widened. "W-wash the sheets?"

"Well, yeah." He scratched his cheek. "It needs to be done, doesn't it? My ma used to say a busy day kept the worry away. And Jesus said in Matthew, 'Which of you by taking thought can add one cubit unto his stature?' Worrying won't bring Mrs. Bingham back."

"Neither will washing the sheets." She sounded argumentative, but she was already marching toward the stairs. "But you're right. I need to have her bed ready. So let's get to it."

Helena

Mr. Nance scooped Helena from the wagon bed and carried her across a patch of bare ground the way a groom carried his bride over the threshold. He'd parked the wagon in a low spot shielded by a sloping rise in the land. A wall constructed from chunks of sod seemed built into the face of the hill with a planked door centering it.

He paused at the door, hooked it with his toe, and pulled it wide. Inside, he dropped her onto a squeaky cot that smelled of mold. Dust rose from the blanket and she sneezed. Sunlight painted a wedge-shaped path across the hard-packed dirt floor, and dust motes glittered in the beam. Helena battled another mighty sneeze and squinted into the shadowed space. The odor of dampness and neglect surrounded her. Was this a cave? Or a burrow?

He stood with his back to her at a square table, his arms moving. Moments later a flash of yellow indicated he'd struck a match, and then he lit a lantern. A soft glow filled the space, and she identified a rusty stove, its pipe extending through the dirt ceiling, and two chairs plus an upside-down barrel tucked in at the table. Cobweb-draped shelves wedged into the wall held a variety of items, all of which bore a coating of dust.

He settled the lantern in the middle of the table and turned to face her. With the light behind him and the sunlight too low to reach his face, she couldn't make out his features, but she remembered his snarling face from across the table at Athol's restaurant. Fear made her mouth go dry. What did he intend to do now? Trussed up like a pig for slaughter, she'd be useless against him if he chose to violate her.

She licked her dry lips and sought a means of distracting him. "What is this place?"

He advanced toward her, stirring dust as he came. "The old dugout, first house built on my property. I use it come brandin' time.

Always stay out here 'til all the calves is marked with my Flyin' N." Sunlight traced a path up his legs and then down as he crossed through the patch of light. He reached the edge of the cot and stuck his hand in his pocket. He withdrew something and gave it a flick. A knife blade appeared.

Helena instinctively pressed herself to the filthy, foul-smelling blanket on the cot. He grabbed her shoulder and rolled her to her side with her face to the dirt wall. She scrunched her eyes tight and waited for the knife to plunge into her back.

But something slid against the skin on her wrist, and moments later, fierce tingling exploded her hands. She flopped onto her back and clutched her hands to her chest, moaning in both pain and relief.

Knife in hand, he straightened and stood over her. "Before I cut your feet loose, you gotta promise not to go runnin' off."

She doubted her feet would hold her up if they were as numb as her hands. "Where would I go?"

A grin lifted one corner of his mouth. "Smart gal. Wouldn't do you no good to run, 'cause there ain't nobody but cows around for miles." He set the knife at a threatening angle. "Do I got your word?"

She nodded.

He flopped her skirts out of the way and sliced the twine holding her feet together. The same tingles now subsiding in her hands attacked her feet with intensity. She gritted her teeth against the discomfort and attempted to sit up.

With a jab of his palm, he flattened her on the cot again. "Stay put."

She chose to obey.

He folded the blade into its handle and returned the knife to his pocket. He scuffed to the doorway, looked out both right and left, then settled the door in its frame. Even though the lantern still provided a yellow glow, the absence of sunshine sent a chill up Helena's frame and she shivered.

He pointed to a crate on the floor next to the stove. "Got a full box o' straw logs ready to burn if you get too cold. Use 'em careful, though. You'll need 'em for cookin', too." He moved around the small space, touching each item. "Matches in the tin, oil in the jug for the lantern. There's canned goods an' such in that crate under the table. Nothin' fancy, but you won't starve."

Obviously he'd planned well for her abduction. She remained flat, fearful of stirring his uncontrolled wrath if she tried to sit, but she couldn't stay silent. "How long do you intend to keep me here?"

Mr. Nance braced his hands on the back of one of the chairs and angled an apathetic look at her. "Well, now, that ain't up to me. I need a wife, but I don't aim to marry up with you. You're a little long in the tooth for my taste. No offense intended."

Relief flooded her, chasing away any offense. If he considered her too old to be his wife, then he would be less likely to take husbandly liberties with her.

"I meant to take that little sassy-mouthed one from the restaurant since she's young enough an' comely enough to be my wife. But I been watchin' an' she never come out alone. So I grabbed you instead. Now I'm gonna keep you until I can work a trade."

Helena propped herself up on her elbows. "A trade . . . You mean for . . ."

A sly grin creased his face. "For the other'n."

Of all the bold, misguided, inappropriate ways to gain a bride. "Mr. Nance, this scheme of yours is doomed to fail. It amounts to blackmail!"

"Call it what you will. I'm needin' a wife."

"You want a sassy-mouthed wife?"

"There's ways to take the sass out o' someone."

Chills broke out over Helena's frame. Athol had been right about this man. She longed again for her reticule and its contents.

He reached into his jacket pocket and pulled out a folded square of paper and a pencil. He slapped them onto the table and yanked out a chair. "Come here."

Her feet were still tingling, but they hadn't lost their ability to hold her up. She stumbled to the table.

"Sit down."

Although her soul rebelled, her body obeyed his command.

"Now start writin'. To . . ." He frowned. "What's her name?"

"Abigail. Miss Abigail Grant."

"All right, then. To Abigail." He jabbed his finger on the paper. "Write!"

Helena put the rounded point on the page and wrote, "Dear Miss Grant."

He scowled at her, and for a moment she feared he might strike her. But then he laughed. "Yeah, that's good. Sounds real fine." He slowly dictated his message, and she recorded every word, gritting her teeth and wishing she was big enough, strong enough, brave enough to tackle him, climb onto the wagon seat, and drive away.

"Now sign it with your name so she knows it ain't a trick."

Helena added her signature.

He dug in another pocket and slapped a rumpled envelope on the table. "Put her name and Spiveyville on there."

Helena did so, then watched him stuff the letter into the envelope. "This isn't going to work. They'll find you out and you'll be in terrible trouble. If you let me go, I won't tell anyone who took me or where you kept me. You'll have your freedom."

"I don't need freedom. I need a wife." He returned the pencil and envelope to his pocket. Then he strode to the door and looked back at her, as cold and unnerving as a snake. "As soon as your little sassy-mouthed assistant agrees to be my wife, I'll let you go. So" — he shrugged — "how long you're here depends on how fast she's willin' to do what needs doin'. I'll be back this evenin' with my boys. We'll need supper, so make yourself useful."

THIRTY

Abigail

With Mr. Cleveland's help, the washing was completed much more quickly than she could have managed on her own. Even so, two hours had lapsed from the time the men set out, and they clipped the last sheet to the line. Not one gunshot had rung out on the breeze.

Sagging in disappointment, Abigail gathered up the extra clothespins while Mr. Cleveland emptied the tub. The sudsy water flowed over and around the dried stems of grass beside the back stoop, leaving a smudge behind that reminded her of melting snow. The air held a sharp enough bite to invite snow, and she aimed a questioning look at her helper.

"Does it snow in Kansas in October?"

"Sometimes. There've been years when we've had blizzards in October, other years

403

when it stayed mild almost up to Thanks-giving Day."

She rubbed her cold, chapped hands together. "What about today? Do you think it might snow today?"

He propped the washtub against the siding and seemed to search the sky. "No. The clouds're all wrong. These are white and puffy, like big balls of cotton. Snow generally falls from thick gray clouds."

Abigail sighed. Her breath hung in a brief puff of fog that quickly whisked away on the breeze. "That's too bad."

"Why do you want snow?"

"Because it would be easy to follow a trail in the snow." When she was a little girl and it snowed, Father went outside and carved a path in the yard by stomping the snow flat. She'd always loved following his footsteps. She wouldn't want to follow his footsteps anymore, though. A lump filled her throat. She hung her head and battled tears.

"C'mon, let's get you inside." He guided her into the restaurant and closed the door behind them.

Warmth enveloped her, a welcome embrace, but she bit her lower lip. "Shouldn't we leave the door open? We won't hear gunfire from inside with the door closed."

"Depending on how far away the men've

gone, we won't hear it with the door open, either. And Athol isn't gonna want that cold air coming inside."

"No, he sure ain't." Mr. Patterson's voice carried from around the corner. "If you got them sheets done, why don'tcha come here an' help me."

With reluctance, Abigail moved into the kitchen, and Mr. Cleveland followed. Potatoes, carrots, and onions formed hills on Mr. Patterson's worktable. He stood at one side of it with a paring knife in hand.

"Figured I'd make up a big pot of soup. Preacher Doan said the men would want a snack, but it's cold outside. Better to give 'em something warm an' fillin', don'tcha think?"

Mr. Cleveland rolled up his sleeves. "Good idea. What do you want me to do?"

"Peel an' slice them carrots. I'll peel an' cut up the taters. Miss Grant, you can chop those onions."

She would have chosen a different task if given the option, but she had no fight left in her. She pushed her sleeves to her elbows, donned an apron, and set to work. The fumes from the onions made her eyes and nose run, but strangely she welcomed the sting. It took her mind off Mrs. Bingham and what might be happening to her.

Mr. Patterson added the chopped vegetables and two large jars of canned tomatoes to a kettle already holding a beef bone and water. He stoked the oven, stepped back, and brushed his palms together. "There. That oughta satisfy the fellas when they come in."

The first group, made up of Mr. Pendergraff, Mr. Bandy, and Mr. Thompson, arrived before the soup was ready to eat. They gathered around the potbelly stove in the dining room and warmed their hands.

"The wind's pickin' up again," Mr. Thompson said. "Near blew us out of our saddles."

Abigail joined their circle. "Where did you look?"

"We went north at least a good mile an' a half. Checked every gully, well, shed, an' ranch along the way."

The fact that they had checked gullies and wells made Abigail's stomach churn. She didn't want to contemplate what they expected to find.

Mr. Pendergraff unbuttoned his jacket. "We stopped at the Double C and asked Firmin if he knew anything about Mrs. Bingham bein' took. He got plenty worked up about it."

Mr. Patterson made a face. "I bet he did.

He wouldn't take kindly to bein' accused o' cartin' off Miz Bingham. Especially if he didn't have nothin' to do with it."

"Nope, that's not what got him all upset." Mr. Pendergraff shook his head, wonder blooming on his lined face. "He was downright scared for her. Saddled up an' wanted to join the search."

Firmin Chapman was what Mother would have called a ruffian, but in that moment Abigail warmed toward the man.

"We told him to stay put," Mr. Thompson said. "No sense in havin' the ranchers all leave their stock unattended. There's plenty o' townsmen out searchin'." He turned to Mr. Cleveland. "Heard anything from Sheriff Thorn?"

"Not yet. But even if he left before seven for Coats, he's probably only just now getting to the town. It's a good five-mile ride." Mr. Cleveland chewed his mustache and glanced at the clock hanging on the dining room wall. "I sure wish —"

The restaurant door flew open, and everyone shifted their attention to Clive Ackley, who clomped in with an air of importance. His gaze landed on Abigail, and he strode in her direction, holding a folded piece of paper out like a shield. "Got a telegram, Miss Grant, from Miz Bingham's sister. Figgered you'd wanna see it right away."

Bill

Bill reined in Patch next to the Coats schoolhouse. He wasn't one for intimidating little children, but neither did he want to spend an entire week trying to track down Elmer Nance. His boys had to know where their pa was.

Kids were huddled in little groups across the play yard, finishing up their lunches. The Nance boys sat off to themselves under a scraggly-looking maple empty of its leaves. He crossed to them. They were sure a sorry-looking pair. Uncombed hair, dirty faces, clothes so wrinkled and stained it looked as though they'd worn them day and night for the better part of a week. Had Nance up and abandoned them? Bill hated to admit it, but it wouldn't surprise him.

He stopped in front of the dark-haired, freckle-faced boys, hooked his thumbs in his trouser pockets, and fixed a smile on his face. "Howdy. Remember me?"

They nodded in unison. The older one spoke up. "You're Sheriff Thorn."

"Yep. You're Dolan, an' your brother's Buster, right?"

They nodded again. Bill went down on

408

his haunches so he'd be on their level. "Wanted to talk to you fellers, if you don't mind. I'm still needin' to find your pa. I'd be much obliged if you could tell me where to look." Suddenly he realized the boys weren't holding lunch tins like every other child in the yard. He frowned. "Didn't you two bring a lunch today?"

The little one hung his head. Dolan slung his arm around his brother's shoulders. "We don't need a lunch. Had a big breakfast."

Bill didn't believe him. They had a hungry look about them. But he wouldn't shame them by pressing the subject. If they had nothing else, he could at least let them keep their pride. "All right, then. Since you're not eatin', you oughta be able to talk. So . . . where's your pa?"

The boys glanced at each other. They set their lips in firm lines and kept their heads low like they didn't even know Bill hunkered two feet away from them.

"Boys?"

They winced, but they didn't look up.

"You ain't in any kind o' trouble."

Dolan didn't raise his head, but his gaze found Bill. "We ain't?"

Bill shook his head. Shook it hard. Convincingly. "No, sir. Just needin' to see your pa. I have somethin' to give to him."

"What is it?"

Now, that wasn't the boy's business. "Somethin' that's rightfully his." He placed his hand on the patched knee of the boy's britches. "Wouldja tell me where to find 'im? It'll ease my mind considerable when I can talk to him."

Dolan opened his mouth. Then his gaze moved beyond Bill to something behind him. He lurched to his feet. "C'mon, Buster, time to go in." He yanked his little brother up, and the two shot off like a bull was chasing them.

Bill stood, his knees popping. "What's wrong with you two? Come on back here."

They darted into the schoolhouse and closed the door.

Bill started after them, but something compelled him to look over his shoulder. Afterward he was glad he did, because Elmer Nance himself was coming up the street in his wagon. Bill ambled out and intercepted him.

Nance set the brake and glowered down at Bill. "Sheriff."

"Nance." Bill braced one hand on the wagon seat and rested the other on the butt of his pistol. "Been lookin' for you."

"What for?" That man could snarl words better than anybody Bill had ever met.

"You left somethin' behind in Spiveyville. I'm wantin' to return it to you." He slid his hand into his pocket and pulled out the handkerchief he'd tied around Nance's coins. He plopped the pouch onto the seat. "There's two dollars and sixty-two cents wrapped in there. Does that match what you put on the table in Athol's restaurant?"

Nance untied the knots and counted out the coins, his lips moving silently. "Reckon so." He dropped them into his shirt pocket and then flipped the handkerchief to Bill. "Thanks." He gripped the brake handle.

Bill grabbed hold of the handle and held tight. "I'm not done yet."

Nance's eyes narrowed to slits, like a poisonous snake's. He sat tense, as if ready to strike. "What?"

"Seems there's some misunderstandin' about you bein' in Spiveyville. Since you didn't get the message last time, I'm re-peatin' it plain an' simple for ya." Bill angled his hat back and matched Nance's squinty-eyed glare. "You're to stay away from Athol's place an' every other business in town. You come in again an' I see you, you'll find yourself sittin' in a jail cell."

Nance reared back and curled his lip. "You'd arrest a man just for comin' in to do some business?"

Bill wanted to smack the contemptuous smirk from his face, but he kept his tone even. "We don't need your kind of business. We don't want it. So you can take it elsewhere. Anywhere but Spiveyville." Or anyplace else he hadn't wore out his welcome.

He looked at Bill's hand still gripping the brake handle. "That all?"

"Not quite." Bill leaned closer and bounced his thumb over his shoulder. "Them two boys o' yours . . . When's the last time you fed 'em?"

The contempt changed to fury so fast Bill came close to taking a backward step. "What'd they tell you?"

"Not a thing. But I know hunger when I see it." Bill huffed, disgusted. "Don't look like they've washed in a month, an' their clothes are torn an' filthy. That's no way to see to youngsters, Nance."

The man sat in silence for several seconds, repeatedly closing and opening his hand. Finally he snorted. "You remember how you told me to stay out o' the businesses in Spiveyville?"

Bill nodded.

"Well, I'm tellin' you to stay outta my business." He pushed Bill's hand aside, jammed the handle forward, and brought the reins down with a smack.

412

Miss Grant hadn't looked up from the telegram even once in the fifteen minutes since Clive put it in her hand. She'd taken it to the table in the corner, sat with her back to the group, and now stayed there with the folded square of paper sandwiched between her palms.

Grover Thompson nudged Clive. "She looks awful upset. What'd it say?" He flicked his gaze between Clive and Miss Grant.

Clive frowned. "I can't divulge the contents of a telegram, Grover. She's gonna have to tell you." He shook his head and backed toward the door. "I hope she tells you soon, 'cause she's gonna need some help." He turned and departed.

The men stood in a circle, shuffling their feet and examining either the floor or the ceiling. Clearly, they didn't know what to do. Neither did Mack. He'd been taught by his mother not to ask snoopy questions, and Miss Grant had told them in the etiquette class to respect other people's privacy, but concern writhed through him. She was troubled, and he wanted — no, he needed — to know why.

He crossed the floor, slow and quiet, and touched her shoulder. "Miss Grant?"

She jumped and raised her startled gaze. Her forehead was puckered into lines of worry, and she held her lower lip between her teeth.

He bounced a glance at the telegram. "Bad news?"

"I . . . I'm not altogether sure."

"Why's that?" He slid into a chair. At the stove, the men all leaned slightly in their direction, turning one ear toward them.

Miss Grant cleared her throat. "Well, the telegram is very short. And a bit unsettling."

"Do you want to show it to me?" Mack held out his hand, palm up.

She hesitated for a few seconds but then seemed to wilt. "Yes. Here." She placed it in his hand.

He unfolded it. Only three words were scrawled on the page. " 'On my way'?" He frowned. "She's coming to Spiveyville?"

Miss Grant shrugged. "I assume so. But is she coming alone? If she's bringing the brides, where will they all stay? What will happen to Mrs. Bingham's business while she's here?" She held her hands outward in a helpless gesture. "I wanted her to know what had happened to Mrs. Bingham, but I didn't expect her to pack a bag and come. I don't know what Mrs. Bingham is going to say to me when she realizes her sister left

Newton."

At least she was thinking positively that Mrs. Bingham would be here to give her opinion. He tapped the telegram on the table. "Do you want me to walk to the post office so you can send another telegram?"

"Do you think I should?"

It warmed him that she asked. It meant that maybe, just maybe, she'd started to trust him. He put his hand over hers. "You know Mrs. Bingham better than any of us. Would Mrs. Bingham want her to come?"

She crunched her lips to the side. "The business means a lot to her. She always prays that the women and men she brings together will be as happy as she and her husband were." Tears winked in her eyes. "She . . . she cares more about other people than she does about herself. I think Mrs. Bingham would want Miss Herne to stay put and see to the business."

"Well, then, let's go send a message."

They both stood. As one, the men around the stove leaned in the opposite direction. She turned to face them, and her chin rose a notch. "Gentlemen, I know you were listening, and I'm going to make a firm request. Keep quiet about the contents of this telegram and my intended response. The last thing we need with Mrs. Bingham in some unknown location is the prospective grooms getting it in their heads that the brides are coming early."

With every sentence, her voice gained strength. "Even if the brides do show up here, there will be no matches made without Mrs. Bingham's personal approval. And please remember we still have classes to complete."

THIRTY-ONE

Helena

Helena paced the small space again. Four wide strides deep, five across. Roughly twelve by fifteen feet. She'd measured her prison two dozen times since Mr. Nance closed the door and left her, and each time it seemed as though the walls pressed a little tighter. No windows. No air moving. She might as well be in a tomb.

What time was it? She absently touched her shoulder where a small jagged tear marked the place where she'd pinned her jeweled watch that morning. Apparently it had fallen off during her scuffle with Mr. Nance. She prayed she would find it when she left this dismal dwelling. Howard had given it to her.

Her head low, she crossed the floor again. Over the course of her lonely hours, she'd observed a sliver of sunlight, which sneaked through a crack in the door, grow shorter and shorter. It had finally disappeared. Its absence pierced her.

She darted to the door and put her eye to the crack. Shadows shrouded the ground directly in front of the wall, but the landscape beyond was still light. So it must be afternoon, and the dugout must face east. In which direction was Spiveyville? If she somehow managed to escape, she didn't want to waste time running in the wrong direction.

She gripped a crossbar on the door and pulled. The door groaned, but it held tight. She planted both palms on the door and pushed with all her strength. The door didn't budge. Grunting with exertion, she banged her shoulder against it until pain drove her to stop. She sank into a chair. Such a useless waste of energy. Mr. Nance had clunked something into place on the outside when he left. Probably a length of wood over the iron hooks she'd seen mounted on the thick doorposts. She'd never break it down.

She paced from the door to the stove and back, restless as a caged animal. If only there was a window, some means of allowing in air and light. Her need led her to stick her face against the crack again. Cold air

418

wheezed in, and she drew one breath after another. In through her nostrils, out through her mouth, praying it would rid her senses of the dead, musty aroma permeating the dwelling.

Her stomach pinched. She hadn't eaten anything since breakfast, and then only a single pancake rolled around a sausage link. She'd already taken inventory of the supplies. A can of lard. Canned beans, tomatoes, peaches, and beef. A good-sized sack of cornmeal and a smaller one of flour. Two dented pots, one crockery bowl, a stack of tin plates, a rusty can opener, and a handful of mismatched silverware made up her kitchen utensils. Rudimentary at best. And yet he'd told her to have supper waiting.

She brought down the bowl, the flour, and a can of peaches from the shelf. It would likely be the sorriest cobbler ever made, but she would give it her best effort. Partly because she needed something to do, partly because she was hungry and cobbler was the only appealing recipe she could glean from her limited resources, and partly because he'd said his boys would be in tow. If it were only the man, she'd let him starve. But children needed sustenance, so she would provide it.

As she pushed the rusty blade of the

opener into the can's tin seal, Mr. Nance's chilling comment — *"There's ways to take the sass out o' someone"* — rolled through the back of her mind. What an evil, unfeeling, selfish man. He didn't deserve a wife or children. Helena couldn't blame his wife for leaving him, but why had she left the boys behind? Apparently the mother had lost her maternal instincts along with any sass she might have once possessed.

Helena peeled back the circle of tin and dumped the peaches into the bowl. The sweet scent seemed improper, considering the foul setting and her unpleasant thoughts. But a conviction filled her. When she escaped this dirt prison and her vile warden, she would do her utmost to rescue Mr. Nance's children from their father. It was the right thing to do.

Abigail

Was she doing the right thing? Abigail tucked the clean, fresh-smelling sheets around Mrs. Bingham's mattress. The scent of ham and roasted vegetables crept between floorboards and taunted her with the reminder of her reason for being in this town. She'd told the men to come tonight for the class on dining because she didn't want to

420

disappoint Mrs. Bingham by not fulfilling her obligation, but now she wasn't sure she should try to teach. Who cared about the proper way to cut a piece of meat or whether or not one buttered tiny bites of bread one at a time when she had no idea what had happened to her only friend?

"Miss Grant?" Mr. Patterson called from below.

Abigail trotted to the head of the stairs and peered down. "Yes?"

"Sheriff Thorn's ridin' in."

Her heart leaped into her throat. "Is Mrs. Bingham with him?"

"He's alone."

Disappointment stabbed with such intensity her knees weakened. She grabbed the wall to steady herself and blinked back tears.

"You wanna talk to him?"

Of course she wanted to. She clattered down the risers at an unladylike speed and darted past Mr. Patterson to the front door. She stepped out on the porch. At the same time, Mr. Cleveland left his hardware store, Mr. Ackley left the post office, Mr. Thompson left the mercantile, and Mr. Adelman left the bank. Apparently everyone had been watching for the sheriff. Waving her hand in the air and calling his name, she took off at a run and met him in the middle of the road.

His horse shied sideways and he pulled back on the reins. "Whoa there, Patch." The animal snorted, but it came to a stop. Sheriff Thorn glowered at Abigail. "Are you tryin' to make him buck me out o' the saddle?"

She gripped her hands beneath her chin. "I'm sorry, but I am so worried. What will you do next to find her?"

The men, including Mr. Patterson, joined Abigail. The sheriff's scowl deepened. He scanned the group. "Find who? What're you talkin' about?"

" 'Scuse me, Miss Grant." Mr. Ackley pushed in front of her. "Didn'tcha get my telegram? I sent it to Coats this mornin'."

He shook his head. "I didn't go into the telegraph office. No need to."

Abigail groaned. "Then you didn't even look for her."

The sheriff shifted his hat to the back of his head. "What in thunderation is goin' on?"

"Mrs. Bingham is missing." Abigail's voice broke on the last word.

Mr. Cleveland put his hand on her shoulder. During the day, he'd been her greatest source of comfort, and she appreciated his presence now. "It looks like someone pulled into the alley behind the restaurant, wrestled

422

her to the ground, and carted her off in a wagon."

Sheriff Thorn swung down from the saddle and gaped at Mr. Cleveland. "When?"

"Early this morning. Before eight for sure."

Mr. Patterson nodded. "Mack an' Preacher Doan sent fellas out to search, an' Clive sent you a telegram. I been keepin' ever'body fed between searches. Tobis here's even put up a reward of a hundred an' fifty dollars to whoever finds her."

The sheriff jerked his wide-eyed gaze to the banker. "A . . . a hunnerd an' fifty dollars?"

Mr. Adelman jabbed his thumb in Abigail's direction and nodded. "Wanted to find out if it was a scheme this thief's daughter concocted to get everybody out searchin' while she went from store to store and emptied cash registers. Figured if there was a reward, an' it was bigger'n what she'd find in any of our tills, she'd take us right quick to Miz Bingham so she could claim it."

Humiliation flooded Abigail's frame. He'd shared her darkest secret. What would the others think of her now?

Mr. Patterson whacked Mr. Adelman on the shoulder. "Here I was singin' your praise when you're nothin' more'n a lowdown dirty snake."

Abigail jolted.

Mr. Ackley stomped his foot and punched the air. "You oughta be ashamed o' yourself."

Mr. Thompson poked his finger at the banker. "We better not find out you hid Miz Bingham away to give Miss Grant some sort o' fool test."

Mr. Adelman put his hands in the air. "I didn't have nothing to do with that woman disappearing."

"Hmph." Mr. Ackley folded his arms over his chest. "You better not've."

Abigail swallowed a lump of mingled joy and anguish.

Mr. Cleveland's hand on her shoulder pressed firm, warm, certain. "Sheriff, don't waste time questioning Miss Grant. She was as shocked by all this as we were. She's spent the whole day worrying. Besides, I saw the scufflin' spot and wagon tracks."

"Yeah!" Mr. Patterson glared at the banker. "An' we all heard Miss Grant screamin' like a —" His face blotched red. "Well, screamin' in fear."

"Tobis," Mr. Cleveland said, "you're always bragging about the plays you've seen on stages in the cities. You ought to know what's real and what's not." His tone hardened. "You've been watching Miss Grant. Have you seen even one thing to make you think she's less than honest?"

The banker ducked his head. "Her pa's a thief." He sounded like a recalcitrant child.

"Her pa's got nothin' to do with this." Mr. Ackley gave him a little shove. "Get back to your bank an' quit stirrin' trouble against Miss Grant. A gentleman never fab— fab—" He squinted at Abigail. "What's that word again?"

"Fabricates," Abigail, Mr. Cleveland, Mr. Thompson, and the sheriff chorused.

Mr. Ackley nodded hard. "Fabbercates tales. Now you best git before I lose my patience."

As the banker scuttled up the street, Abigail slid a wobbly smile across the remaining men. "Thank you." Would she have expected to find trustworthy men in this tiny, unpolished town? No, but they were here, and how she appreciated them.

She turned a firm look on Sheriff Thorn. "What are you going to do to bring her back? She's probably frightened out of her wits." Tears stung. "She's the kindest person I know. We have to get her back before whoever took her does her harm." The tears she'd held back during the long day of watching and worrying found their way to the surface. And it seemed perfectly natural to turn her face into the front of Mr. Cleveland's plaid shirt and let them flow.

Helena

When she was alone again, Helena would let the tears pressing behind her lids flow, but for now she needed to be brave. But, oh, she found it hard. Dolan and Buster Nance dug into the sorry excuse for cobbler as if they hadn't seen food for days. She longed to wash the dirt from their thin faces, dress them in fresh-smelling clothes, hold them to her heart and assure them they were safe. But she couldn't do any of that with their father looking on. So she pasted on a smile she hoped would give the boys reassurance and dipped the spoon into the half-empty pot of cobbler.

"Would you like some more, boys?"

The younger of the pair of scruffy waifs thrust his plate forward. "Yes'm."

Mr. Nance whacked the boy on the back of the head with his open palm. "Stop bein' greedy. You ain't the only one wantin' more."

The boy hunkered low.

Helena gasped. "Shame on you, Mr.

Nance. You're the greedy one, taking food from the mouths of children." She tipped the pot and scraped a good-sized portion of cobbler onto Buster's plate. Then she added more to Dolan's. A small amount remained, and she thumped the pot onto the table in front of the man. He could serve himself.

She flounced to the stove, which still emitted warmth thanks to the twisted straw logs and dried cow chips. A bucket rested on the floor near the stove, and she picked it up. "I'll need water to wash the dishes. Is there a well nearby?" She started for the door.

Mr. Nance leaped into her path, tipping his chair in the process. "There ain't no well out here."

"Then what am I to do? I can't be without water." Too late she realized the sassiness in her tone. The boys sent wary glances at her, and the man's eyes narrowed. Although it galled her, she bowed her head in a show of submission. "Would you please show me where to fetch water?"

He grabbed the bucket and shoved it at the older boy. "Go fill the bucket."

The boy jammed one more bite in his mouth, then grabbed the rope handle and trotted out the open door.

Mr. Nance took her by the arm, guided her to the stove, and released her with a rough shove. "You'd do well, woman, to remember your place."

She rubbed her arm where his fingers dug in. She sent up a silent prayer for protection and chose her words carefully. "Will you and the boys expect breakfast in the morning?"

He stared at her for several seconds with his brows low and his lips curled into a snarl. Finally his stiff stance relaxed. "No. They can't get all the way out here an' then back to town in time for school." He snorted. "I don't put much stock in book learnin', but my wife was set on them two finishin' out all the grades. Made me promise I'd send 'em, so that's what I do."

Helena could scarcely believe what she'd heard. He was keeping a promise to a wife who'd abandoned him and the boys? Perhaps there was some small element of decency deep inside him.

Dolan shuffled in, the bucket gripped in both hands. One side of the bucket was dark and dripping, the other side dry, indicating he'd scooped water from somewhere. A stream, perhaps? Or a stock tank? He plunked the bucket on the ground next to Helena's feet, then stood and heaved a sigh. "Here you go, ma'am."

"Thank you, Dolan. I appreciate your

428

help." She reached to smooth his hair, but he ducked away with a look of fear and scuttled to the table. Her chest panged. Never should a child be fearful of a simple touch. The feeble bit of warmth she'd felt toward the father whisked away like a bit of dust in a stout breeze, and she inwardly cursed not only the man's penchant for violence but also the mother's cowardly decision to leave the helpless children alone with him.

She faced him and forgot about tempering her tone. "Do you intend to feed them in the morning? Growing boys need a good meal more than once a day."

His hands balled into fists, and his face contorted with rage. He leaned close, his foul breath searing her cheeks. "Don't be tellin' me how to raise my boys." He turned and waved his arm. "Dolan, Buster, git in the wagon."

The boys jumped from their chairs and scrambled for the door, bumping into each other in their haste. Dolan grabbed Buster by the sleeve and pushed him ahead, and he glanced over his shoulder as they crossed the dirt threshold. Helena would remember forever the mix of resentment and pleading in the boy's dirt-smeared face.

Mr. Nance stomped after them but paused

in the doorway. "We'll be back again tomorrow evenin' for supper. Fix somethin' besides sweet next time." He reached for the door.

Helena hurried after him. Her dignity would take a beating, but she hadn't relieved herself since morning, and her need was greater than her pride. "Mr. Nance, I . . . I require the use of an outhouse." What a foolish request. If there wasn't a well, would there be an outhouse?

He cupped his hand beside his mouth and hollered, "Buster, get that bucket out from under the wagon seat an' bring it here." Moments later the boy trotted to the doorway, bucket in hand. Nance pushed him toward Helena. "Give it to her."

Buster handed it over, his gaze darting everywhere but on her face. She smiled anyway and thanked him. He scuttled out without a word.

"Tomorrow evenin'." Nance barked the simple farewell and slammed the door into its casing. A *thud-clunk* sealed her inside.

THIRTY-TWO

Mack

Mack sat on a chair next to the restaurant's front door and listened in on the final dining class. Despite the circumstances, he battled a grin. Miss Grant had a lot of gumption. More than she probably even realized.

If Mack hadn't known about her distress over Mrs. Bingham still being missing despite two days of searching, he wouldn't guess there was even the slightest thing troubling her. She addressed the group of students — Sam Bandy, Cliff Lambert, W. C. Miller, and Grover and Harriet Thompson — with the same confidence and poise as in previous classes. The students were a lot more subdued than previous ones, though. Even W. C. stayed quiet and followed her directions. Another time, Mack might have found W. C.'s quiet cooperation

431

amusing. But not tonight. Everyone in town was on edge over what had happened to Mrs. Bingham.

A part of him wished he could be out on a scouting detail. The sheriff declared they'd search 'round the clock, day and night, until they found the kidnapper and brought Mrs. Bingham back to safety. He felt cowardly staying behind, but he couldn't rebel against Sheriff Thorn's authority. Plus there was some truth to the warning he'd given the handful of men left behind.

"We don't know if the kidnapper was after Miz Bingham or just any woman an' she happened to be available for snatchin'. Until we know for sure, every female in Spiveyville is in danger. We need some men stickin' in town to protect 'em."

So Mack, Athol, Clive, Grover, and Tobis stayed behind while nearly every other able-bodied man took an assigned amount of time on horseback, roaming the countryside, searching for Mrs. Bingham. The sheriff came close to canceling school, but Mrs. Doan convinced him the children were safer in the schoolhouse than they would be running around free. Mack was glad the woman spoke up. At least the children in town would have their normal routine.

"Mr. Miller?" Miss Grant's tone turned

sharp, and Mack automatically perked up even though she wasn't talking to him. "If you must pick your teeth, wait until you are away from the table. And kindly do not use your finger. It's considered gauche."

W. C. frowned. "What's that mean — 'goash'?"

She tipped slightly in his direction and raised one eyebrow. "Lacking in social graces."

He nodded. "Ah. All right." He wiped his finger on his pant leg and raised his hand. "May I be excused? I got a chunk o' ham caught an' it's hurtin' me."

Uneasy laughter rolled. Miss Grant sighed, but a grin twitched at the corner of her mouth. "Yes, you may."

W. C. bolted for the corner of the room, digging in his pocket as he went.

Miss Grant cleared her throat, and the diners shifted their attention from W. C. and his pocketknife back to the teacher. She linked her hands and let them fall against the front of her dark-red dress, a relaxed, feminine pose. "Now that our meal is finished, let's discuss the proper use of the napkin. Please remove it from your lap." She mimed the action. "Let it drape from your hand, holding a clean spot between your fingers, and wipe your mouth — one smooth motion. No, no, Mr. Lambert, no mopping."

A few guffaws rolled.

Cliff's face blazed red and he followed her directions.

She smiled. "Much better. Now, are there any questions?"

W. C. clomped back to his table and slid into his seat. He poked his hand in the air.

"Yes, Mr. Miller?"

"You still plannin' to start the dancin' lessons tomorrow? 'Cause I'm kinda thinkin' we shouldn't be dancin' an' carryin' on when Miz Bingham ain't here to join in."

Miss Grant hung her head for a moment. Mack braced his palms on the edge of the chair, ready to jump up and stand beside her if she needed some support. He'd spent pretty much all of the past two days staying near, and he admitted he liked being close to her. Looking out for her. Offering an encouraging word if she needed it. He liked that she seemed to appreciate it, too. So if she looked at him with any kind of pleading, he'd be at her side before W. C. could say *dance*.

She raised her head, and her gaze drifted across the room to him. He left the chair and headed in her direction, but before he reached her side, she started talking. "I've had the pleasure of Mrs. Bingham's friendship for three years. She's a strong, gracious, giving woman who certainly did not deserve to be overtaken in the alley and carted away to who knows where."

Tears flooded her eyes, but she blinked rapidly and they cleared. "She finds great joy in bringing men and women together as husband and wife, and I am sure that, wherever she is right now, her greatest concern is causing yet another delay in bringing the wives to Spiveyville to meet their prospective grooms. I think, if we could ask her, she would tell us to finish the classes. And even though it is . . . difficult . . ." She gulped.

Mack placed his hand on her shoulder. A touch meant to tell her, *You're not alone.*

She flashed a watery half smile at him and faced the class. "We must persevere. If not for ourselves, then for Mrs. Bingham."

Cliff shook his head. "I admire your starch, Miss Grant. Goodness knows you've got reason to hightail it back to Newton an' forget all about us here after what's happened, but how're we gonna finish the classes with so many of our fellas out huntin' for Miz Bingham? We gotta leave some men at the ranches, an' we gotta leave a few here in town for you ladies' protection. Will there be enough folks to even have a dance?"

"Well . . ." She looked up at Mack.

He shrugged. "Sheriff Thorn's worked out a schedule for coming and going so the searchers have a chance to rest. I reckon we can hold the classes for those who're in town and able to come. Over five days, hopefully there'll be at least one that works for all the grooms."

Athol came out of the kitchen and moved to the other side of Miss Grant. "Circumstances bein' what they are, I doubt Miss Grant's gonna keep anybody from marryin' up just 'cause they couldn't get to a dance. But havin' the dances — havin' something to keep our spirits up — seems like a good idea to me."

Miss Grant nodded, a genuine smile gracing her freckled face. "Yes. Something to keep our spirits up. That's what we need. It's exactly what Mrs. Bingham would want for us. So starting tomorrow evening, unless Mr. Briggs has any objections, there will be a social-dancing class at the livery starting at seven for whoever is available and desires to attend."

She could scarcely believe she was making such important decisions on her own, yet it felt right to continue the classes. The townsfolk needed the distraction. She needed the distraction. Mrs. Bingham would wholeheartedly agree. And if the prayers everyone was offering were answered, Mrs. Bingham would be back to participate in the dancing. The woman dearly loved to dance.

Oh, please, Lord, let her be here to dance.

This internal prayer didn't take her by surprise. She'd sent up twenty or more since finding the circle of flattened grass in the alley, and with each communication with God, it seemed more natural to speak to Him. Deep inside, a part of her still wondered if He was listening, if He cared. Just in case, she repeated the internal prayer as the students left and she began to gather the dirty dishes. Both Mr. Patterson and Mr. Cleveland helped, and then Mr. Cleveland asked her if he could stay and help wash dishes.

Abigail looked to Mr. Patterson for approval. It was his kitchen, after all. She held her breath while waiting for his reply, uncertain whether she wanted to hear an agreement or a refusal.

Mr. Patterson shrugged. "I reckon it's up to you, Miss Grant. If you ain't tired o' him hangin' around yet, then tell him yes. If you'd rather he went on home, then tell him no." He ambled to the stove and started banging pots around.

Abigail looked at Mr. Cleveland, who looked at her. She read hope in his eyes. The corners of her lips tugged upward. "Yes, please. And thank you."

His beaming smile nearly melted her heart.

She washed the dishes, and he dried them and made a neat stack on a nearby table. They didn't talk while they worked, but she was keenly aware of his presence. The mundane things — the steamy water, the sharp scent of the lye soap, the squeak of her fingers on a wet plate, even the sounds of Mr. Patterson's grumbling about how hard it was to scrub baked-on grease from the stove top held a significance. Would she think of Mr. Cleveland each time she smelled lye soap carried on steam or her finger played a discordant note on a wet plate or she overheard a growly male voice grumbling under his breath?

Suddenly her eyes welled, and tears rolled. She pulled her hands from the water and searched desperately for something on which to dry them. Mr. Cleveland held the only towel in close proximity. She reached for it, and he captured her hands inside the cloth, his larger hands cradling hers.

"Miss Grant, what's the matter?"

She'd cried the morning of Mrs. Bingham's disappearance — desperate, fearful tears. She'd cried when the townsmen defended her against Mr. Adelman's accusation — relieved, grateful tears. But these tears she couldn't identify. She shook her head. "I . . . I don't know."

Mr. Patterson sent a wide-eyed look in their direction and darted into the dining room. She couldn't blame him. She'd overwhelmed him yesterday morning with her near hysteria. She expected Mr. Cleveland to leave, too. Father had always been uncomfortable with tears, whether hers or Mother's, and the one time she had cried in front of Linus, he rolled his eyes and shoved a handkerchief at her, advising her to "dry up" because she was embarrassing herself. She'd already wetted Mr. Cleveland's shirtfront once. He wouldn't have the tolerance for yet another crying jag.

Mr. Cleveland released her hands, and she expected him to flee the kitchen. But he snatched a clean wiping towel from the basket and, while she tangled the damp towel around her fingers, he gently dabbed the tears from her face. And that only made them rain all the faster. He stood close, not saying a word, but his nonjudgmental expression and tender swipe of the rough cloth against her skin soothed her.

Finally the weeping subsided and he tossed the tear-stained towel in the wash basket. He aimed a half smile, half sympathetic grimace at her. "Better now?"

She turned her gaze aside. Linus was right. She had embarrassed herself. "Yes. I'm so sorry. I don't know what came over me."

"Sowing tears."

She met his solemn gaze. "What?"

"Sowing tears. That's what my ma called them when she got hit with a wave of crying she couldn't explain."

"Sewing . . . as in . . ." She pretended to stitch a seam.

He grinned. "No, sowing . . . as in . . ." He flipped imaginary seeds across the floor.

"Oh." She sniffed and pushed her hands into the now-tepid water. "Why did she call them sowing tears?"

He propped his hand on the washstand. "Psalm 126:5 says, 'They that sow in tears shall reap in joy.' ' Ma said when she got overwhelmed and needed to have a cry, she could be sure joy would follow the tears. That the tears watered seeds of joy. I've had some of those tears myself."

She paused in scrubbing a plate and gawked at him. "You . . . cry?"

He chuckled. "Well, sure."

"But you're a man!" She'd never seen Father cry. Not even when they led him from the courtroom in chains. If ever there was a time to cry, that was it. She and Mother had cried themselves to exhaustion.

His expression turned serious. "Miss Grant, I don't know where you got the idea that men don't have deep feelings, but that's wrong. Oh, we might be better at hiding them. But we get sad and scared and doubtful, the same as anybody else. I can tell you I cried lots of sowing tears when my uncle died after I came to Spiveyville. Here I was, far away from anybody I knew, and I was all alone."

Abigail understood that feeling far too well.

"But like Ma said, the tears sowed seeds of joy. I found a new home and people I call my friends." He took the plate and ran the cloth over it. "If you trust God and are patient, you'll find out. Those tears you just shed, there'll be healing behind them. Wait

441

and see."

She washed the last dish slowly, contemplating all he'd said. Men had deep feelings, which they hid. That day in the courtroom, when Father had stood stoic and seemingly uncaring, had he only been hiding his remorse?

Something deep in her heart seemed to splinter. Not a break, not even a crack. But some of her resentment toward her father shifted to . . . sympathy. How far he'd fallen from the respected businessman and revered husband and father. She would need to spend more time considering whether she'd misjudged his hardness as a protective cover to hide his real feelings.

She handed Mr. Cleveland the dish, and he meticulously wiped away every bit of moisture. He placed it on the stack, draped the towel on a hook to dry, and caught her watching him. A light stain of pink lit his tanned cheeks.

He rubbed his finger under his nose, smoothing his mustache into place. An unnecessary gesture. It always lay quite politely across his upper lip. A nervous grin lifted his lips. "What is it?"

Perhaps it was the quiet of the kitchen, maybe the leftover effects of her tears, maybe her loneliness for Mrs. Bingham, but she opened her mouth and heard herself say the most unexpected thing. "Do you suppose all would be well if I called you Mack and you called me Abigail?" Heat flooded her face. Oh, she'd never been so bold. Was Mother rolling over in her grave? Yet she needed the informality. She needed a friend.

"Are you worried that somewhere out there a mountain will crumble into a hundred pieces and fall into the sea if you don't follow the dictates of polite society?"

If he had asked such a question a week ago — maybe even a day ago — she would have given him a look of superiority and advised him to keep a civil tongue in his head. But looking into his eyes, which glittered with mischievousness, she could only giggle. "Maybe."

"It won't happen, and I'd be very honored to call you Abigail." He grinned. "In fact, I might even call you Abbie."

She wrinkled her nose. No one had ever shortened her name. "Well, then, I shall call you . . ." She tipped her head. "There's no way to shorten Mack, but it must be the shortened version of something. What is your given name, Mack?"

He choked out a guffaw and shook his head. "Oh, no. Let's stick with Mack and

Abigail."

Mack and Abigail . . . She liked the way it sounded.

THIRTY-THREE

Bill

The three-quarter moon glowed behind a thin patch of clouds. No night birds sang. Cows stood in little groups, heads hanging, none of them lowing. The only sound was the muffled *clip-clop* of horses' hooves. Bill wasn't one to let the idea of ghosts and goblins bother him, but the evening felt eerie. Unsettling.

He hunched lower into his jacket. The movement made a muscle twinge in his back. Grimacing, he rubbed the spot. He'd spent so many hours in this saddle, they might need to pry him out of it when he reached the livery stable. He glanced at Millard Fletcher, whose horse clopped alongside his. The man slumped forward so far his nose almost touched the back of the horse's head. Was he sleeping?

"Millard."

"Huh?" The rancher jerked upright. "What?"

"You were about to fall off your horse."

Millard's mouth hung open. "Nah. I was?"

"Now, why would I tell you that if you wasn't?" Bill shook his head. Millard was a nice enough fella, but sometimes Bill wondered what he used for brains.

Millard snuffled, shifted a bit on the saddle, and stayed upright. "Was hopin' maybe you'd seen her or somethin'. Been three full days already, Sheriff. How long're we gonna keep lookin'?"

Bill brought Patch to a stop. Millard reined in, too. A few cows released some nervous moos, but they'd settle down soon enough. "Lemme ask you somethin', Millard. What if it was your mama or your sister or your wife who got took? How long would you look for her?"

The man blinked. " 'Til I found her, I reckon."

"An' that's what we're gonna do. We're gonna look 'til we find Miz Bingham." And if the Good Lord was on their side, they'd find her alive and unharmed. The longer it took, the less likely it became, but that's what Bill was praying. He clicked his tongue on his teeth, and Patch started forward.

Millard and his roan fell in beside Bill.

"Well, she sure ain't anywhere around Spiveyville or somebody would've come across her by now. We gonna push farther out now? Maybe Cullison, Coats, or Sawyer?"

Bill would go as far as Isabel, Pratt Center, and Sun City if need be. His back twinged again. He jammed his fist against the cramping muscle until it released. He was getting too old to ride this horse for hours on end. Maybe it was time for him to turn in his badge, settle down, have himself —

Now, what was he thinking? At his age, starting a family? Thunderation, if some woman birthed him a son tomorrow, he'd be past sixty by the time the boy was old enough to set out on his own. He had no business even thinking such thoughts. Funny how hard it was to squelch it, though. Still, he could make a change. Turn in his badge, maybe open a little shop where he could use his papa's woodworking tools. He wouldn't mind that. Not a bit.

Millard pointed. "Spiveyville's just over the ridge. Reckon the other fellas have come in already?"

"Could be."

"Reckon they found Miz Bingham?"

Bill hoped so. For her sake, and for his, he hoped so.

As their horses left the pasture and fol-

447

lowed the road up the rise, he thought he caught a few notes from a fiddle. He reamed his ear with his finger, frowning. But when he popped his finger free, he heard it again. He glanced back at Millard. "Do you hear —"

"Sure do!" The young rancher broke into a wide grin. "It's comin' from the livery. Sounds like Joe Booth's got his fiddle playin'. Do you s'pose they're havin' a celebration dance 'cause they found Miz Bingham?"

Bill didn't know, but he wanted to find out. He gave Patch a solid nudge with his heels, and the horse broke into a trot. Millard's spotted gelding kept up *clop* for *clop,* and the two of them reined in near the livery corral. Lanterns glowed behind every window in the loft, and the fiddle song drifted out sweet and inviting.

Millard looped the reins over the fence rail and took off in a clumsy trot. Bill followed a little slower, his hours in the saddle making him walk like he carried a bucket between his knees. He climbed the loft ladder and stepped into the middle of a dance the likes of which he'd never seen before. Not a square dance, but some kind of circling dance with folks' feet following a boxy one-two-three step in time with the melody.

Millard bounded to Joe and stood beside him, swaying faster than the music played. Bill scanned the dancers, hoping he'd find a stately looking woman with white-blond hair swept back in a twist. He spotted the Thompsons, the Doans, the Pendergraffs, half a dozen men hanging on to each other with sheepish looks on their faces, and Miss Grant dancing with Mack.

He plodded across the hay-strewn boards to Mack and tapped him on the shoulder. The younger man stopped and aimed a glance over his shoulder. He broke into a smile. "Sheriff Thorn."

Miss Grant released Mack and crowded close. "Did you have any luck? Did you find her?"

So Miz Bingham was still missing. Then why in thunder were they up here dancing like there wasn't a care in the world? Had they all lost their senses? "No, I didn't find her. When I heard music an' saw the lanterns burnin', I thought you'd found her an' were all celebratin'. Why're you havin' a party if she's still lost?"

Miss Grant put her hand on her hip. She lifted her chin, and her eyes sparked fire. "This is not a party. It is a class. The social-dancing class I promised Mrs. Bingham I would teach."

Joe stopped his playing, and everyone shifted to listen in.

Miss Grant gave them plenty to hear. "She isn't here, but I am, and it's my responsibility to finish what she started. So, Sheriff, if you'd be kind enough to get out of the way, we will continue learning the steps to the waltz." She nodded at Joe. "Go ahead, Mr. Booth. Where you left off — one, two, three . . ."

Joe slid the bow on the strings, and a sweet tune sang. The dancers started again, some smoother than others, but they all joined in.

"Take your eyes off your feet," Miss Grant called out, moving just as easy as if she glided on ice while holding on to Mack. "Look into your partner's eyes."

Guffaws and giggles broke loose.

"And no laughing!" But she laughed while she said it.

Bill watched for a while, not sure he believed what he saw. He thought folks got crazy only when the moon was full. The moon was near three-quarter, but these folks were full crazy, dancing when Miz Bingham was lost.

He climbed down to the lower level. Hugh Briggs was up there hanging on to Ike Rose

450

from the Tumbling R, so Bill would have to put Patch into a stall on his own. He'd see to his horse and then head to his office. If Vern O'Dell and Sam Bandy had come in already, they'd be waiting for him. If they hadn't come in already, he'd wait for them. Get a report.

The music stopped and clapping broke out.

"All right, change partners. Ladies, if you wouldn't mind dancing with one of the single men, let's give them a chance to prove they can lead."

Laughter.

More music.

Bill shook his head again. Crazy. They'd all gone plumb crazy.

Helena

Helena pressed her eye to the crack in the door again. The front yard was completely in shadow. Evening. Finally. Trapped in the small, windowless space, all alone, with not even a book to read, never had hours crept by so slowly. Where was Mr. Nance? Supper waited. Beans and a mealy corn bread made from cornmeal, lard, water, and a bit of flour. It would probably taste awful, but she'd discovered from previous encounters

451

that the Nance children were hungry enough to eat the soles of their boots. They wouldn't complain. If they came. Mr. Nance had never arrived so late.

Her stomach clenched. More from loneliness than hunger. She pushed away from the door, releasing a little grunt. Was she now looking forward to the vile man's arrival? She laughed at how far she'd sunk in such a short amount of time. Perhaps she was going mad.

She'd passed the morning alternately praying and using one of the butter knives to hack at the sod blocks in the corner opposite the table. But after carving away several chunks, she realized her mistake. Where would she hide the clumps of dirt? What if her digging caused the wall to collapse? She could bury herself alive. So she'd cleaned the knife on her skirt and paced. Prayed. Paced. Prayed and paced at the same time, pausing repeatedly to peek out the little slit that served as her only connection to the world outside the dugout.

Maybe he wasn't coming at all. If the letter she'd written had reached Spiveyville, maybe Abigail had met up with Mr. Nance. If he had Abigail, he'd have no reason to come back for Helena. Fear rattled through her, but then she shook her head, dispelling the thought. Mack and the sheriff would never allow Abigail to take Helena's place, but the letter would give the sheriff and the men of the town a clue where to look for her. That meant her rescue would come. But would she still have full possession of her senses when that finally happened?

Her stomach rumbled and cramped. Mr. Nance hadn't told her she had to wait for them to eat, so she sat at the table by herself and ate a spoonful of beans and a crumbly lump of corn bread. She grimaced. So bland . . . She pretended she was cutting into one of Athol's beef steaks with roasted potatoes and carrots, and she managed to fill her belly. Only a little bit of water remained in the bottom of the bucket, and even though the dry corn bread stuck in her throat, she didn't dip it out to drink. She'd wait for fresh. She shouldn't have to wait much longer. The Nances would surely come soon.

She scraped her plate clean with a fork and crossed to her peephole. She drew back in alarm. Night had fallen. Something must have happened to Mr. Nance. Maybe the sheriff caught up with him, fought with him, killed him. If the man was dead, would his children tell the sheriff where to find her? Her heart thudded so hard she felt dizzy.

She sank onto the cot and put her head in her hands.

"Dear God, don't let me die in here all alone."

I'm never alone.

The thought swooped through her mind with such power she almost believed it was an audible voice. She lifted her face to the dirt ceiling and smiled through tears. "You will never leave me nor forsake me. I was so sure I would wither up and die when Howard died, but You were with me. You helped me fill my house with young women and helped me send them out into their new lives. You're here with me now. Forgive me, Father, for thinking for even one moment that You've abandoned me." She thanked her Lord again and again for His presence, and by the time the rattle of wagon wheels penetrated the thick wall, her spirit had been restored.

She darted to the stack of plates and set them on the table with spoons, then brought the pans of beans and corn bread. As she set them down, the door squeaked open and Mr. Nance shoved the boys inside. The younger one's left cheek bore a red mark, and tears had washed clean trails on both boys' cheeks. Alarm propelled Helena forward, and she crouched low to examine

454

Buster's face. She recognized the clear impression of a handprint.

Fury filled her. She stepped past the boys and met Mr. Nance head on. "How dare you strike a child in the face."

He pushed her aside.

She stumbled but caught her balance and whirled on him again. "Why are you so late? Is it because you were beating your children?"

The boys cowered in the little space between the table and stove. She didn't mean to frighten them, but her anger overwhelmed her. She wanted to be big enough and strong enough to pummel Mr. Nance into the ground, to show him how it felt to be weak and powerless. All she had were words, and she must use them to build the boys up.

Drawing herself to her full height, she stepped in front of the boys and held out her hands as a shield. "Children are gifts from the Lord Himself. They are to be cherished and loved as His precious creation. Parents are called to teach their children with patience, not to stir them to wrath." She'd seen resentment in the older boy's eyes. How long until he began striking out at others the way his father struck at him? "You are wrong to mistreat them,

Mr. Nance, and I will not tolerate it."

Mr. Nance glared at her for several seconds, then growled low in his throat. "Dolan, fill her water bucket. Buster, dump the slop bucket out in the field and rinse it in the creek."

Helena clapped her hands to her face. "Don't give such a disgusting task to the child. Let me take care of my own slop bucket."

His eyes narrowed. "You ain't goin' nowhere." He snapped his fingers at the boys. "Go!"

The boys slunk past her, grabbed the buckets, and dashed outside.

Now without an audience, he advanced on her, inch by inch. She held her ground until his foul breath touched her face, and then she couldn't resist taking a step backward. Her palms connected with the hot cookstove. She yelped and locked her hands at her waist.

He leaned in, forcing her to bend backward over the stove. "I smacked the boy because he let the milk cow loose an' we had to chase her down. It kept me from gettin' out here before dark. The only way young'uns learn is if they pay for their mistakes. It's how my pa taught me, an' his pa taught him. An' it works. I can tell you it works for women, too, an' you'll find out if you keep pushin' me."

I'm never alone.

The reminder brought a rush of confidence and peace that made no sense, but it emboldened her. She stepped sideways away from the stove, away from him, and met his steely gaze. "I'm sorry your father chose to batter you into obedience. I'm sorry no one intervened to prevent him from hurting you. But I am telling you, there are better ways to raise children. And I don't care how many times you threaten me, I will not stay silent when a child is being mistreated."

The boys appeared in the doorway. Buster chewed his lip and stared at Helena as if he were gazing upon an angel, but Dolan hung back, his frame stiff, wariness etched into his features.

She held her hand to them. "Thank you, boys. Now please come in and have a seat at the table. We're having beans and corn bread. Does that sound good?"

Mr. Nance remained as if rooted in place. Helena eased past him and filled all three plates. She set the pans aside and the boys picked up their spoons, but she shook her head. "No, you need to wait for your father. Mr. Nance?"

He still didn't move.

She held her breath and gazed at the back of his head. The hair was mashed, as if he hadn't combed it in a while, and for reasons beyond her understanding, sympathy washed through her. At one time he had been a little boy, an innocent child, abused by his own father. He was full of wrath because he'd been a product of wrath.

Her breath escaped on a gasp of discovery. Had God brought her into Mr. Nance's life to help point him to a better way of living? If so, she should take full advantage of the opportunity.

"The beans are getting cold, Mr. Nance. Are you ready to eat?"

He jolted as if he'd suddenly come to life. He yanked out a chair, sat, and picked up his spoon.

"Bow your heads, please." She ignored his startled glare and closed her eyes. "Dear God, thank You for this food. May You bless it to nourish our bodies and give us strength to do Your will. Amen."

The boys' spoons clanked against their plates, but Mr. Nance didn't reach for his spoon. The whole time the boys ate, he sat and stared at her with a smoldering glare.

THIRTY-FOUR

Abigail

Abigail hurried through her morning ablutions and then entered Mrs. Bingham's room. For a moment she stood just inside the door, a fist against her trembling lips. Would Mrs. Bingham come back to this room? At the close of last night's dance, the participants had joined hands in a circle and prayed for her safe return. With so many people storming heaven with the request, would God grant it? She couldn't know for sure. She recalled a scripture stating God's ways were not man's ways, and she surmised it meant He had reasons beyond men's understanding for doing or allowing certain things. Abigail prayed that if it was God's way to never bring Mrs. Bingham back, He would give her the strength to endure. In the meantime, she would cling to hope.

She touched the watch waiting on the

dresser top and then fluffed the pillow on the bed and straightened the coverings even though they hadn't been touched since she'd made the bed Tuesday morning. Satisfied the room was as neat and welcoming as it could possibly be, she pattered down the stairs to the dining room and into the kitchen. She removed an apron from the hooks by the door and tied it on as she crossed to the stove.

"Good morning, Mr. Patterson."

The cook continued stirring something in a large kettle. "Mornin', Miss Grant. Sleep well?"

"Yes, amazingly well." Better than she'd expected to.

"Prob'ly 'cause the dancin' wore you out. You an' Mack moved real good together." He winked.

Remembrances of gliding around the dance floor with Mack's hand on her waist swept in and warmed her from within. Despite their height difference, they'd moved as one. She would cherish memories of that simple barn waltz for the rest of her life. She poked her nose over the kettle so she could blame her rosy cheeks on steam. An unappealing glob of something gray bubbled in the pot.

She straightened. "Oatmeal?"

"Yep." He reached for his cinnamon jar on the shelf. "Not gonna wear myself out this mornin' keepin' up with pancake orders or fryin' bacon. Oatmeal's good an' fillin', an' it's somethin' the fellas can eat in a hurry an' get back to their search."

Oatmeal held no appeal for her, but Mr. Patterson deserved an easy morning. And she wouldn't oppose anything that would expedite the search. Her last conscious thought before falling asleep was a prayer asking for Mrs. Bingham's safe return. *Please, please, God* . . . "What a good idea. I'll put out bowls this morning instead of plates."

"Before you do that, go down to the cellar. Find the sack o' raisins an' scoop three or four cups o' walnuts from the barrel. Those'll make good stir-ins for the oatmeal."

Raisins and walnuts? Her mouth watered. She might have some oatmeal after all. She grabbed a lantern, lit its wick, and made her way down the dirt stairs. She easily located the walnuts, but the raisins were hidden behind sacks of flour. Using the apron skirt as a pouch, she carried her small burden up the stairs. She extinguished the lantern and dumped the bag of sticky raisins and unshelled walnuts on the worktable.

"Where is your nutcracker, Mr. Patterson? I will shell the walnuts for you."

"Nah." He handed her the wooden spoon. "Them shells are hard to crack. I'll do it. You stir."

She held the spoon like a sword, uncertain she'd heard him correctly. She remembered Mrs. Bingham's chuckling taunt the night Mr. Patterson had joined the dining class. *"Your stove will survive one night with a different cook at its helm."* He'd let her cook, but the entire evening he'd cast sorrowful glances toward the kitchen.

Abigail waved the spoon. "Are you sure you trust me?"

He scowled. "Just stir, wouldja?"

She stifled a giggle and stirred.

Mr. Patterson unlocked the door at six thirty and several men, including Sheriff Thorn, were already waiting to come in. A couple of them grumbled when Mr. Patterson announced the morning special, but none of them turned down a bowl of oatmeal topped with raisins and chunks of walnuts.

Abigail collected the dirty bowls as the men finished, and when she reached for the sheriff's bowl, he held his coffee cup to her.

"Fill me up one more time, Miss Grant, before I have to head out in the cold."

She scurried to the kitchen, retrieved the pot, and poured steaming dark liquid into his cup. The man's eyes bore dark circles, and his shoulders slumped. She couldn't resist touching his shoulder when she gave him his full cup. "Can't you let the others search today, Sheriff, and take a day of rest? You've hardly been off your horse since last Monday."

He took a slow draw on the cup, his eyes half-closed. Then he lowered it to the table, braced his palms around it, and gave her a determined look. "I'll rest when we know for sure what happened to Miz Bingham. This badge on my chest ain't for show. It means I'm accountable for the folks who live in an' around Spiveyville. Just 'cause you an' her ain't real residents of the town don't mean I'm any less responsible for makin' sure you're safe."

He made a horrible face. "I sure bumbled it by not bein' here when she got took. My office is right next door. If I'd been in there 'stead o' off tryin' to return money to that no-good scoundrel Nance, I might've been able to stop it."

Abigail slid into the chair next to him and wove her fingers together. "It isn't your fault. Mr. Patterson and I were in the kitchen. We didn't see or hear a thing. Blam-

463

ing ourselves won't bring Mrs. Bingham back. What's done is done, and we have to look forward now instead of trying to find fault." She'd meant to reassure the sheriff, but the truth of her words bolstered her, too.

He sighed and placed his hand on her wrist. "Ah, I know, missy. It's prob'ly the tired talkin', but I can't help but think mebbe a younger sheriff would've made a differ'nt choice an' mebbe kep' her from goin' through such a scary ordeal." His watery gaze collided with hers. "You're bein' brave, an' I'm proud o' you for it, but I know you're scared." His fingers curled tight. "I am, too."

"We all are." Abigail sniffed and blinked hard. "But Preacher Doan is praying, and Mack is praying, and I'm praying, and — well, the whole town is praying. I know Mrs. Bingham is praying, too. We have to trust that God is hearing our prayers and will answer in the best way for Mrs. Bingham and for all of us."

Sheriff Thorn lifted the cup and drained it in one long, noisy series of slurps. He slapped it onto the table and rose. "All right. I'm settin' out again. Gonna take a couple o' men an' head toward Sawyer. There's some ridges an' hills east o' Sawyer where rustlers've hid out in the past. I'm wantin' to take a look-see over there."

Abigail stood, too, and reached for the sheriff's hand. She cradled his dry, calloused hand between her hands. "Good luck, Sheriff Thorn. I'll pray for your safety."

He nodded, sniffed, and plopped his hat over his gray-streaked black hair. "You do that." He strode out, looking a little taller than he had coming in.

She picked up his empty coffee cup and bowl and carried them to the kitchen. Mr. Patterson had heated a pot of water for washing dishes, so she readied the washbowl and rolled up her sleeves. While she washed, Mr. Patterson dried, and she smiled, remembering Mack's comforting presence and their easy conversation about sowing tears.

She never would have imagined feeling so comfortable with a man. She'd been engaged to marry Linus Hartford, and more often than not, she'd found herself on edge, worried about displeasing him somehow. Not once had Mack given her a reason to guard her words or worry about her behavior. She appreciated being able to relax in his presence.

She recalled something, and she jerked her hands from the water. "Mr. Patterson,

465

did Mack — I mean, Mr. Cleveland — come in for breakfast this morning?"

He scratched his cheek, his lips puckering. "Hmm . . . nope. Don't think I saw him."

"That's rather out of the ordinary for him, isn't it?"

"Well, he is partial to my cookin', but he keeps some canned goods an' dried fruit an' so forth in his apartment, an' he sees to his own needs now an' again." A sly grin climbed Mr. Patterson's cheeks. "But if you're worried about him not havin' a good breakfast in his belly, you can go tap on his door an' see if he's ate somethin'."

Abigail raised one eyebrow. "Mr. Patterson, you're being impertinent."

His grin widened. "Why, thank you."

She frowned. "For what?"

"For callin' me important." His chest puffed.

"I said impertinent. It's not the same thing."

"Well, thank you anyway. Go on over an' check on Mack if you wanna. Them dishes'll keep."

She plunged her hands into the water and finished every bowl, studiously refusing to acknowledge the cook's ridiculous chortles. She dried the last bowl and carried the stack to the shelf. As she placed them in their proper spot, the dining room door opened and someone hollered her name.

She nearly tipped the stack of bowls. Mr. Patterson reached to stabilize them, and she ducked beneath his arm and entered the dining room.

Mr. Ackley trotted toward her, waving an envelope. "Mail stage just come by. Found a letter in the bag for you. I figgered you'd want it right away."

Nervousness smote her, and her hands trembled as she reached for the crumpled envelope. She peered at its front and gasped.

The postman grabbed her upper arms. "Your face just went white as a ghost." Still holding her, he tilted sideways and bellowed, "Athol! Bring some coffee, quick!" He guided her to a chair, then stood close, his hands on his knees, and his face level with hers. "What is it, Miss Grant?"

Her hands shook so badly the letters seemed to jump around on the tan-colored paper. But she recognized the writing. She'd seen the neat round script on dozens of notes and in the pages of ledgers. She knew from whom the letter came, but fear kept her from opening it and discovering what the woman had written.

Mr. Patterson scurried out, cradling a cup

467

of coffee. "What's wrong?"

Mr. Ackley grabbed the cup and held it under Abigail's nose. "Dunno. She looked at the envelope an' went all white in the face. Thought she was gonna faint."

The pungent aroma of the brew filled Abigail's nostrils. She angled her head aside. "Please, it's nauseating me."

Mr. Ackley frowned at the cook.

Mr. Patterson nodded wisely. "It's makin' her sick. Miss Grant don't drink coffee."

She groaned. "Doesn't drink coffee."

"I know." Mr. Patterson leaned down, patting her on the back. "What's got you all white faced, Miss Grant?"

She sucked in a steadying breath and showed him the envelope. "It's from Mrs. Bingham. She wrote to me. What . . . what if this letter is telling me she went away on her own and left me here by myself? She's always been kind, but I know I've been a burden to her. She could never find a match for me because . . . because . . ."

"How come?" Mr. Ackley's round, curious face remained only inches from hers.

She swallowed a knot of shame. "Because the men always sent me back. They didn't want to k-k-keep me."

The two men exchanged open-mouthed gapes, then zipped their attention to her

468

again. Mr. Ackley patted her hand. "Well, now, I don't know how any feller could be so coldhearted as to send you away. You're right purty, Miss Grant, an' so smart. Them men just didn't show good sense, that's all."

Mr. Patterson squeezed her shoulder. "An' lemme tell you, I seen how Miz Bingham looked after you while she was here. She's right fond o' you, Miss Grant, so I don't think you need to worry that she left you behind. It's gotta be somethin' else."

"That's right." Mr. Ackley stood up straight and put his hands on his hips. "You open it an' see. All them worries you're holdin', they'll be set to rest."

Abigail's fingers convulsed on the envelope. She sent a hopeful look across both men. "Do you think so?"

"Sure do." They spoke at the same time, their tones matching in volume and certainty.

She offered them a grateful smile and held up the envelope. "Do either of you have a pocketknife?"

They both produced one, but Mr. Ackley was quicker opening his. He used the blade and slit the top flap.

"Thank you."

He nodded. "You're welcome." He flicked his hand at Mr. Patterson. "Come on, Athol, let's leave her alone. Remember? Folks isn't supposed to butt into other folks' privacy."

When they'd disappeared into the kitchen, Abigail pulled a wrinkled sheet folded into a square from the envelope and slowly unfolded it. The letter began "Dear Miss Grant" in Mrs. Bingham's familiar handwriting, but it was written in pencil. Abigail frowned. Mrs. Bingham never wrote in pencil.

She continued reading, and the more she read, the more her pulse pounded until she could scarcely draw a breath. She crushed the letter to her chest and bounded to her feet. She needed Sheriff Thorn. But he'd left — for Sawyer, wherever that was. She whirled toward the door to the kitchen, but then without conscious thought, she spun the opposite way and charged out the front door.

THIRTY-FIVE

Mack

Mack's stomach growled. The crackers and hard cheese he'd eaten for breakfast an hour ago hadn't satisfied him nearly as much as one of Athol's hearty meals. But he'd chickened out from going to Athol's for breakfast. Because he knew he'd see Abigail. And he feared she'd read something in his face he wasn't ready to let anyone know.

He'd always said if he was meant to love someone and get married, God would bring the woman to him. Well, God had. Last night, moving around the dance floor with Abigail Grant in his arms, his heart made its choice.

He wanted Abigail.

But what a foolish choice. She was a city girl. She had a job with Mrs. Bingham, and she took the responsibilities of the job seriously. So seriously she continued even without Mrs. Bingham's supervision. She'd made it clear from the beginning she wasn't one of Mrs. Bingham's bevy of brides, so it was foolhardy to think she'd changed her mind. Especially now, with Mrs. Bingham missing.

Someone pounded on his front door. An insistent pound that brought him out of his apartment at a run. A glance through the glass sent his heart into his throat. Was God trying to torture him? He twisted the key and opened the door. "Good morning, Abigail."

She fell through the opening and jammed a wrinkled sheet of paper at him. "Read it."

If his senses had fled, they'd taken her manners with them. "What is it?"

She flapped it against his chest, her expression fierce. "Read it!"

He took the paper and crossed to the counter, where an overhead lamp lit the space well. She stood beside him, chewing her thumbnail, while he flattened the page on the wooden top. He glanced at the greeting, flicked a startled glance at her — she wanted him to read her personal mail? — and then read the letter, one word at a time.

Dear Miss Grant,
    I have been took by someone who

472

wants to marry up with you. He will let me go as soon as you say you will marry him. If you say no, write it on a paper and leave it at the old Addison well house. If you say yes, take yourself to the well house and wait. He will meet you there. Don't tell anybody about this because if anybody else goes to the well house you will never see me again. This ain't a joke.

Helena Bingham

Mack broke out in chills. The final sentence, "This ain't a joke," had to be a lie. Why would Mrs. Bingham send such a message to Abigail? "Are you sure this is from Mrs. Bingham? It doesn't sound like her at all."

"It's not her voice, that's true, but it is her handwriting. I'd know it anywhere." Abigail's brown eyes were wide and moist with unshed tears. She steepled her hands beneath her chin. "It seems as though she transcribed exactly what someone told her to say. But it's good news, isn't it? She was alive and able to write this letter, and whoever this person is, he wants to use her as a trade, so won't he continue to keep her alive?"

Mack fingered the paper, worry rolling

through his gut. Any man who was dishonest enough to kidnap a woman and hold her for ransom was unlikely to keep his word about letting her go. But he didn't want to scare Abigail. Not when she was gazing at him with hopefulness shining in her doe-brown eyes. "Have you shown this to Sheriff Thorn?"

She shook her head. "He left at least a half hour ago for Sawyer."

Mack groaned. Sawyer was the opposite direction from the old Addison place. And he probably wouldn't be back until late. "So we're on our own."

"We don't need Sheriff Thorn. We know what to do." She drew herself to her full height and lifted her chin, like a bantam rooster preparing to take control of the henhouse. "Where is the old Addison well house?"

He jolted. "Why?"

"So I can go there, of course."

Protectiveness struck with enough force to buckle his knees. He braced his palms on the counter and glared at her. "You aren't going anywhere near that well house."

"Mack!" She stomped her foot and moved into her stubborn pose — head cocked, shoulders square, fists on hips. "I have to go. It's the only way we can get Mrs. Bingham back. The letter says so."

"I don't much care what the letter says. You aren't going." Determination to keep her safe gave his legs their ability to hold him upright. He stood tall and glowered at her, but underneath he battled the urge to take her in his arms and never let go. If he reached for her now, though, she might smack him and run.

He forced himself to be calm. Bullying her wouldn't work, but pleading might. "This is a dangerous man, Abigail. You can't reason with dangerous men. If you go there and ask for Mrs. Bingham, he's likely to grab you, too."

"I didn't intend to go reason with him." She flung her arms outward. "I'll go and give him what he wants."

Mack's jaw dropped. "W-what he wants? Did you read the letter? Did you see what he's asking?"

"Yes."

"Then are you telling me you want to marry this man, whoever he is?"

She crinkled her nose. "He won't marry me." Suddenly her brave front wilted. "Believe me, once he gets to know me, he won't want me anymore. He'll send me back." She jerked her chin up in an arrogant angle. "But if letting him think I'll marry

475

him will ensure Mrs. Bingham's freedom, then we'll have to let him think he's won. It's the only way."

Mack groaned. "Abigail . . ."

She released a little cry and grabbed his shirtfront. "Please, Mack, she's taken care of me since my mother died. Even when I was nothing but trouble to her, she didn't send me away. I owe her. She — she's more than my friend. She's my only family."

Mack caught her wrists and gently set her aside. He turned his back on her and ran his hand through his hair. Why couldn't the mail have arrived before Sheriff Thorn took off? He might have to tie Abigail to a chair until the sheriff returned.

He whirled around and caught her by the shoulders. "All right. I'll help you, but on one condition."

Her fine brows descended and her gaze narrowed. "What condition?"

"You need to wait for Sheriff Thorn. He'll want to follow —"

"The letter says —"

He tightened his grip. "Will you listen to me?"

She set her lips in a firm line. Her eyes sparked with fury, but she stayed silent.

"The sheriff'll want to follow you from a ways back, keep an eye on you, keep watch

476

for Mrs. Bingham. He'll want you both to be safe. He's the law, Abigail, and whoever sent this letter has broken the law by stealing Mrs. Bingham and using blackmail to gain a bride. We can't do this without Sheriff Thorn knowing what's happening."

She folded her arms over her chest. "How long do you expect me to wait? She's been gone three whole days, and she's probably wondering if anyone will ever come." Her chin quivered and tears swam in her eyes. "I can't bear to think of her alone and frightened for another day, Mack."

He might regret it later, but he grabbed her close and held tight. She clung to him, her shoulders shaking in silent sobs. He rested his chin on her silky brown hair and closed his eyes. "Mrs. Bingham's a strong lady." He remembered her pointing her derringer at him her first night in Spiveyville, and despite the dire circumstances, he couldn't hold back a chuckle. "In fact, if I was a betting man, I'd put my chips on Mrs. Bingham over any kidnapper."

He brushed his lips over her hair and set her aside. "There's no sense in Sheriff Thorn going all the way to Sawyer now that we have a better place to look. Hugh Briggs has a saddle-broke stallion that he says could win the Kentucky Derby. Let's go to the livery and ask Hugh to go after the sheriff and bring him back. While we're waiting for him, we'll let Preacher Doan know about this letter." If he kept her busy and in his sights, he wouldn't have to worry about her asking someone else for directions to the Addison well house. "He'll want to pray for safety for Mrs. Bingham and you."

She nodded slowly. "All right. But when the sheriff comes back and Preacher Doan has finished praying, you won't get in the way of me going?"

Mack gritted his teeth. He let his gaze drift across her features inch by inch, memorizing the soft arch of her brows, the curl of her thick lashes, the gold flecks in her eyes, the pale freckles dotting her nose and dancing across her cheekbones. His examination reached her rosebud lips, and agony writhed through him. Would he taste their sweetness someday? Or would some evil man steal her from him?

He grabbed her close once more. "If you'll do it my way and you're bound to go, I won't stop you."

Bill

Bill's back was aching like a bad tooth.

When he found Miz Bingham and brought the foul kidnapper to justice, he would tell the townsfolk he was done with sitting in saddles. Wind howled and sent dirt and tumbleweeds rolling. He shivered. He was done with spending his time outside in the wind, too. He scanned the landscape in both directions, hoping against hope he'd see something that led him to Mrs. Bingham's kidnapper.

"Sheriff Thorn! Sheriff Thorn!"

The voice came from so far away, for a minute Bill thought the wind was tricking him. But Jerome Reed, today's fellow searcher, turned backward in his saddle and frowned.

"Somebody's hollerin' for ya, Sheriff."

They turned their horses the opposite direction, and a gust nearly took Bill's hat from his head. He clamped his gloved hand over the top of it and squinted ahead. Moments later the fancy stallion from Briggs's livery with Hugh Briggs on its back topped the rise. Bill and Jerome galloped up to meet him.

"Sheriff, glad I caught you." Hugh panted like he'd been running alongside instead of riding the horse. "You gotta come back to town. Miss Grant got a letter, somethin' the kidnapper made Miz Bingham write. He's wantin' to make a swap at the old well house on Addison's land for Miss Grant, an' Mack says come as quick as you can 'cause he's having trouble holdin' Miss Grant back."

There wasn't one thing funny about the situation, but Hugh's words painted such an image in Bill's mind, he threw back his head and laughed. "I like that little gal more every day." He yanked his hat low over his ears, grabbed his reins, and jabbed his heels into Patch's sides. "C'mon, fellas, let's go."

Helena

The sun hadn't yet moved far enough to send shadows in front of the dugout when the rattle of a wagon caught Helena's attention. Hope exploded in her chest. Had someone discovered her hiding place and come to rescue her? She pressed her eye to the little gap, and the hopes plummeted so quickly that tears threatened. The pair of old swaybacked horses pulling the wagon belonged to Mr. Nance. But why had he come so early?

She skittered away from the door and positioned herself near the stove. The squeak of the door hinges broke the silence in the dugout, and Mr. Nance stepped in,

480

followed by Dolan and Buster. She frowned. Shouldn't the boys be in school?

Mr. Nance caught Dolan by the collar. "Get the water bucket and fill it up. There's two more buckets in the wagon. Fill them, too, an' bring 'em in here." The boy scuttled to obey. The man aimed his scowl on Buster next. "See to the slop bucket. Then help your brother." Finally he looked at her and quirked his finger. "Come with me."

She dug in her heels. "Where?"

His lips formed a snarl. He stomped forward and grabbed her arm. His fingers bit in as he pushed her out the door. After days of being trapped in the dim dugout with only a single lamp for light, the bright sun was an assault. She brought up her hand to shield her eyes. Cold wind raced across her, welcome in its refreshment. She hadn't done more than wash her face and hands since he'd brought her here. She and her clothes needed a thorough washing.

He pulled her to the rear of the wagon and lifted out the gate. A basket of eggs and a crate with various items rested in the bed. He handed her the basket. "Take these inside."

Squinting, she cradled the basket in her arms and returned to the dugout, moving slowly and sending a surreptitious glance in

481

both directions as she went. Gently rolling land, overgrown with dry grass, stretched for as far as she could see. No other structures, no people, only cows in the distance. Helplessness swooped in.

He thumped up behind her and planted his hand in the middle of her back. "Get in there."

Why couldn't she stay outside a little longer? He'd chosen a perfectly isolated spot as her hideaway. Who would see them out here? But his push sent her through the door. She set the basket on the table, and he placed the crate next to it. He began pulling things from the crate and plunking them on the table.

"Brought more lamp oil. More foodstuff, too. Enough for all three of you for a couple o' days."

She shot a sharp look at him. "Three of us?"

He didn't lift his gaze from the crate. "You an' the boys. They're stayin'."

"Why?"

"Because I say so, that's why." He emptied the crate and slid it under the table. He brushed his palms together and glanced around. "There's only the one bed, but the boys can sleep on the floor. Won't bother 'em any."

There were two blankets on the cot. She would willingly share, but couldn't he have brought bedrolls along with the food? And why had he brought the boys? She fingered a bag with granules of sugar caught in the rolled-down top. "Is today Saturday?"

"Nope. Friday."

He'd snatched her Tuesday morning, so she had been in this dugout for only three days. It seemed much longer. "If it's Friday, why didn't you send the boys to school?"

He moved to the door, cupped his hand beside his mouth, and hollered, "Dolan! Buster! Hurry up!" He faced her again. "Got things to do away from my ranch an' might not be back at night. Couldn't leave 'em on their own. So I brung 'em here." He looked out and yelled again. "Boys? What're you doin' out there?"

He'd brought a cast-iron skillet. It lay on the table in the middle of everything else, inviting her to pick it up. Her fingers inched toward the handle while she kept her gaze fixed on the back of his head. If she was stealthy yet quick, she could bring the skillet down on his skull. Then she could lock him inside and leave with the boys. Her hand closed around the handle, her pulse pounding.

"We're here, Pa." Dolan waddled to the

door, a full bucket hanging from each hand. "Buster's fillin' the other'n."

Helena released the skillet and reached for the buckets. "Here. Let me help you."

Surprise registered on the boy's face, but he let her take them.

Mr. Nance snapped his fingers. "Tell your brother to hurry up. I got places to be."

He'd left the door open the entire time, and cool air had whisked inside the dugout, but Helena experienced a chill unrelated to the weather. "Where, exactly, do you need to be, Mr. Nance?"

He angled a sly grin over his shoulder. "Dunno why you're askin', 'cause you already know. Gotta get to the well house. Gotta wait for my answer." His expression turned smug. "Guess we'll find out whether or not you'll get to leave this place or whether it'll be your burial tomb."

THIRTY-SIX

Bill

Word had sure spread fast. Bill entered Athol's restaurant — sent there by Hugh Briggs — and men swarmed him, all talking at once. He glanced around the crowded room in amazement. Seemed every able-bodied man in and around town had left their home, ranch, or workplace.

Miss Grant got swept along in front of the throng, and she held both hands to him. He took hold and tipped his head to catch her words.

"I'm ready, Sheriff. Let's go."

She might be ready, but he had some planning to do first. He squeezed her hands, then let go and waved both arms over his head. "Quiet! You hear me? Quit your yammerin'."

It took a few seconds, but the noise dimmed. Took another second or two for

485

Bill's ears to stop ringing. The fellas had sure raised a ruckus. He planted his fists on his hips and pasted on his sheriff face. "All right, Hugh filled me in on the kidnapper's demands, an' I reckon you're all here thinkin' you're gonna be part of an army who goes after Miz Bingham."

Vern puffed out his chest and patted his sidearm. "We're ready, Sheriff. You just say the word." The crowd murmured in agreement.

Miss Grant stuck a piece of paper in Bill's face. "You have to make them stay here, Sheriff Thorn. The letter says if I don't come alone, I'll never see Mrs. Bingham again."

Bill yanked off his hat and tossed it onto the nearest table. "We ain't sendin' an army."

Miss Grant sagged. "Thank you."

"But neither are you goin' alone."

Her spine went straight. "But —"

Bill pointed at her freckled nose. "An' I ain't gonna listen to so much as a word of argumentin'."

She clamped her lips, but boy did she glower. And that was just fine. No little gal's frown would change his mind. He held up his palms. "Ever'body, find a chair. Or a leanin' spot. Wherever you can land, get there. Then I needja to listen."

Grumbles and mumbles broke out, but the men obeyed. Miss Grant didn't seem inclined to budge, though. Mack whispered in her ear and then led her to a table. She sat, and Mack stayed close, his hands on her shoulders.

Bill caught himself fighting back a grin. That Mack, he was real took with Miss Grant. No sense in trying to keep him from going along on the rescue. But Bill had thought it over on the ride back to town, and he had a plan. If his plan went well, neither of the ladies would be hurt and he'd be able to arrest the kidnapper.

Now that everybody was calm and paying attention, Bill let himself smile a little. "Don't think I don't appreciate you wantin' to help. You're good men — all o' you — an' Miz Bingham would be right proud o' the way you're steppin' up. But if we all go ridin' in there, the kidnapper's likely to panic. Might start shootin'. An' when bullets start flyin', people get hurt. I ain't gonna risk that. Not with two women involved."

"So," Mack said, "you're gonna let Miss Grant go to the Addison well house?" He sounded plenty disbelieving, and Bill couldn't blame him.

Bill scrunched his face. "I ain't happy about it, Mack, but I don't see no other way. He's wantin' to trade, so Miss Grant here is what it'll take to coax the kidnapper into the open."

Mutters started up again, and Bill sliced his hand through the air. "Don't get your danders up. I ain't gonna send her alone no matter what the letter says."

The men calmed. W. C. pushed off from his place along the wall. "Who's goin' with her? Needs to be somebody with a sure shot, just in case. I'm willin'."

"Me, too."

"I'll go!"

"Count me in, Sheriff."

Bill stifled a groan. "Fellas, fellas, will you listen to me, please?" He waited until everybody got quiet again. "I already picked who I'm takin'. Doc Kettering in case Miz Bingham needs some doctorin' when we find her, an' " — he hoped he wouldn't regret the second choice — "Mack Cleveland."

W. C. grunted and bounced his fist on the old bar. "Why Mack? I'm a better shot'n him." Several others echoed W. C.'s claim.

Bill stared them down. "I picked Mack 'cause he ain't already married or on the list o' grooms waitin' for brides. Things could get ugly out there, an' I don't aim to leave widows behind." He turned a look he hoped asked the right question on Mack. "Unless somethin's changed."

Mack's jaw muscles twitched. He shook his head. "No, Sheriff. Nothing's changed."

If Bill hadn't lost his ability to read faces, there was hurt in Miss Grant's eyes. If things worked out all right, the two young people could sort out their feelings later. For now, they needed to stay focused on the rescue.

"All right, then. Tomorrow mornin', well before daybreak, me, Hiram, Mack, an' Miss Grant'll set out." Bill gritted his teeth. His next request might be considered lily livered by some, but he'd make it anyway. "The rest o' you who ain't goin', you can help us out by prayin' ever'thing goes smooth." He sure didn't want to lose anybody in this trade.

Helena

"I won!"

Helena couldn't hold back a smile even though tears stung her eyes. The elation on Buster's face — a face that normally reflected sadness and apprehension — cheered her more than she could measure.

After supper, with little else to do to pass the time, she'd drawn cross marks on the floor and engaged the boys in tic-tac-toe. For an hour they'd sat in a circle on the floor, taking turns scratching Xs and Os in the dirt with a butter knife. She or Dolan had won every game not claimed by the cat. Until this one.

She pointed to the game board. "Draw a line through the Os to show your victory."

His tongue sticking out of the corner of his mouth, Buster used the butter knife and carved an uneven line from top to bottom over the Os. Dolan frowned.

Helena touched Dolan's tousled head. "Aren't you going to congratulate your brother?"

Dolan folded his arms over his skinny chest. "Ain't fair. He's littler'n me. He hadn't oughta beat me at nothin'."

Buster blinked, his smile fading.

She arched her brows. "Well, now, you're littler than me, and you won in at least two of our contests. Should I say those matches weren't fair?"

He curled his lip, a perfect imitation of his father. "Aw, that ain't the same."

"Why?"

" 'Cause you're a girl."

The scorn in the boy's tone stung. Helena

490

tipped her head. "Are you telling me you believe girls are inferior to boys?"

Both boys scrunched up their faces. Buster said, "What's inferior?"

"Not as valuable."

Their expressions didn't clear.

She searched for a simpler explanation. "Unworthy. Not important."

Dolan nodded. "Yeah, that's what I'm sayin'. Girls . . . they don't matter much."

Helena didn't need to ask to know where he'd learned such a lesson. "You listen to me, Dolan and Buster. Girls matter. As do boys, whether big or little. Every person matters. Do you know why?"

They shook their heads in unison.

"We are all created in God's image. He crafted male and female, and He breathed His very own breath of life into them. He loves His creation. What God sees as valuable and important is valuable and important."

Dolan squinched his eyes to slits, distrust oozing from him. "How do you know?"

"Because it says so in the Bible, which is God's holy book. Has anyone ever read to you from the Bible?"

Buster nodded hard. "Uh-huh. Our ma did."

Dolan nudged his brother on the arm, and

491

Buster hung his head.

Such an intriguing piece of their puzzle. A woman who wanted her boys to be educated and who read to them from a Bible didn't match one who would abandon those same children. She put her hands on the boys' shoulders. "Well, then, you should know that the Bible doesn't lie. If the Bible says all men and women are important, then it's true."

Dolan stared at her for a long time, as if trying to discern her importance, then snorted and grabbed the butter knife from Buster. "I bet not even God thinks Pa matters. Pa's nothin' but a —"

She cupped his chin and lifted his face to her. "You're wrong, Dolan. God loves your pa. The same way He loves you and Buster and me." The same way He loved these children's mother despite her unfathomable decision. "Remember what I told you about the Bible?"

Dolan ground his teeth together, but Buster nodded. "If the Bible says it, it's true."

"That's exactly right." Helena flashed a smile at the younger boy and then pinned her attention on Dolan again. "This is something else the Bible says, John 3:16 — 'For God so loved the world, that he gave

his only begotten Son, that whosoever be-
lieveth in him should not perish, but have
everlasting life.' *The world,* Dolan." She gave
his cheek a gentle stroke with her fingers.
"That means God loves everyone who has
ever been born and will ever be born. He
loves them so much He sent His very own
Son into this world to take the punishment
for the sins, the wrong things, that we do."

The truth of God's grace swept through
her with a warmth she couldn't deny. Oh,
how she wanted these boys — and their
irascible father — to understand the depth
and breadth and fullness of God's love. "In
Hebrews 8:12, God tells us, 'I will be merci-
ful to their unrighteousness, and their sins
and their iniquities will I remember no
more.' The sins of anyone who believes that
Jesus is God's Son, sent to be the Savior,
will be forgiven. Wiped away!" She leaned
forward and scrubbed out the tic-tac-toe
game with the heel of her hand. "Just like
that. Forgiven . . . and forgotten."

Buster stared at the smooth spot in the
dirt. "All the wrong things? Even the really
big ones?"

Helena followed her instincts and pulled
the little boy into her lap. She hugged him
hard, and to her joy, he snuggled against
her. "Every single one, Buster. There's noth-

ing we can do that's so bad God won't forgive it, because God's love is bigger than any sin."

The boy tilted his head and stared straight into Helena's eyes. He licked his lips. "E-even killin' one o' God's creation?"

Dolan jumped up and clenched his fists. "Pa made us promise not to tell! You broke a promise, Buster! You're gonna be in so much trouble not even God can save you."

Buster burrowed his face against Helena's throat. She wrapped her arms tightly around the boy and stared at Dolan. "Wasn't supposed to tell what?"

Dolan growled and pressed his fists against his temples. "It don't matter. She don't matter. Pa can get another one. He said so. But we wasn't s'posed to tell. Now Pa's gonna . . ." The boy moaned as if gripped by unbearable pain.

Helena shifted Buster from her lap and grabbed Dolan's cold hands. "Did . . . did your father . . ." She couldn't complete the sentence. She didn't want to complete the thought.

Dolan's face contorted horribly. "I killed Ma."

Had she not been sitting on the floor, she would have collapsed. She tugged Dolan's hands, and the boy dropped to his knees.

494

He began to sob, and Buster joined in with the most heartbreaking wails.

"I — I forgot to close the cellar door. I'm always s'posed to close it when I come up, but my hands was full, an' I figgered I'd go back an' close it, but I forgot, an' Ma . . . Ma was holdin' a basket o' dirty clothes an' she didn't see the hole an' —" He fell forward, rear in the air, and buried his face in her lap. "I'm sorry. I'm sorry."

Buster huddled against Helena's side, still crying. She rubbed Dolan's heaving back, stroked Buster's hair, and inwardly prayed for guidance. She didn't try to hush their expressions of grief. Deep hurts needed purging. Purging came from tears. And oh, such a deep hurt the boys held. Deeper, even, than she'd imagined. But God could heal, if only the children would accept His loving touch.

It seemed hours passed until the boys ran out of tears. Dolan sat back on his haunches and swiped his nose with his sleeve. Buster snuffled and rubbed his face on Helena's dress. She opened her arms, and the children scooted in. She closed her arms around them, the way a mother duck sheltered her ducklings beneath her wings. The boys smelled of sweat and dirt and tears, but she deposited a kiss first on Dolan's head and then on Buster's. With them snug in her embrace, she sent up one more prayer, gathered her courage, and spoke as gently and sweetly as if they were newborn babes.

"Dolan, you did not kill your ma. The fall killed her."

He shuddered. "Pa said I did. He said I'd hafta go to jail if folks found out what I done."

"Your pa was probably shocked and hurting. When people are hurting, they say things they don't mean. But no matter what he said, you won't have to go to jail because you did not kill her. You're only a boy, and boys sometimes forget things. They make mistakes." She pressed her lips to his sweaty temple. "Did you leave the door open with the idea that someone might fall and get hurt?"

"No." The word choked out.

"Then you can't say you killed her. Killing is intentional — done on purpose. This was an accident, Dolan. Only an accident."

He slumped against her, his chin quivering. "But she's gone."

"I know, and I'm so sorry." She kissed him again, wishing it was enough to cure his hurt. "But if your ma read to you from the Bible, then she must have believed it, including what it says in John 3:16 about

Jesus. People who believe in Jesus have eternal life with Him. She's gone from earth, Dolan, but she's alive in heaven, and if you believe in Jesus, too, you'll see her again someday."

The boy sat up abruptly, the first hint of hope she'd witnessed glimmering in his tear-filled eyes. "I will?"

"You will."

Tears spilled down his face, but his lips formed a quavering smile. "Thank you, ma'am."

Thank You, God.

THIRTY-SEVEN

Mack

Mack gripped the reins as tightly as he
wanted to hold Abigail. He'd never been so
scared. He'd never prayed so much, so hard,
so persistently. The prayer lifted again.

Dear God, keep her safe.

Could his prayers get through to heaven?
Cloud cover hid the egg-shaped moon.
Every now and then, the clouds shifted
enough to let a few stars peek out, but their
light didn't reach the landscape. He kept
his gaze on Patch's white rump, just a lump
of whitish gray against a black backdrop.
He couldn't see Abigail at all, but he imagined her slender form on the back of Sheriff
Thorn's horse. He'd lifted her up before
they set off from Spiveyville just after
midnight, and he'd never forget the look of
longing she turned on him before slipping
her arms around the sheriff's waist and rest-

ing her cheek on his shoulder blade.

Doc Kettering trailed behind Mack. His horse occasionally snorted, interrupting the nearly silent night. None of the men talked. They'd talked it all out over supper, and in another half mile or so, they'd all divide and go to their separate locations. Mack would hunker down in the thick grass east of the well house, and Doc Kettering would do the same in the west. Sheriff Thorn would give Abigail a lantern and let her walk the final quarter mile while he rode a wide circle to the rear and worked his way in on foot as close to the well house as possible. He'd said, *"If anybody's gonna be in the range of pistol shot, it's gonna be me."* Nobody said anything, probably so they wouldn't scare Abigail, but she'd be in the range of pistol shot, too.

Dear God, keep her safe. Ma always said the fervent prayers of a faithful man were answered, so he'd keep praying.

Patch stopped and Mack pulled back on the reins. Doc's horse bumped his nose on the back of Mack's leg. The sheriff's gravelly voice drifted on the chilly breeze. "Gonna light that lantern now an' send her on ahead. Just in case somebody's lookin', you two branch off so the light don't touch ya. No sense in givin' this feller the idea Miss

Grant's got company."

Mack urged his mare up close and touched Abigail's elbow. "Are you sure you want to do this?"

"Yes." Her pale face and wide eyes reflected fear, but her voice came out strong.

"Go on now, Mack," the sheriff said.

Mack gave a gentle squeeze he hoped communicated everything his heart held and then tapped the horse's sides. Doc Kettering pulled his reins and aimed his horse in the opposite direction. Mack risked a glance over his shoulder and saw the flash of light from a match. The illumination touched Abigail's face and then faded, leaving her in shadow again. He prayed it wouldn't be the last glimpse he received of her precious freckled face.

Abigail

Abigail gripped her shawl at her throat and held the lantern in front of her. Her shawl's tails flapped in the breeze, and the lantern light flickered, casting otherworldly shadows across the grass. The heavy clouds had finally started to clear, changing to filmy ribbons that seemed to float like the tails of a dozen kites. Moonlight glowed behind the gossamer layers, and her heart caught, a

500

childhood memory rising without warning.

When she was six, maybe seven, she'd awakened in the middle of the night with the need for the outhouse, so she tiptoed up the hallway to her parents' room and tapped on the door. Father answered it.

She danced in place. "I need to go."

Without a word, he scooped her up and carried her outside. In the dark yard, she clung to his neck and whimpered, and he asked her what was wrong.

"It's dark. I'm scared of the dark."

Father chuckled. "You don't need to be scared. I'm here."

She drew back slightly and tried to memorize his smiling face. "Because you're awake. But mostly you sleep at night."

He stopped and pointed to the moon overhead. "Look, Abigail, do you see the moon?"

She examined the round yellow ball way up high. "Yes."

He'd slid his warm finger lightly along the curve of her jaw. "Well, the moon guards the night, and beyond the moon, God's looking, too. He never sleeps, and He sees as well in the dark as a cat. So He's always watching, and you needn't ever be afraid when nighttime comes."

Abigail loosened the ties of her bonnet

and let it slide from her head against her spine. She lifted her gaze. With nothing around her but swaying grass and the gray cover of night, she searched the sky. The men were out of sight. Mother was gone, Father locked away. How she needed to know God was there, was watching, would always be watching.

A breeze rich with the scent of earth lifted a strand of her hair and brushed it across her cheek, the touch like a Father's gentle finger.

She smiled and whispered, "Thank You."

Turning her gaze forward, she continued her trek beneath the prairie moon.

Bill

Bill angled a glance at the night sky. Couldn't those clouds clear all the way off and let the moon shine down? If he could make out shadows, figure out for sure whether that was a wagon parked alongside the old well house and not his imagination playing tricks, it would sure help. The last thing he wanted was to find himself walking straight into the muzzle of Nance's gun.

He let himself think the name Nance even though he hadn't said it out loud to anybody. Mostly because he wasn't completely sure yet himself. But of all the folks in and around Spiveyville, Nance was the only one Bill could call lowdown enough and bold enough and contrary enough to come up with such a scheme and carry it through. And Nance had lied to Miz Bingham, saying his wife served him with divorce papers. A man who lied, ignored orders from the law, and mistreated his family wouldn't think twice about nabbing a woman and using her as bait to trap another one. If the kidnapper wasn't Nance, Bill would be mighty surprised.

Hunkering low, knees bent, he scuttled a few feet closer to the well house and paused, his pulse thundering worse than the way the ground shook during a buffalo stampede. The bob of a lantern crested the rise on the other side, and he sucked in a breath and held it. Miss Grant, finding her way just like he'd told her to. His chest went tight. Such a brave little gal, determined to rescue Miz Bingham. If she did everything like he'd told her, didn't let on she'd brought anybody with her, she should be all right.

He swallowed against his dry throat, braced himself, and made another zigzagging scuttle across the grass. He was close enough to make out a wagon and a pair of horses drowsing in their traces. Sure enough, the kidnapper had posted himself for Abigail's arrival. Their coming at night instead of during the day would catch him by surprise. Surprise was good, as long as it was Bill giving the surprise and not getting it.

The wagon was parked in front of the north-facing well house door, so Bill sent up a quick prayer and made one last bent-low advance. Safe on the south side, he plastered himself to the wall. Then he slipped his pistol from his holster, laid it flat against his chest, and waited.

Only minutes later one of the horses blew air, and the wagon creaked. A scrambling noise reached Bill's ears, and a man's sleep-thick voice called, "Who's there?"

Bill's heart pounded like a bass drum. Yep, that was Nance. Maybe he should've prepared Miss Grant for the possibility. If the shock of recognition made her forget what she was supposed to do, he'd —

"It's me. Abigail Grant."

The wagon squeaked again, an eager sound, and boots hit the ground with a dull thud. "How'd you get here?"

"I walked."

Clump, clump, clump . . . Boots carrying Nance across the ground. Bill imagined the man scanning the area, and he stayed as still as a statue. "All the way from town? It's more'n three miles."

"I know. That's why I set out when I did. I didn't expect to get here until sunrise."

"How'd you know the way?"

Bill gritted his teeth. They hadn't practiced for that question. He held his breath, fearing the whole plan was about to collapse.

"I asked Mr. Patterson. I knew he'd tell me without asking why I wanted to know. He's not terribly bright."

Bill stifled a chortle. Smart girl. Nance resented Athol. He'd accept her answer out of pure spite.

"Come on in closer."

"I'll come closer when I know Mrs. Bingham is all right."

Relief temporarily slumped him forward. She had to know it was Nance, but she was following his instructions like a stage actress with a script.

Nance grunted. "You ain't the one callin' the shots, little gal. You come on in here right now."

Impatience deepened Nance's tone. While he was talking, Bill took advantage and cocked his revolver. He eased to the corner and peeked out. Miss Grant stood at least thirty feet away, holding the lantern like a beacon. Mack and Doc would be able to see her without any trouble. If they had to start shooting, they'd know to avoid the circle of yellow light.

"Your letter said you'd trade Mrs. Bingham for me. I'm here, but unless you set Mrs. Bingham free, I'm not moving. If you want me to keep my part of the deal and marry you, you have to keep your part and let her go."

"An' what if I don't?"

Bill's flesh tingled at the man's sneering voice. He waited for Miss Grant to launch her threat in return.

"Then I shall throw the lantern on the grass and run."

They'd planned the threat 'specially for Miss Grant. Every man in the county knew the danger of an uncontrolled prairie fire. The kidnapper would reason a city gal'd be foolish enough to do it, and he'd keep his distance to protect the precious grass needed to feed the county's cattle. Now that Bill knew for sure it was Nance, he hoped the threat would still work. The man wasn't known for looking out for anyone but himself.

Nance burst out laughing. "I was right about you. You're a sassy one. I like a woman with a little bit of sass. That's how

506

my Susie was. Just sassy enough to add some sparks. But she also knew when it was time to put aside the sassin' an' do as she was told." A menacing edge entered his tone. "Like now."

The moon had slunk below the clouds as night inched toward morning. Miss Grant raised the lantern, melding the moonlight with the lantern light. "Where is Mrs. Bingham?"

The man growled low in his throat. Both horses snorted and shifted in the traces, making the metal rings clink. "Gal, you are tryin' my patience."

"That isn't my intention. I'm merely asking you to honor your word and do what you said you would do. You said you would trade Mrs. Bingham for me. I'm here. Where is she?"

THIRTY-EIGHT

Abigail

Her arm was so tired. She wanted to put down the lantern, but Sheriff Thorn had warned her about the danger of touching the hot globe to the grass. The past week's fierce winds had dried everything, and the slightest spark could start a fire. So she should blow out the lantern and then run through the dark if the kidnapper made any advance toward her. Mack, Doc Kettering, and the sheriff promised that the moment the light went out, they would gallop in and keep the kidnapper — Mr. Nance — from harming her. But she didn't want to run. She wanted Mr. Nance to send Mrs. Bingham to her.

"Is she in the well house?" She took a step closer and angled the lantern to the side so she could see the small wooden structure lurking in the middle of the seemingly endless prairie. No larger than an outhouse, it presented a dismal dwelling for someone. "Mrs. Bingham! Mrs. Bingham, are you there?"

"Shut up, you." Mr. Nance stomped forward five long strides. He stood like a matador preparing to defend himself against a bull. "You got one more chance to do what you're told before I make you real sorry you didn't listen."

Abigail shifted the lantern to her other hand. Her shawl slipped off her left shoulder, pulling at her arm. "I'm already sorry. I should have known I couldn't trust you." Sheriff Thorn might be angry about her veering from the specific phrases he'd given her, but she was too angry to care. Clearly, Mr. Nance had never intended to release Mrs. Bingham. "Anyone who would steal a woman and concoct such a ridiculous ransom does not possess a sound mind."

A hint of palest pink disrupted the dark-gray sky at the eastern horizon, bringing the promise of dawn. Of a new day. Of a new beginning. Such an incongruous image juxtaposed to Mr. Nance viciously slinging off his jacket.

"By the time I'm done with you, you're gonna rue the day you was born." He tossed the jacket on the ground.

509

"No, Mr. Nance, you are going to rue the day I was born, because I am going to be your downfall." She raised the lantern with the intention of extinguishing the flame, but a gust of wind struck her. Her weak fingers lost their hold and the lantern fell to the ground. The globe shattered on impact. Oil splattered and flames immediately spread across the liquid, catching the grass as it went. The tail of Abigail's shawl dipped into the licking tongues, and fire climbed the wool.

With a shriek, she turned to run, dragging the shawl with her.

"Stop! Stop!"

Mack's panicked order carried across the ground. Assuming he was speaking to Nance, she continued running. Heat scorched the backs of her calves. Had her dress caught, too? Oh, please, not this dress, the deep-russet organdy Father commissioned for her betrothal party. She couldn't let it burn up. She spun in circles, trying to escape the greedy flames.

A solid body slammed into her and forced her to the ground. Large hands prowled all over her, rolling her this way and that way, slapping at her. She caught a peek at her attacker's face, and she screeched in alarm.

Mack pounded up and threw Mr. Nance

510

away from her. "Nance, help with the fire!"

Mr. Nance took off at a stumbling run, and Mack smacked her skirt with his gloved hands until every flame was extinguished. He helped her up, grabbed her damaged shawl, and gave her a little shove away from the well house. "Go upwind and stay there!" He ran back to the snapping patch of burning grass.

Abigail scrambled several yards away, then turned and watched the four men use their jackets and her shawl to beat down the flames. As pink and yellow grew across the eastern sky, the orange and yellow flames succumbed to the men's battle.

Mack tossed her shawl aside and came at her in a staggering run. With a little cry, she ran to meet him. He slung his arms around her and held so tightly the embrace stole her breath, but she didn't mind. She pressed her cheek to his chest. His heart thrummed in her ear, a steady, comforting beat.

Eyes closed, she savored the security of being cradled in his arms. Not since she was a little girl had someone held her with such tenderness, such concern. Tears stung, but she smiled, receiving his embrace as a gift. She clung equally hard, silently communicating her gratitude.

Far too soon he pulled back and took her

face in his hands. The smell of soot clinging to his warm leather gloves stung her nose, but the sweet, possessive pressure was too welcome for her to resist. "Did he hurt you when he knocked you down?" He scanned her length, grimacing when his gaze reached the hem of her dress. "Did the fire burn your legs?"

She curled her hands around his wrists. "No, no, I'm all right." The heat had touched her, but the layers of her petticoat surely protected her. That, and the quick action that extinguished the flames before they could climb higher or reach underneath.

Doc Kettering plodded up to them. "Miss Grant, you all right?"

She tucked herself under Mack's arm. "I am now." Then she gave a jolt. "But Mrs. Bingham . . ." She turned a frantic look on the men. "Is she here?"

Doc scowled over his shoulder. Near the charred patch of ground, Sheriff Thorn was tying Mr. Nance's wrists together behind his back. "Nope. Nance says he'll tell us where to look as soon as the sheriff promises to let him go." He snorted, shaking his head. "Sheriff Thorn's done making deals with him."

Abigail pressed her fist to her lips, worry

descending. Mr. Nance was so stubborn. Would they ever find Mrs. Bingham? She turned her face to lean against Mack again, and the pale white moon against a soft blue-gray sky captured her attention. *"Beyond the moon, God's looking, too."* Peace eased through her. God had watched over her. He was watching over Mrs. Bingham.

She whispered, "I choose to trust."

Mack looked down at her. "Did you say something?"

She blinked back tears and smiled at him. "I was speaking to my Father."

He gave her a quick squeeze, his smile filled with approval. "Been doing that quite a bit myself."

Doc started down the rise. "Come on. Sheriff's got Nance in the wagon. We better get him to town. Sooner he's behind bars, the sooner we can all rest easy."

Mack kept his arm snug around her waist and escorted her to the well house.

The sheriff was tying his horse to the back of Nance's wagon. "Miss Grant, you ride with me. Mack, Doc, follow behind."

Mack gripped her waist and lifted her onto the wagon seat. He gave her one more lingering look before trotting to his horse and swinging himself into the saddle with a movement as graceful as a deer bounding across the prairie.

The sheriff climbed up beside her, bouncing the seat. He pushed a rifle into her hands. "Hold on to that an' keep it aimed at Nance."

She gulped. Sheriff Thorn had tied the prisoner's hands and looped a rope from ankle to ankle, limiting his stride. How would he escape even if he tried to leap over the side of the wagon? "Is . . . is it necessary?"

"I wouldn't ask you to do it if it wasn't necessary."

Abigail settled herself sideways and angled the gun across her lap, its barrel pointed beyond Mr. Nance's left ear. Despite the chill morning air, sweat broke out over her body. She prayed she wouldn't be forced to fire the weapon.

"Hee-yah!" The horses jolted and the wagon creaked to life.

Abigail never moved her gaze from Mr. Nance the entire drive to Spiveyville. The rocking wagon bed jarred him from side to side, throwing his shoulder against the hard wooden box again and again. If it hurt, he didn't let on. Abigail kept watching, hoping she might see some softening in his expression, some hint that he would bend his stubborn pride and tell them where he'd hidden

Mrs. Bingham. He held his sullen expression the whole distance.

The wagon rattled to a stop outside the sheriff's office. Sheriff Thorn set the brake and took the rifle from her. His blue-eyed gaze settled on her, and an approving smile formed beneath his thick gray-and-black mustache. "Miss Grant, you done real good out there."

She hung her head. "Sheriff, you're very kind, but I failed. I dropped the lantern. I didn't get him to trade Mrs. Bingham for me."

The sheriff grunted. "Droppin' the lantern was a accident. Coulda happened to anybody who'd been holdin' it for as long as you did. As for the tradin' . . . he prob'ly never meant to make the trade. That ain't your fault. We can blame it on his cussed hide." His expression turned grim. "Maybe sittin' in a jail cell for a day or two will loosen his tongue. Reckon we're about to find out."

Another day or two . . . Abigail closed her eyes and envisioned the prairie moon, then God's face beyond it. *Keep watch over my friend, dear Father.* When she opened her eyes, Mack was waiting beside the wagon. She held out her hands and allowed him to help her down.

515

Townsfolk spilled out of the stores and crowded near as Sheriff Thorn guided Mr. Nance to the sheriff's office. Chatter and questions filled the air, but the sheriff didn't respond. When the door had closed behind Sheriff Thorn and the prisoner, Doc Kettering waved his arms in the air.

"Folks, the kidnapper's in custody. He hasn't told us yet where he's keeping Mrs. Bingham, but Sheriff Thorn knows how to do his job. Let's all return to our businesses an' let him work in peace."

People ambled off, some casting curious looks over their shoulders, others jabbering. Mack offered Abigail his elbow. She took hold, clinging with both hands. They strolled up the boardwalk, tiredness making her drag her feet. The scorched hem of her dress hooked on her heels, and she battled a wave of sorrow. How silly to mourn the loss of a dress. Only fabric and thread and lace. But she'd already lost so much. Her home, her friends, her lifestyle, her mother, her —

She gasped and stopped.

Mack gazed at her in concern. "What is it?"

"I didn't lose him."

His brows furrowed. "Who?"

Tears flooded her eyes, distorting his image. "My father. Ever since he was taken to

516

prison, I've told myself he was lost to me. But I was wrong, Mack." She smiled, an unexpected joy weaving its way through her very soul. "I have my memories of him — good memories. I'd pushed them all aside because it hurt too much to remember, but now I want to remember. I want to remember the man who carried me on his shoulders, who taught me to cipher before I started school, who took me to church and taught me to pray."

The air chilled the wet tracks on her face. "He was a good father to me before he stole from his partners. I don't know what brought him to make such a choice, but God forgives. God can forgive my father, and He can forgive me for turning my back on Him out of anger and confusion." She bit her lip and searched Mack's face, seeking signs of disgust. She saw only compassion and — her heart rolled over in her chest — affection.

She swallowed against more tears. "A guard at the courthouse told Mother and me we could write to Father at the penitentiary, but we didn't do it. We were wrong. Father needs to know he isn't irredeemable. He needs to know I . . . I still love him." She straightened her shoulders, resolve filling her. "As soon as I've finished helping

Mr. Patterson with the breakfast cleanup, I'm going to write Father a letter. A plea for forgiveness for abandoning him."

To her surprise, Mack started to laugh. "Do you find my plan amusing?" If he said yes, she would deliver a scathing diatribe and make him regret the word.

"Some of it." He chuckled again and pulled her close. "After what you just went through, you're gonna wash dishes." He planted a kiss on the top of her head. "You're something else, Abigail Grant."

She sucked in her lips to keep from laughing. Then she angled a teasing grin at him. "You know, I could get to my letter much faster if someone dried the dishes and put them away."

He squeezed her shoulders. "All right. I don't reckon it'll hurt to leave the store closed this morning. But before I dry dishes, I want to dirty one up." He slapped his flat belly. "I'm ready for some breakfast."

Mr. Patterson served them fried eggs, ham, and grits, plying them with questions about their midnight rendezvous the whole time they ate. When breakfast was done, she and Mack saw to the dishes, and then Mack walked her to the base of the stairs. He touched her cheek with his fingertips, tenderness in his expression.

"Why don't you take a nap? I know you're tired."

Yes, she was tired. More tired than she'd ever remembered being. But she needed to write to her father. "I will." He offered another smile of goodbye, and she trudged to her room and closed herself inside.

For an hour, she poured her thoughts onto paper, recording cherished moments from her childhood, openly divulging the pain of seeing him taken from her and Mother, and ending with a bid for forgiveness for not writing sooner and a humble plea for the chance to renew their relationship as father and daughter.

When she finished, she folded the pages and slipped them into an envelope. She started to rise from the edge of the bed, but the soft mattress invited her to recline, to close her eyes, to give in to the weight of exhaustion. She looked at the envelope in her hand. She hadn't spoken to her father for five years. Could it wait another day? She shook her head. A nap could wait.

She changed out of her russet organdy and into her brown plaid serge, tied her red wrap around her shoulders, and set off for the post office. The wrap did little to block the wind. Perhaps she would visit Mr. Thompson's mercantile and ask to look at the Montgomery Ward catalog. Her good shawl lay out on the prairie, scorched and smoke damaged, and she would need a good covering to see her through the winter.

Her feet came to a halt as reality descended. Where would she spend the winter? When the men had finished their classes, she wouldn't be needed in Spiveyville any longer. She was almost past the age to remain in Mrs. Bingham's program. Assuming, of course, the business didn't close. What would her future hold? She didn't know. But for the first time in a long time, she believed that Someone knew and cared.

With a lighter step, she entered the post office and crossed to the counter. "Mr. Ackley, may I have a stamp, please?"

He opened a little drawer and poked around in it. He withdrew a stamp and a small glue pot and brush. He glanced at the envelope. "Mr. Mortimer Grant, Deer Island House of Correction, Massachusetts. Writing to your pa, huh?"

She clasped her hands together and nodded.

He looked up and met her gaze. "I think that's a real good thing, Miss Grant. Betcha he'll be right pleased to hear from you."

She blinked in surprise. If her former friends from Boston knew she'd penned a missive to her father in the penitentiary, they'd whisper behind their hands or openly condemn her. Fondness for the whisker-faced man washed over her. "Thank you, Mr. Ackley."

He grimaced. "Well, you might not be thankin' me with your next breath." He dropped her letter in a wooden tray marked "Outgoing" and trudged to the back counter. He carried a scrap of paper between the forefingers and thumbs of both hands, as if he feared it might sting him. "There must've been a line down somewhere between here an' Massachusetts, 'cause the date on this telegram shows November 7, but it only just come through this mornin'. Three days late." He shook his head. "Hope this ain't gonna trouble you too much."

He handed her the paper and she unfolded it.

Miss Grant, arriving in Pratt Center 8 a.m. Sunday, Nov. 11. Will rent conveyance for drive to Spiveyville. Marietta.

She clapped her hand to her cheek. Marietta Constance Herne would arrive tomorrow. What would she say when she discovered how Abigail had failed to rescue her sister?

THIRTY-NINE

Bill

Bill pointed at the man who sat on the edge of the simple rope bed with his arms crossed and glower intact. "You better thank the Good Lord Almighty that I'm not prone to fits o' rage, Nance, 'cause otherwise you'd be in a broken heap on the floor."

He whapped one of the door's iron bars with his palm. The iron rang, but the satisfaction didn't remove the sting from his hand. Fool move, but he had to hit something. He couldn't hit Nance. Not unless the man swung first. And that man wasn't swinging. He wasn't talking, neither.

Bill rubbed his palm against his thigh and stomped into the office portion of the jail. Slumping into his chair, he cradled his head in his hands. Tired. So tired. What he wouldn't give to stretch out on the cot in the corner and sleep the rest of the day. But what kind of sheriff slept when a woman was still missing? By now she was most likely dead. The thought pained him worse than the whack on the iron had hurt his palm.

In all his years of sheriffing, he'd never lost anybody. Oh, he'd shot and wounded a few rustlers. He'd returned fire on a would-be bandit trying to take off with Grover Thompson's cashbox back in '76 and drilled a hole through the man's shoulder, but nobody'd ever died on him. Wasn't right that Miz Bingham, who hadn't done one blamed thing wrong, could be the first.

To stave off sleep, he rose and paced the room, making himself think, think . . . They'd scoured the countryside, checked barns and sheds and gullies and wells. He couldn't come up with another place where Nance might've hid her. Mostly because he didn't know Nance well enough. But there was somebody who knew him. Those two little scared-faced boys. He'd seen something more than fear in their faces. They held a secret, something they'd been warned not to share.

He swung a glance toward the jail half of the building. Nance was locked up tight. Nobody in town would try to bust him out. He could leave the man untended if need be. Just in case, he'd pop in at the post office, let Clive know where he was going, and then head to Coats and convince Dolan and Buster Nance to tell him where their pa had hid Miz Bingham's body. The woman at least deserved a decent burial.

Helena

Helena used the inside of her skirt, the only part of her dress that wasn't stained from the reddish dirt walls and floor, to clean one of the wormy apples Mr. Nance had included in the food crate. "Here you are, Buster. Now, please eat it slowly. Chew well before you swallow so you won't have a bellyache." The smell in the dugout was nearly unbearable with all all three of them making use of the slop bucket.

Buster sank onto his bottom on the floor and chomped into the wrinkled apple.

She returned to the table and arranged the remaining items in the crate. In their very short time together, the boys had consumed more than half the food Mr. Nance said was meant to cover a couple of days. She should have rationed it. He'd indicated two days, but who knew whether he would honor his word? From now on, they would have to eat only at mealtime, and then only what she put on their plates.

She turned to inform the boys of her decision, but she glanced at Buster, who chewed, smiling, his eyes half-closed like a sated cat. He might have been eating divinity for the pleasure he took in the wilted fruit.

Helena's heart constricted. Rationing meant denying them. She couldn't do it, not when they were so hungry. She suspected not only had their father been negligent in seeing to their needs, but they had probably spent two or three days in shock — days when they didn't want to eat — after their mother's death. Helena would starve herself before she took food out of their mouths. Because in their hours together, they had won her affection.

She shifted her attention from Buster to Dolan, who lay sideways on the cot and drew pictures in the dirt with his finger. Such hapless waifs. They no longer had a mother. Their father, regardless of what he believed, would not evade punishment for kidnapping her. He would most likely end up behind bars, if he didn't end up getting shot. She cringed. As distasteful as she found the man, she hated to think of the boys losing their father in such a violent manner.

Please, Lord, preserve his life.

Using her skirt to protect her hand, she opened the stove door. The fuel box still held several straw logs. She added one to the small flame within the stove's belly, then stared at the licking tongues of fire, imagining Mr. Nance's large chapped hands twisting the lengths of straw that would keep her warm in her hideaway. Such a despicable individual, yet he'd seen to her needs. The little bit he shared of his childhood tiptoed through her memory and stirred an element of sympathy. Certainly he'd gone about it the wrong way, but his desire to secure a wife so his boys would be cared for was admirable. There had to be some good in him, somewhere. Buried deep, perhaps, but present.

Bring it to the surface, Father, for the boys' sakes.

She closed the door and turned, her gaze drifting from Buster to Dolan. What would happen to the boys? If she were twenty years younger and if Howard were still alive, she would take them to Newton with her and raise them as her own. But, of course, that wasn't possible. She was fifty-nine already, too old to keep up with two young, active boys. She had a business to run, one she was committed to and that took her full concentration. The boys deserved more than she could give.

Dear Father, find a home for Dolan and Buster where they will be cherished and raised to honor You.

She'd done more praying in the past five days than in the former three months combined. Too often the demands of her business stole her focus and filled her hours. Although she hadn't pushed God out of her life, she'd relegated her communication with Him to mealtime prayers and short requests sent up in moments of need. How sad that it had taken something so extreme to drive her to her knees and back into close fellowship with Him. When she finally left this dugout, she wouldn't forget the joy she'd experienced in leaning fully into her Father's arms for strength, peace, and comfort.

"Miz Bingham?" Dolan sidled up next to her, twisting his dirty fingers and looking hopefully into the crate. "Since Buster's havin' a little somethin', can I —"

"May I," she prompted with a smile.

The corners of his lips pulled up in an embarrassed half grin. "May I have one, too?"

She flipped the top layer of her skirt over her knee. "Yes, you may, but let me wipe it off first, hmm?" It seemed ridiculous to clean the apple and then place it in his filthy hands, but she'd cleaned Buster's apple, so she would clean Dolan's, too. She held it out and he took it eagerly. But he didn't bite into it right away.

Rising on his tiptoes, he peered into the crate. A frown creased his face. He settled back on his heels and passed the apple from hand to hand. "Um, there ain't no more."

She already knew that. "Yes."

"Well, then . . ." He slowly extended his hand to her. "You can have it."

She grabbed him in a hug. One quick squeeze and a peck on his dirt-smeared cheek. Then she released him and smiled. "Thank you, dear one, but you go ahead. Enjoy it."

The boy plopped down next to his brother and took a big bite.

Helena bit the end of her tongue to hold back tears. *Oh, dear Lord, give these boys a worthy home.*

Bill

A cow lowed from the barn, but no one answered Bill's knock on the front door of the Nance house. He wandered to the back door and pounded on it. Waited. Still no answer. Were those boys hiding, or were they

528

off somewhere else?

He took a slow walk toward the barn. Chickens pecked at the ground around their coop. Through the windows, he spotted eggs in the nests. Those should've been collected that morning. Just outside the barn, four pigs grunted in a pen, jamming their snouts against the ground. Their food trough was empty. He stood for a minute, looking into the pen at the rooting animals, an uneasy feeling in his gut.

The cow was bellowing for all it was worth. He entered the barn and crossed to the stall. "What'samatter with you, huh?" Then he got a look at her distended udder. The poor thing stood straddle legged and rolled its eyes. Another mournful low echoed from the rafters. Bill gave her neck a quick pat. "All right, all right, I'll take care of ya."

He located a stool and bucket and sat down. The cow's complaints faded away as he emptied her milk sack. He filled the bucket to the brim, but he wasn't sure what to do with it. He recalled the pigs and made a face.

"Pains me to feed this to critters, but there ain't a soul around here, an' there'll be more milk by mornin', so . . ."

Gritting his teeth, he emptied the bucket

into the pigs' trough. They dug in and slurped it up, tails whirling. Bill rested his arms on the top fence rail and watched the animals. If those boys were somewhere around, they'd have seen to the livestock. So they weren't just hiding. They were gone.

Who might know where to find the boys? He slapped his thigh. The schoolmarm. Most schoolmarms knew as much about youngsters as their folks did. If he recollected rightly, Miss Alexander took a room above the Coats mercantile. He'd pay the teacher a visit. He pulled himself onto Patch's back, groaning with the effort, and aimed the horse for town.

The mercantile owner's missus fetched the schoolmarm for Bill, and the minute she rounded the corner from the stairs, he asked if she knew where to find the Nance boys.

Miss Alexander pinched her lips as if she'd tasted something spoiled. "Sheriff Thorn, I wish I could help you, but Dolan and Buster didn't come to school yesterday. I don't know where they've gone."

Bill curled his hand around the stair rail and tried not to frown at the young schoolmarm. Wasn't her fault the boys were missing, so he shouldn't growl at her, but it was hard. He was near asleep on his feet. "Is it usual for 'em to not show up at school?"

She shook her head. "Oh, no, sir. Dolan and Buster are very faithful in attendance. Their mother wants the boys to learn to read, write, and cipher. It's important to her."

Bill started ciphering in his head. Something wasn't adding up. "When's the last time you talked to the boys' ma?"

"Oh, my . . . Four, maybe five weeks ago? We encountered each other here in the mercantile on a Saturday morning and chatted a bit. She's a shy woman who's been sickly since Buster was born, but she's always been very friendly with me."

Bill fiddled with his mustache. "Um . . . you ain't heard any rumors lately about Miz Nance, have you? 'Bout her maybe takin' off an' leavin' her youngsters?"

"No, I haven't, and I can't imagine her doing such a thing. She's a very devoted mother. But . . ." She folded her arms over her waist and shivered. "You know, I've been worried about the boys. The way they've looked lately . . . so disheveled, dirty, always sad and hungry. I wondered if their mother fell ill again. I thought about driving out to their house and checking on Mrs. Nance, but to be honest, their father scares me." She hung her head. "I suppose that doesn't sound very caring."

Bill gave the woman a little pat on the shoulder. "Now, it's clear you care about 'em. An' as for that pa o' theirs, you're right smart to stay away from him."

She offered a crooked smile. "Thank you. But what about the boys? Are you going to look in on them?"

"Yes'm, but before I go, mebbe you can help me with something." Bill squinted, trying to find the best way to ask. "Have the boys ever mentioned a special spot they or their pa like to visit?"

She tapped her lips, rolling her eyes upward. She brightened. "You know, last year Dolan wrote an essay about a place he liked to go to be alone and think. I believe he called it his dugout."

Tingles exploded across Bill's scalp. "Dugout?"

"Yes, sir. I don't have the essay anymore, of course, but I'm certain I'm remembering correctly." She tilted her head, and her smile turned sad. "He added a little note at the bottom for me not to pin the essay on the class board. Quite often Dolan's essays appear there — he really is a very intelligent boy. But he wanted his dugout kept secret."

Bill backed up, easing toward the front door. He tipped his hat. "Thank you, ma'am. You've been a big help."

She stepped onto the first riser, peering at him over her shoulder. "When you see the boys, please tell them I miss them at school."

"Will do." Bill left the store and trotted to Patch. He swung into the saddle and gave the horse's sides a bump, his mind whirling.

Way back when folks first settled the land, lots of them cut cave-like hollows into the hills and built a single wall over the opening for shelter. He couldn't think of anyone who still lived in a dugout, but folks used them to store grain or as a place to duck in if they got caught out in the weather. If there was a dugout on the Nance property, it'd be a mighty fine place to stash a woman.

Excitement chased away his sleepiness. At the edge of town, Bill gave Patch his head and let the paint break into a canter. He'd search 'til he found that dugout. Then, no matter how he found Miz Bingham — dead or alive — he'd have answers.

FORTY

Abigail

Abigail draped a clean wiping cloth over the tray holding a bowl of chicken and dumplings, a plate of biscuits, and a cup of milk. Balancing the tray on her palm, she headed for the front door of the restaurant. She reached for the doorknob, but the door opened before she could turn the knob. Mack stepped in, sweeping off his hat in the way she'd come to associate with a man bowing. She almost curtsied.

His gaze landed on her, and his familiar smile formed, lighting his blue eyes. He glanced at the tray. "What's this? It's a little chilly for a picnic."

She smiled in reply, unable to help herself, even though a dozen diners were probably watching every move they made. The townsfolk had become very interested in observing her whenever Mack came near. After all

534

the lecturing she'd done about not staring and about honoring other people's privacy, she should be dismayed or disgruntled. But their inquisitiveness inspired fond affection instead.

"Mr. Ackley came in a few minutes ago and said the sheriff had gone off on an errand midmorning. No one's seen him return, so Mr. Nance has been sitting in the jail all day without food. I thought someone should bring him something to eat." If she'd known about the sheriff's departure earlier, she would have taken lunch to the man. No one — not even Elmer Nance — should have to spend the day without a meal.

Mack settled his hat in place and took the plate from her hand. "I'll see that he gets it. You stay here."

"No." She lowered her voice to a whisper, unwilling to give the curious group behind her fodder for gossip. "I appreciate your concern, but there's something I need to tell him."

He opened the door. "Then I'm going with you."

There wasn't any need. Mr. Nance was secure behind a wall of iron bars and she no longer worried about being accosted by any of the Spiveyville men. But she enjoyed Mack's company. His protectiveness made her feel treasured. "All right."

They moved from the boardwalk to the street because others were heading for the restaurant. She would have enjoyed conversation, but every townsperson they encountered greeted them by name, and it was impolite to ignore them. By the time they reached the sheriff's office, she was eager to duck inside and be alone with Mack. Oh, such a shameless thought, but an honest one. She couldn't deny it. She'd given her heart to Mack Cleveland.

He slid his finger underneath the windowsill and extracted a key, which he used to unlock the front door.

Abigail gazed at him in amazement. "The sheriff leaves a key outside?" She whispered lest any of the passersby overhear.

Mack grinned. "The whole town knows it's there. He told us, in case somebody needed to get in while he's away." He slipped the key back into the little crack between the window frame and siding and opened the door for her. "Small towns're a lot different than big ones." Suddenly his tone seemed sad.

She wanted to ask what troubled him, but a clanging from the rear of the building sent him clomping across the floor. He opened a door centered on the wall and stepped through.

"Nance, quiet down."

The man tossed the tin cup he'd been using to bang against the iron bars. " 'Bout time somebody got here. Sheriff locked me in an' took off. Haven't had —" His steely-eyed glare landed on the tray Abigail held. He jammed his arms through the bars. "Give it here."

He'd never draw the tray through the narrow gap, and she would not ask Mack to make use of the key to the cell. She glanced around, biting her lip. "Mack, bring that crate over here, please."

Mack dragged a wooden crate from the corner and positioned it in front of the cell.

"Mr. Nance, if you'll pull your cot up close, you can use it as a chair, then reach between the bars to eat your supper."

To her surprise, he scurried to follow her directions, screeching the cot's metal legs across the planked floor. She set the tray on the crate and whisked the towel aside. He grabbed the fork and stabbed into the dumplings as if he was starving. His greedy gulping betrayed every dining rule, but her heart hurt watching him. No one should suffer such hunger.

"If you're still hungry when you've finished, I will bring you another bowl."

He paused, his cheek bulging with a bite, and glared at her. "Why?"

"Why . . . what?"

He bobbed his head in a mighty swallow. "Why're you feedin' me after what I done?"

She gazed steadily into his resentful eyes. "Because there's been enough unkindness. Someone has to, shall we say, turn the tide. Jesus instructed His followers to repay evil with good. I suppose I'm trying to do what He said. Besides . . ."

She inched forward, not yet within his reach but close enough to let him see the sincerity in her eyes. "I owe you a debt of gratitude for attempting to put out the fire in my clothing this morning. It was foolish of me to try to outrun it. I could have been badly injured had you not pushed me down and tried to extinguish the flames."

Mack gaped at her as if realizing for the first time what Mr. Nance had done.

"You could have run instead, escaped while Sheriff Thorn, Mack, and Dr. Kettering fought the blaze, but you stayed and helped. You did the right thing, Mr. Nance, and I'm grateful."

He stared at her through narrowed eyes for several seconds, his lower jaw working back and forth. Then he jammed the fork into the food and resumed eating.

Mack took Abigail by the elbow and guided her into the sheriff's office. He closed the door, sealing off the jail, and gave her a dumbfounded look. "How did you know he wasn't trying to hurt you when he threw you to the ground?"

She hung her head. "I didn't at the time. I feared he was attacking me. But he didn't strike me or . . . or otherwise hurt me. He rolled me against the ground and slapped at the flames." She glanced at the door, remembering something she'd just seen. "Did you notice his hands? They're burned. We should bring him an aloe plant."

He threw back his head and burst into laughter.

And Abigail found herself laughing with him. Ah, such sweet music they made. Her heart caught. If only . . .

Bill

Bill buttoned his jacket. The air was getting cooler and the sun's light dimmer. Seemed as though he'd been riding an ever-widening circle around the Nance property for years instead of hours. Weariness weighted him, and with evening getting swallowed up by night, sleep tugged hard. Another half hour and he wouldn't be able to see well enough to know if he ran smack into a dugout. He wished he'd brought a bedroll, because it sure looked like he'd be staying out under the stars and waiting until morning to finish his search.

Patch nickered and Bill patted the animal's splotchy neck. "I know, boy. Sure wasn't usin' my head when I set out. But if you an' me snug up tight, we'll make it through the night." At least the horse could eat some grass. Bill's stomach wouldn't get filled until he made it back to Spiveyville.

He flicked a look at the sky. Stars were starting to twinkle, and the moon sat like a fat toad on the horizon. He wouldn't waste one minute of light. He tapped his heels. "Come on, Patch, keep goin'. Take me to the dugout."

He swallowed a snort. He talked like the horse knew what he was saying. Would he spend the rest of his life talking to a horse instead of a wife? Way back on her first day in Spiveyville, Mrs. Grant had asked him, *"Might you be interested in securing a wife?"* He'd scoffed at the notion then. But he wasn't scoffing anymore. He was plumb tired of being alone. Of being lonely. He might be too old to be bringing babies into the world, but he wasn't too old to enjoy the company of a wife. Maybe he'd look into ordering up a bride after all.

Patch nickered again, bobbing his head. Then the horse snorted.

Bill pulled the reins. "What's the matter with you, fella, huh?" He searched the graying landscape. Was there a coyote somewhere, laying low? Wily creatures — not prone to attack a horse, but they could sure make one nervous. He didn't spot any eyes peering from the clumps of grass, but a rise in the land, growing higher than any others he'd encountered so far, caught his eye.

His scalp prickled. Maybe it was lack of sleep making that hill seem bigger. Maybe it was wishful thinking. But the height of the rise and Patch's strange behavior gave Bill the first ray of hope he'd had since he left Nance's house.

He angled Patch toward the rise and clicked his tongue on his teeth. "C'mon, let's go see what's there." If nothing else, a hill that high would block the wind. It'd be a good place to bed down for the night.

Helena

Helena tucked the edge of the blanket under Buster's chin. If the boys lay tummy to back on the edge of the mouse-eaten blanket, there was just enough flap remain-

541

ing to wrap around and over them. She knelt on the hard ground and placed a kiss on each of their heads. "Sleep well, now."

"We will. Good night, ma'am." Dolan snuffled and closed his eyes.

Buster's big brown eyes stayed fixed on Helena as she struggled to her feet, but before she took a step away from him, his lids slid closed.

She eased around the boys and headed for the table, where the plates from their simple supper of fried eggs and stewed tomatoes still awaited cleanup. As she reached for the plates, an odd sound intruded. Her heart leaped into her throat. Someone was sliding the board from the brackets outside the door. She hadn't heard a wagon, so it couldn't be Mr. Nance. Dolan had told her earlier in the day that some rustlers had hidden in this dugout a year or so back. Was a rustler out there now?

Instinctively, she grabbed up the now-cool frying pan and stood guard in front of the boys' sleeping forms, ready to swing hard at anyone who tried to accost them. The door creaked open, and Sheriff Thorn took a step into the dugout. Too stunned to react, she froze in place with the iron skillet gripped in her hands like a club.

His gaze scanned the space and landed on

her. He drew back and held up one hand. "Here now, put that down before you hurt somebody." A huge grin formed on his weary, whiskered face. " 'Specially me."

Her arm dropped, relief nearly toppling her. "Oh, Sheriff . . ." She inched away from the boys and placed the frying pan on the table. Her entire body trembled and tears threatened. "I've never been so happy to see anyone in my life." She sagged into a chair.

He clumped to her, glancing at the boys as he came. "You all right? Nance didn't . . ."

"He didn't molest me."

He blew out a breath, and his shoulders slumped. His obvious relief touched her.

Helena released a light laugh, joy of rescue overtaking the worry from moments ago. "I'm so glad he told you where we were. He left food and water, but we're going through it very quickly. The boys . . ." She turned her gaze to them. "They haven't been well cared for since their mother —"

She jolted to her feet, gestured to him, and led him outside. For a moment, she forgot her purpose in bringing him to a private place to talk. After hours of being closed in with the slop bucket, the fresh air was heavenly. She inhaled, allowing the breeze to cleanse the foul stench from her nostrils.

Sheriff Thorn creaked the door closed, sealing away the boys and the light from the lantern. They stood beneath a star-studded sky while somewhere in the distance a cow released a low moo and an owl replied with a lingering *whoo*. The sheriff's horse, tethered close by, nickered, and the sheriff crossed to the animal.

Helena trailed after him. "Sheriff, did Mr. Nance tell you what happened to his wife?"

"Nance ain't told me about nothin'. That's why it took me so long to find you. Hadda do it on own thinkin' " — he tapped his temple — "an' Patch's instincts."

"I'm grateful for both." She glanced at the dugout, envisioning the pair of sleeping boys, then sighed and faced the sheriff again. Blinking back tears, she repeated what the boys had told her about their mother's fall. "They're terrified Dolan will be prosecuted for her death because their father told them they'd go to jail unless they kept what happened a secret."

Although the shadows were heavy, she saw the man grimace. "Probably 'cause he figgered, given his reputation, most folks would think he done her in an' blamed it on the boy." He frowned. "You don't think

544

them boys are tellin' a story, tryin' to cover up their pa's doin'?"

She shook her head hard. "Absolutely not. They were too distraught, too broken. They told the truth."

"Well, then, I'll make sure to write a death report that don't put the blame on anybody. No child should have to carry the weight of his ma's death on his shoulders."

"Thank you, Sheriff." She shivered. As much as she enjoyed the scent outside the dugout, she needed warmth. They should get to Spiveyville as quickly as possible. She turned toward the shelter. "I'll rouse the boys and —"

He began unbuckling the horse's saddle straps.

She stopped. "Why are you unsaddling your horse?"

"Gonna bed down out here with Patch. First thing in the mornin', we'll head for Spiveyville."

She stared at him. "We aren't going now?"

He swung the saddle to the ground, then reached for the blanket. "Ma'am, Patch an' me've been up since before midnight an' we're both plumb tuckered out. Patch's gonna hafta carry the three o' you, an' I'm gonna hafta walk to town. Not sayin' you're an over-burdensome load, but this ol' feller deserves a rest before he makes that trek. As for me, if I set off walkin' without getting some sleep, I'll likely fall an' bonk my head on the ground. I got no desire to bonk my head on the ground." He flopped the blanket across the patch of grassless dirt in front of the dugout and lay down, using the saddle as a pillow.

"But Abigail will be so worried. And we're nearly out of food. And —"

He slid his hat over his face and crossed his arms. "G'night, now." Almost at once, a snore rumbled from underneath the hat. Patch snorted, nodded his great head, and then folded his legs and lay down next to his master.

She stood shivering, staring at him in shock. Then giggles, no doubt brought on by relief after days of tension, built in her chest. She clamped her hand over her mouth to hold them back and darted inside. The smell from the slop bucket struck her hard and chased away every bit of amusement. She set her lips in a determined line and marched to the corner where the awful bucket took up residence. If they were going to stay in this dugout another night, the bucket was going outside.

FORTY-ONE

Mack

Mack lit the final streetlamp. He stood for a moment under its glow, looking up the road in hopes the sheriff might ride in. But not a single *clop* of a horse's hoof carried on the night air.

With a sigh, he trudged up the boardwalk to the gap between Athol's and his businesses. The restaurant lamps had gone out five minutes ago, and the streetlamps didn't reach the alleyway, but he found his way to his back stoop, then sank down, unwilling to close himself inside yet. His weary body groaned for sleep, but his mind refused to quiet.

When he'd committed to being Abigail's friend, he hadn't expected to fall in love with her. But here he was, chin deep in it. But what to do about it? She wasn't one of Mrs. Bingham's bevy of brides. She hailed

547

from the city. She'd consented to calling him Mack, and she'd let him hold her — twice — when she'd been very upset. So upset she might have let Clive Ackley hold her if he'd offered. So it didn't really count.

Did the times she let him put his hand on her shoulder, stroll her around the church, and help with the dishes mean anything? He put his head in his hands. Yes, it meant she saw him as a friend — the very thing he'd set out to achieve. So he should be happy. Grateful. Feeling successful. So why was he disappointed, dissatisfied, and admittedly disgruntled?

He aimed his gaze at the twinkling stars and sighed. "Because friendship might be enough for her, but it's not enough for me. I want . . . more."

As if spoken on the breeze, Mack heard his mother's voice reciting Hebrews 13:5, one of her favorite scriptures. *"Be content with such things as ye have: for he hath said, I will never leave thee, nor forsake thee."*

He hung his head and closed his eyes. "Thank You for the reminder, God. You're right. I need to be content. You've given me so much. I know You're always there. You'll always be my Enough. And if this love I feel for Abigail is only meant to be a friendship, then I will accept that, too. But, Lord?" He swallowed against the salty taste of tears. "Would You help me, please? Because I don't think I can do it on my own."

Bill

Something warm and moist snuffled his cheek. He shrugged, and the snuffle came again. And this time it snorted. Bill sat up, knocking off his hat. He glared at Patch. "You crazy ol' horse. What're you tryin' to do?"

Patch blew air and bumped his nose against the top of Bill's head.

"All right, all right, I'm up already." He yawned, stretched, and then gave a second jolt. Two boys stood next to his saddle blanket, their dirty faces half-lit by the morning sun peeking over the horizon. Bill rubbed his nose and blinked at the pair. "Mornin'."

"Mornin'." The older one dropped his arm around the younger one's shoulder. "Mrs. Bingham says if you want breakfast, you better come quick 'cause me an' Buster are big eaters."

Bill's stomach growled. "Whatcha havin'?"

"Everything that's left," Buster said. The boys darted through the open door into the dugout.

Bill groaned and rolled to his feet. He stretched again, trying to work out the kinks in his shoulders and neck. When he got back to Spiveyville, he'd spend a whole day and night in his warm, soft cot. He hobbled after the boys.

Miz Bingham had laid out plates and forks at the table. She smiled and then hustled to the stove. "Good morning, Sheriff. Please sit down. We've got eggs, canned beans, and peaches for breakfast." Her voice wobbled like she was trying not to laugh. The boys were grinning and hunching their shoulders. What was so funny?

He rubbed his nose again and sat. "Thank you, ma'am."

She carried a pot of beans and a skillet of hard-fried eggs to the table. Her lips twitched and she sent warning looks at the boys, who were giggling worse than a couple of little girls.

Bill couldn't take it anymore. "What is it?"

The boys guffawed, nearly falling out of their seats. Miz Bingham touched their shoulders, shaking her head, but she let loose a little chortle, too. She pulled in a breath and finally looked full at Bill.

"May I use a bit of water and smooth down your hair? It's" — she cleared her throat and touched her fingers to her lips — "standing up like the feathers in a Comanche chief's headdress."

He explored and sure enough, his fingers found several tufts sticking up. Grunting, he finger-combed his hair, but it shot back up like spring grass. So he marched outside, snatched up his hat, and jammed it on his head. He came back in and the boys laughed again. Bill tried to glower at them, but his mouth just wouldn't stay turned down. His cheeks twitched, his chest went light, and the next thing he knew, he was laughing with them. And it was the best way he'd started a day in more years than he could count.

He grinned while Miz Bingham served up the breakfast. He grinned while the boys folded their hands and recited a thank-you for the food. He kept grinning even though there wasn't coffee and the plates didn't look quite clean and his stomach really wanted bacon or sausage.

When they'd finished eating, Bill leaned back in his chair and sent a hopeful look at Miz Bingham. "Ma'am, when you asked if I was innersted in takin' a wife, did you mean it?"

Her jaw dropped open for a second. Then she clamped it shut and nodded.

551

"Is there any woman in your bevy o' brides that has enough years on her to match up good with me?"

She scrunched her eyebrows and seemed to inspect him. "How many years would that be, Sheriff?"

He tapped the overgrown whiskers on his chin, hoping he wouldn't scare her off. "Turned forty-four last August."

Her head tipped, spilling a straggly strand of white hair over her shoulder. Her lips turned up real slow into a smile that reminded him of a fox laying its eyes on a fat rabbit. "It's possible."

"Well, good. 'Cause when we get back to Spiveyville, I'd like to talk to you about gettin' a bride for myself."

Abigail

Every time the restaurant door opened Sunday morning, Abigail's heart gave a hopeful leap and then plummeted when the arrival was someone other than Sheriff Thorn. Mack came in around seven thirty, and even though he wasn't the sheriff, her chest went light and fluttery. At once she turned her back, stacked dirty plates and cups, and shot for the kitchen.

She dropped her load on the washstand.

"Mack is here, Athol." She couldn't explain why he'd suddenly become Athol instead of Mr. Patterson, but she decided not to explore the reason. It put a smile on the man's round face, and it gave her a feeling of kinship to address him in a friendly rather than formal manner.

Athol cracked an egg over the sizzling skillet and winked at her. "Well, go find out what he wants to eat."

Her face went hot. "But I . . . I . . ."

"Oh, go on. Ain't no harm in it."

She raised her chin and gave a nod. He was right. She marched out of the kitchen, past the spattering of diners, to Mack, who remained just inside the front door as if uncertain what he should do next. "Good morning, Mack."

"Morning, Abigail." His lips curved into a smile, but it didn't reach his eyes. "Sheriff Thorn not back yet?"

"We haven't seen him." She chewed her lip, the same worry that had tormented her during the night returning. "I don't know what I'm going to say to Marietta when she arrives this afternoon. She tends to be . . . morose . . . under the best of circumstances. I fear she will be devastated to discover we haven't located her sister."

As she'd come to expect, Mack placed his

hand on her shoulder and offered a little squeeze of reassurance. "We'll all be here with you. You won't have to face her alone."

She shook her head. "I'm not worried about me. I'm worried about her." She angled a hopeful look at him. "Will you and Preacher Doan pray for her?"

"Of course we will."

She'd known he would agree, and warmth flooded her. He was such a considerate man, such a giving man, the kind of man with whom she wanted to spend the rest of her life. Why couldn't he have written one of the letters to Mrs. Bingham so there would be a chance of her being matched with him? Tears pricked and she turned her face away so he wouldn't see.

"Athol has eggs with bacon or ham and grits or biscuits. What would you like?"

He leaned down slightly and met her gaze. "Are you taking my order?"

She shrugged and giggled although her face heated. "Yes. I suppose I am."

His grin reached his eyes this time. "Two eggs over easy with ham and biscuits, please."

She started to scurry off, but he reached out and caught her arm. She looked at him expectantly.

"Have Athol fix a second plate, too. I'll

carry it over to Nance when I'm done eating."

Yes, such a considerate man . . . She gulped back tears, nodded, and hurried to the kitchen before she broke the rule of protocol concerning public displays of affection.

Bill

Bill squinted against the bold morning sun at the trio of riders on Patch's back. "All right, now, ever'body set?"

Miz Bingham gave Bill a sorrowful look. "Are you sure you can walk the full distance to Spiveyville, Sheriff? I don't mind walking part of the way."

If Joseph could walk all the way from Nazareth to Bethlehem, Bill figured he could walk from Nance's property to Spiveyville. "I'll be fine, ma'am. You let me know if you need to get down an' move around some, though. It's a tight fit up there."

He'd told Miz Bingham to take the saddle and she'd done so — astride — without a word of complaint. The little Nance boy sat in front of her, and the bigger one held on from behind. If all three of them didn't look a sight, filthy from head to toe. Probably no worse than him, though, after his night on the ground. At least he could keep his unruly hair hidden under his hat.

Buster wriggled, a grin stretching across his face. "This is fun. Never rode horseback before. Can you make Patch gallop?"

"No." Bill and Miz Bingham answered at the same time.

Miz Bingham put her arm around the boy's middle. "It's a long way to the ground, Buster, and galloping might bounce us off."

Dolan leaned around and bopped his brother on the arm. "Fallin' ain't safe."

Bill hadn't said a word to the boys about their ma, waiting for an opportunity that felt natural. The time arrived. So he stepped close to Dolan and put his hand on the boy's leg. "You're sure right about fallin', Dolan, an' you're a smart boy to warn your brother. Seems to me the accident at your house learned you somethin'. When we let accidents teach us things that help us make better decisions down the road, then somethin' good comes out o' the mistake."

Dolan stared hard at Bill, his dark eyes serious and turning moist. The boy gave a slow nod. One tear rolled down his cheek and he looked the other way, but not before Bill saw gratitude in his face.

'Nough said.

Bill gripped Patch's reins in his fist and turned his face to the sun. Straight east to the old Addison place, then north to Spiveyville. He figured if they covered two miles every hour, they'd reach the town an hour or so past lunchtime. He hoped Athol would have something left in the pots on his cookstove. Walking built up a terrible hunger.

FORTY-TWO

Abigail

Abigail and Athol hurried through the kitchen cleanup and then, instead of attending church service, they set to work cleaning the upstairs rooms. Marietta could stay in Mrs. Bingham's room, but if the brides came, too, they'd need places to sleep. Some of the men thought they'd be able to take their brides to their ranches the moment they arrived in Spiveyville, but Abigail ended their speculation with a firm reminder that they hadn't yet completed their classes and Mrs. Bingham was the matchmaker. They would have to wait. To her surprise, not even W. C. or Vern protested. At least, not where she could hear.

Yesterday afternoon, after contemplating the best way to accommodate the arrivals in the four available rooms, Athol had asked Grover Thompson for eight bedrolls. Mr.

Thompson delivered the bedrolls as well as feather pillows, sheets, and quilts. He'd grinned as he flopped the last armload on one of the beds.

"My wife got the church ladies involved. When the wives've gone on to their homes, the ladies'll come in an' claim what they loaned."

Abigail had thanked him profusely, and he'd shrugged, red faced.

"Ah, ain't so much. It's what neighbors do . . . be neighborly."

Now Athol grimaced as he spread the first of the bedrolls across the fresh-swept floor. "It don't seem very neighborly to put ladies on the floor, but at least it won't be for long. Another week or so, right, Abigail?"

She wanted to immediately agree, but should she? What if Mr. Nance remained stubbornly quiet about where he'd taken Mrs. Bingham, and the sheriff couldn't locate her? What if — how she hated to even consider such a thing — Mrs. Bingham was never found? Abigail could finish teaching the classes, but she didn't know how Mrs. Bingham selected matches. Marietta probably didn't either. Who would take responsibility for placing this man with that woman? She shuddered, considering the ramifications of unwise pairings.

559

Athol stood with a pillow in his arms, waiting for her answer.

She forced a smile. "I'm sure the accommodations will be fine, Athol, for however long they're needed."

His gaze narrowed, but he returned to preparing the makeshift beds without a word.

They finished just as diners began arriving for lunch. Because of their time spent in the rooms, Athol hadn't been able to prepare something hot. So he served a choice of ham or cheese sandwiches, pickles, boiled eggs, and leftover spice cake or dried apple pie from the evening before. No one complained about the simple fare. The entire town was aware of Sheriff Thorn's absence and chose not to add more tension to an already tense situation by requesting a more substantial lunch.

By a quarter after twelve, it seemed half the residents of Spiveyville had gathered in Athol's restaurant. The other half wandered up and down the boardwalk or huddled in little groups, talking quietly. Nervous anticipation filled the air like electricity before a lightning storm, and Abigail found herself repeatedly stepping outside to peer up the street, ever hopeful for Sheriff Thorn's return with Mrs. Bingham. With each excursion, townsfolk greeted her, asked how she was "holdin' up," and offered words of encouragement. Her heart warmed and tears stung. She would miss these simple, good-hearted people when she returned to Newton.

When Athol's wall clock showed ten minutes past one, the front door burst open and someone bellowed, "Wagon's comin'!"

People swarmed the door. Abigail got caught somewhere in the middle of the crowd and flowed out the door with the rest of them. Outside, she fought her way to the edge of the street. Mack was already there, and she pressed close to him. He pointed to a cloud of dust, signaling a coming conveyance, and she clasped her hands beneath her chin.

Oh, please, God, let it be the sheriff and Mrs. Bingham. Her knuckles digging into the underside of her chin, she gazed with hope beating a thrum in her heart until a team of horses crested the rise, and an unfamiliar wagon followed it with a strange man and a well-dressed woman on the seat. More than a dozen women filled the bed.

Chatter broke out across the waiting crowd, and Abigail grabbed Mack's sleeve. "It's Marietta and the brides."

Mack nodded. "Go greet 'em. I'll keep

everybody else back." He held out his arms. "All right, folks, stay where you are, please. Everybody, stay back so we don't spook the horses."

With whispers and murmurs filling her ears, Abigail moved to the middle of the street. The driver brought the team to a stop several yards from her. At once, Marietta Constance Herne climbed down and darted to Abigail. She grabbed Abigail's shoulders, leaned down, and seemed to search Abigail's eyes. Then she sighed.

"She hasn't been found, has she?"

"Not yet. I'm so sorry. Sheriff Thorn is still out looking." She held her breath, waiting for Marietta to collapse in a heap or dissolve into wails.

Marietta curled her hand through Abigail's elbow and steered her toward the wagon. "Well, then, it's up to us, Miss Grant."

Abigail's breath eased out on a sigh of wonder. She trudged along with Mrs. Bingham's sister, curiosity writhing through her. What had happened to bring out this staunch, unflustered side of the woman?

"We'll do our best by these brides and grooms. I've become acquainted with the women. You've become acquainted with the men. If we put our heads together, we'll still probably do only half as well as my sister, but regardless, we will do our best not to disappoint her, yes?"

Tears filled Abigail's eyes. "Yes. With God's help, we will do our best."

Marietta squeezed Abigail's arm and released her. "All right, then. Where will the ladies stay? We've traveled day and night, and we would like a chance to rest a bit, even if we have to sleep on the hard floor."

Abigail started to answer, but a collective gasp behind her stole her focus. She whirled around and discovered that everyone else gathered on the street was now facing south. She shifted her gaze to the opposite end of the street and clapped her hands to her mouth, stifling a cry of elation.

Marietta gave her a puzzled look, then turned. She gasped and threw her arms in the air. "Praise God!" Repeating the phrase again and again, she gathered her skirts in her hands and began a clumsy run down the center of the street.

Bill

Bill squinted up the street. The whole town was there, all gaping and pointing and smiling like it was Christmas and everybody's birthdays all rolled up in one. How'd they

563

known he was coming? And who was that yellow-haired woman in the fancy dress and flowery hat barreling toward them?

"Marietta!" Miz Bingham squealed the name.

Dolan slid down Patch's rump, and Miz Bingham slid off after him. Buster held on to the saddle horn and stared with as much confusion as Bill felt. Who in blue blazes was Marietta? Miz Bingham went running to meet her, and the women embraced right there in the middle of the street, rocking each other and crying.

Dolan stepped close to Bill and poked him on the arm. "Who's that?"

Bill shrugged. "Dunno, son." He grabbed Buster under the arms and swung him to the ground. Bill handed off Patch's reins to Dolan and took a step toward the women.

At the same time, the pair broke apart and the one new to town shifted her gray eyes on him. A smile that rivaled an angel's lit her face, and she came at him with her arms held wide. Before he hardly knew what was happening, she wrapped her arms around his neck and kissed him full on the mouth. The hug knocked off his hat, brought his arms up like a pair of springs, and earned a roar from the watching crowd.

She stepped back, still smiling. "Sheriff

Thorn, you're my hero for bringing Helena safely back to me." She held out one hand. "I'm Miss Marietta Constance Herne, Helena's baby sister."

Bill grasped her hand and gulped, his lips still tingling. "Nice to meetcha." He saw a little bit of Miz Bingham in the woman's tall, slender frame, pale hair, and pale eyes, but she didn't have as many years on her as Miz Bingham. And she'd said she was a miss.

He held tight to her hand and leaned sideways a bit to catch Miz Bingham's eye. "What I said back at the dugout about wantin' you to find me a wife?"

She nodded.

"Well, ma'am, I sure didn't expect you to act so fast." He chuckled, slipping Miss Marietta's hand to the bend of his elbow. "You're one right fine matchmaker."

FORTY-THREE

Mack

Mack held his palms to the crackling flames of a bonfire and smiled at the happy noises filling the air. What else could the town do with their happiness except throw a party? Hugh Briggs's livery overflowed with people. Folks danced in the loft — not the slow waltz they'd learned from Abigail, but lively jigs and hornpipes. Between songs they helped themselves to sandwiches and cakes and cookies carried in by Athol and every woman in town, and they chatted around the three bonfires glowing in various places in the yard.

Everywhere — from every corner — laughter rang. So much joy. The lost had been found. Mack fully understood the biblical father's desire to host a party when his runaway son came home again. He was joyful, too. Seeing Sheriff Thorn return with

Mrs. Bingham and the Nance boys was an answer to prayer, and he praised along with everyone else. But underneath the joy ran a ribbon of sorrow.

Now the brides were here, and Mrs. Bingham had told the men she and Preacher Doan would arrange a joint wedding ceremony for the Wednesday before Thanksgiving. That'd give Abigail time to teach the fellows about courtship and conversation, and the fellows would have a chance to practice the new skills on their intendeds before everybody said "I do." Then the whole town would come together again for another celebration on Thanksgiving Day, officially welcoming the women to the community. After that, Mrs. Bingham planned to return to Massachusetts. And she didn't say so, but he figured Abigail would likely go with her.

Clive Ackley and a tall, thin woman with schoolmarm glasses perched on the tip of her button nose strolled past the fire in the dignified way Abigail had taught the men. Mack couldn't help returning the smile Clive beamed at him. Earlier he'd encountered Norm Elliott and a petite, kind-faced young lady sitting side by side on a short bench inside the livery, petting the barn kitten she'd lifted onto her lap. The rapt expression on Norm's face had matched the one Clive now wore.

Across the yard, Athol and his future bride roved up and down the food tables, the robust woman giggling and sampling from every tray. Athol looked on and grinned as proudly as a new father. Another couple approached the tables — Sam Bandy and his intended, who clung to Sam's elbow like a baby possum held to its mother. The four began an animated conversation. Mack didn't catch their words, but from their smiles, he knew they were having a good time. Jealousy nibbled at him, and he angled his gaze away and came face to face with Otto Hildreth and a shy-looking young lady.

"Mack, guess what?" Otto bounced a grin at the woman, then turned it on Mack. "Jessie here is a seamstress. She's always wanted to own a dressmakin' shop. Spiveyville's never had a dressmakin' shop, but it's gonna have one now, 'cause her an' me are gonna make my tailor shop a tailor-and-dress shop. We'll call it" — he slid his palm in the air as if envisioning a sign — "Hildreth an' Hildreth Custom Wearables." He waggled his eyebrows. "Jessie come up with that. Clever, huh?"

Before he could answer, the two headed for the food tables and joined Clive, Sam, and their intendeds. Mack watched them for a few minutes, shaking his head. Mrs. Bingham sure knew her business. Seemed as though she'd found the perfect helpmeet for every one of Spiveyville's bachelors. He must have some ability in matchmaking, too, because he'd found his own perfect match. Where was she?

He turned his head, and his gaze landed on Abigail standing in the wide doorway of Hugh's barn, talking with Sheriff Thorn, Miss Marietta, and the Nance boys. His chest went warm. Funny, considering how many people swarmed the livery's grounds, he'd found her on his first sweep, as if his heart automatically knew where to direct his eyes. He swallowed a knot of agony. He didn't want her to go back to Newton.

The sheriff and Miss Marietta entered the barn, and the two freshly spit-shined boys trotted after them like a pair of faithful puppy dogs. Abigail turned slightly and her gaze collided with his. For a moment she seemed to freeze, her bearing stiff, but then a soft smile curved her lips and she glided toward him, stepping around others and offering a sweet "Excuse me" as she came. She stopped on the opposite side of the bonfire and fixed her smile on him.

The dancing flames ignited the golden

flecks in her brown eyes and brought out the pale freckles that seemed permanently in place on her cheeks and nose. Everything within him longed to reach out, grab her close, and plant a kiss on every one of those freckles until he found her lips, but he wasn't as bold as Miss Marietta Herne. He'd never do such a thing in the middle of a town party.

"Mack?"

He swallowed. "Yes?"

"I was hoping you'd ask me to dance."

He shot a puzzled glance toward the upper-level windows, where shadowy figures moved to the fiddle's lively tune. "But it's not a waltz."

"There's a time for waltzes and a time for jigs. Considering the wonderful happenings this afternoon, don't you think this is a time for jigs?"

Maybe for everyone else. They were all getting something — the brides their grooms, the grooms their brides, the towns-folk their sheriff, and Abigail her friend. "I" — he sighed — "don't much feel like dancing a jig, Abigail."

She slowly rounded the fire, holding her russet skirt well away from the writhing flames. No sense in adding more scorches to the dress she wore more often than any other. She stopped beside him, tilted her head, and gazed steadily into his eyes. "Why not?"

She must have eaten some of Athol's pickles, because he smelled vinegar on her breath. Such an unlikely scent to cling to such an attractive woman. But from now on, every time he ate a pickle, he'd think of her. He groaned and let his head fall back. The nearly full moon, with its shadowy craters, seemed to stare down at him.

Abigail touched his jacket sleeve. "Mack, what's wrong? I thought you'd be happy to see our prayers answered."

He took her hand and guided her away from the fires, away from the townsfolk, away from the barn to the deeply shadowed patch behind Hugh's toolshed. He leaned against the sturdy wall and captured both her hands in his. "I am happy for Mrs. Bingham. I'm happy for Athol and Clive and all the others."

Her fingers tightened. "The sheriff was just telling me that Buster and Dolan are going to stay with him while their father is in jail."

"How can he keep track of the boys with all his other duties?"

"Marietta is going to help."

"She is?"

"Yes." He couldn't see her face, but he heard the burble of joy in her voice. "She loves children, and she's quite taken with the sheriff, and he with her. So she's going to stay here in Spiveyville. With all of them."

So even the sheriff was taking a bride. Mack's stomach ached. He lowered his head, and to his surprise, his forehead nearly touched hers. When had she moved so close?

"Mack, do you really want to be the only bachelor in Spiveyville?"

The spicy scent of pickles tickled his nose. The thought of being alone tormented his soul. "No. No, I don't."

"So what do you intend to do about it?"

He needed to see her before he answered a question like that. Walking backward, he tugged her out to the middle of the empty street. Under the nearly full moon, he let his gaze search her uplifted face. The same longing filling his chest was reflected in her eyes. His pulse picked up speed. "I intend to take a bride."

Instantly her eyes sparked with impishness. She jerked her hands free and folded her arms over the chest of her short red cape. "Well, I can tell you right now, if you choose anyone besides me, I can't be your friend anymore."

He battled a grin. "Are you blackmailin' me, Miss Grant?"

"Will it work?"

"I think it might."

She reached out and caught hold of his hands. "Then will you ask me?"

He glanced around. "Here?" On a dark street, with a cool wind tousling her hair and the smell of pickles surrounding them?

"Yes, out here, where God is watching and smiling."

Still holding her hands, he bent down on one knee. "Miss Abigail Grant, will you do me the honor of staying here in Spiveyville and becoming my wife and helpmeet for the rest of my life?"

She launched herself into his arms. "Yes!"

He rose, lifting her at the same time, and the fiddle music stopped. The whole town fell still. Even the breeze seemed to cease. And then the music started again with a gentle, flowing tune. Mack lowered Abigail's feet to the ground. Her small hand found his shoulder, and he placed his palm on her waist. Teary eyed but smiling, she danced with him beneath the prairie moon.

ACKNOWLEDGMENTS

First, as always, *Mom* and *Daddy* — thank you for being patient and understanding about my forays into imaginative worlds rather than telling me to get my head out of the clouds. Thanks for believing in me, especially when I didn't believe in myself.

Don — thanks for seeing to your own needs and letting me escape into story-world. I'd never finish a book without your willingness to handle the mundane.

Kristian, Kaitlyn, and *Kamryn* — I am so grateful God gifted me with each of you. You are my best blessings and my joy. (Thanks for giving me much story fodder. Heh, heh, heh.) I love you muchly.

Alana, Connor, Ethan, Logan, Rylin, Jacob, Cole, Adrianna, Kaisyn, and *Kendall* — I pray someday you will open the pages of one of Gramma's books, read the story, and come away with the realization that your gramma loved Jesus with all her heart. And

I pray each of you will grow deeply in love with Him, too.

The Posse — my friends, my prayer partners, my sisters in the Lord. Thank you for taking this journey with me and encouraging me every step of the way. Special thanks to *Eileen Key* for gifting me with *Manners and Morals of Victorian America* by Wayne Erbsen, which provided the rules Abigail so stringently followed.

Shannon and *the incredible team at Water-Brook* — thanks for partnering with me and making the stories shine.

The *readers* who read *A Hopeful Heart* and asked me to write another "mail-order brides" story — thank you for your enthusiasm and prompting. Abigail, Helena, Mack, and Bill also thank you for the chance to come to life.

Finally, and most importantly, *God* —You are ever faithful, ever available, ever my source of strength, wisdom, peace, and encouragement. I would not want to take one step in this life without You. May any praise or glory be reflected directly back to You.

READERS GUIDE

1. Abigail's world crumbled when her father chose an unsavory pathway. Have you ever suffered as a result of someone else's choices? How do you overcome the feelings of betrayal and unfairness?

2. Abigail lost her mother, her home, her beau, and her circle of friendships. Only one thing remained: the manners her mother taught her. She clung to that scrap of her former life with fierceness, fearful that if she let go, she would lose herself. Was this understandable? Did it benefit her? How can we determine when we need to hold on and when we need to let go of things from our past?

3. Helena began her matchmaking business after her husband's untimely death, and she wanted others to experience the marital bliss she had enjoyed. Abigail wanted

marital bliss, but her standards got in the way. Why do you think Helena didn't remove Abigail from the list of prospective brides? Was her idea to let Abigail teach manners to the ranchers in Kansas a good one? Why or why not? Do you think Helena sent Abigail to teach or to learn? What makes you think that?

4. Helena made an assumption about the men from Spiveyville based on the crudeness of their letters, and Abigail seconded the assumption when she met them in person. First Samuel 16:7 tells us "the Lord does not see as man sees; for man looks at the outward appearance, but the Lord looks at the heart" (NKJV). What is more important: outward appearance or character? Why? How can we as Christians look beyond others' exteriors to what lies beneath?

5. Mack was in strong opposition to the men's sending away for brides. Why was he so against it? Was he right to distrust all mail-order brides based on the actions of one? Why or why not? How do we set aside preconceived ideas about people? Is

there a difference between being cautious and being close minded? Explain.

6. Mack made a determination to befriend Abigail, partly because of the biblical admonition to "love thy neighbour as thyself." What made this difficult? Why did he persist? When you are rebuffed, do you give up or keep trying? Why?

7. Bill had put off marriage and family. Why? What made him change his mind? Do you think he made the right decision? Why or why not?

8. If you were to apply attributes (for instance: bravery, recklessness, stubbornness, and so on) to each of the characters, what would you choose and why? Which of the attributes would you want others to use to define you? Why?

ABOUT THE AUTHOR

Kim Vogel Sawyer's titles have garnered awards including the ACFW Carol Award, the Inspirational Readers Choice Award, and the Gayle Wilson Award of Excellence. Kim lives in central Kansas with her retired military husband Don. She enjoys spending time with her three daughters and a bevy of grandchildren.